REFORGED

SPARX LUMINARY BOOK II

REFORGED

SPARX LUMINARY BOOK II

K.B. SPRAGUE

GaleWind BOOKS An imprint of Whisperwood Publishing | Canada

REFORGED, SPARX Luminary Book II by K.B. Sprague

2022 First Print, Trade Paperback Edition
© 2021 by Kevin Sprague. All rights reserved

ISBN: 978-1-988363-13-4 (paperback)
ISBN: 978-1-988363-14-1 (epub)
ISBN: 978-1-988363-15-8 (kpf)

Cover designed by Damonza
Maps by Josephe Vandel of MapForge

Published in Canada by GaleWind Books,
an imprint of Whisperwood Publishing, Ottawa.

www.galewindbooks.com

Of wolves and men

To Glace Valley
Western Tor
Dim Lake
Dim River
Harrow
Harrow's Gate
DEEPWEALD
Upper Malcousin River
WHISPERWOOD
BEARDED HILLS
Webfoot
To Scarsands
Turnsby
The Mire
The Crossing
Doncaster
Blacknuk Creek
THE FLATS
Lower Malcousin River
Akeda Ruins
ABANDON BAY
Fort Abandon
Dory Crossing
Abindohn Ruins
Green Island

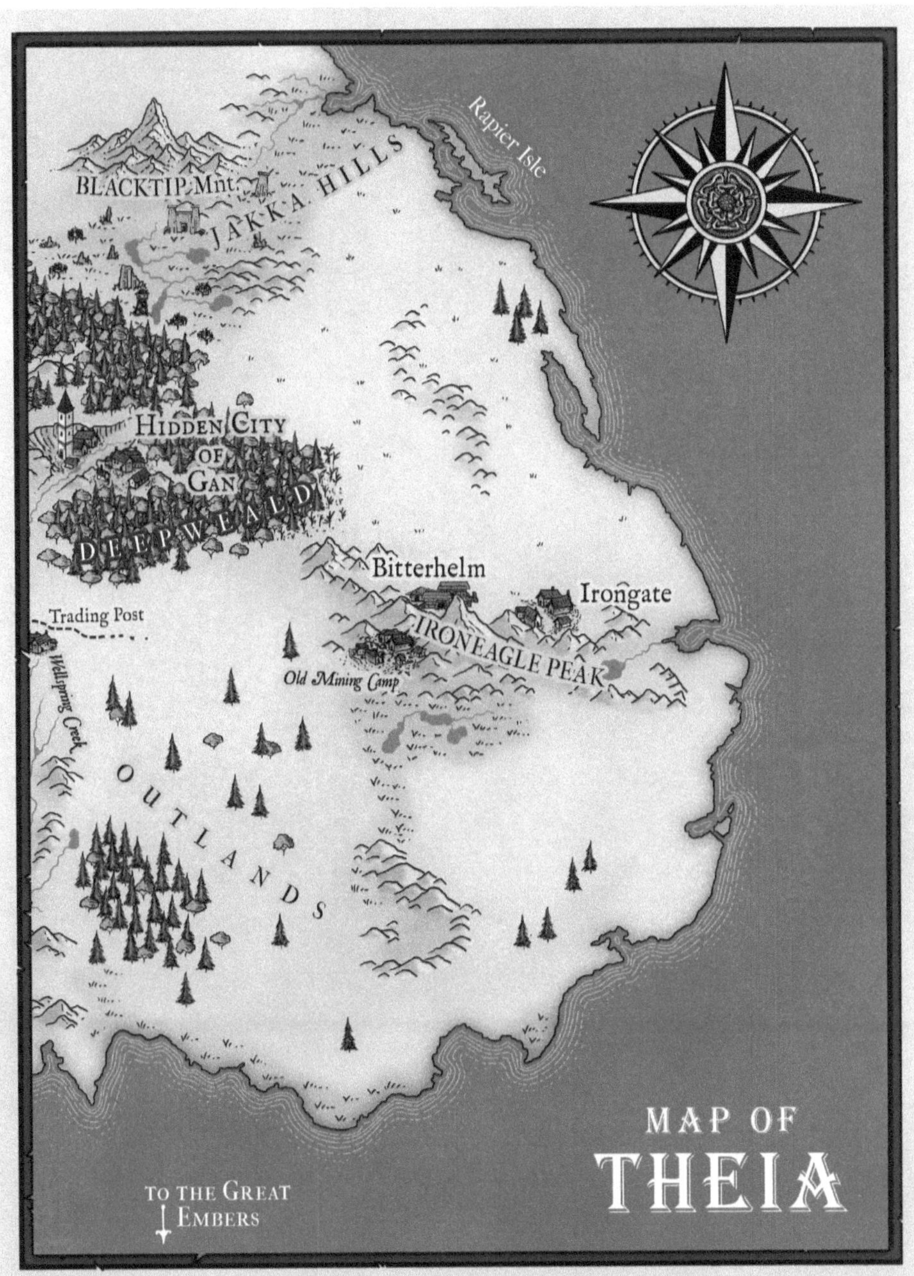

BLACKTIP Mnt.
JAKKA HILLS
Rapier Isle
HIDDEN CITY OF GAN
DEEPWEALD
Trading Post
Wellspring Creek
Bitterhelm
Irongate
IRONEAGLE PEAK
Old Mining Camp
OUTLANDS
TO THE GREAT EMBERS
MAP OF THEIA

PROLOGUE
THE LONG ROAD HOME

RISE OF THE GREEN DRAGON

THE BOG STONE on the tip of Nud Lenokin's staff began to flicker wildly.

No. Nud stopped himself. *Not this time.*

The Shaper quickly voided the thought from his mind before it could lead to consequences; before it could lead to something he might regret. At his age, he knew better… usually.

Look away.

Nud closed his eyes to avoid seeing the back of Backslap's stupid, ingrate, hooded head. He concentrated on his own steps… one foot in front of the other.

Left. Right.

He concentrated on the beat of the horse's hooves ahead of him.

One. Two. Three. Four.

And he concentrated on the sounds of the queensman leading the beast of burden: Jens Haulik's plated armor clinked and his chainmail swished as he strode alongside Backslap. Nud could walk a fair distance with his eyes shut, carefully feeling out the way forward with every step. He did just that until slowly the grip on his walking stick loosened. Yet still, when the councilor opened his eyes, he had to set his gaze to the ground. *Can't let myself get so worked up about such things,* he scolded himself.

The longer walk already behind them, a long walk yet lay ahead. Nud's legs ached terribly as weary bones craved for relief. Fallow fields to the south stretched out like a rolling bed of pale gold, fluid in the wind and bearing the promise of soft earth and gentle sunshine amidst the invigorating air of the low country. Only Val'shira among their small party had sped ahead to Turnsby, taking with her the most critical tomes destined for the Crimson Tower of the Grey Quarter. Nud's last image of Val'shira was her long dark hair flowing behind her as she leaned into a gallop, like the streaming mane of the swift, dark stallion that bore her.

Jens had argued that Val'shira should take Nud along with her, even saying it was for *her* protection, but the councilor would hear nothing of it. To leave behind the lion's share of the hard-earned collection of books, scrolls and tablets in the hands of a career cutthroat and a naïve nobleman was nothing short of pure foolishness. Nud had already proven that point true: without him acting as a buffer between the two, Backslap and Jens would've been at each other's throats by now. And there was nothing to worry about concerning Val'shira. She was of the sturdiest Abindohn stock and could take care of herself.

Backslap shifted sideways on the hard-packed trail, stepped in close to the queensman. Gusts rippled the dark cloak draping his form, head to toe. He leaned to the right until his hood completely engulfed the greater part of Jens' face.

He's about to say something. Nud was old, not deaf, but lagging behind nonetheless. So, he took care to pad softly, keen ears pricked to the fullest. He raised "Shatters" too – his burlwood staff – until it hovered just above the road.

The Blackdagger spoke in a low, raspy voice. "They eat their horses when it suits them, you know," came the muffled words across the howling winds. It was another attempt to crawl under Jens' skin. "I've seen it with my own eyes. Scarsanders can be as brutal as Outlanders. They'll work a horse near to death, but they don't *kill* it swiftly before they roast it. No, they *butcher* the poor creature alive and laugh while it screams, or mount it on a log-spit while it writhes and squirms to free itself." Backslap scoffed at the leather-bound goods being hauled. "Garbage like that is for the firebox. No one will ever make sense of those writings. Nonsense, all of it. We left all the useful ones behind."

Backslap coughed, hawked up a shot. He swiveled his head to the left, away from the queensman. With a raw sounding "thwuk" he launched the projectile into the air. It caught the wind and whipped back on a wicked arc.

Nud sidestepped the main ball successfully, cheek catching the tickling spray in its wake. With the sleeve of his shirt, he wiped the spittle off his weathered skin and white beard. The old Pip snorted air through flared nostrils in short, fast pulses, then redoubled his grip on Shatters. His eyes narrowed on the dark figure ahead of him. *Disrespectful, sniveling little…*

"Such a waste," Backslap egged on. "That fine mount of yours was worth a thousand times more than the packhorse and the worthless junk we're hauling now, and way more use to the world alive than in the belly of some wretched Scarsander. I'd sooner have set her free and brought back none of it."

Poor Jens. He'd spent the first half of the trip gloating about his hardy and well-tempered courser before having to give her up, before having to leave her behind in the Scarsands. The majestic beast had been bred by his horse lord uncle.

The queensmen responded with measured reserve in his tone. "Did you ever consume the flesh of a horse prepared in this manner?"

Backslap nodded slowly. Jens turned away, focused straight ahead as he strode. Without wavering, he asked a second question.

"What exactly do you want, assassin?"

Backslap didn't answer right away.

Although the boy's pinkish face was hidden, Nud could visualize the narrow eyes and dirty look painted on it – he saw the image in his mind. He'd witnessed the same look a dozen times over, and a Pip never forgets. And although Nud knew that the boy's forked tongue would do nothing to turn an honor-bound man like Jens against him, the fact he even tried made the councilor's blood boil. The boy had no respect for anyone. Nud scrunched his brow, glared at the back of Backslap's stupid hood, despite himself. He felt his face flush with hot vessels. The sensation was invigorating. His heart began to race.

And then it came. It came in a rush just like the old days, pounding behind the eyes and burning in his veins like pulsing magma. The rage welled up inside Nud and the fire of it swept over him. Jens spoke in the midst of the building pressure. The fury.

"That Scarsander got a bloody-good deal," Jens said, measured cheeriness in his voice, deflecting Backslap's remark with his usual blend of good sense and unbridled optimism. "Still, it would be the most expensive meat he ever ate. Even nasty Blackdagger will not roast that one. He is a businessman, after all. I would not be surprised if *Valiant* is sold and traded ten times over until she eventually ends up right back in the East, where she will fetch top dollar. My dollar, with Ekkon's luck."

Fortunately for Backslap, Jens' words did much to curb Nud's frustration with the malcontent, and the feeling did not escalate beyond an unspoken vow of reprisal. *That brat will get what's coming to him, soon enough*, Nud assured himself. But the councilor should've known better than to think even such a small contrivance, trivial as it might seem. He should've known better than to program such a thought so soon after anger. In the heat of the moment, you can't always help what you think.

The devoted Queen's Guardsman held steady his demeanor for a few long strides, then made a sideways glance at Backslap. He spoke into that awful hood.

Whatever Jens muttered, Nud didn't hear the soft-spoken words in full. But something of the tone carried to his ears, jolting his thoughts. *Was that a polite threat?*

Backslap jerked his head back abruptly, as if to rebut.

An insult? Ultimatum?

A gust filled the Blackdagger's enveloping hood, pushed it off. He cursed, arms flailing to gain control of the inflated cloth. Nud chuckled to himself. The boy didn't like the sun and the sun made no excuses for him. He glowed as pale and pink as a newborn rat. And in that brief moment, Backslap glanced back at the trailing Pip, all squinty-eyed.

He saw that Nud was watching and he took note of the raised staff. He quickly muttered a curse against Aelish the Resplendent as he fought with the wind to pull his hood back over his head. Jens wouldn't like the blasphemy either – yet another attempt to get under his skin.

In all Nud's dealings and negotiations in affairs of state, he'd seen and read a thousand faces a thousand times over. That boy's eyes were bitter with contempt. *Good one, Jens*, he told the queensman, in his mind. *Whatever you said to make Backslap react that way, I approve.*

Anyone watching the aging Pip would've noticed a sizable smirk creep across his face as he reflected on the moment, and they would've seen his eyes twinkle ever so bright.

That satisfied his thirst.

And anyone that could've read his mind would have known that many soft thoughts danced behind those eyes.

That kept his shaping hands steady.

But no one watched and no one read his mind, and Nud remained alone and unseen both in body and in spirit. Such is the way with the mortally aged in the company of youth that never die, or *should* never die.

≪

Jens was still distraught about leaving the steed behind; there was no mistaking that. But she, the draft horse and the carriage had fetched a fair price under the circumstances. Nud had need of coin after spending every last skull and every last griff on acquisitions, with more to come. Promise notes hadn't been worth the parchment scratched upon, having fallen out of use in the West. Were his legs not so stiff and sore, Nud could've kicked himself for not having considered that before departing.

The decision to commission a Blackdagger – an unofficial decision – had not been Nud's own. He'd only done so out of obligation to an old friend of a friend, and because he needed someone who could deal with black market smugglers. Unease had crept in during the time since, and dark whispers haunted him on the matter. Nud now regretted not making a bigger fuss about it back in Turnsby while there was still a chance to alter the arrangements.

Despite putting forth solid arguments to the Fourfold Alliance, the councilor had departed the annual speaker's gathering with little more than token backing. The Tri-town members had been too busy worrying about how Harrow was scheming to annex the northern reaches of the Bearded Hills – rich mining territory – to take proper notice of the serious threat of an arms race, not to mention the mass book burnings. After all Nud's years of service, the politics of the day had done him in. He'd made more enemies than friends on the Council of late, and so was spared only a few horses, a carriage, one aide with imperfect memory, and a gentlemanly, but grossly inexperienced champion on the fencing circuit. The Tri-town members – whom he'd known all his life – had refused to dedicate even a single person of their own to "his" cause, citing moral difficulties with the venture. The champion had been posted in from Gan to gain experience in the wilder reaches of the world, and Val'shira had been offered up by a grig named Feleg attending from Aokwan, to fulfill an ulterior motive of his own.

"That's the Fourfold way," Nud muttered to himself, mid-stride. It was not a complement. "Four ways screwed, every time."

Backslap glanced back over his shoulder, sneering. "What was that old man?"

Nud just waved him off.

The longer the councilor walked, the better his legs felt, and once he found his stride his steady pace kept the other travelers honest through morning. As one-by-one his footsteps marred the earth, Nud let his thoughts drift to earlier times – adventurous times – in youth long passed on the same trail he now traveled, and many others far and wide. But by mid-afternoon, his back had begun to ache and the sun beat him down.

Backslap suggested they rest under one of the first full-grown trees that came into view on the trailside. They stopped for cheese, salted fish and cranberry juice. Jens shared his last half-bottle of wine generously. After the meal, Nud knew he could go no farther that day. With immense pain shooting down one leg, the Pip could do little more than lie down with his head on his pack. It was an old injury. And the jostling about that comes with riding was out of the question. Taking the saddle would only serve to do in his lower spine for days if not a week. And so, Jens and Backslap worked together to make camp for the night. Backslap picked an out-of-the-way spot behind a knoll on the south side of the road. Jens took over from there, eager to show off his fresh wilderness skills. "Kith-trained," he insisted. Their guardian set up a simple lean-to shelter and piled the books inside under a canvas tarp. The Blackdagger set the horse grazing, then went looking for some special herb he thought might grow in the surrounding fields.

Jens built a smokeless fire. While alone with Nud, he proposed his plan for the night watch. "I shall take the first until midnight," he said. "And if you could take the second…"

Nud nodded. *Makes sense,* he thought. Nud was always awake in the middle of the night anyway. Jens regarded the councilor squarely.

"On Backslap's morning watch, nudge me, and I will keep one eye open."

"You're wiser than you look," Nud replied. "We should leave at sunrise to make the Bearded Hills by nightfall."

Jens nodded. "I will be awake."

⚜

When the hammer fell, Nud thought of Val'shira. Something about her reminded him of his first love, Holly.

Jens fought valiantly for one so far outside of his usual fencing lane. Given half a chance to learn a little more about *actual* combat before the night's ambush, he might've even prevailed.

Backslap fought well for such a young Blackdagger, and in his final moments showed his worth. Deft movements. Quick thrusts. And he didn't flee. Not so bad after all. It wasn't his kind of fight though: open conflict against giants. They simply overpowered him.

The scrolls. Damn it Val'shira, please come back for the scrolls.

When the hammer struck again, everything went black.

⚜

Nud opened his eyes and found himself surrounded by friends and family. He smiled, or thinks that he did. At least, he felt like smiling. Then everything went black once more.

When Nud opened his eyes a second time, he lay in a woodland grove gazing up at the stars. He did not feel fully material. The air was cool. Hazy lights surrounded him.

Flickering lights…

I do not mean to say the path is 'meant to be' in the sense of the greater cosmos or the grander scheme of things, heavens no. How could I even speculate on such a thing? I mean to say it happens along in the sense of what might be the next best thing though… a higher consciousness in our midst, one just out of grasp. We do not tap into it, not usually, but it is no less there because we are naïve to its presence.

—*Fyorn the Wilder,*
on the Selection of Spirit Hurlorns

Chapter I
WOODLAND TRAIL
(Amot)

Amot was thirteen, cocooned in his blanket in the Sacred Grove. He couldn't sleep. Everyone else in the encampment could though.

As the night wore thin, an uneasy feeling crept into the initiate's gut. It lingered there, churning, like bad meat.

I need more time, he thought. Amot had gone backwards in his studies, confusing things he once knew.

A bat swerved overhead, arcing across the grey-lit clouds, dawn only hours away.

Amot glanced to the two blackened tusks that marked the gateway to the ritual – an ancient rite of passage, the last trial before becoming a full-fledged scout. Jutting out of the hard-stony earth, their ivory tips met some dozen or so feet into the air, glimmering in the night. Amot felt tense, twitchy. A wave of heat flashed through him, left to smolder on his forehead. He made a tight fist. Fingernails bit into his palm.

Damn Overseer! Amot pounded the ground, then glanced about. No one stirred.

The ancient Kith Master had sprung heaps of new material on Amot last minute, piling onto what he already needed to practice. The second trial of the Eightfold Way fast approached, and his rehearsals hadn't gone well. He wanted to run crazed through the wild, leave it all behind.

Amot got up to clear his head, left his bedroll behind and crept away from his slumbering Kith brothers. Unnoticed, he slipped past the Sunrise Arch and descended the hillslope.

Striding through the dark, Amot came upon a small open area. He felt out a mossy boulder to sit on, lit a torch and sized up the place. The clearing screamed "build a fire" to the teen, so he got started.

~Foolish.

The crackling blaze Amot built was small and compact, but it burned bright and steady in the still night air. And as the flames wavered and danced fluidly in yellowy-orange, the heat washed over his face. The coming ritual involved, among other wilderness skills, communicating in the native tongue of Hurlorns, or Treesong. He wondered how it would go.

The complexities of all the musical phrases and greetings swam through his mind. He contemplated the Overseer's training. The navigation and survival chants he could handle, but the elemental comms... there were so many, made no less difficult by the fact that Amot was not a musician or linguist by any stretch.

~Incompetent.

The initiate's thoughts had barely drifted into the mysteries of Treesong before he heard a rustling in the bushes. A whipping sound came with it, then a shuffling drag over the ground.

A curious Sprigg popped into the clearing, probing and insect-like in its treeform guise, bursting with red berries. Amot put his newfound knowledge of Hurlorn lyrics to the test. He conjured up a greeting...

⌘

That was the moment, Amot recalled, as he plodded on in the real world. It happened five years ago. *That was the moment I should have stopped myself... too risky... too soon.* His boots crunched over the parched earth as he traversed a sharp ridge along the woodland path; the same path he'd taken years ago on that fateful day. Amot knew the forest wouldn't stay dry for long. Overhead, through the branches, the sky was Djinxar-grey. Dark clouds loomed over the hills to the west, rolling in and smelling of rain.

Guided by little more than decades-old axe blazes, the scout had set off early morning to the Spirit Hurlorn grove, alone but for Howler. Snout to the ground, the patchy brown and white spaniel had already scared up fowl and sent a dozen squirrels scurrying up trees. Every so often the pooch circled about some invisible find of great interest – until he forgot what he was doing and bounded off into the forest.

Amot ignored the distraction that was Howler. He pondered his current errand – as if he didn't have enough to worry about already. He needed to get this task for Lumen Hadamard out of the way so he could get back to the main mission at hand: retrieving the striker and maybe, just maybe, avoiding the military tribunal for losing it in the first place. But Amot knew there was more at stake. More than getting himself out of hot water for losing a prototype dancing sword – a sword with powers that rivaled the legendary brightswords of the Jhinyari warlords, no less. *Why else would Hadamard have gone out of his way to insist I be part of the mission, especially with my record of screw-ups?*

It wasn't the first time Order Lumen had taken special interest in Amot. At the half-dozen or so ceremonies and social functions every year that brought luminaries and Kith rangers together, Amot was always singled out, pointed to in conversations, and inquired about. Meanwhile, his peers watched on, baffled by the buzz of activity surrounding him. Perhaps the attention had something to do with his uncle's connection to the Order. But whatever it was, both groups – as opposite as they were – relied on the Hurlorns. And that meant they had to rely on each other.

Lumen Hadamard had sparred with House Ralador over his involvement in the weapon recovery mission. And it was Hadamard who'd insisted that Amot alone engage the Hurlorns in this matter, though the scout didn't quite grasp why. The request was vague: ask the guardian of the forest realm to reveal the origins of the elemental stones, for the sake of developing new weaponry. Why would the Hurlorns know this?

Not my concern, Amot told himself. What mattered was that one way or another, completion of the two tasks could mean redemption. Acceptance. A proud moment for the Kith Overseer to draw upon. A shared success for Wilders and luminaries.

Never mind that the coming mission could be damn near impossible.

Never mind that he'd have to enter dangerous woods and enemy territory. That's the sort of thing he'd been trained for all along.

I'll make amends, get this done right and impress the Overseer, like Lumen Hadamard and Uncle Feleg said I should. The Green Dragon will lean my way. He'll have to.

His mind barely cognizant of what lay ahead, Amot let the painful memories bleed through to the surface. But the memories themselves were not the worst of it. The worst of it was the sober realization of his own imperfections.

Maybe it wasn't the Overseer's fault after all.

If only he'd listened as a young spotter. The top Kith had warned the class of initiates not to experiment beyond the simple chants they'd practiced.

It was supposed to be a casual thing, Amot reminded himself… *friendly and rewarding.* At least that's how communing with Hurlorns had been portrayed. But there were simply too many new concepts clogging up his mind. He winced at the mere thought of the words that had spilled out of his mouth next, calling out to the young Sprigg who'd happened upon Amot's lonely fire. If only he could turn back the clock, enact the day over again, the right way. He'd remind himself that he was speaking to a collective as opposed to only one, and he'd remind himself to stick to phrases he knew best. And lighting a fire in densely-wooded Hurlorn country? Maybe not such a good idea after all.

His mind drifted back…

✄

In the glow of the blaze, Amot sounded out his Treesong greeting to the red-berried Elder, one he'd made up on the spot.

"Ready to burn, kindling?"

The Sprigg jerked back, branches flinging. It let out a fluty screech.

Gnarled roots burrowed into the earth and wrapped themselves around a protruding rock.

Amot's mind raced. He spoke gently, in his own tongue, "Why so jumpy?"

The Sprigg froze, blended into the surroundings like a tree.

Amot shrugged. *What's gotten into him?* He shook his head, turned his gaze back to the fire. *Did I greet him respectfully?* The phrasing was still all mixed up in his head, and no wonder.

Slowly, he began to piece together what'd transpired. In Treesong, the melodies underlying both "ceremony" and "kindling" are very nearly the same, and those for "arch" and "burn" are identical, distinguished only by context. Then it dawned on him. Asking the Sprigg if he'd come to bear witness to the arch ceremony had turned into something wholly malevolent – a common problem with Treesong. Sing one word wrong and the entire meaning collapses. Errors cascade into nonsense.

- Thoughtless.

Amot stood up, turned to apologize. The Sprigg didn't budge.

Out of nowhere, something large came barreling through the woods, cracking and splitting branches, ground thumping as it neared. Amot backed away as a ten-foot Elder crashed into the clearing, then halted.

The Sprigg animated abruptly, pulled up its roots and skittered behind her. For a long and tender moment, the tall Elder smothered the sapling in the confines of her enveloping roots. Her ropey tendrils twisted about the two of them, caressing and snakelike.

"Sorry," Amot fumbled, speaking in his native language. Few Hurlorns understood though.

Everything seemed fine for the moment, touching even. Amot sighed at the inspiring display of affection. But the Sprigg pushed away from the tall Elder's embrace, let out another screech, then darted off, piping into the woods.

The tall Elder stayed behind, gaze tracking the Sprigg's hasty departure. Slowly, the Hurlorn shifted her stance. She swung around to glare straight at Amot, anger shaping in every branch. Her burlwood brow furrowed, and her ebony eyes narrowed on him.

Amot was no idiot. He knew what was up.

"I was just trying to… *strike* up a conversation," he told the Hurlorn in her own tongue – another innocent remark that didn't translate well.

The Elder sized up Amot for what he was, then swiveled to regard the blazing fire. She stood there, transfixed by the hot flames. Evaluating. A fresh log caught, crackled, and split before her. It was only deadwood, but it made an impression. The misunderstandings multiplied.

A surge of fire leapt up, nipped at her low-hanging boughs. The Elder tucked them in, backed away. And when a gust of wind arose suddenly out of the calm, wild tongues of flame rushed towards her and licked the nearby bushes. The Elder's limbs began to tremble, bow, and creak. But not of fear.

A low rumble sounded. Leaves in her canopy began to shudder. Red berries dropped. Amot's chest began to vibrate.

In sudden fury, the air cracked with a deafening blast of woodwinds.

Enraged, the Hurlorn lifted a mighty mass of roots and stomped. The ground shook. Amot stumbled back.

Murmurs of confusion arose from the encampment. A scratchy adolescent's voice called out, "Has anyone seen Amot?"

And as the young initiate scrambled to escape the clearing, the Elder kicked moss and dirt onto the fire to douse the flames. Sparks flew through the air. And while thick smoke billowed up from beneath the spirals of her smothering roots, the woods surrounding Amot came alive. Leaves suddenly took flight, swarmed around him; twigs crawled and snapped to pierce his flesh. The trees themselves began to close in, pinning him down. Frantic, he swatted at the attackers and brushed them off his body. With rasping breaths, Amot broke free, sprang to his feet.

"I didn't mean anything by it!" he tried to explain, fending off the critters. But it was too late for explanations and he spoke the wrong tongue.

Fire smoldering under the Hurlorn's root collars, the Elder glared back at Amot, fierce eyes black as coal. Accusing. *How dare you*, they seemed to say. With a loud snap, a hollow opened in the Elder's trunk.

It widened to a gaping maw, jam-packed with long splinters that could tear a man to shreds.

Amot's heart began to pound. A burst of energy jolted him into action. He ducked away from the flying leaves and the biting sticks, spun out of the clearing and bolted blind into the woods. Branches whipped and lashed at his body as he made his getaway.

Amot outran the Elder. He outran the swarm and he outran the stick creatures. He ran wild through the woods and never looked back.

❧

Back in the real world, Amot scolded himself. "Strike up? Really?"

He'd blackened half the hillside for those who actually did undergo the ritual, three days late. The scout rubbed his forehead as he continued his trek along the woodland trail. He cursed *Ekkon the Wanderer* while he was at it, as though that watchful beast had something to do with it. The council of Kith chieftains were mortified when they found out what'd happened. They sent all manner of apologies to the Green Dragon of Deepweald to pass on to the Elders. To the Overseer, Amot's offensive language was just another mess adding to an already long list of messes to be cleaned up, with the troubled understudy dead center of it all. The high-ranking Kith fumed when he confronted Amot about the incident. The bald spot on his head pulsed beet red; scathing words spat out of his grey-speckled beard.

"Foolish! Incompetent! Thoughtless!"

The Overseer had gone on to lecture the young spotter about the Battle of Ironeagle. It was hardly a battle at all, really, by the old druid's account. A massacre more like. Outlanders torched Sleepers and Spirit Hurlorns alike by the thousands. They called the young Spriggs "kindling" before tossing them into massive bonfires, fueled by the charred husks of parents and kin. Sleepers, although docile, are no less sentient than their Spirit Hurlorn cousins and no less active in the group's consciousness.

"She's burning low," Outlanders would say to the helpless Spriggs, then "throw on the kindling" before heaving them onto the flames.

"She's ripping hot again!" they'd say, as the Spriggs burned alive, squirming to free themselves or dashing through the woods like living torches.

The long-lived Hurlorns never forget such things. How could they? And their strong connection to one another imparts an awareness and persistence that reaches deep into their psyches. "Too strong, almost," according to the Overseer, reflecting on that very point. "They feel one another's sufferings as vividly as they would their own, and never wholly let go. You must have really touched a nerve."

Many seasons passed before the opportunity came for Amot to once again exchange lyrics with a Hurlorn.

The scout shook off the memory. Amot had enough to worry about in the present, never mind the past. His commander's words resonated in his mind – words he'd spoken just before Amot had departed Seventh Kaeda: *Overly aggressive actions towards a member of the Queen's Guard during an exercise.*

Amot felt flush behind the brow just thinking about the accusation, heat building up inside. It wasn't his commander's fault, he knew – the Lord of the March had made the declaration. Berendt was just the messenger. That only made things worse. Tribunals never went well when Wilders were judged by outsiders not of their own kind – it was an unfair process. The Judiciary never understood the Kith Quarter. Never. Yet they had no trouble locking up his people over circumstances they'd let their own walk free on.

Balance. Stability.

Amot huffed, drew a calming breath. *I can still keep things from going south,* he reassured himself. The decision rested with the Overseer about whether the proceedings would fall under the purview of the Blue Tower or his Kith brethren. A glimmer of hope, but he knew better than to count on it.

Nothing ever goes smoothly, he reminded himself. There's always some screw-up, some apology to be handed out on a silver platter by himself and others on his behalf. No one bothered to tell him it would be that way when he joined the Kith Quarter. Instead, recruiters had filled his head with stories of grand adventure, great deeds, and the gratitude of kings. Well, it didn't quite seem to be panning out that way. He had half a mind to just up and quit.

To the Spirit Hurlorns and the Wilder tribes, everything he did was wrong anyway, and now it was the same with the Queen's Guard. They called him unfocused. They called him careless. They said his mind was everywhere at once, except where it needed to be. The worst part was that they were not completely wrong.

What would happen if they labelled me "Unchosen" – blocked from Kith thaumaturgy and banished from the Wilder tribes forever? Would the Hurlorns still collect my soul, in the end? If not, where to? Ekkon's Wheel? Shroud's Well? Who could know?

The scout peered ahead, checking for markers on the trail. He was coming up on the last turn that would bring him back to the Sacred Grove. The visit was long overdue. But this time his clumsiness with Treesong wouldn't be the problem. This time, Amot wondered if he'd be accepted by the mighty Hurlorn that dwelt there. He forced himself to focus.

What do I say? How do I start?
Do I apologize for the past first?
Do I apologize for the present?
How much do I tell the Hurlorns?

Amot drew in another breath. *I've been through worse. I'll get this done right. I will not screw this up. I will make a good impression.*

Howler broke Amot's train of thought again. The dog padded up alongside, nudged his thigh. Something wet soaked through his pant leg.

"Pffh!" Amot jerked sideways, halted to swipe the dog's grime off himself. "You need a bath," he grumbled. The spaniel was hopeless, his fur so matted and grungy no one could tell for looking that his legs and hindquarters were supposed to be white.

Howler barked at the suggestion, bounded along the path for a short stretch, then dashed off into the woods again.

Amot shook his head, smirked, then set his sights back on the trail. Trusty hatchet in hand, he kept a sharp eye out for the next blaze to refresh.

The path he'd been following ended abruptly, overgrown.

From about ten paces back where Howler had left the trail, swishing branches sounded.

You missed the blaze, Amot scolded himself. *Back to spotter's school for you.*

The scout retraced his steps and entered an unnatural V-shaped parting of bushes. The new path that opened up before him had no blazes to mark the way. This trail was born out of the free will of the forest. Foliage of all kinds bent to one side or the other, to create a parting of the woods for his personal traverse.

Amot spotted a giant leaf insect stirring on the gentle bend of a bowed branch. He started on his way. Farther along another appeared, then another. Soon the trees were crawling with them and the stick insects too. No doubt, he was nearing the grove.

I will not screw this up, he told himself one last time.

That would be a first.

CHAPTER II
AERIE OF THE GRYPHONS
(Galewind)

GALEWIND HALTED AT the wide steps carved into the base of Icy Blue – the glacier-polished neck of an extinct volcano. In the morning sun, its craggy black peaks stood in sharp contrast to the autumn-colored lowlands from which they emerged, and from the glistening gorge waterfall that formed the backdrop.

Six portico columns fronted the massive structure, each the girth of a giant oak. Double doors led in. Rapids to either side hissed in Galewind's ears as the water rushed past, while eddy currents swirled beneath the translucent walkway she stood on. The rough-hewn *glace* let the light pass, but distorted the view underfoot.

Icy Blue was one of three great monoliths in Gan. For millennia, they defied the fast waters and high winds that rushed between the steep, rocky walls of the gorge, while softer ground eroded and washed away. The first host of Elderkin to look upon the deep valley had undertaken the long, slow process of sculpting them into towers. Great towers. Legendary towers.

Galewind breathed deep, stretching the elastic limits of the supple leather constricting her chest, snug-fitting under her fur-lined cloak. She filled her lungs with the cool, misty air, and delighted in the tingle of icy droplets depositing on her face. *It's good to be back*, she told herself. A part of her missed the excitement of the Aerie, while a part of her was glad to have moved on.

Instinctively, the knightmaiden glanced up at the rock's jagged summit, to gauge the climb ahead. The grueling rise of a thousand stone steps awaited, narrow and winding through the cavernous interior. The monolith's many peaks and sheer sides gave it a natural fortress-like appearance. Lynx and eagle carvings adorned the two top corners, facing. Between them a spur balcony jutted out, resting atop the hewn back of a majestic gryphon, wings spread for takeoff.

Galewind knew the tower inside and out. She ought to have. Before being posted to the palace as a royal liaison and trainer, she'd been stationed at Icy Blue for three decades, although she didn't look or feel a day over thirty-five since her latest rejuvenation cycle. The only person with a longer term in the tower was Lady Apsarla, who'd summoned her hence.

Does she know yet? wondered Galewind. The Judiciary Council had been set to rule on the knightmaiden's case yesterday, while she herself was a world away in Seventh Kaeda. Her knees felt weak, shaky, as she replayed in her mind the cold stares she'd received at the hearing. *I can't have that,* Galewind told herself. *Worrying about the ruling won't help, and it won't change my briefing to Lady Apsarla.* She double-checked her cloak pocket for her notepad, pushed her trepidations aside, then started up the wide steps to the double doors.

The knightmaiden glanced at the bronze plaque by the entrance as she passed: "Justice Tower" in block lettering – Icy Blue's more formal title – together with the names of the four divisions within. Each hosted a myriad of halls, chambers and stairwells on various levels, gutted out of the rock's innards. The topmost level of the monolith, Galewind's destination, was home to the Gryphon Aerie. In some sense, the beast's presence among the peaks rekindled an ancient past, for the location was also the resting place for the timeworn bones of a prehistoric, avian-like Colossus, bonded to the stone by ancient river sediments that long ago poured over its remains.

The gryphons were like a resurrection.

ᔐ

Legs quivering, Galewind climbed the last flight of stairs. She huffed, then braced herself against the rock wall to catch her breath. She could hear the winds outside and see the light of day. *Fresh air, finally.*

Heavy footsteps sounded and a familiar, deep-throated humming carried to her ears. Beastmaster Lorenz stopped to greet Galewind at the cave mouth that opened to the gryphon hollow.

"Knightmaiden!" came his grating voice, above the dull rumble of the falls. "You have finally come to visit your lonely friends up here on the mountain!" He was just passing by. In one arm, Lorenz cradled a sack held against his massive chest. At nearly seven feet, he hulked over her.

"I will help you in a moment," he went on, "Lady Apsarla awaits in the Wing Chamber, here since the dawn with her favorite new spear-maiden. At least two others have already arrived. I heard Rainsong's voice, sweet as a bird. She was with another that I did not see or hear… unless Rainsong finally went completely mad and was talking to herself. I always wondered when that day would come." Lorenz's ebony arms were streaked in blood that soaked through the sack he carried – a fresh carcass from the abattoir.

Feeding time.

The knightmaiden tilted her gaze up to meet his. She jolted back. The long locks of jet-black hair that Galewind always remembered Lorenz by were gone. In their place, tight white curls, cropped short against his dark scalp. *When did that happen?* He smiled a toothy smile.

Galewind smiled back, hoping to disguise her shock at the beast-master's dramatic aging. "That would be Catwings, whom you didn't see or hear with Rainsong; she's soft-spoken and light-footed." Catwings had gone through celeste training only recently. Rainsong not so long ago either, for that matter.

His free hand rose to his square chin. Lorenz reflected on the encounter for a long moment, then nodded. "I thought it might be her, if the wind hadn't carried her off yet."

Galewind watched as a drop of blood beaded, then fell. "You're dripping," she said.

He glanced at the rock floor. "Did I get any on you?"

"No, not a drop."

"No worries, Knightmaiden," Lorenz said, with a flap of his hand. "The rain will wash away the blood." He switched arms, re-adjusted the load he carried.

Galewind said, "And there's no need to escort me, Beastmaster. I still know the way to the Wing Chamber; I was stationed on this rock long before you set foot on it. Is your memory beginning to fail you?" Hers was a friendly dig, referring to the choice he'd made over twenty years ago not to undergo rejuvenation.

The man grinned fully. "Getting older, yes, but still as virile as ever." His eyes widened for an instant when he spoke the word "virile."

"I'm too old to blush at such come-ons," Galewind said, staring at him coyly.

Lorenz grunted. "Time has been kind to you."

"And you look the wise man, now."

The beastmaster laughed heartily. "I am. Age does that to a man – fills the heart and soul with the wisdom of time passing, and of time to come… Speaking of what is to come, a big day is on its way for you, isn't it? Back in the saddle?"

Galewind nodded. "I suspect as much. All I ask while I wait for confirmation is that my greatest friend be well-fed."

"I am very well fed, thank you," quipped Lorenz.

Galewind groaned. "Just whisper to the 'old Gold' for me, if you will. Tell her that I will visit her later this morning."

"How long has it been since you flew a cat?"

"Not as long as you might think. I flew a few months back – you were on a supply run, but before that…" Galewind sighed. She rolled her eyes upwards and thought back. "Years. Five… six maybe. I'm tied up with liaison duties and a new batch of recruits that have yet to set foot in the Aerie. My job now is to teach them how to fly using nothing more than words and a blackboard."

Lorenz grunted. "Put them on a gryphon's back and let them figure it out for themselves, I say."

Galewind felt a pang of guilt, a dagger twisting into her heart. "That's how I learned. That's how we all learned, until…"

"I know… tragedy." The beastmaster's gaze fell to his enormous feet. "Maybe it is best. I regret my words, Galewind. Sorry. By now, I should have learned to keep my big mouth shut."

She reached out, rested her hand on his upper arm. "No. It's all right." She paused. "About my Gold…"

Lorenz raised his eyes to meet hers again. He was smiling that toothy, contagious smile. "For you, Knightmaiden, the moon, and the elemental winds that ferry it across the sky." He raised the bloodied sack in his arms. "But as for this lamb that I carved up for my beasts so lovingly, your old Gold will receive an extra cut of loin from me, no more."

One thing about him hadn't changed. "So, you are still on about that Wind God of yours?"

"Breeze, Norwin of the Dawn, the Great Eagle," he responded, "however you wish to name Her; the Wind carries us all through life. She has a temper though, be careful, hence the other name She is called that I try not to mention very much: Cold Death. Three days ago, it was gusty and I cursed Her name into the wind. She blew me clear off the Aerie before I could take my foolish words back, and I plummeted."

Galewind played along. "Why did you curse her name?"

"Cut myself on a talon; your old Gold, in fact." He raised his right arm at a right angle, revealing the flesh on the underside of his wrist and a deep, six-inch scrape that ran along it. His eyes grew wide. "Those things are razor sharp."

Galewind replied, "Believe me, I know. How did you survive the fall?"

"I called out Her name the moment I tumbled over the edge, and She took pity on me. She cupped me in Her icy palms and raised me back to the Aerie on a cushion of air. What do you call a force that coincides with an element of nature, other than a god? No Colossus can do as much."

Galewind shook her head. "It's called 'updraft'..." She turned away slightly, raising her hand to her lips to hide the smirk growing there. "And a vivid imagination."

The beastmaster scoffed. "You are too skeptical for one with a call sign such as yours. How do you think I read the weather to come?" He paused for her to answer, then resumed when she did not. He brought his free hand to one side of his mouth, and spoke with covered words. "The Wind God *whispers* it to me."

"Lorenz. You look at the skies, you look at the wind sock, and you guess, like everyone else. You're just better at it than most."

"Hmm... do I accept the compliment, or contest your accusation that I am a liar? You leave me with no good choices, Knightmaiden Galewind." Lorenz shook his head with a feigned look of disgust. "Never have. I am not talking to you anymore. I have hungry gryphons waiting on my return. You know how they get."

"I can't argue with that. Thank you, Beastmaster, and an extra cut of loin will be quite adequate."

Lorenz grunted, then set off for the stables. Galewind stood a moment longer in the mouth of the cave, her only company the howling winds. She stepped out onto the bare summit. The sheer roar of the cascading waters overpowered her senses. Mist-laden winds rippled her cloak and tousled her dark hair, throwing about her wing-shaped hairclips in the process. She strolled farther out onto the spur balcony and gazed at the Elderkin River flowing a thousand steps below, the only stretch of the otherwise subterranean waterway naked to the sky. Her eyes tracked the network of graceful walkways that crisscrossed its rapid course, swooping between towers and buildings to connect Gan's many districts. She tracked them all the way to the opposite end of the gorge, to the royal spires of the Hidden City. Galewind breathed deep again, then turned to face the Aerie.

Nothing had changed in the years she'd been absent. Apart from the mounting platform, the sunken hollow was barren and bowl-like. The jagged peaks encircling it still reminded her of the stone teeth of some colossal golem's mouth. Massive bones lay resting, embedded in the floor, blackened and protruding like stone blood veins of the living rock. The hollow was otherwise empty.

A cacophony of high, piping calls erupted over the exterior wall of the stables, followed by the sounds of ripping and tearing into flesh, then the guttural hiss of a large, angry cat. *Testy-testy,* she thought, shaking her head. *Always a scuffle at feeding time.* Galewind pulled her cloak tight around her and proceeded to the Wing Chamber.

CHAPTER III

THE WILL OF AELISH

(Eriff)

"WAIT HERE, SIR."

The queensman's escort approached the door of heavy oak to the Lord of the March's daily affairs chamber. She appeared small but sturdy in her blue cloak and sparkling chainmail. The decorated polearm the palace guard carried seemed more ceremonial than practical, with the flag of the March hanging limp beneath the blade – a white tree adorned with the three-starred crown of the Hidden City, shining bright against a true-blue sky. When she reached the door, her gauntleted hand rapped a polite knock with the iron knocker. After a respectful pause, she slid open the speak-through panel and called mellifluously into the metal grating behind it.

"Pardon, your Lordship, you have a visitor." The palace guard's voice was young, strong-lunged, and easy on the ears. *A natural caller or singer*, thought Eriff. The young woman glanced to Eriff, a slight grin forming on her lips. She had a pleasant, round face under her helm and a well-mannered demeanor. She spoke into the grating again: "That Horse Lord's son who keeps coming around—"

"Yes. Yes. Let him in," a man's voice called from within. The guard shot Eriff another glance, playful and devious, then undid the catch and pushed on the thick wood. The door creaked open. She held it for Eriff to enter. After a polite nod of appreciation, the queensman stepped inside. Early morning rays of sunlight beamed into the chamber through high windows, illuminating the plush interior to its fullest.

The Lord of the March sat at his fine desk, eyes lowered, pouring over a scroll. Neat stacks of bone tubes sat to either side. Administrative manuals and notebooks lay strewn about the desktop, some open and some closed, interleaved with bookmarks and scraps of scribbled-on paper. Silvery, blue-feathered quill in hand, Lord Ralador's entire right forearm suddenly looped into a series of wide arcs as he inked his fanciful signature.

Without raising his eyes, the March Lord gestured to a stiff, wooden chair. "Be seated, Gallant Eriff Haulik," he said, his tone formal and infused with authority. He inspected the document from top to bottom as he spoke. "We must discuss the will of Aelish the Resplendent, with regards to the matter of Operation Diamondback."

The door shut behind Eriff as he took his seat. "Has the Chamber convened, my Lord?"

Satisfied with his handywork, Lord Ralador set the quill on its ornate, silver stand, gently blew on the signed document to dry the ink, and then rolled it up. He glanced at the blue candle beside him, burning bright, and the accompanying wax seal stamp. With a sigh, and without setting a seal on the document, he grasped an empty bone tube, popped the document in and corked it. Lord Ralador tilted back in his seat to finally meet Eriff's gaze.

"The Chamber of Aelish, at large, is unaware of the mission. I personally briefed Pristine Channeler Nawry Katena. She already knew something of the event, in fact, and was kind enough to provide words of 'guidance.'" The last word, he said with a hint of disdain. "News travels faster than glide boats, apparently."

"Her meaning, I take it, is that the task falls fully to you, my Lord."

"Hmm. Yes, I suppose it does. You know Aelish as well – or should I say better – than I do. If you could…"

Eriff considered the request for a long moment. As his father-in-law to be, Lord Ralador knew more about Eriff than Eriff cared for any commander of his to ever know. For one, the Lord of the March was keenly aware of Eriff's failed candidacy at the Royal Citadel as a *diviner*. And although a strong affinity to Aelish the Resplendent had been verified at a young age, which he was quite proud of, and rightly so for it is a rare and wondrous thing, his candidacy was ultimately rejected by a secret and uncharacteristic Chamber vote. Instead, Eriff had been relegated from adept to a mere battlefield healer –radiance channeler in polite company. That meant little more than a common squire with some enhanced capacity and training to apply battlefield first aid. The decision had come as a complete surprise and disappointment. Regardless of the slight, the Lord of the March treated Eriff in every respect like his very own personal diviner.

Lord Ralador began tapping his fingers on his desk. "Are you communing now? Have you obtained insight on the matter?"

"No, my Lord." *It does not work that way, and the rhythms are weak lately, if they are present at all.* Eriff forced himself not to come off insulting or to raise unwarranted concerns. "The skill is delicate – almost beyond me – and of late Aelish's will is veiled."

"Were you trying hard enough? You had a far-off expression on your face."

"A proper divination could take hours." *And really should be attempted by a member of the Chamber… not me.*

"Hmm… I see."

"Shall I then?"

Ralador considered the offer briefly, then shook his head. "Another time, perhaps. Just lend me your thoughts for now. I need something that will give me an edge in follow-on discussions with the Pristine Channeler. She has a tendency to go off on a wild tangent every now and again."

Eriff took a deep breath, thought about what he should say. He trusted his instincts.

"His Radiance, being suffused with positive energy, will see striker weapons, such as the sword we seek to recover, as integral to promoting the elder leviathan's values of defending life, health, and the pursuit of wholeness. He may go so far as to decree them veritable swords of power for the coming age. And the light emitted from them, by the flicker of the slider charm encrusted into each pommel, is likely to become a symbol of life energy for combating darkness in all of its many forms. His Radiance may even see strikers as an integral part of the epic battle prophesized against those shadows of life that persist beyond death – the Undying, of course, who hate the natural living."

The March Lord nodded slowly in response, pensive. "I see these things coming to pass as well. Amazing." He looked squarely at Eriff. "You have brought forth images that hithertofore lay dormant in my mind's eye."

"Perhaps your thoughts were just waiting for confirmation."

"Perhaps. It all seems so clear now."

"And," Eriff continued. "I am certain of one thing." He paused.

Lord Ralador leaned forward on his seat, ears pricked. "And that is…"

Most of what Eriff had said was just good sense, adjusted slightly for alignment with the March Lord's mindset. The queensman could do more, though. *Yes,* Eriff told himself, *this, both he and I can use.* He spoke gently.

"I am certain that Aelish does not wish this striker weapon – as I said, a veritable sword of power – to fall into the hands of the Harrowians, who would seek to twist such power into an instrument of terror and oppression."

Lord Ralador grunted his approval. "Splendid. That will do very well, in fact. Thank you, Gallant Eriff Haulik. You bring honor to your house. My *adopted* daughter could not have found a better suitor."

"Thank you, my Lord. I am humbled by your words." Not quite humbled by one of those words though, which he'd spoken with inflection. A question came to mind: Were she his biological daughter, would he still have thought a horse lord's son good enough? *Not likely,* Eriff decided, *which is probably why he pointed that out.*

Lord Ralador stood up, chair scraping against the floor's smooth tiles. Eriff also rose, adjusted his cuirass.

The March Lord extended his hand over the desk; in it, the bone scroll tube he'd just signed. "Take this note," he said. "Read it to yourself before you depart, for planning purposes, but don't let anyone else know about the scroll's contents until you touch down between the two rivers."

"Touch down, my Lord?"

"Yes. Order Valkyrie will be handling the drop-off. I've just received the rendezvous instructions by raven."

"I see." Eriff shifted his stance. He'd expected a larger contingent. "Is that all that can be spared for this mission, my Lord, four gryphons and those which they would carry?"

"Speed and secrecy are of the essence."

"Of course, my Lord. Myself and three queensmen, then."

"And don't forget the rangers."

"Of course."

"That should be sufficient. The note states that you are to meet Order Valkyrie a short ride out of the gorge, at a pair of hills…"

"The Kiranis Hills, my Lord. I know them well."

"You should leave early – send your assault group trailing after, if need be. I want you to hobnob with the valkyries; get on their good sides before the rangers show up. Charming and such, right?"

Eriff nodded. Lord Ralador stooped over the desk, extended his arm, and firmly knuckled Eriff's plate-armored shoulder.

"That's my boy," he said. "And don't forget to warn the good ladies about those scoundrels they are about to deal with." He paused to raise his index finger. In silence, he held it suspended for a long moment.

"And one other thing," he went on, finally. "I want to know the look on Ranger Berendt Garondi's face when you read the scroll to him aloud. He was such a pain at the exercise – it would have been much better if the Kith Overseer had just attended like he was supposed to."

"Too easy, my Lord."

"And I have it on good authority that Knightmaiden Galewind is due to attend this mission. She may have made some assumptions about command that I am afraid will be shattered by the scroll's contents. She is likely to conspire with that ranger Garondi the entire flight in. No bother. I want to know the look on her face as well, when you read the words aloud."

"My Lord, I will report back every grimace and every clenched fist.

I will report every flushed shade of red that appears on their faces, and every throw of the arms in frustration and disbelief."

"Splendid. We cannot let these singing birds and ranging rogues run operations that are this important. Imagine what would result. Pure and utter chaos, no less."

"Understood, my Lord." Eriff tucked the scroll tube away into his sidebag. He turned partially, aiming to leave.

Lord Ralador raised a staying hand. "One more thing, before you go, if you please." He gestured to the wooden chair, while he himself retook his plush seat.

Eriff stalled out of instinct, then slowly sat back down. "Of course, my Lord."

The March Lord met his gaze. "I put in a special request to the Kith Commander. One of the young rangers caught my eye at the exercise, a spotter by the name of Rix Caledon."

Eriff remembered the youth, barely old enough to be enlisted: "The redhead that you did not allow to compete?"

"Yes," Ralador said, then muttered, "Rules are rules, after all." He cleared his throat. "I have seen his ilk before, back when I captained a Lancer company."

"The thirteen sixty-second, my Lord. A battle cavalry."

"Yes, very good. Did my daughter tell you?"

"The cavalry commands during the Outland Wars are mandatory reading. I can only dream of leading such a fine unit one day."

"You will, I am sure." Lord Ralador narrowed his eyes, nodded slowly, and gave the queensman a measured look. He spoke softly, with an encouraging tone. "You have that fire in you. Bide your time, young man. Now here is something for you to chew on. Keep this to yourself: the command elements at Gallant and Captain level will be shaken up soon enough. I have been conversing with the Earl on this matter. Too many in the Lancer battalion have become too comfortable on their high horses for too long. Only the expeditionary units have any real experience these days. The Lancer's lack of vision and prepared-ness is disturbing, as was reflected yesterday in the mock battle against the rangers." He winced and shook his head, visibly upset. "Those rogues never should have lasted near as long as they did. That was not your fault though. I do not blame you. Not yet anyway, you had just been promoted."

Eriff stiffened. "I thought so as well and felt the Guard's honor at risk. The match was invalid though. Nevertheless, I will put my utmost into retraining those under my command to address this issue. It will not happen again."

Lord Ralador nodded in agreement. "This will be your top priority upon return. I will ensure that the first six of Order Lumen's white-metal swords are assigned to your quick reaction force. You will perform martial miracles during your command, young man. You will revitalize the Queen's Guard, and this is how you will do it: train your men on this radically new weapon, then proudly demonstrate its capabilities to the First Assembly and to the citizens of Gan in the course of your premier away mission as commander."

"Away mission, my Lord? You mean other than the one we are currently discussing?"

"Yes, yes. Diamondback does not count. No one can know it even happened." He paused. "You see, something is brewing to the East, my young Gallant, beneath Ironeagle Peak… those brutish Baruush, of course. And in the swamps of Jakka, the slithering Nali. I am certain of it. I can feel it in my bones. They are up to no good and Harrow is behind it all. Our expeditionary forces are having great difficulty maintaining captured territories near Jakka, and the Wilder tribes can no longer hold the Baruush line of control. You will lead an elite force of your best fighters to deal with the problem areas swiftly and surely." He paused, leaned forward over the desk, then lowered his voice to a firm whisper. "News of your great deeds will boost enlistment, and, if carefully laden with the right mix of rumors, the news will spread to our neighbors and both astonish and horrify them. Harrow will think twice about any schemes they are cooking up on the eve of the union between our two city states. As you know, my whisperers tell me a covert takeover of Gan is imminent."

"Takeover?" That raised Eriff's eyebrows. He pretended not to be surprised. "Ah… the Union, yes." Then he ejected the obligatory pleasantries. "Blessings of Aelish to both of them, Queen Xara and King Taeglin. May they discover long-lasting love beyond duty and sacrifice." Fishing for more intelligence, he asked, "Have you heard new tidings from your whisperers, my Lord? There is much hearsay circulating. The Wilder tribes are also having trouble on the Harrow front." Eriff had heard nothing of the sort, but he suspected tensions would be on the rise there as well.

"Unfounded speculation." Lord Ralador scoffed, waved the notion off. "All of it. The problem on the northwest line with Harrow will disappear once the Union is made." Then he grinned out of place, nodding the way he always does when relishing a thought. "Call it a farewell parting gift between old rivals, if what you say is true."

Eriff nodded back, "Ah, yes, perhaps."

Ralador hesitated. "Now, where was I before we got onto this track..." He slumped back in his chair, made himself comfortable, then spoke gently. "Ah yes. That young ranger I was talking about would have been Spotter Rix Caledon's great-great-uncle that I rode with... maybe one hundred and twenty years ago, scouting the Ironeagle Mountain Range off the southeastern tip of Deepweald." He paused, reflective. The air in the room went dead. Eriff watched as tiny specks of dust, visible only within the thin sheets of sunlight that beamed through the high windows, slowly sank from the ceiling. "One hundred and twenty-one years, six months, twelve days. Has it really been that long?"

Eriff hoped his eyes had not glazed over noticeably. Equally, he hoped his future father-in-law would not break into another long-winded account of a battle long-forgotten. Not much of the content of such stories seemed to apply anymore. It was a different world back then.

Lord Ralador continued. "Ranger Taarix Caledon, that was his name. If this Rix is half the man Taarix Caledon was, he will be indispensable for your away missions to Ironeagle and Jakka. Be sure to secure his services. A fantastic marksman... went on to become the renowned Ranger Knight-Errand Taarix Caledon; especially proficient at picking off enemy spies, once our patrols flushed them out. Slippery targets, they were: small, agile, always on the move and making expert use of cover, and deadly with poison darts. This all occurred in the numbered days preceding my battle cavalry's charge on Irongate, which had been overrun by Outlanders – the Baruush, of course. With insider backing I'll have you know."

Lord Ralador paused again.

Please be over.

Then Eriff's father-in-law-to-be cleared his throat and continued. "Ahem… yes. There is an interesting story behind that one…"

Eriff gulped, grinned outwardly, and bore the pain.

CHAPTER IV

WINDSWEPT

(Wind)

SAILING HIGH ABOVE the world, Norwin of the Dawn basked in the raw energy of the sun. A familiar vibration arose within her, above all others, carried by the Nexus. "Ah yes," she muttered to herself in a language not of Theia. "The big one." She favored this man and the beasts he tended to. *His connection is strong.* Norwin knew he spoke aloud when he addressed her and that he called unto the open skies. The two together helped twist and propel the threads of his utterances, so that they wove their way with forceful determination through the Aether to her. But the man took a risk, she noted, for a message so closely guarded as this one.

I will send him a Spirit Raven, to teach him Avian, the tongue of my flock.

The Great Eagle dipped a wing, eyes on the Bundle the man had spoken of, and banked towards it. First, she examined the jumbled paths with her mind's eye, her third eye, to determine if intervention was warranted. The paths leading in were many and fateful. *A dark forest*, she could see, *where those who enter will collide dramatically, and those who exit will shape the future.* The knots and twists within the bundle of events in that forest were impossible to sort out from high above, writhing and pulsing even as she observed. But what emerged from the convergence of folds was purposeful, yet wispy thin on any one path and widely spread in purpose. *A tipping point*, she concluded. The one some call the Wind God angled her great wings against her momentum, beat them gently to halt her advance. She would hover over this place. She cocked her head, fixed all three eyes on the bundle within the forest. Tipping points require careful scrutiny.

Norwin of the Dawn did not like what she saw in the spectrum of outcomes for that tipping point. No indeed, it did not suit her. Not at all. The fibers pulsed. Frayed ends flailed without closure, and they drew on and on with senseless waste. And she saw the flicker of what might grow to become a beacon for destruction on a grand scale, even transcendent. So, the Great Eagle beat her great wings strong and altered the skies, but she shrieked in outrage at what she saw unfold. Again and again, she beat her wings with ferocity and determination, to no avail. At a loss, to vary the mix, she instead gathered air masses and set them on a path of convergence to the bundle. She would forge an unseasonable storm at the risk of leaving more to chance than to her will.

Norwin of the Dawn settled on the only acceptable pattern she could find. She was convinced it would come to be, for no other Colossus, material or otherwise, was likely to be drawn to this event, given its small footprint and the veils of secrecy surrounding it. Try as she might though, a gryphon would be lost to the world. A sacrifice to the Wind. But that much was inevitable, and that particular facet of reality to come saddened her deeply. Her heart sank into her stomach with the grief of such a loss. Yet, she took some comfort in yet another gryphon joining her flock. It had been so very long. The Great Eagle swept her gaze back to the Elderkin man who had called her name to the Wind.

As reward, Norwin sent the man a sensation of profound calm that one only attains while hovering high above the world. She sensed his meditation on the feeling thus granted. But there was more. This man had chosen to be mortal, and the choice convolved with every fiber of his being, and every thread that he sent into the Aether, to Chaos' end.

Norwin proclaimed aloud, "Do not fret, mortal-by-choice! When your path folds and knots with the inevitable, your essence will soar with me above the skies!" She craned her head to behold and admire the supreme collection of windswept souls that propelled her through the heavens. "Yes! Fly with me, Beastmaster Lorenz!"

Norwin of the Dawn sent the man just enough knowledge of the weather to make him look good, but not so much as to spoil her clever designs.

Chapter V
WIND RIDERS
(Stormbringer)

STORMBRINGER SHARED THE Wing Table with her two wind riders – one beside and the other diagonally across – together with the head of Order Valkyrie, Lady Apsarla. The Lady sat wingtip, a place of honor, respect, and focus. She demanded no less. Her spangled headdress and jeweled accessories reinforced her status, colorful and vibrant against her dark hair and smooth, sandy-beige skin. Being the second most senior in attendance, Stormbringer sat adjacent to Lady Apsarla, back to the cave wall. The seat across remained vacant – reserved for the final attendee, late in arrival.

The room was stark, the hearth cold that morning, for lack of wood. There was no escaping the damp chill that seeped in from the outside. Lanterns lined the rock walls but only half were lit, spilling their yellow light across the polished stone surface of the table. The spearmaiden's eyes rested on the crisscrossing shadows cast by the table's protruding centerpiece: a large, fossilized bone cut from the heart of the Aerie.

A pause had come over the valkyries as they waited in silence, lulled by the hollow sounds of wind in the chimney-shaft, anticipating the approaching footsteps from outside. Lady Apsarla hadn't revealed who the final valkyrie might be. Stormbringer had her hopes up though:

another rising-star wind rider to command, perhaps, or one of the newer spearmaidens. Nor had Apsarla spoken much about the mission particulars. Her firm poise and placid composure did little to betray her inner devices.

Stormbringer looked forward to her command, particularly with regard to Rainsong. She glanced at the brown-skinned woman beside her, eyeing the chiseled cheekbones and the striking white braids tight to her scalp. Rainsong was a top performer: strong, practical and gregarious, young enough not to have any serious bad habits, and she possessed enough raw talent and athletic prowess to be jealous of. *She'll make a capable spearmaiden, someday*, Stormbringer knew. Then she glanced at Catwings, who sat comfortably slumped with her back to the door, relaxed, lost in thought.

Catwings was a different sort altogether and harder to gauge. Her pleasant features and easy-going style made her a natural go-between. And she had a mischievous demeanor about her that played off well against her petite build and pixie-cut hair, platinum-blonde. Yet, she seemed distant at times, private even. Stormbringer wasn't exactly sure how best to use Catwings. She'd have to try her out for size and get a feel for her strengths and weaknesses.

The footsteps stopped; the door to the Wing Chamber whirled open. Propelled by a rush of air, the iron-bound oak thudded against the cave wall, then slowly grated back with the drawn-out groan of heavy hinges. Knightmaiden Galewind stood in the doorway, dark hair wind-whipped in front of her oval face. Her fur-lined cloak flapped behind her, revealing the soft leathers she wore underneath, black and body-hugging. She strode in with the grace of a disheveled duchess.

Palace lapdog, thought Stormbringer straightaway, who wore her wings on her combat helm as opposed to in her hair as an accessory. Irritation burned through her and she firmed up her composure. She leaned forward, straining her eyes to look past Galewind, to see who the knightmaiden had brought with her to offer up for this mission. No one else was there.

Galewind addressed her superior. "My Lady, a pleasure as always." She offered the top valkyrie a polite curtsey. The woman's mannerisms carried hints of Gan's pampered affluent. *Speaks to her roots,* thought the spearmaiden, disdain building up inside. Even though valkyrie backgrounds are hidden in order to protect their identities, she knew it had to be true.

The Lady accepted Galewind's greeting with a kind nod, face beaming with smiling grace.

Stormbringer burst out, "Norwin's Breeze, what is *that woman* doing here?"

"Spearmaiden!" Lady Apsarla scolded back, eyes glaring. "That *woman* is your superior."

Heat flushed behind Stormbringer's eyes. "She has no right." The spearmaiden folded her arms, stiffened in her chair, then scoffed at the woman. "How dare she even show her face on this mountaintop." Stormbringer glanced at her two wind riders for affirmation. Both shrunk in their chairs. The spearmaiden turned back to Lady Apsarla, avoiding Galewind's stare. "She can't just waltz into a warm welcome like that, not after what she did… or failed to do."

Everyone knew what Stormbringer was talking about – the circulating accusations, the fact Galewind was in charge during the recent tragedy that saw two talented valkyries and two novice celestes plunge to their deaths in a catastrophic in-air collision. All for the sake of a banned flyby maneuver: passing the flag of the Aerie while barrel-rolling past one another within a wingspan. *Stupid.*

The knightmaiden looked to Apsarla, waited. Remaining composed, the Lady Valkyrie delayed her response. No reaction could be discerned by her expression. And as the seconds ticked by, the tension mounted.

Stormbringer didn't care if the incident was the victims' own fault, if they knew better. Surely, the young celestes understood they were tempting fate. But that's what initiates do and it's up to the instructor to be firm on points of safety, recklessness. And to anticipate. *No, that's not an excuse. You can't just tell them. You have to drill it into their heads.*

Stormbringer shrugged at the silence. "Well, I want to know." She glanced to her wind riders again, then back to the head of the table. "We all deserve to know. This is a command confidence issue." By rights, Stormbringer stood next in line to command the away missions. Only one person could challenge that pecking order, and that person was standing across from her. Unbelievably.

Lady Apsarla kept her gaze steady, her tone firm as she gave answer. "I never said who would be in command."

Galewind broke in, "I didn't come here to command anything."

Stormbringer narrowed her eyes. *That's right. Back off, Princess.* The spearmaiden's time for a command had come; no, it was overdue. And Galewind was, well, out of practice, to put it mildly. Unlike the knights of other orders, the title "Valkyrie Knightmaiden" was more honorary than anything else. As the biting thoughts roiled in Stormbringer's mind, she noticed Lady Apsarla had been reading her expression all along.

"What ill brews within you now, Stormbringer?"

The spearmaiden said nothing.

The Lady huffed, "Isn't it always *something* with you?" She paused. Again, Stormbringer gave no answer. "Whatever it is," the Lady continued, "I implore you to drop it, or I shall find a spearmaiden who can fulfill her duties faithfully and without prejudice."

The words stung more than they should have, more than Stormbringer wanted them to. She'd held the belief that Lady Apsarla valued her efforts highly, especially of late. Stormbringer had been as dependable as could be throughout the recent crisis and had taken on heavy duties to help the Order cope with shortages, all the while maintaining operational tempo. She'd kept the wind riders organized, focused and productive. She'd worked long hours, fatigued, and had done odd jobs that weren't hers to do. She was proud of all she'd accomplished. *And now this?* The lead valkyrie's cutting response brought all of that appreciation, all of her efforts, into question.

Stormbringer could summon little more from herself than to keep her mouth shut. She didn't even try to hide her defiant expression.

The Lady measured the spearmaiden's visage again, sighed heavily, and in the same gesture quickly shed the imbalance in her disposition. Her voice softened. "I personally invited Knightmaiden Galewind. She possesses critical information. Do you care to contest, Stormbringer?"

The Lady didn't wait for an answer. Instead, she reached out to the knightmaiden, wiggling her stretched fingers. Galewind approached. Apsarla firmly grasped the knightmaiden's wrist. Eyes still fixed on Stormbringer, she continued. "Galewind, my sweet and loyal sister, has been cleared of all wrongdoings."

Galewind clamped her eyes shut, let out something between a gasp and a soft laugh. When she opened them again, she gazed at Lady Apsarla, eyes glistening. She tightly squeezed the hand of her superior. "Thank you so much. I was hoping you'd heard… you can't imagine…"

Stormbringer interjected, "So, she's off the hook and on the mission then?"

Lady Apsarla responded with measured firmness, "Off the hook, yes. The rest you will find out, Spearmaiden, soon enough: precisely when I decide to tell you. Remember, we are all sisters in this Order. We stand arm-in-arm, as one."

With a light tug on Galewind's wrist and a sincere locking of the eyes, Lady Apsarla urged Galewind to the adjacent chair. "Please sit with us now, Knightmaiden, we have much to discuss."

"How about shutting the door first," Stormbringer said.

Catwings got to it first. "It's freezing out there," she complained.

Before reclaiming her seat, the wind rider made a display of pulling out the chair meant for Galewind, next to hers. The knightmaiden politely accepted.

"Welcome, Knightmaiden," Catwings said.

Rainsong regarded Galewind, "Yes, welcome. You must feel so good to be vindicated."

"Relieved is all," Galewind responded. "Now I can get on with my life. But nothing takes away the pain of the loss. A terrible loss."

As all nodded in agreement, the room suddenly seemed small and crowded to Stormbringer, and she felt more on the peripheral of the group than belonging to it. She sat wondering if it was even possible that this woman really had done no wrong, given her role and given the circumstances. It went contrary to everything she'd heard about the Judiciary's investigation.

Galewind withdrew a notepad from her cloak pocket, opened it, and flipped to a page of scribblings. She paused to read it to herself, then addressed Lady Apsarla. "Before we begin the discussion, my Lady, I have a message to relay from Lord Ralador."

Apsarla clenched her jaw. "What does the Lord of the March want this time?"

"My Lady, he has requested immediate surveillance from the eastern tip of Deepweald, bearing southeast, along the mountain range as far as Ironeagle Peak. He claims that according to Irongate, after prolonged dormancy the Baruush Outlanders have increased their military enrollment, training cycles, and intensity of training. They are also constructing new war engines. Irongate believes they are massing an invading force. Lord Ralador asks that we, Order Valkyrie, provide evidence to validate these claims."

Apsarla's perfectly arched eyebrows drew close together. "To invade where, exactly?" she asked. "They have a long way to go to get anywhere."

Galewind responded, "He did not say, my Lady."

Lady Apsarla shook her head. "How dare he. Ralador, I mean. These are all side concerns. Has the Asph changed sex yet? Has the leviathan's new mate been ascertained?"

Galewind sighed softly. "No one knows for sure, my Lady. Or at least, it wasn't part of the March Lord's message."

"Completion of the change is the indicator we have all been waiting for. Without evidence of such an occurrence, collecting such information will have to wait. Lord Ralador is well aware that we do not have enough resources to conduct simultaneous missions, especially not now, and especially not at opposite ends of Deepweald." Lady Apsarla let out an exaggerated sigh. "Four gryphons and missions enough for a fleet. No. This mission I am about to convey to you is the priority. The Earl will back me on this."

Rainsong cocked her head, narrowed her eyes. "So, what is this mission exactly?"

CHAPTER VI
AS PERFECT A PLACE AS ONE MIGHT FIND

(Amot)

AMOT PAUSED AT the summit, ribs tight, squeezed even. It felt like his insides were quivering. He took a deep breath and glanced up. Jagged clouds raced by on a low plane of fast wind. Behind them, the unmoving dullness of early morning shaded the backdrop. He glanced back over his shoulder, cocked his head to listen for Howler. The dog had disappeared, as usual.

Tension mounting, the scout eased out of the gloomy woods and emerged in the Sacred Grove. At its heart sat a flat boulder with glyphs incised upon it. Behind it, a huge and squat-looking tree.

A crow gruffed out a caw, left. Amot swung his gaze to the greyed and dried-out pines there, leaning over the bluff like suicidal skeletons. A score of the forest's small, feathered beguilers eyed Amot as if they knew something he didn't, plumage gleaming like black velvet. Their tilting heads and sharp eyes tracked every motion with bold inquisitiveness.

Amot ignored their prying eyes, turned his attention straight ahead to the flourishing maple that stood just beyond, too gargantuan to be real. The base of its trunk flared out in a tangle of roots. Amot's breaths accelerated; lungs constricted by the tightness in his chest. With careful steps, he passed the Sunrise Arch to his right and approached the Runestone.

The scout's keen eyes zeroed in on the leaves in the high branches. A quiet gust had set them to flutter. They didn't move quite right – heavy, like flaps of leather. And on lower boughs, sheltered from the wind, the leaves shimmered more than they should. More light passed through their fleshy matter than was normal. Amot stepped cautiously towards the Spirit Hurlorn, peering up between its branches. The crows erupted in screeching protest. Amot ignored them, stole another step. The shrieks grew harsher, louder. Urgent.

The maple's leafy crown began to stir and shudder. The crows went silent. A rolling voice billowed forth from somewhere in the high branches, slow and calming. It labored in deep tones, rasping and guttural and rough as old bark.

"Do you smell rain in the air?" boomed the voice.

Something in the sound hit Amot like a wave. Soothing reverberations flattened the tension in his chest, as though scoured away by its rough edges. "I do," Amot replied.

"I feel the moisture in every leaf this fine morning," the voice continued. "Every bough… I so miss the *smell* of rain." The Hurlorn paused.

High branches quivered. Loud creaks sounded. The trunk began to shift.

"Stand clear now, young *Wiffler*."

Amot stumbled backwards as the massive tree toppled forward. In the plunge, two great forelimbs shot out, slamming the earth with a thud that shook the hill. Thick, heavy scales of bark jostled with the impact. Roots tore out of the ground and what remained of the trunk ripped apart into two hind legs, creeping tendrils swirling about them. A long and sinuous tail whipped free of its coil.

The Colossus that stood on all fours before Amot looked like something straight out of a legend, much different than the drowsy Spirit Hurlorn he'd tended to with his grandfather, years ago. The process was complete. The man had fully incarnated the beast.

The whipping vines and tendrils gently came to rest. A long

moment of stillness followed, so much so that the creature once again appeared surprisingly natural and tree-like, in complete harmony with the surroundings except for the oddity of four trunks instead of one to support a single, dense canopy. Amot dared to approach again. This time, the old crows held their tongues.

With a sudden rustling, the leafy crown parted directly above Amot. A face peered down from between the branches. Gnarled and wood-grained, with a little imagination it could pass as vaguely lizard-like. Amiable and kind though, like shared wisdom, with a slight grin and a definite smiling of the one eye that was clearly visible, the other overgrown by a burl gone wild. The creature scrunched its grainy brow, perplexed, and spoke once more.

"I knew your father and your grandfather," the old Hurlorn graveled. "I am wholly surprised you returned to serve in Deepweald. Not many do, of those who leave. And less, of those who tend to offend."

"Apologies," Amot said. "I did n—… I mean I do not mean to offend, only to serve and inform. That is my duty. I am Kith, at your service."

"And studying to become a kithblade, the Whispers tell me."
Amot nodded. "Someday."

"Hmph," resounded the beast with a woodwind snort. "I believe you have come for more reasons than just to inform."

On a silver platter, the scout reminded himself. *Explain what happened. My apologies on a silver platter. The Green Dragon will understand.* But the instant Amot opened his mouth to speak his mind, to offer his side of the "Sprigg and kindling" incident from years back, the foremost of all Hurlorns burst into wild Treesong.

The lyrical verse caught the scout off guard. Amot could do little more than stand before the beast in wonderment, in awe. Yet, he resisted being drawn into the song's gentle rhythms and soothing tones. He attempted to dissect, decipher, decode. But the harder he tried, the more the Treesong charged through his being, permeated his soul, yet remained elusive in its every meaning. And although Amot knew that true words had to lie somewhere within, the moment he thought he had one in his grasp it melted away and dribbled between his fingers. In his mind's eye, Amot was whisked away to wherever the forest creature willed to carry him – faraway places beyond the edge of consciousness. Dark reaches. Such a foolish thing.

Its unrelenting grip now solid on Amot, the Treesong pulled the scout in two opposing directions.

The first wave pulled him in profound and sorrowful ways, drawn from the deep and tragic earth. The turmoil of his upbringing, the disappointment of the Overseer, blood-soaked ground and the scorn of his brothers, the tragedy of new love, a raging sea, and the death of his heart. Only the first two were known to him. The rest had never happened, nor should they ever happen, but they were present nonetheless, building and shifting under burdening, heavy tones that made his stomach sink and his feet weigh like granite. But even while anchored so by calamity to the hard, stony earth, the second wave played in to free him of it: airy and wind-woven melodies lifted his spirits. But there was only one matter of substance in the counter-offering there, among past and present. He would grow a new heart. These things made perfect sense to Amot, in the moment.

The sensation of being caught between the two waves was one of being "stretched out" – so thin he felt he would rip at the seams. And when he reckoned his being could be stretched no further, musical moments both pleasant and inviting drew him closer to the core of the Treesong, like the warm voice of an old friend, only to circle back in betrayal; full of bitterness, spite, and utter disbelief. The duality of its superposed beats and melodies was ever-present and complex. A blending of autumn colors into song was the last thing Amot fully remembered, as the tune melded into a pale yellow hum.

Time had passed out of memory during the experience. Some unknown duration after entry, the scout found himself on his way to exit the grove. He felt drained. Footsteps slow and heavy, he shuffled ahead, half in a trance as though sleepwalking. Coming to this realization suddenly, Amot blinked his eyes twice, shook his head, then stopped to look back. The Sacred Grove appeared to him as silent and natural as when he'd first arrived. And as his eyes fixated on the great maple and the Runestone, an unparalleled sense of purpose welled up inside. The ubiquitous presence of a higher order filled his being. For a brief moment, he saw himself together as one with the subtleties of Time and Fate laid out before him. But the feeling washed away before he could appreciate it fully, as non-specific as a bygone dream minutes after waking.

Amot wanted to tell the Green Dragon so much more: Hadamard's message, the lost striker sword, the wonders of Jhin he'd witnessed. And he wanted to ask the Hurlorn – his grandfather's good friend – he wanted to ask the Hurlorn about his father. But the specific things Amot had on his brain told him that somehow he'd accomplished the tasks charged to his doing, and that somehow the answers he needed now lay rooted within his being. For one, after the mission, it was in his thoughts to make a slight detour to Turnsby on his way back and obtain supplies for writing. Then he would report back to the grove. And there was something on the tip of his memory about old friends, and Hurlorns, and a sword of black metal, together with the drawn-out clinking sound of a long chain being dragged over the ground. He couldn't make sense of it all.

A crow rattled off a croak, Amot's way. A farewell croak.

The next instant, a border hedge parted in front of him. It was almost rude.

The young Kith obliged. Still in a daze, he stepped through to the other side of the parting. Back to reality. Back to the solitude of the forest.

"Howler," he called straightaway, his voice shaky. Amot cleared his throat, called again. He descended the slope and followed up with a whistle. "Come here, boy!"

In the distance, Howler responded to his master's call with a single bark, then started crashing through the bushes in the exact wrong direction.

Amot just shook his head. *What am I going to do with a dog like you?*

When the scout finally did catch up with Howler, the answer to his question was obvious. The dog stunk and was covered in even more grime. On top of that, it would be a long run to Elgar's Pocket. They'd both need a swim.

CHAPTER VII

TWO WINGS AND A TAIL

(Galewind, Stormbringer)

GALEWIND FLIPPED THROUGH the pages of her notebook to the mission particulars she'd recorded back in the Netherdome, then nodded to her superior. She wondered how much the lead valkyrie already knew. *News travels fast.*

One by one, Lady Apsarla made eye contact with the other valkyries at the table, then began her explanation. "As the knightmaiden will surely elaborate on, it seems one of our Wilder friends has lost something important that belongs to Gan."

Galewind nodded knowingly. "Yes, a sword. I saw it happen."

Rainsong deflated, dropped her shoulders, made a saucy remark. "And they want us to find it?" She shook her head and huffed in disbelief. "No, not again. Let them conduct their own search. We can't see a damn thing through the canopy, and even if we could, the leaves are already falling. One windstorm and the ground will be covered. Don't they have something else for us?"

Lady Apsarla endured the mild outburst, then continued. "As I understand the mission, dear Rainsong, Wilders will be conducting the search alongside special operatives from the Queen's Guard."

Stormbringer scoffed. "I can't imagine anything going wrong with *that* combo."

Catwings turned her gaze to Stormbringer, eyes wide and eyebrows raised, with a perfect O forming on her lips. "Ohhhh, ya," she whispered loudly.

Lady Apsarla sighed, flicked her gaze to the hard rock ceiling and back.

"Order, sisters," Galewind stated, in place of her superior.

Stormbringer and her wing riders fell silent and still.

Apsarla went on without further hesitation, skin shining like burnished clay in the lantern light. She regarded each sister at the table equally, in turn, while dictating their duties.

"Valkyries, this mission needs two wings to get off the ground, and I need each of you to fulfill your assigned roles. The left wing is transport, the right wing is reconnaissance and quick response, but be prepared for more – a tail, we shall say, so three parts in total. But if the tail drags, cut it loose."

She eyed the exterior door and the single, shuttered window, then paused to choose her words with care. "This mission is highly secretive. To begin with, we… no *you*, pardon … will have to rendezvous outside the city, away from crows' eyes, and transport the payload to Whisperwood. I chose the Kiranis Hills. They are out of the way and not far from the palace. As we speak, Beastmaster Lorenz readies your mounts."

Stormbringer said, "The payload… do you mean queensmen and rangers?"

"And all of their gear," Galewind added.

Rainsong leaned forward, eyes glowing. "What's the next part? The tail?"

Lady Apsara smiled, "I appreciate your enthusiasm, Rainsong, but I have yet to convey the right wing."

Catwings snickered. Lady Apsarla ignored her.

"The right wing is sealing the border between Greater Harrow and the Forest Between Two Rivers, also known as Whisperwood, depending on which map you are looking at. This should only be needed for a few days, maximum. During that time, no one must be allowed to enter or leave the northern boundary of the forest. You will have full freedom in this matter to deter travelers or woodsmen by any reasonable means, and to engage Harrowian forces, *but only if absolutely necessary.* Use your judgement. No one passes in or out while the operation is afoot. Understood?"

Galewind and Stormbringer both spoke up at the same instant. Lady Apsarla regarded Galewind.

"Whisperwood extends past Harrow's Gate, my Lady," said the knightmaiden. "As you may recall, decades ago the Harrowian Guard used to run foot patrols through that territory on a regular basis. Officially, it's still a line of control, but is largely ignored in that context."

"I can't recall a single incident along that L-O-C." Lady Apsarla swept her gaze to Stormbringer. "What does my spearmaiden have to say on the matter?"

Stormbringer provided more current information. "Harrow *is* running patrols, at *irregular* intervals. Rainsong, Catwings?"

Catwings shifted in her seat, but it was Rainsong who accepted the cue. "They've stepped up the pace, m'Lady. Two or three a day between the rivers. The only incidents in the area lately involve smuggling of one sort or another, usually with no trace of Harrow's involvement. We don't believe they use the forest."

Galewind asked, "How far south do the patrols run?"

Catwings spoke up. "Not far. They like to skirt the northern edge of the forest. I don't think they have any desire to enter."

"At least not without force," Stormbringer added.

Galewind nodded. "Yes. They won't go in. They believe it's haunted, just like everyone in Turnsby does." Keeping to her purely professional tone, she addressed Stormbringer. "Air?"

Stormbringer again looked to the faces of her wind riders, this time to confirm. They both shook their heads. She swung back to regard Galewind. "We have suspicions they send cloakers on patrol at night as far south as Abandon Bay, but we don't really know."

Lady Apsarla asked, "Cloakers?"

Galewind addressed her question. "Also called stone ghosts. Flying mounts of the Il'kinik from deep underground. Blind as bats. They originate from beyond the Catacombs and the Dim Sea – Dromeron Odoon, in particular."

"And cloakers can get *huge*," Rainsong added.

Catwings teetered back and forth slightly in her chair, knees up. Her brow wrinkled. "Can we hide from them?"

Galewind shrugged. "From what I know, they have poor eyesight or none at all, but they home in on their targets like bats, so don't expect to gain cover from darkness."

Lady Apsarla spoke next. "I said this mission needed two wings to get off the ground. There is the tail that I would now like to discuss. Over the course of your interactions with the Kith Quarter, I want you to scout for a good ranger."

Rainsong's hands clutched together. "Good *looking* you mean? Handsome, with rugged good looks?"

Catwings added her two coppers worth. "Yet sophisticated, and gentle with the ladies?"

Rainsong shook her head. "Not necessary." She chuckled at herself and then smiled wide. "I'll be the brains and put the man in his place."

Catwings smirked back at Rainsong. "I bet you would."

Lady Apsarla responded to the wind riders, forcing an even tone. "We need someone who knows the lands we surveil."

"A Wilder then, not some Stout or fort boy," Galewind stated. "Wilders know the forest like the handles of their hatchets."

"Choose the lightest," Stormbringer said. "We don't want some lug dragging us down."

Rainsong asked, "Aren't there female rangers?"

"A few," Galewind replied, "but don't let that be the driver. There are other requirements I can think of straightaway. Mounted archery training would be nice to have in certain situations."

Rainsong's eyes widened again, excitement brewing. "The Whisper. Can you imagine what communications on the fly would do for us?"

Galewind shook her head. "I don't think it works up high. The Hurlorns pass the Whispers from one to the next, using tiny vibrating hairs on their bodies that emit sound we can't hear."

Catwings jerked her head back slightly. "How do you know all that?"

"It's in the new course that I teach, in the Hidden City. I believe we need to gain a better appreciation of how the other orders and guards operate."

"Maybe I should take it."

"You're welcome to."

Rainsong tilted her head to one side. "Back to the Whisper. How do the rangers hear it then?"

Galewind furrowed her brow in response. The real experts who'd trained her on the subject, the luminaries, had skipped that aspect. "I'm not sure exactly," she said, "but from what I understand the Hurlorns work together as one to focus the sound at rangers who are trained to listen for it, and who happen to be in the path of the Whisper. It can even find them."

"We could swoop down," countered Stormbringer, "pass messages at predetermined intervals during a patrol."

"Hmm." Galewind shrugged, nodded slowly. "Maybe. You might need to straight-out land though – it takes some time, stillness, and concentration to pick up a Whisper."

Catwings' face lit up, "We need two rangers for messaging. One on each end."

The knightmaiden smirked. *Wishful thinking, young wind rider.*

Stormbringer addressed Lady Apsarla. "How many cats are we sending on the mission? And who is going?" She took a deep breath, exhaled slowly, readied herself for whatever answer might come her way.

Lady Apsarla responded to the young wind rider's comment first. Stormbringer tried not to take it as a slight.

"Catwings dear, we will start with just one ranger for now." Rainsong's lip curled into a feigned pout at the remark. The Lady turned to regard the knightmaiden. "Galewind, you were present at the exercise during which the *item* was lost."

The knightmaiden nodded. "As a distinguished observer, my Lady."

"Then you must have an idea who might be suitable among the ranger cadre."

"I do, my Lady. Unfortunately, the most impressive ranger who comes anywhere near the lightweight requirement is also the one being blamed for this entire mess. Lord Ralador despises him." Galewind flipped through her notes, found her entry on him. "Amot Rixin: a strong fighter, considered unpredictable – wildcard, use caution."

"Stormbringer?"

"Yes, m'Lady."

"What is your opinion of this ranger."

"I know nothing of this ranger or what happened… m'Lady."

"And?"

Stormbringer started her answer, "And…"

What does she want to hear?

Then it came to Stormbringer. She glanced at Galewind, then back to Apsarla. Her shoulders dropped as she sighed, lowered her eyes.

"And we should wait to hear his side of the story before we judge."

Apsarla hesitated. Catwings flashed wide eyes and a slight nod to Stormbringer from across the table.

Stormbringer took the prompting. "My Lady," she added.

Lady Apsarla smiled back. She seemed genuinely pleased with Stormbringer's coming around, like a patient mother who'd just gotten through to her stubborn teenage daughter.

Apsarla said, "Perhaps then, we can scoop him up if he runs into too much trouble with the Kith or the Queen's Guard." She swung her gaze back to the knightmaiden.

"Galewind, you will accompany the mission, personally command the tail and oversee Stormbringer's command of her two wings. You will personally transport the Kith Commander – I believe it will be Berendt Garondi – and confer with him on the matter of supplying a ranger that matches our requirements, and any other requirements that you come up with between now and then. Keep an open mind and do not allow any queensmen to ride with you. We do not need them meddling. Understood?"

"Yes, my Lady. I know Berendt well."

"I am counting on it. And if, during the course of the mission, you catch wind of anything… distasteful… ordered by whoever is in charge on the ground – I assume that will be Champion Eriff Haulik – feel empowered to overrule him. Remember, yours is the senior rank on this mission. Therefore, you are ultimately accountable for whatever transpires, for good or ill."

Next, Lady Apsarla regarded Stormbringer. "My spearmaiden, you will lead the way to the rendezvous point and, from there, organize transport to Whisperwood. I have already notified Lord Ralador via raven. You will have to track down Ranger Garondi some other way, and within the hour. After the drop-off, with an assigned ranger's help, you will select an appropriate staging ground to organize sealing the border. Choose an appropriate 'line in the sand.' You will also support the needs of the forest landing party, whenever and whatever they require, and organize a return rendezvous for transport back to Gan. Is everything clear?"

"Clear as the blue sky," Stormbringer replied. "Thank you, m'Lady."

"Use your wind riders, Spearmaiden. Do not try to do everything yourself."

"Yes, m'Lady."

"If you do this right, you will make full valkyrie. I promise you that much."

Relief poured over Stormbringer. At the same time, she felt a pang of embarrassment. She couldn't help but feel she'd been a little… petty.

Rainsong directed her gaze to the knightmaiden's notepad, tilted her head to one side. "So, why is this sword such a big deal?"

CHAPTER VIII

OVER SUCH A SIMPLE THING

(Catwings)

"CATWINGS. SO, IT was you I did not hear lurking about."

Catwings jumped at the baritone voice, caught off guard as she stumbled past the stables gate, already flustered. Her heart pounded in her chest. The pail she'd kicked clanged and rattled over the rock floor. She looked about hurriedly, but saw only gryphons shuffling in their stalls, spilling woodchips and hay into the common area.

Beastmaster Lorenz slowly stepped out from the shadow of a partial rock wall, the one that always had pitch forks and shovels leaning against it. He spoke evenly in his deep voice, enunciating every consonant. "I am sorry for startling you."

Catwings put her palm to her chest, let out a huge sigh. She met the beastmaster's gaze. "You are too quiet, for one so enormous."

His face appeared relaxed, his expression calm as polished stone. The ebony-skinned man folded his hands together.

"Forgive me. I was meditating."

Catwings blurted out, "Oh. Did I disturb you? Please, continue. I can wait." *Why did I say that?* She bit her upper lip, pulled and twisted at her fingers. *No time to wait. I must get moving.* The smell of dander, sweat and manure hung heavy in the air.

The beastmaster glanced up to the sky, then back down to her. He gave Catwings a measuring once-over. "There is no need. I am finished. How can I be of service, Wind Rider?" He paused, tilted his head and narrowed his eyes. "I see you have your riding cloak, and there is a glint of steel underneath. I have never seen you in armor before today."

"Oh, that." With his steady gaze on her, Catwings fidgeted with the clasp of her mottled grey and white cloak, patterned to match the markings of her Harpy gryphon. Finally, she released the clasp, swung the cloak open, and posed perfectly.

"It isn't much, really," she said. Her scaled armor shimmered in the grey light of the day, well-fitted and low-cut, styled more like a dress than protective gear. It barely felt like armor at all.

Lorentz raised an eyebrow. "Impressive." He nodded his satisfaction. "Not bulky in the least."

Catwings pulled her cloak in, glanced to the line of small caves across the common area – the gryphon stalls. "Are the cats ready?"

Lorenz grimaced. "The Harpies are ready, but the Golds are taking their sweet time."

"That's fine. I only need my Harpy."

A throaty rattle filled the air. Lorenz turned to the caged ravens he kept off to one corner. "Oh hush," he scolded. "I'll get to you in a minute." He mumbled something about a miserable bird under his breath, then regarded the wind rider.

"What is it you need her for today?"

"I need to track down a ranger," she told him.

Lorenz nodded. "Then you have a big day ahead of you. Rangers are the trackers, which means they know how to cover their trails."

Catwings smirked. "I have an eagle eye that they don't know about."

"Did you say 'eagle' or 'evil'?"

"Eagle."

"Good. For a moment you frightened me." Lorenz shivered in jest. "I will saddle her up for you. Follow me." He waved Catwings alongside as he strode over to the tack room. The tall man stooped to avoid knocking his head on the low doorway, then entered. Catwings followed two steps behind. Each wall in the small cave was dedicated to a particular gryphon, with its own set of saddles, harnesses, headgear, and reins, and other riding gear that might be needed.

"I could have passengers," Catwings said.

"How many?"

"Two. Or one. Plus gear."

Lorenz shook his head slowly. "Tsk. Tsk. You should fly a Gold then. Three's a crowd on a Harpy Gryphon."

"Everyone has to take two passengers."

"All four cats?"

"All four."

"I see then. You should take the lightest ones." Lorenz turned to his left, halted next to a metal plate with the name "Spree" embossed in gilded lettering. He scanned what he had available for tacking up the gryphon, then grimaced and muttered to himself as he sorted through the many pegs and hangers. Catwings fixated on his white hair as he did so, then her eyes wandered over his firm build. He seemed as strong and stocky as a young queensman, except one-and-a-half times the size. She cocked her head. *Not bad for an older gentleman.*

Hand on a saddle, the beastmaster pursed his lips. "And you are the wind rider who refuses to carry a weapon, aren't you, Catwings?"

She hunched her shoulders, palms up. "Why would I use a puny sword? No. I fight with my gryphon instead. She's much bigger than me. And those talons..."

The beastmaster boomed laughter. "Why indeed?" An amused expression washed over him. He yanked the saddle free, tucked it under one arm. "You should tell that to Stormbringer. She wants to fight everyone herself. One day, I fear, she will leave the spears behind."

"You fear? What do you mean?"

"To fight with her bare fists."

Catwings nodded. "Yeah, she has anger issues."

Lorenz grunted. "And sweet Rainsong is going to be just like her someday, you wait and see."

Catwings shrugged. "Maybe."

He grunted a second time. "I have seen enough wind riders pass through these gates to know it isn't 'maybe.'" Lorenz raised a hand to his chin as he contemplated his next grab.

"No spear; single bridle then, for you, Catwings." The beastmaster sorted through the bridles, selected one, then grumbled to himself as he gathered more gear, addressing each item in turn. When he seemed done, he paused, nodded his head in satisfaction, then pivoted to face her.

"I'm serious. A wind rider should take something along to defend herself. You never know what you might meet out there."

Catwings didn't answer.

"Have you not learned how to use a weapon?"

"You know very well, Lorenz, that I am trained on every sword and spear in that armory."

Lorentz grimaced. "Do you not have passion for any one of them, spear or sword? How can you become a spearmaiden without a spear?"

Catwings reverted to her defiant silence. She didn't like the weaponry and, frankly, she'd never needed them either.

The beastmaster prodded on. "If you came to the conclusion that you need to wear armor, then you probably need to carry a weapon as well." He looked her up and down in a measuring sense, like a tailor might. "I have something special for you, Catwings. Three things, in fact, neither sword nor spear among them."

Catwings shifted her stance. In sparring classes, she'd always felt intimidated by others. But on her gryphon, she was ferocious.

The beastmaster prodded her on. "I insist."

She nodded reluctantly. "Okay then. Show me what you have."

"Wait here," he said.

Through an opening in one of the long walls of the chamber, hewn round for reasons unknown, lay the armory. Despite Lorenz's arms being absolutely full, he ducked his head again and stepped through. Catwings waited as he clattered about inside, muttering to himself. A heap of metal fell and clanged. Eventually, he emerged, clenching between giant fingers two gloves with steel contraptions attached. And looped on one of his wrists was a coiled whip that dangled like a huge, leather bracelet.

"Kindly take these retractable daggers from me, before I drop one. The design is a favorite of mine, but they are too small for my liking."

Catwings grasped the gloves.

"Be careful." Lorenz pointed to a thin metal swivel on one of them, in the palm of the grip. "That is the safety." Then he pointed to a push button. "That is the spring release mechanism. You can activate them both with your thumb. When you're not planning on using these daggers, keep the safety on. When you feel you might have a fight on your hands, flick the safeties discreetly to ready the spring action, and when you need them—"

"Push the release button," Catwings broke in.

The beastmaster nodded. "Make a fist first."

"How do you know so much about weapons?" she asked. He'd always helped out with the combat training.

"I served three tours in the Scarsands as a weaponeer, back when I was young and foolish. I am lucky to be alive."

Catwings pulled the fingerless gloves on. She paused, pointed the left glove away from her in the safest direction possible, flicked the safety, then made a fist and pushed the release. With a soft metallic schwing, three metal blades sprang out like retractable claws. She did the same to the other glove, then examined the blades carefully. They were long and thin with a silvery, wicked curve and whirly engravings along their lengths.

"I call them 'talons,'" said the beastmaster, watching and grinning. "But they could equally be called claw-daggers. They match that dress you call armor, don't they?"

"Oddly, they do. Thank you," Catwings said.

A wide smirk crept across Lorenz's face. "I have an eye for fashion. It is one of my many talents."

The giant man was right. They appeared almost elegant. She flashed him a grateful smile. "I kinda like them, actually."

"To retract the blades, just hold the release again and press them firmly against a hard surface. Be careful not to let them slip though. You will hear them lock back into place, spring-loaded. See here..." Bracing the load he carried against the round doorframe, Lorenz took her small hand in his massive one and motioned to the end of one of the blades. "There's a tiny flat extension near the tip that keeps you from putting pressure on the sharp points when you push them back in."

"To keep them sharp," Catwings said.

Lorenz nodded.

"I see." Catwings strode over to a heavy wooden table in the center of the tack room. She tightened her fist, jammed the claw-like blades into it. They slid back easily into their sheaths. She flicked the safety on.

"Good. And there are some attachments as well." The beastmaster hunched up his shoulder to reveal a small wooden box tucked under his arm. "I'll add them to your saddlebag. They don't weigh much."

Lorenz readjusted his load and approached Catwings. He raised his other arm, the one that held the whip. "Now, take this as well, Catwings. It is my finest whip. The cord is light and strong, with just the right weight on the end. You need something with reach."

The wind rider sheathed her other claw-dagger the same way she did the first, then took the whip from him and admired it. She pivoted her head up to see Lorenz gazing down on her.

"I don't have time to practice using this before departure," she said.

He shrugged. "Practice when you have the time, Catwings. I cannot teach you much about the whip anyway. The whip teaches you."

The beastmaster smiled wide. His teeth were neatly stacked, strong, and bright against his complexion. He laughed even as he spoke, wild amusement in his eyes. "Ha! Now that I have given this 'cat' that purrs before me her claws and her tail, it is time to ready her 'wings'! Come now, 'Cat-wings.'"

She shook her head, smirking. "You are a strange man, Lorenz, but you are a kind one."

Lorenz ducked out of the cave through the tack room doorway and proceeded towards the gryphon stalls, dumping the load of gear in a pile along the way. With soothing words of encouragement, he unhooked Spree's stall clasp, slid the gate open, and stooped to attach the leg tether before the beast stepped out. In the midst of his well-rehearsed utterances – promises to the other gryphons in neighboring stalls, all scratching and bumping about as they vied for attention – the beastmaster gently coaxed the Harpy into the common area. Lorenz had an odd way of dwarfing the otherwise imposing beast.

"She's skittish today," Catwings observed, as Spree angled herself contrary to her trainer, swinging her head slightly and testing the draw on her reins.

The wind rider shrugged, turned her attention to her glove-daggers. *Spree's in good hands. She'll calm down.* While Lorenz placated the beast and readied it for flight, Catwings practiced rapidly tripping the safety then springing the action. After a few tries, she let out an exaggerated battle cry, lunged at a nearby tie post and raked the soft wood with her new claws. Grunting with effort, she scratched again and again. Catwings caught Lorenz eyeing her, a half-hidden grin forming on his lips. She smiled to herself. *I knew he'd like that.*

"The kit contains a sharpening tool," Lorenz informed her. He continued working on his task.

Satisfied with her performance, Catwings meowed loudly, held the release firm, then jammed the daggers into the post to retract them.

Lorenz bellowed out a laugh. "You had me going," he said, shaking his head at her.

Next, she took the whip and put in a more serious effort. On her first try, Catwings successfully coiled it around the post, gave it a tug, then unwrapped it by hand. She stood farther back and tried flicking the whip a few times to make it crack – no success.

"It's all in the wrist," the beastmaster called out.

Catwings focused her mind. With a powerful fling, she hurled the point high, then jerked back the instant before full extension. The whip snapped loudly. Her gryphon let out a guttural rattle in response. Catwings swung her head and watched as Spree reared against Lorenz. He struggled to keep her down.

The beastmaster swept his gaze to Catwings, eyes glaring as he fought to subdue the gryphon. His voice boomed like thunder. "Not here! They do not like whips." He wrestled the Harpy into a hold. "A previous trainer was unkind to the cats, I believe. Cruel, in fact."

Catwings grimaced. "Then when am I supposed to use this thing?"

The Harpy gryphon reared again, broke away from Lorenz,

half-spreading its grey wings as it stumbled over the pile of gear. A saddlebag strap caught Spree's talon. She let out an ear-piercing squawk. And as the Harpy tried to shake it off, a chorus of "chealping" noises erupted from the other gryphons, shifting uneasily in their stalls.

With sturdy pulls and firm commands, Lorenz finally managed to rein in Spree. Then with soft assurances and a slow approach, he calmed her down, coaxed her to fold her wings. Only then did he remove the caught saddlebag.

Catwings was still waiting for an answer.

Lorenz took a deep, slow breath, exhaled heavily. "Wind Rider, you have to build trust. Start small, with kind words and kind strokes, and a measured number of treats to offer. Snap the whip casually as part of the process. Make it a routine."

Catwings nodded. "I can do that."

Lorenz tightened a few straps on the charmed animal, added the saddlebag, double-checked everything he'd done, then regarded the wind rider. "Your girl is ready, Catwings." He paused, a quizzical look building on his face.

"Did you tell me the name of that ranger?"

"No," Catwings said. "His name is Berendt Garondi. Do you know him?"

"Not personally, but I have seen his name. The Fort Abandon base sends us ravens now and again, as you know. You have a long flight ahead of you."

"Actually, he's somewhere in the area. I just have no idea where. I need to pass him our rendezvous coordinates: the Kiranis Hills."

"Wait one minute." The beastmaster's posture stiffened. He raised a hand to his chin. "A raven brought news from the northern outpost during your meeting with Lady Apsarla, about a dozen miles beyond the falls. It mentioned a gathering point – the old trapper's cabin at Elgar's Pocket. Noon. The message was signed 'Hallman' – a name I often see. I sent Celeste Dana to deliver the message by hand to the Wing Chamber."

"What?" Catwings guffawed, staring at Lorenz. Lorenz stared back, expression blank. She added, "You're joking, right?" He remained expressionless. *Just what I don't need.* She responded with a vigorous shake of her head. "We didn't receive the message."

"Hmm… Dana can be a shy one. I will have to have a word with her. I believe she did not want to interrupt. She sneaks around quietly like you, Catwings. I see extra stall duty in her future."

"If the rangers already left… damn. The hills are a long way from Elgar's Pocket." Catwings huffed. "And if the queensmen already left and I have to change the rendezvous point… Argh. I have a lot of flying to do – stops in Gan and who-knows-where in Deepweald before I even sort this out. What a mess! Over such a simple thing."

Beastmaster Lorenz shrugged. "What can you do?" He turned to the Harpy, gave it a once over. Satisfied she'd settled down, he offered to lift the wind rider into her saddle. Catwings accepted. Lorenz gently grabbed her under her ribs and raised her into the air. She felt like a child again, to be held so high by his long, strong arms. Once up, she scrambled into the saddle. Spree shifted nervously beneath her. Lorenz undid the tether.

"My old girl's a little testy this morning," Catwings said, stroking the beast between its furry lynx ears. "Do you think it's the whip?"

The beastmaster curled his lower lip, shook his head slowly. "No, the whip is long forgotten. This is something else. She feels your anxiety, I believe, and she smells the approaching weather. Putting the two together is what makes her testy." He reflected for a long moment. "Don't you worry, Catwings. It is not so bad. At worst, you and your fellow valkyries will have two pickup zones. If so, load the rangers first. The queensmen are a heavier lot and carry more than they need."

"That'd be backtracking," Catwings countered. "The hills are closer, and from there the lake is on the way to Whisperwood; plus stopping and starting again will take more time." Catwings ran her hand over her forehead, flicked her hair up away from her face.

"You could send the two Golds to the Kiranis Hills to pick up the queensmen – they can handle a heavier load, and send the two Harpies to Elgar's Pocket to pick up the rangers."

"Hmm. Not bad." Catwings sighed heavily. *Except Galewind rides a Gold, and Lady Apsarla insisted that she only carry rangers.* Catwings clenched her jaw and grunted in frustration. "I'll figure something out."

"I am sure you will, Catwings. Tell your comrades a storm is brewing. A mean one. The first ill breath of winter, perhaps. Rain, snow, hail, you name it; could get real nasty, real fast. Tell them to make haste."

Catwings nodded.

Beastmaster Lorenz led Spree to the launching pad in the main Hollow, then coaxed her up its three steps. Over the edge, a sheer drop. With the gryphon at the top, he handed the reins to Catwings and slowly backed away. And as Catwings redoubled her grip and positioned for lift off, out of the corner of her eye she saw the beastmaster suddenly jerk back. She swung her gaze to him as a flurry of wings thumped directly in front of his face. Small wings. White.

"Whoa, who are you?" Lorenz boomed. With one hand he shielded his face, with the other he readied a swipe to knock the creature away. The flapping bird set down on his outstretched forearm. There, it croaked once, teetered forward then back.

The beastmaster addressed this newcomer with a kind voice. "Who sent you?" he asked.

By the bird's size, its curved beak, and its shaggy throat feathers, Catwings surmised the visitor was a raven. A white raven. An anomaly she'd never seen before. It hopped along the beastmaster's arm towards his shoulder, stuck its neck out, then screeched into his ear. Lorenz winced, raised a slow and gentle hand to force the raven to back off.

Catwings said, "Another message?"

The beastmaster shook his head. "I have never seen this blinding white bird before, and it bears no message… unless that horrible noise was the message. Odd. Messenger ravens never fly to me directly unless I happen to be standing next to the cages. I've had one land on my head before…"

With a twist of his arm, he tested the bird's balance. The white raven adjusted its stance. It wasn't going anywhere. The beastmaster shrugged, let out a loud, rolling chortle. He waved Catwings off.

"No concern of yours, Wind Rider. I can handle this winged beast. Ride the winds and be off! May the Eye of the Eagle guide you."

Catwings swiveled on her saddle to face straight ahead.

"Yaw!" she shouted, kicking her mount into action.

The gryphon spread its great wings, leapt from the windy summit of Icy Blue to soar over Gan. Spree tracked the Elderkin River before Catwings had her doubling back. The wind rider swooped overtop the monolith, past its northern spires, then plummeted straight down past Lorenz, who was already on his way back to the stables. Catwings spun into a tight roll and then arced her gryphon up in front of the falls. Glancing back over her shoulder, she glimpsed a surprised look on the man's face. With a smirk of her own, she guided the Harpy out of the gorge. Catwings had a ranger to catch.

CHAPTER IX
ELGAR'S POCKET
(Amot)

THE SCOUT TORE through the pine-thick lowlands, then whipped along the boulder-ridden course of a dried-up riverbed. He made good use of his long stride to traverse Brillyerd's Vein: an age-old path of goliath rocks, flat and mossy like the stepping-stones of giants.

Amot worked up a good sweat by the time the bright patch in the sky reached its zenith. It had been on the horizon when he'd set out. And as he soldiered on, no matter how hard he tried to account for hours spent in the hilltop grove, the time always came up empty. An uneasy sense lurked in the back of his mind from the encounter… ominous.

Vil'nyan? Something about Vil'nyan? Amot couldn't quite place the thought. In his mind, he replayed their time together in the crystalline gardens of Seventh Kaeda, bathed in the flickering glow of the Starshine. *But that was good.* His thoughts wandered to the night before, camped out with her under the stars. *Even better.*

Suddenly ahead, light filtered through the trees. An opening. He could smell the lake air.

Amot's reckoning had been dead-on. He broke through the tree line onto the open lakeshore of Elgar's Pocket, just as the sun peaked out from the grey. Heart pounding in his chest, he slowed to a stop, hunkered down on the pebbled beach. Legs aching from exertion, the scout drew deep, fast breaths. Sweat dripped off his brow and splattered onto the coarse sand at his feet.

Overheated, Amot looked about. To his left, the old trapper's cabin slumped in its place, tired and dilapidated. The structure was nestled between the forest pines and the small inlet stream that ran past it. By all appearances, it hadn't been used in years. He swept his gaze up and down the shore and saw no one, then over the lake's jittering surface to the high dome of bedrock across the narrows, its craggy surface pierced by slim jack pines and marred by fissures like the claw marks of some mythical bear.

The place was utterly empty until Howler traipsed out of the bush, snout to the ground. The quirky spaniel zig-zagged between small boulders and knobby driftwood, wove a winding path to his master, then nuzzled.

"High noon," Amot told the dog, scrubbing him behind the ears. Tail and tongue slowly wagging, Howler panted heavily. The scout shook his head in disbelief. "I know Berendt told me high noon. Where are they?"

A breeze startled Amot, prompting him to rise to his feet. He nodded to himself. There was one way to maybe get an answer. So, while Howler took to sniffing about, the scout closed his eyes and stood absolutely still for a long minute, just listening. He focused his mind on the sound of the wind hissing through the trees behind him. But try as he might he could hear no Whispers beyond the normal sort of tribal chatter. And so, he wove his own voice into the chorus. In Treesong, he uttered a brief message for his fellow rangers on their westward journey, revealing his location and querying theirs. He waited again for a minute, and then another.

A strange bird call broke his concentration, from across the water – one he hadn't heard before.

Amot sighed at the Whisper silence. *They could be miles away*, he thought. And with queensmen to slow them down, there had to be ten good reasons why his Kith brothers might be late. The scout's eyes fixated on the rippling surface of the lake water and the promise of a refreshing dip. He turned his gaze to Howler, let out a sharp whistle. The dog's ears perked. Amot stooped to pick up a stick, then flung it into the water. Howler dashed after it, bounding and splashing and rolling out growls like a silly puppy one-fifth his age. Amot got started undressing.

Chapter X
Northeasterly
(Galewind)

Hours after Catwings' departure, the remaining harpy gryphon and two golden gryphons lifted off into the grey sky. Wayward gusts buffeted the pride of Gan and their riders as they rose above the protection of the gorge, above the falls and then over the forest rim. The ceiling above them was low. Galewind glanced down behind her. Lorenz stood watching their departure, waved a farewell with one hand while the other rested on a rake. He turned back to work the stalls alongside the new celeste. Galewind smirked, tucked in tight to her Gold, then turned her attention ahead.

Unusual, she thought, when she felt the push of the open winds, blowing from the northeast. She hadn't expected a northeasterly. Electra's wings inflated with the chill air. The knightmaiden rode the current as her gryphon rose higher.

Stormbringer veered her own Gold westward. "Wind riders, fall in," she called. Her voice rang loud and clear.

Galewind's and Rainsong's mounts fell into a casual wedge-shape behind Stormbringer, the default formation for three cats. With the winds at their backs, it would be a short flight to the rendezvous.

"Wind riders, ascend," Stormbringer called next, and led them into the low-hanging clouds. The spearmaiden was hungry for command, that much was obvious, by her strong voice shouting orders across the airy expanse. A part of Galewind wanted her to have it. The knight-maiden had already decided she'd be as lenient as she could stomach. She'd try not to take offence at small slights, such as Stormbringer's use of the term "wind riders" in her commands instead of "valkyries." Wind rider was fine for Rainsong, but ranked three stations below knightmaiden. *I'll mention it in passing,* she decided, *after we land.*

Galewind glanced over the side. The forested terrain appeared in patches below, through the cloud cover. According to Beastmaster Lorenz, their destination had already changed from the Kiranis Hills announced by lady Apsarla to a small glade in the vicinity of a nearby lake. The locale happened to be natural hunting grounds for the gryphons, where a sighting would not seem out of place. *I hope Lorenz stuffed Electra right full,* she thought. The last thing she needed was to wrestle a hungry Gold into submission. After several minutes of flight, Stormbringer called out again.

"Rainsong, spot."

Rainsong's "Ashes" dipped down so the agile wind rider could have a look. The grey and white plumage of the Harpy Gryphon would be difficult to spot against a backdrop of clouds.

"I see the objective," Rainsong called back, then swung up to rejoin the formation.

A long minute later, Stormbringer called out her final command of the flight, "Valkyries, descend."

Hmm… she got it right that time, thought Galewind. *Must've read my mind.*

As the trio swooped down from the cloud cover, Galewind first spotted the lake. She caught glimpse of a small to medium-sized animal dashing along the shore there – maybe a coyote. Next to the lake, footing a rocky ridge, lay the glade. Horses had already arrived; rangers and queensmen busily unpacked and carted their gear. The knightmaiden smiled secretly when she saw Kith Commander Berendt Garondi among them. "I can spot you from a mile away," she said to herself.

The gryphons glided in for a soft landing. Moments later, Catwings joined them from the southeast.

⁕

After hitching her Gold, straightaway Galewind sought out Berendt. He was with Tall Hallman, the two of them admiring their neat stack of packed gear. The Kith commander had his pipe out, but unlit. He greeted her kindly on arrival.

"You're flying on *my* cat," she told him.

"Sounds good to me," he replied. "What about Bigfoot here?"

Galewind made an apologetic face. "I'm sorry Tallman," she explained, calling him by his more common nickname. "You can't come. You're too heavy."

Tallman's jaw dropped. He looked to his commander.

Galewind chuckled, then lightly grasped his bicep. "I'm only kidding. Take your pick – any valkyrie would be glad to have you aboard." Then she remembered Apsarla's words. "In fact, fly with me."

Tallman breathed a sigh of relief, shook his head and replied in his sonorous voice. "You had me going."

Galewind turned her attention to Berendt. "Are we all here?"

Berendt shot Tallman a glance. "Better check on Rix," he said.

The burly ranger excused himself and headed for the edge of the glade where his lanky comrade, with fiery orange hair, had already discovered Catwings. He was chatting her up.

The Kith commander tapped his pipe, then responded to the knightmaiden's question. "Everyone on my team is present except for my scout, Amot. We're missing one on the Queen's Guard side as well, Champion Eriff Haulik."

"Aren't Eriff and Amot the ones who caused this mess in the first place?"

Berendt grunted. "Yep. Afraid to show their faces, I say."

Rainsong overheard them, chimed in. "Good riddance then," she said, "unless they're handsome."

Berendt grunted again. "Cute as buttons." He laughed outright, and the laughter spread throughout the glade.

After Berendt composed himself, he said to Galewind, "I don't know about the queensmen, but Amot had an early morning errand to run. He'll be arriving on foot from the north. I told Rix to spot for him and keep an ear out for Whispers as well." Berendt stole a glance at the ginger. "Seems like he might have become… ahh… preoccupied though."

Galewind nodded. "Yes, I noticed." She paused. "You should know that I spotted something at the lake. I think it was just an animal though."

Berendt rubbed his beard. "Hmph," he gruffed. "Could be my scout and that damned mutt of his." He barked out to his rangers: "Rix, Tallman. One of you check for Amot by the lake."

Rix responded, calling back over his shoulder, "A valkyrie already disappeared up the slope."

Galewind's eyes darted about the glade. He was right. Stormbringer was missing.

"And bring that damn pack I gave you," Berendt barked.

Tallman shoved Rix away from Catwings. "Get on it," he grumbled. He shoved Rix again. A playful shove, not a serious one. "Move, spotter."

Rix obliged, smirking a parting apology to Catwings for having to leave so soon. The wind rider covered her mouth as she smirked back.

Berendt called after his men, "I'll join you in a minute or two. I've been meaning to take a gander at the lake anyway."

"And have a good long puff?" Galewind suggested.

Berendt nodded, began stuffing the bowl of his pipe with choice weed. "You know me too well, Knightmaiden."

Chapter XI
ROCKY SHORE
(Stormbringer, Amot)

Stormbringer's climb wasn't as easy as expected, up the rocky slope to the ridge overlooking the lake. She was forced to used her polearm to steady herself over the uneven ground, littered with splintered deadwood and wobbly stones. It would've been quicker and easier to just fly over. The spearmaiden and Rainsong had heard what they thought was a whistle, and Stormbringer had gone to investigate. As she neared the top of the bluff, a stick snapped behind her.

The spearmaiden looked back over her shoulder, took note of the scrawny ranger starting at the bottom. She watched as he struggled to keep his footing, nearly tripping over his feet, then almost tipping by the weight of the heavy pack he bore. He couldn't have been more than seventeen by the looks of him. Certainly eye-catching though. His bold wilder ink and spikey orange hair would've been enough to set him apart, but combined with the bright, leafy green cloak he wore over the usual brown ranging leathers, there was little doubt he was spirited. The white-metal piercings on his eyebrow, ear, and lower lip – tokens of the eastern Wilder tribes – gave his angular face an added edge. *Catwings and Rainsong will be keen on that.*

Sensing the boy was about to look up, Stormbringer quickly turned away and continued her trek.

When the spearmaiden reached a good vantage point to see the lake on the other side, she paused. Through rugged pines, she glimpsed a dog swimming in circles in the middle of the channel below, stick in mouth. Plus, something else – fair reward for her suffering. On the opposite shore a young man, twenties maybe, was in the midst of stripping down on a narrow stretch of beach.

Stormbringer raised an eyebrow. "Well, well," she said in a low voice only she could hear.

The young man – the misguided ranger presumably – one-by-one dropped his garments onto a lone boulder. When he was finished undressing, he proceeded to roll his clothes up into two tight bundles, then stuff them into his boots.

Curious, the spearmaiden watched the buff ranger, well-muscled and raw as new life, as he stepped tender-footed over the stony sand, entered the lake, then sloshed his way through the shallow water. All the while he carried his boots against his chest. A hatchet handle stuck out of one of them. He waded into the channel waist-deep, then tossed the loaded footwear across the water to her side of the lake.

Not bad, Stormbringer thought, puckering her lips slightly. She nodded to herself, impressed at how he'd handled the problem of getting his clothes across the lake without getting them wet, and how he'd tossed his axe onto the rocks without a clang.

The ranger called out to his dog, "Look out, Howler. I'm coming for you!"

Howler rawled back in response from the middle of the inlet channel. The young ranger dove in, swam to meet his dog. Treading water when he got there, he teased the animal playfully, tugging at the prize stick in its mouth. Howler seemed determined not give it up without a fight.

"You'll tire yourself out," the ranger told the dog. With a quick jerk, he wrested the stick from Howler's jaws, then flung it towards the bedrock. "Go fetch!" he hollered. The stick hit the rock face and deflected back into the lake with a plop. The dog craned its head to its master, snorted, and then growled an elaborate, undulating protest before dog-paddling in pursuit.

The ranger ducked under the surface and disappeared. Stormbringer chose that moment to step out onto the rock dome. She glimpsed the ranger's nude form propel underwater, aiming to cross the narrow channel fully submerged. She started down the slope towards the water's edge. A private smile crept across her lips as a devious thought crossed her mind.

Amot felt the gentle draw of the lake's current when he passed through the deepest part. The chilled water pressed against his ears as he made his way. After holding his breath near to his limit, the outstretched fingers of his left hand contacted a slimy, submerged boulder. He arced upwards, broke surface. Standing chest-deep, he shook the water from his hair, slicked it back. Blinking and rubbing his eyes, his water-blurred surroundings slowly came into focus. Before him, blotches of red and gold.

A queensman? He rubbed his eyes again.

As his vision cleared, the image that took shape was nothing like a queensman. Instead, a stern woman, neither old nor young, stood glaring back at him. She was not just any woman. She wore a winged helm and carried a long spear. *Order Valkyrie.*

The woman squatted to pick up one of his boots, lying haphazardly on the shore with a pant leg dangling out. She rose, holding it pinched between two fingers like something untouchable, crinkling her nose. She lifted it in front of her eyes, examined it carefully, then swung her gaze to him.

"Is this yours?"

The exposed scout felt his ribs close in. Unable to form a sentence, he shrugged in response. Discreetly, he angled his torso slightly to limit her field of regard.

Howler chose that moment to slip out of the lake. Amot cringed as the dog beelined towards the woman, halted beside her.

"No! Howler!" he called, but too late. The dog shook himself.

The woman gasped and turned away, one hand raised to shield herself from the radial spray.

When the shower was over, she held a look of disgust on her

face. And when Amot apologized, she took on a steady, unimpressed demeanor. Howler looped around the woman, sniffing and nudging at her ankles. In all his grace, the dog plunked down at her feet and starting licking his balls. Amot rubbed his forehead, shook his head. The valkyrie's only response was to let the boot she was pinching drop.

Rix Caledon, or "Quick Rix" to his Kith brothers, appeared on the summit just then, lugging Amot's pack over one shoulder. His composite shortbow was in its usual side holster, unstrung along with a dozen or so arrows. He was training to be a deadeye. His freckled face went wild with amusement as he put together the scene before him.

Rix waved at Amot from behind the woman's back, raised a thumb to her feminine attributes. "Go for it," he mouthed as a silent cheer, then stooped over to contain his vibrating gut.

Amot shifted his gaze back to the woman. Two long, golden braids spilled out from beneath her winged helm. Her outfit possessed a decorative quality to it, with tailored padding snug-fitting to her arms and legs. She wore a lighter variant of the usual guardsman armor, plated grey with high shoulders and an intricate collar. Above her heart was the golden emblem of her order – a gryphon carrying a spear-bearing rider, sun blazing in the background – embroidered into the scarlet red doublet that kept her adequate chest in check. She held a spear of sorts in one hand, a custom weapon so tall the tip rose well above her helm. It bore the triple-headed threat of a spearpoint, hammer, and prong.

The valkyrie had an impatient air about her. She shifted her stance, raised her spear. The wicked curve of the black-iron prong stood out against the sky like the beak of some predatory bird. Then, with a loud knock, she firmly tapped the butt-end of the weapon onto the bedrock. She spoke with a strong, cutting voice.

"Get yourself dressed, Kith-boy," she ordered. "My gryphons await. They do not like to linger."

"Gryphons? Where are the horses?" A wave of foolishness washed over Amot in the asking. The valkyrie's unwavering stare made him feel doubly so. Her eyes dug into his. Rix chuckled from atop the rocky hill.

"Don't delay," she reiterated. "My gryphon is getting a little… hmm…"

The woman paused, leaned forward and with a sly glance peered down into the water, tilting her head slightly for a better view. The tingle of blood-heat began to spread over Amot's face, but he didn't budge just the same. The glimpse obtained, the winged woman's eyes slowly crept upwards to meet his. She cocked her head, raised one eyebrow.

"Let's just say that the *bird* is getting a little *testy*," she finished, with a subtle smirk.

Amot flushed. Rix burst out laughing. The valkyrie swiveled her head, glared daggers back at the ginger. Her tone was sharp.

"Is there a problem, *colorful one*?"

Rix straightened, folded one hand over the other in front of him, froze in place. Even with all the edgy piercings and honor markings, his blankly innocent composure reminded Amot of a misbehaving child who thinks he can fool his parents at the dinner table.

"No Ma'am, not at all, m'lady… bird," he said.

Ladybird? Amot scrubbed his face with both hands.

The woman huffed, and the scout caught the tail end of her eye-rolling expression as she swung her gaze back to the lake and to him – the ranging skinny dipper. Her previous smirk had already been wiped clean. Her harsh demeanor resurfaced, doubled. She spoke in a toneless voice.

"We have the weather to beat, Kith-boy, and I'm sure the queens-men will be more than happy to embark without you,"

Amot had another question.

"Well… do the gryphons like dogs?" he asked, again feeling a bit foolish. But he wasn't going anywhere without Howler.

The woman tilted her head, scrunched her brow. She shook her head. "Canine is not their favorite, but it will do in a pinch… if they are hungry enough."

The exchange might have been humorous if she'd smiled. But her words were crisp and her expression unbroken. On that note, the valky-rie broke off their paltry exchange, turned her back and made her way up the slope. She fully ignored Rix as she proceeded to the outcrop's summit. Rix wasn't the only one she snubbed.

No way.

Amot's commander, Berendt Garondi, stepped out from the scraggly tree line and onto the bare rock.

The woman made a fast remark to him as she passed. "I'll tell the others your men are all accounted for." She took a few steps and, without glancing back, raised her voice. "You might want to consider dressing them yourself next time. I assume your man has armor somewhere in that heap?" The woman loosely waved one hand in the general direction of Rix, a vague reference to the pack he carried.

Berendt nodded grimly to her in acknowledgment. He knew how to take a hit. His gaze tracked the valkyrie as she passed into the woods behind him.

Eyes wide, Rix puffed a sigh of relief, long-held. His lanky arms dangled by his sides. He passed sheepish glances to his Kith brothers. "Tough ladybird."

Amot dragged his sorry self out of the lake, frisked the water off as best he could. He pulled his clothes out from his boots and got busy dressing. After fumbling with his smallclothes, he peered up the slope to the Kith commander, then sighed.

With surefooted steps, Berendt descended the rock dome towards the lake. Halfway, on a narrow ledge, he stopped to spark up his bogwood pipe, cupping and hunching over the flame to protect it from the wind. After a few quick puffs he took a long drag, then set the shank to hang out of the corner of his mouth, bit clenched between his teeth. Berendt seemed his usual self. Not being a Wilder and not one to get caught up in tribal mysticism, he was one of the few Kith rangers who'd dispensed with the ink and honor markings altogether. His sandy brown hair was messy and speckled grey, and his beard more of the same. He let out a smoky sigh, pipe waggling as he spoke.

"Don't take the spearmaiden too seriously," he gruffed, sounding as grim as ever. But grim was normal for Berendt. "I'll smooth things over with Galewind. She's in command. And that golden-boy-Queen's-Guard hasn't graced us with his presence yet either. Just wait and see if they take off without *him*."

Berendt swiped the pipe out of his mouth, looked to Rix. "And don't call her 'Ladybird,'" he grumbled, a hard edge to his voice. "It's disrespectful and it makes you and me look bad. It makes us all look bad."

Rix infused his own voice with unbridled cheeriness. "Look! I brought your stuff!" he told Amot, grinning in his attempt to turn the criticism on its end. The spotter held up Amot's pack like a prize catch as he half-slid, half-pranced down the remaining bedrock to hand it over.

The scout put his shirt on. "Did you bring the striker too?"

Rix cast a sideways glance at their commander, shook his head. "No," he said, speaking low. He gestured to Berendt. "You'll have to ask him about that."

The commander addressed his spotter from up the slope. "Rix, there's nothing more for you to see here. Head back and finish loading. Better get a move on it, before that valkyrie pricks you in the arse with her nasty spear."

The spotter bit hard on his lower lip. "Commander's right," he said to Amot, "she's brutal." Rix plunked the pack down on the bedrock beside him. "I'll see you on the other side." Without another word, he flapped a feeble wave, climbed the steep slope past Berendt to the outcrop's summit, and disappeared into the tree line.

The Kith commander sat down on the rock dome, silent for a long minute. He flipped up his eyepatch, scratched at the wrinkled skin underneath. Berendt looked as though he'd aged since Djinxar and added a rough night of drinking on top. The scar that began over his left eyebrow and ran down his cheek didn't help. Nor did the glazy eye in its midst. The worry lines on his face seemed more prominent than ever. But his leathers, in contrast, were as unflexed and immaculate as an initiate's at First Confluence – too stiff and spiffy, it seemed, for a seasoned outdoorsman like himself to be wearing.

Berendt chewed on the bogwood in his mouth. He took it out, grunted, and spoke in his usual gravelly voice. "I heard your Whisper, Scout, but I was in the middle of packing. I can't concentrate on a damn thing with all the racket down there."

Amot explained himself, "I didn't see anyone. I thought—"

"I figured as much," Berendt cut in. "We're in the glade just over the ridge, in case you haven't noticed."

"But I thought—"

"I know, I know. It's been a dry summer. Makes a perfect landing pad – not boggy in the least." The commander puffed his pipe again. "Listen Amot, why don't you start getting ready before the next curious valkyrie shows up."

Amot nodded his acceptance.

Berendt grunted. "I brought Hallman too. That makes four of us."

Tall Hallman was a solid ranger. Rugged. Athletic too, despite his rather deceiving middle-age body type.

Amot shrugged. "Still thin on the ground though, wouldn't you say?".

"Bah!" Berendt growled. "That should be all the rangers we need." Howler slunk over to Berendt and lay down, gnawing on his recovered stick. Berendt reached out, gave the soggy dog a good rub. Eyes fixed to the lake and his expression slightly pained, the commander pulled the bogwood from his mouth again, cleared his throat.

"Unfortunately, Amot, bringing along a striker was not possible. Last minute, your biggest fan – the Lord of the March, of course – put a stop to you *ever* handling a striker again. Yes, 'ever.'"

"He can't do that," Amot said. "It was a done deal. And I promised Lumen Hadamard."

Berendt scoffed. "He can and he did. That royal pain-in-the-ass has the backing of the Earl." The Kith commander raised the eyebrow over his good eye, slowly shook his head. He met Amot's gaze. "Hadamard should've known something like that would never get the royal stamp. That mystic thinks he owns the strikers. He doesn't, I tell you. The Royal Quarter does – they paid for them. Luminaries are just tools to those bastards." He grunted. "So are we, for that matter." Berendt paused to take another draw from his pipe. He puffed a few times to hold the burn, then continued. "Anyhow, that's just the way it is. Some people are born into power and the rest of us just have to learn to live with it, even when said people are complete jackasses."

"What were Ralador's reasons?"

"He doesn't need any reasons. But he did mention there are too few strikers to be wasting any more on rangers. I'm guessing what he really wants is to buy some glory for his precious Queen's Guard, even if it gets us all killed."

Amot's shoulders slumped at the words. He took a deep breath. The scout had been counting on the striker's farseeing capability to help him locate the lost sword, and he'd promised to report to Hadamard about how well it worked for homing in on a target.

Don't complain, Amot told himself. *Berendt hates that.*

Berendt grunted. "And that's not the worst of it. Once that was out in the open, Lord Ralador made the argument that if you weren't going to be given a striker to use, you shouldn't be a part of the mission at all. I put a stop to that. After all, this *is* a ranger op by all definitions, and you're one of my best."

Amot lowered his gaze to his feet. "Thanks for the vote of confidence." He grabbed a boot, slid it on.

"None of that nonsense ended up mattering anyway," Berendt gruffed. "As it turns out, the second ship from Tetherport never made it out of the Otherworldly Realm – had to turn back after a mishap. Well, guess what? Apparently, the strikers were on board."

"Shit. The *Hyperion*? So, no one has a striker on the outside?"

"That's what they tell me. Now look, this mission is a good opportunity for you, so don't screw it up. A damn good command for my part too. I'm looking forward to the minute we lose those queensmen."

"How many?" Amot asked.

"Same as rangers, four. That's all the gryphons can carry. The queensmen and the valkyries are going to make sure nothing makes it out of Whisperwood into Harrow, or vice-versa. That's the real worry. They'll be up the Malevuin a ways keeping watch, while we stir things up with the Wulvers."

Amot lamented internally for a long moment, distracted by Lord Ralador's concerted efforts to shut him out of the mission. Howler chose just then to perk up, rush over, and then promptly stuff his nose in the scout's groin.

"Damn it, Howler!" Amot shooed the dog off. Berendt let out a mild chuckle.

Nose down, Howler slunk away from Amot's scolding, back towards dependable, but ultimately disposable, Berendt. Part-way, the spaniel stopped to peer back at his master, as though struggling with some monumental decision.

"Ah… come back here," Amot told him.

Howler barked once and sat. He whimpered and pawed at the stony ground.

Carrying his other boot, Amot went to the dog instead, consoled him with a solid rub and sturdy side-pat to the belly. "Don't worry, Howler. I won't let any gryphons eat you." He dumped the hatchet and his knife out of the boot, then pulled the footwear on.

Berendt interrupted. "I hate to break up you two love birds, but can we get on with it?"

Amot returned to the gear that Rix had left for him, grabbed the pack and slung it over his shoulder.

"No, no. Better armor up right here and now," Berendt said. "We don't know exactly what we're up against. I want everyone ready to fight the minute we land."

"They're just Wulvers," Amot protested. "They'll probably bolt the moment they see us."

"You might be right," Berendt replied. "But do it anyway."

Amot sighed, shrugged off the pack and got started. There was no arguing with his commander.

Berendt gave Amot a measured look as the scout pulled the various pieces of armor out of his pack and laid them out in a row on the bare rock. Berendt was staring at the lake when he finally spoke. His low voice was barely audible. It was the voice he used when he didn't want anyone else to hear.

"Don't be so worried about losing the striker," he said. "The reason you lost it is because you were the only one who could figure out how to use the damn thing. You and that damn uppity queensman who thinks he's better than everyone."

"Eriff?" Amot offered.

"That's right, Golden Boy – Eriff Haulik. Ralador's lackey. You kicked his royal lily butt though, didn't you?" Berendt let out a gruff chuckle to himself. "That's what scares the likes of those two. You proved that Hadamard was right – the weapon should go to rangers. Technically, a dancing sword like that is a ranged weapon, and it's also a stealth weapon – sneak attacks and all, never mind the farseeing. That puts it in ranger territory, or maybe assassins – I shudder to think – but certainly not the Queen's Guard. It isn't for defending honor and it isn't for glorious charges on the battlefield, or any of that nonsense.

Lumen Hadamard should have accounted for this possibility and come up with contingencies – that's *his* responsibility, not yours. Just remember that. You were the lab rat in his little experiment that went south."

Amot nodded as he packed away his hatchet. He kept his knife handy though. Then he pulled his waterskin out of his pack and filled it with lake water.

Berendt snuffed out his pipe with the palm of his hand, then grunted. "I should check on Rix and Tallman." He flipped his patch back over his eye. "Rix can help you tie your gear in to speed things up. Don't plan on taking a heck of a lot with you. The valkyries are hard bargainers when it comes to loading up their birds." He stood up. With stiff steps, the commander began his climb to the summit. "I expect you there in five."

"Gryphons? Really?" Amot huffed. He'd never ridden a gryphon before and wasn't particularly looking forward to it.

"That's right," Berendt said. "We're lucky to have them. They'll save us half a day, at least, and no one will see us pass – at least not with the weather we're about to get."

Berendt departed with a quick nod, leaving the scout alone with Howler. The dog curled into a wet ball and licked himself, while Amot donned his ranging armor. The supple leather had overlapping scales and plates sewn into it, and there were bracers for his forearms, greaves to cover his knees, and heavy shoulder pauldrons. By the time he was done strapping everything on, Howler had passed out, completely bushed. They both were.

Amot donned his cloak. Hearing a stream of soft yelps from his companion, the scout squatted down next to Howler, gently rubbed its side, then whispered, "Chasing squirrels in your dreams?" The spaniel's ears perked, but his eyes remained shut. "Stay right there." The scout patted the dog's belly. *He'll come when I call.*

Amot left Howler in his place to climb the rock dome. He took a long minute to gaze out over the lake, turned his back, then descended into the hidden glade. Chatter, bird calls and clinking noises welled up from below.

Chapter XII

OF A FEATHER

(Amot, Galewind, Stormbringer)

Warm wafts of boggish air filled the scout's lungs as he skidded down the uneven slope. Pines thinned to standing deadwood nearing the bottom. Summer drought and a withering fall had transformed the basin's usual goopy floor into a motley of baked mud and patchy tussocks, with wet patches only here and there. The location was a good choice for the rendezvous point, Amot conceded. A great choice, really. Not just because it was hidden. No one would ever think to go there.

When Amot stepped into the clear, the scene in the glade unfolded, far from ordinary.

"Chealp… chealp… chealp." The weak, uncertain calls were pitiful compared to the glaring majesty of the beasts that made them. Gryphons, larger than life, lay crouched in the glade. Great wings tucked, black-tipped tails short and bobbed.

Three were grouped nearby. A fourth crouched across the field. Their markings varied. Fore-portions were all eagle-like, propped up by straight and solid avian legs with gripping talons that could snatch a deer. But rear portions were all cat-like, with muscled legs and oversized paws in the manner of a lynx. Their giant-sized beaks were wickedly hooked and perfect for tearing into flesh. Leather hoods covered the eyes, with owlish ears sticking out in long tufts. The ears twitched independently, homing in on the sounds around them.

A valkyrie tended to each gryphon: armor-clad women ranging in apparent age from late teens to mid-thirties, with body types ranging from petite to tall and slight to brawny. As Amot crossed into the glade, the nearest one – a shapely, brown-skinned woman with contrasting white hair – passed Amot a casual glance. She hoisted a heavy pack onto her shoulder. The woman wore little else than a flowing poncho open at the sides, together with low-cut boots. Bare skin and hints of scant armor flashed from beneath the loose-fitting weave. Her neck and arm muscles flexed smoothly as she shoved the pack into place on her mount. Beside her, gripping the reins, a solid-built queensman in plated armor steadied her grey and white beast. A second queensman accompanied them, in his recycled forties. Standing off to one side in his chain armor, hand raised to his chin, the man's narrowed eyes kept watch over the maneuver.

Elsewhere in the glade, fellow rangers and a queensman packed their gear for the flight, all of whom he knew or recognized from Diamond Saber. Fragments of practical conversation filled the air as busy squires darted to and fro, running errands. Horses, some in light barding, grazed a careful distance from the gryphons, tied up at the far eastern edge of the field. A second look confirmed the horses were all queensman Coursers. His Kith brother's Farizans must've already departed.

Amot's eyes were drawn to the woman from the lake. She stood apart from the others with her gryphon, adjusting its harness. *Pretend you didn't see her and head over to Berendt,* was Amot's first instinct, but the heavy feeling in his gut told him that wouldn't do. Instead, the scout halted, sighed, and then headed her way, despite himself.

Should I apologize? he wondered, as he approached. *For what, exactly? Maybe I should just talk about the trip… or the weather?* Amot had gryphon questions he could ask her, but she'd probably already heard them ten times over if not twenty. He didn't get very far before the queensman in his forties intercepted him.

"Hello there, Chap," the man said, approaching with a brief, easy smile. "We haven't been formally introduced." The queensman extended a firm hand to the scout. "Duelist Haulik," he offered. "You can call me 'Marec.'"

Amot recognized the surname – an outer house of the Horse Lords with breeds well known to the Kith Quarter. Especially the Farizan, a light and swift riding horse.

"Amot Rixin," responded the scout as he grasped the duelist's hand, exchanged a strong handshake.

"Tremendous fight back at Diamond Saber," Marec complemented. "I have never seen anything like it." His neat-cut hair and clean shave gave him a well-groomed appearance overall. But offset to some degree by his rough, creased face and weak chin. Folds of skin rolled underneath. *Not the typical look for a queensman,* Amot couldn't help but judge. *An Aelish clergyman, maybe.*

"Thanks," Amot replied, unsure where the conversation could be leading. The man's outright friendliness – for a queensman, that is – caught him off guard.

The duelist continued. The rhythm of his voice bore a meandering quality. "Are you ready to face the man-wolves? Ready for another fight?"

Amot merely shrugged, not wanting to mention that he wouldn't be bearing arms. Marec kept on.

"I have it on good authority that when addressed in a civilized manner, Wulvers do not have the slightest clue about what they are being told. They simply growl back, unintelligibly."

This queensman clearly didn't know the wild. "Wulvers are not your typical canine," the scout retorted. "Don't underestimate them. They're more human than animal." Adrenaline flared slightly, firing up Amot's memories. While he'd never encountered a Wulver personally, his grandfather had shared many fireside stories about the beasts, some of which perhaps he shouldn't have. "In fact," Amot added, "Wulvers have been known to be involved in the slave trade, and they've bartered with Outlanders."

"I will educate you both," a valkyrie called out. It was the dark-skinned woman, now strapping a second pack onto her gryphon. Her voice carried easily above the other noises in the glade, strong and smooth. "Danus, don't move," she said, commanding the queensman next to her. Then she swung her gaze to Amot and Marec.

"Give me a moment and I will tell you the real trick of these Wulvers." She spoke with emphasis as though every syllable counted. The valkyrie returned to her task momentarily, muscled legs tensing as she held the pack firm against her gryphon with one hand while attempting to tie a sturdy knot with the other.

Marec asked her, "Rainsong, may I help?"

She huffed. "Does your horse roll? Fly upside-down?" Her tone had a bite to it.

The queensman shrugged, feebly. "I hope not, but surely I can tie a knot better with two hands than you can with only one."

She grunted. "Better that I do it, so I know it is done right." Rainsong flicked her gaze to Danus. "Just hold the reins steady, keep her calm."

When the valkyrie finished with the ropes and the straps, she casually strode over to a dead tree. Her helm hung in its lichen-coated branches and her spear had been set to lean against the snag's greying trunk. The weapon had a long, sleek shaft of shining black metal, with red feathers tied below the spearhead. Rainsong grasped her spear. Leaving the helm behind, she strode over to Amot and Marec. Her words were careful and precise as she scanned the two of them.

"I must tell you this," she started. "On my patrols over the Forest Between Two Rivers, I have heard the Wulvers howl and I have seen them hunt. They feast on raw flesh; yours and mine being no exception." She paused to examine Amot's physique, smiled at him like he was dessert. "I suspect they might find yours *delectable* – especially with such broad shoulders to gnaw on."

Marec's expression went completely blank at the remark.

Rainsong's right ear twitched. She eyed a patch of ground near her, scrutinizing.

"What is it?" Amot said.

Without answer, Rainsong widened her stance, tilted her spear to the marked aimpoint, and brought her body into perfect alignment with the shaft. The tip traced to a tuft of grass sprouting from the hard-packed mud. She held the weapon still and waited, then shifted her gaze to Amot.

"The man-wolves are not like us," she went on, waiting, still as can be. Her voice had become hushed. "They dig dens with their claws to live in, they raise their young like wolves, and I'm sure they hump like dogs." Rainsong tilted her head, glancing sideways as though in thought.

"But you might be right," she conceded, with a slight shrug. "There is one thing they do that is very much human."

"And what is that?" Marec asked.

Rainsong plunged her spear into the grass, then released. It stuck there, firmly planted. She straightened up, turned to Marec.

"They plan their kills with the utmost of precision," she stated coldly. "Every detail. The whole pack contributes. It is their obsession."

Hearing a rustling sound, Amot and Marec glanced down to where the spear had impacted. Grass twitched. She'd impaled a snake, body still twisting. Amot looked back to her. She faced him squarely. Her large, intense eyes held the scout's gaze in check.

"A snake could send these cats into a frenzy." Rainsong grasped Amot's wrist. Her palm was warm. "You heard that I am Rainsong?"

Amot nodded.

"My squadron commander tells me you are 'Amot.'"

"Yes," he answered, assuming Rainsong meant the woman at the lake had told her.

The valkyrie glanced to her gryphon, then back to him. "Well, Amot," she said, "I have to return to my cat – 'Ashes.' Something has gotten her spooked. Perhaps the snake. Come talk to me after we land." She followed with a single nod, prompting him to respond.

Amot returned the gesture. "I will." The valkyrie let go his arm, made her exit, abandoning her spear and the impaled snake coiling around it.

Galewind tracked Amot as he strode across the glade, heading towards Stormbringer. The knightmaiden shifted her gaze to another ranger – the scrappy-looking redhead, back to distracting Catwings. Last, her eyes wandered to Tallman. She watched as he approached a queensman and laid in on him with an earful about reducing his load. Galewind turned to regard Berendt, beside her.

"You picked quite the assortment of rangers for OP Diamondback," she said. "Tell me about them." She flicked her gaze to the one talking it up with Catwings. "The redhead's young."

The Kith commander maneuvered away from Electra to get a clear view of what his men were up to. He settled his gaze on the ranger in question. "That's Rix Caledon," he gruffed. "A damn good spotter. I trust his eyes and ears more than I trust my own. And he fills a capability gap in my team – best deadeye I've seen at his age. Wilder to the bone though, which comes with a rebellious streak, no less. Nothing I can't handle." Berendt rubbed his beard, then fixed his gaze on another. "And Amot Rixin… well, you've seen him in action at Diamond Saber. He's talented. Another Wilder and a third-generation ranger, with strong connections to the Hurlorns. Knows how to use a complex environment to his advantage. The trick with Amot is to keep him from getting himself killed long enough to learn some common sense."

Berendt grunted. "And you already know Tallman."

"I do," Galewind replied. She'd worked with him before on recce ops.

"Every commander's dream," Berendt went on. "Strong, determined, reliable, and does exactly what you tell him to do. The only thing with Tallman is to make sure you put him in a straightforward situation. Clear-cut objectives, I'm saying."

Galewind smiled. "You know your people."

"Yep. Have to in this sorry business." Berendt sighed, nodding as his one eye scanned the glade, from one ranger to the next. "We rely on each other out here." He turned back to her. "How about yours?"

Galewind sighed. "Well, my Rainsong is your Tallman. I'd only add 'highly adaptable,' like your Amot. Every time she flies, she wrestles our most compact and feisty gryphon into submission – Ashes has an attitude and is solid muscle. Catwings, well, she might not look like much in a warrior sense, but she's determined and she can fight her cat better than anyone. Those are my two wind riders."

"And the tall one…"

"Stormbringer. She's my up-and-coming leader. There's a fury about that one."

"Like you used to be?"

Galewind scoffed slightly. "I was never quite like that. When she doesn't get her way…"

Berendt mixed a chuckle in with his grunt. "Watch out."

Galewind nodded.

Despite herself, a heavy, somber feeling welled up inside Galewind. The knightmaiden lowered her eyes. "I don't know them as well as I should. Not for this kind of mission."

Berendt paused, grasped the knightmaiden's hand in his. With his other hand, he gently tilted her chin up, lock eyes with her. He spoke in a low voice. "I know it's been hard, Galewind. I know you got a raw deal. I wish I could've… you know… been there for you."

She placed her free hand lightly on their shared grasp. "You were there. I mean, I thought of you all the time. And I should have been there for you when…"

"We both have duties."

"I know." She forced a smile. "I've been exonerated."

Berendt sighed heavily. "I knew you would be."

Galewind lifted her hand, stroked the side of the Kith commander's face, gently caressing his scar with her finger tips. She grimaced. "Does it hurt?"

Berendt chuckled. "Itches like hell, is all."

"Can you see out of it?"

He shook his head. "Not much. Healer at the 3rd Institute says I need to take the patch off a bit longer every day to get the eyeball moving again – to exercise my vision – and give the wound some air."

Galewind firmed up her voice. "Listen to the healer."

Berendt scowled slightly. She shot him a stern, motherly look of concern.

Berendt's shoulders dropped. He sighed. After a long moment he finally conceded. The Kith commander raised a hand to his eye, flipped up the patch. "That healer doesn't know what the hell she's talking about. I'm sure of it."

The knightmaiden gave him a warm, encouraging smile before averting her gaze to Electra. She drew a deep breath, then started fussing with the tie ins. It was all she could do not to stare at the wound. *One step at a time,* she told herself. *One step at a time.*

Stormbringer glanced up at the darkening sky. The weather was shaping up just the way Catwings had said it would. Winds gusted in the high pine branches and the air that swirled down into the glade carried with it a newfound chill. Her mount stirred. The spearmaiden whispered into Ladybird's tufted ear, one hand gently stroking the gryphon's nape. "What's wrong, Lady?"

Out of the corner of her eye, Stormbringer noted Amot casually making his way over, backpack slung over one shoulder. She released her grip on Ladybird and pivoted full around to face the scout. His dark hair had already dried some, and now fell loose to his shoulders. And he was fully dressed, tall and wide-chested in his scuffed leather armor and heavy shoulder pauldrons, looking much the combatant. She called to him.

"Hey, Kith-boy. Come to help?"

He slowed, hesitating.

"Come on," she reassured him, gesturing. "I won't bite."

When he came near, Ladybird shifted in her place, then tried unsuccessfully to scratch off her hood.

Amot halted beside Stormbringer. "Will *she* bite?"

The spearmaiden smirked. She grasped Ladybird's reins in one hand to steady the beast, returned to stroking her with the other. "She probably hears thunder in the distance. Storms make her testy." Stormbringer turned to meet Amot's gaze. He'd taken a step closer. She couldn't help but notice his wilder ink.

Stormbringer wasn't normally one to hold any admiration whatsoever for such markings, but straightaway she thought that, in his case, something about the particular pattern of fine, faint lines and intricate swirls suited him. Like a winding sense of purpose. She shook off the wayward thought.

He asked, "What's wrong with a little weather? A good ranger never minded a bit of weather."

Stormbringer replied in a flat tone. "Rain will bring us crashing down. That's what's wrong."

"It can't be that bad." Amot sized up the mount. "Strong animal. Nature knows best."

"Pff," Stormbringer scoffed. "Nature has little to do with gryphons."

She extended her arm, grasped a handful of golden fur from the underside of the beast's neck. The scout leaned in, peering, as she showed him the quill-like shafts and downy barbs at the base of each one.

He raised his eyebrows. "Oh. That's different."

"And see here," she said, pointing to the nearest wing, where the coat's feathery pattern was more obvious to the eye.

He scrunched his eyebrows together. "How…"

Stormbringer explained, "The original *Shapers* in Fortune Bay were experimenters. They gave these steeds great wings and warm pelts, but they seem to have forgotten one thing: no one considered how heavy water-soaked fur can become. It might not make much of a difference for a land animal, but it is critical in the air – especially loaded with rangers and bulky queensman."

"I get it," Amot said. "And there was no time for a do over, was there?"

Stormbringer shook her head. "They were heralded 'abominations of the flesh,' same as Outlanders – outlawed before the Shapers could complete their work. The Shapers were forced to stick with what they had, with their experiment." She paused. "So, who's been coaching you?"

"My detachment in Fort Abandon is dedicated to enforcing the treaty."

"So, Order Lumen then?"

Amot nodded. He looked to the other gryphons. "Have I slowed down departure?"

Stormbringer shook her head. "No, not at all." She gestured. "Here, give me your pack."

The scout shrugged the pack off his shoulder, handed it to her. She took it and tested its weight. *Clothes and a hatchet,* she figured.

"Not bad," she said. "Much lighter than a queensman's gear." The spearmaiden eyed a space on Ladybird for it, towards the rear. She hushed to her gryphon, "Keep still," she said, and left the reins to dangle. Amot took them up.

"Did you know that there were originally six gryphons?" she asked him.

"No, I didn't know that," Amot said. He began to stroke the animal the same way Stormbringer had been doing. He found just the right place to make Ladybird purr a gravelly purr.

Stormbringer began strapping in the pack, then continued, "Two were lost during the battle for Fortune Bay – the only males: one Harpy and one Gold. Felled by swords that appeared out of thin air, as the story goes."

"Really?" Amot said.

The spearmaiden nodded. "I'd say scorpion heavy arrows are the more likely culprit. Apparently, the male gryphons were the larger targets and more aggressive, so the Jhinyari took them out first." She pulled the straps tight, grunting as she spoke. "The other four – these four – … ugh… were scattered. Ladybird still bears the scars of that battle."

"Makes you think, doesn't it?" Amot said.

Stormbringer nodded. "What could've been."

A long pause followed. The spearmaiden puffed out air, turned her gaze to Amot.

"Phoof. Done," she said, then adjusted her collar to protect her neck better from the newfound chill. Her eyes darted to the other gryphons.

"Actually," she said, "everyone's nearly ready, except…" She surveyed the edge of the glade, across the field, "… except we're still waiting on a queensman. Let's just say if he falls off his horse and doesn't make it, I won't shed any tears. There isn't a lot of space or weight to spare."

Amot tugged and fidgeted with the saddle straps and some of the gear tied on, as though double checking her fastenings.

He's stalling, she thought. "What is it?"

A long moment of silence followed. Amot sounded sincere when he finally spoke his mind.

"Sorry about… earlier," he started, sounding more than a bit awkward. "And Rix, well, he's just Rix – no one takes him seriously. Honestly, I didn't know about the gryphons…"

Stormbringer laughed. "Don't even try to explain," she said. "I see you showed up with your pants on this time, at least."

The scout took the hit solidly, without emotion. A glancing blow to his ego. The spearmaiden got the impression he'd been hardened to criticism.

"Smart to leave the dog behind too," she added. "You don't want to scare the gryphons. Besides, we promised our cats they could hunt a bit of wolf. What would your dog think of that?"

Amot made a pained expression. He didn't answer.

CHAPTER XIII
KITH CHAOS

(Eriff, Amot)

STALLION IN TOW, Eriff Haulik craned his neck around to catch a glimpse of the horse and rider struggling behind him. Another sharp grunt sounded, accompanied by the jangle of shifting gear hauled on the trailing Kurstern's back. Eriff peered through the scattering of colored leaves, still clinging to their branches. His squire was at a rough patch. The ground had degraded to nearly impassable since breaking north from the flat stream bank they'd been following. Heavy bush, fallen logs, and rocky terrain made for rough riding. Over his shoulder, Eriff grumbled to the young girl.

"Those wretched rangers are to blame for this mix up, I am certain of it, Lorri. Whenever they are involved, chaos rules. 'Order Kith' is self-contradictory, if you ask me."

"Pardon, Gallant?" Lorri replied. "Chaos rules, you say?" Her mount snorted in defiance. "Oh, come on, Big Baby. Step now… you can do it… step."

She is faring better than I. Eriff had given up the saddle right then and there, surrendered himself to leading his noble steed by the reins. The squire's riding horse had been no match for Eriff's mount on the open trails in and out of Kiranis Hills, but along Elgar's Creek and over the seldom used forest path cutting north from it, Lorri's sturdy mare had made gains on him, and not surprisingly: Kursterns often double as packhorses. It was the first time Eriff and his squire had been in earshot that day since the two met while traveling in opposite directions, at the tip of the gorge that descended into Gan.

Eriff shook his head, scoffed quietly to himself. *Unbelievable. I cannot even trust my own kin to organize anything past their noses. A squire on a pack horse? Hours late? What was my uncle thinking? Shroud's Well, lend the girl a Courser and send her on her way.*

On his future father-in-law's advice, Eriff had departed the gates of the Hidden City early that morning, unattended, to secure an early and private audience with Knightmaiden Galewind of Order Valkyrie. He'd also intended to reserve a seat on her golden gryphon for the journey to Whisperwood. For his grand arrival, Eriff had selected a proud Akedan Lord Horse to showcase, freshly trained at his family's stables and in need of some gentle, off-estate trail experience. The sheer majesty of the beast would draw in the valkyries, he was sure, and would stimulate conversation. And if his knightly presence spawned feelings of envy among the have-not rangers present, all the better.

That was the plan, at Lord Ralador's urgings. Eriff never imagined he'd be forced to double back to Gan in utter frustration after no one showed up at Kiranis Hills. He also hadn't anticipated that he'd meet up with his squire on the way back, and be forced to change direction yet again after learning the new location of the rendezvous point. And it certainly hadn't dawned on Eriff that he might need to urge his prize horse ahead one step at a time along a trail meant for pack animals. The queensman had to be especially careful with his mount. After all, he was only trying it out for size before delivery to a Harrowian Tor Lord within weeks. *One bad step…*

Eriff huffed. *Everyone will be there by now. Instead of being the first, I will be the last.* He squeezed his eyes shut momentarily. *Aelish, lend me strength.* When Lorri finally made it through the rough patch, she interrupted her commander's train of self-defeating thoughts.

"Gallant Haulik. Did you say 'chaos rules'?"

"Yes, Lorri, I did," Eriff replied. "And it surely does."

"It's those rangers, isn't it?"

"Yes, Lorri, it is the Kith. Clean out your ears."

"Pardon?"

How did I get stuck with this one? – Oh yes, my charitable soul. Conversing with Lorri could be tedious. Eriff had taken her on because, frankly, no one else would take on the girl who dreamed of being a queensman.

"Never mind," Eriff said.

"How long were you waiting, Gallant?" the squire asked.

Eriff sighed heavily. "I watched the sky for two hours. All I saw were dark clouds."

"Gallant," Lorri continued.

"Yes, Squire?"

"Order Valkyrie only received the ranger coordinates *after* Lady Apsarla had sent out her own different ones, and the Palace Guard never received a message from Northpost at all."

"Could the Northpost raven have been intercepted?"

"I suppose, Gallant."

"Hmph. More likely some ranger with a pounding head after a night of drinking sent out the wrong bird, or an untried one."

"Yes, Gallant."

Eriff paused for a moment, pondering. "Lorri, might I ask that you do not call me 'Gallant' for the remainder of this trip? 'Sir' will do just fine."

"Whatever for, Gallant – *Sir?*"

"For sport, Lorri, at Lord Ralador's behest. They must think me a lower station."

"But…"

"Never mind why."

"Very well, *Sir*. And… and look ahead."

Eriff peered through the stand of pines and yellow-leafed alders. Beyond the trees, the trail opened into a grassy field. It spread out gradually to a low mound that marked the entry point into a small, protected valley.

"Good eye, Lorri. That must be the place. My armor, squire."

Eriff halted and, with Lorri's assistance, spent a few minutes donning the entirety of his protective gear.

"No, not the helm," Eriff told Lorri as the squire was about to pull it out of a saddlebag. "That would be overdoing it, but be sure to brush the mud off the horses' legs and unfurl the house banner."

While Lorri fussed over the final details, the queensman mounted the Akedan Lord Horse. And as soon as Eriff settled into his saddle, the horse pawed at the ground beneath it, ears pricked forward and stiff. *He wants to get moving.* The white stallion's temperament had improved in eye of the open terrain. Restless himself, Eriff waited another long minute for Lorri to get ready.

The squire nodded to her patron. "All done, Sir."

The queensman grinned as he gathered the reins and kicked his mount to a canter. With the cool wind rushing through his hair, the gallant leaned forward and patted his steed on its side. Feeling nearly breathless, he spoke softly to the Akedan. "Time for that grand entrance, *Poet.* Impress the ladies, now."

Before Amot could ask the spearmaiden about strapping Howler onto her gryphon, out of nowhere Rix interrupted, voice cracking.

"Is it true valkyries charge into battle topless, to distract the enemy?"

A flushed feeling swept the back of Amot's neck and across his forehead. *Shit, Rix, show some restraint.* Before him, Stormbringer's face tensed, her casual expression wiped bare. An awkward pause filled the air as her cold eyes glared past Amot to Rix. Amot swung his gaze to the spotter. The orange-topped wonder kept a straight face; straight and bright with puckish provocation.

Before the spearmaiden could even respond to the spotter's ill-placed remark, the sound of thudding hooves sounded throughout the glade, from the far side.

The two rangers and the valkyrie turned to watch as a member of the Queen's Guard rode into view, swift and well-poised atop his high-bred horse. Behind him trailed yet another scrawny squire, sitting tall and straight and bearing the banner of the Horse Lords. Amot recognized the lead queensman straightaway. It wasn't so much the golden short-cropped hair, the snob-nose, or even the signature Royal Quarter armor that he wore, custom made for a self-inflated braggart of medium build. It was his attitude, projecting ahead of him like a cone of arrogance. Yes, Amot recognized him all right. The man rode in like he owned the place: fast, proud and poised for showmanship. A spread of fallen logs lay directly across his path. Rather than skirt around, by all appearances he would jump it.

That moment a gryphon let out a low, guttural growl, more to Amot's expectations than the weak chealps earlier. He cringed at the sound reverberating in his chest. It shook his insides all to hell.

Then a bark sounded.

The scout whirled around as the dog – his dog – barked again. Body and ears erect, tilted forward, Howler stood his ground at the heels of Rainsong's beast.

Ashes jerked its head low, clawed off its hood.

"Howler?"

A hand pushed against the scout's shoulders, launching him forward.

"Go!" Stormbringer urged. "Hurry. If Ashes doesn't shred your dog, Rainsong will carve it up herself."

Poet had executed a perfect leap into the protected glade, soaring over the deadwood obstacle in its path by half an arm's length. And this despite the thunderous rumble that occurred while airborne. It wasn't the first time Eriff had heard the loud and throaty growl of a gryphon, but never one so near. *A fitting opener for my arrival,* he decided.

"Apologies," Eriff cried out to all, as he brought his steed to an abrupt halt. He spotted Galewind to his left in the company of a scruffy ranger. *I'll rescue you from that bore,* he decided. Eriff cleared his throat, projected his voice her way.

"Ah, Knightmaiden Galewind," he started. "The Lord of the March kept me until late morning, and then of course the trail coming in was treacherous. I ran into a bloody tripvine along the way. Just one, thankfully…"

Eriff's voice trailed off when he noticed Galewind's eyes staring past him, narrowed as though in confusion. He quickly turned, scanned the scene that had her captivated. He spotted his duelist uncle standing with a petit blonde, while a brown-skinned valkyrie and two chargers, Danus Leigh and Spratt Devine, backed away from a disgruntled gryphon. Instead of all eyes homing in on Eriff and his grand horse, they'd fallen on an emerging crisis.

What's wrong with that thing? The gryphon slowly weaved back and forth, bobbing its massive head up and down, all the while maintaining eye contact with a dog barking at its heels. With wings slightly spread, the beast tested the limits of its leash. Out of the corner of one eye, the queensman glimpsed a ranger dashing towards the perturbed gryphon.

"How-ler!" the ranger yelled. "I told you to STAY!"

Eriff tracked the man as he ran. "Is that… Amot?" The queensman's shoulders slumped. He rolled his eyes. "Well, that figures."

The dog's barking intensified. The gryphon hissed back, feigning strikes.

Lorri pulled up beside Eriff on her Kurstern. "Sir?" She too fixed her eyes on the center of attention. The squire jerked her head back, did a double take. "The ranger from the exercise in Seventh Kaeda… the one who lost the striker."

Eriff let out a heavy sigh. "Lord Ralador *assured* me that Amot had been axed from the mission."

Lorri said, "That's him all right. I'd recognize that bastard anywhere."

Her cutting tone surprised the queensman, but it lined up with his own sentiments. "I hate these backwoods," he complained to her, "and I hate dealings with rangers."

A gasp to his left caused the queensman to swing his gaze back to Galewind. She'd grabbed the arm of the ranger standing next to her — the Kith commander from Diamond Saber, Ranger Berendt Garondi. The expression on the rogue's battle-scarred face hardened as he took in what was happening.

"I should go before this gets ugly," he told Galewind in a gruff voice.

She nodded in agreement. The commander started off across the glade, making haste.

"Glad you could make it," he grumbled to Eriff as he passed.

Eriff scoffed. "I was lucky to get here at all." The man's wound looked even worse up close. "That eye looks terrible. For the sake of Aelish, it's oozing! Can't you cover it up?"

The Kith commander grunted at the suggestion, then flipped his eyepatch down. The queensman called after the departing ranger. "Who is responsible for this mess of a rendezvous?"

Berendt continued on his way without an answer.

Perfect, thought Eriff, opportunity blossoming in his mind. He dismounted, sauntered over to Galewind, while Lorri took the reins of both horses and led them to an area where they could graze and drink with the other horses.

"Knightmaiden Galewind, so nice to find someone reasonable in this…" Eriff glanced about, made a face, "… in this *charming* glade. Shouldn't a ranger, above all, be able to control his animal?"

Galewind inhaled sharply and cringed, eyes still fixed on the gryphon. "That was a close one." She shook her head, shifted her gaze to Eriff. "Some animals are easier to control than others," she replied. "Each has its quirks. They get their heads filled with silly ideas, like 'I can take on a gryphon ten times my size.'"

Eriff snickered.

"Champion Haulik," said the knightmaiden, with a slight bow of her head, "so glad you could join us." Galewind sounded a tad more sincere than the ranger had. "Your duelist uncle is already among us. Your timing is perfect."

"Everything at once, it seems. Looks like I am in for a show." Eriff repeated his earlier remarks about why he was late, then positioned himself beside the knightmaiden. They both watched the fretful bird and the disobedient canine. Everyone else had crowded around. Some to watch; others poised to intervene.

The dog was in Eriff's direct line of sight. It lay crouched to the ground, barking and growling at the gryphon. *Not ten,* he thought, *but twenty times the dog's size, at least.* The dog completely ignored Amot's repeated commands to "get out of there."

Eriff sighed. "Let me guess, Amot's dog?"

"Correct," Galewind replied. "The Kith use dogs for tracking all the time."

"A terrible way to begin a mission: one ranger and his dog, eaten."

The knightmaiden raised one eyebrow, smirked. "Yes, it would be terrible."

Eriff turned his gaze to her. "Might I trouble you for a seat on the journey over?"

Galewind paused. "I'm sorry, I'm all full up with rangers, and none of mine are about to be eaten. You'll have to find another."

Eriff snickered, thinking her remarks were a jive. An awkward silence followed.

"Really," she continued. "Electra is at capacity. My spearmaiden will have a seat for you on Ladybird, the other Gold. She only has one ranger packed so far."

Eriff scoffed. "Surely, one of the rangers on Electra can be displaced."

"I think not, dear Eriff," Galewind replied. "I need to have words with Commander Garondi, and Tall Hallman is packed and too heavy to pair up with a queensman. Had you arrived earlier..." Galewind raised a hand to her chest, drew in a quick breath. "Oh dear."

The dog lunged at the great beast, skidded beneath the eagle fore portions and nipped at its toes. The gryphon backed away, rearing in terror, talons flailing. It made an awkward turn on its hinds – wings spread and off-balance, beak wide open.

Amot lunged into the foray, "No!" he cried, putting himself between the dog and the gryphon. He waved his arms. "Back off!"

"Don't challenge the gryphon!" called a valkyrie in red.

Poncho flowing about her, the brown-skinned valkyrie yanked a spear out of the ground. Taking a low stance, she tilted the butt end towards the threatening canine and advanced. "Shoo," she said, feigning thrusts at the dog.

Amot raised a staying hand to her. "No. It's all right," he said. "They're just... intimidating one another. We can walk them back."

"Get that mutt away from my Ashes, Scout," the valkyrie responded.

Eriff glanced over the ranger's light armor, sized up the gryphon's massive beak and talons. *That's all we need. Casualties before we even get started.* The queensman called out to the scout.

"Walk away, rogue, while you can. That gryphon will tear you in two." Given Aelish's condition, Eriff doubted his ability as a radiance channeler to put Amot back together again, if it came to that.

Berendt took charge. "Everyone back-off," he bellowed. His voice carried a hard edge. "Leave it to Amot to handle the situation. My scout knows what he's doing."

This isn't your command. Eriff held his tongue on that front though, for the time being. Instead, he called out to his men: "Danus, Spratt." The two queensman responded immediately.

The two heavily armored chargers waved their arms at the gryphon, drew its attention, then got in the way as much as they could. Amot used the distraction to successfully remove his spaniel from the Harpy's presence. The chargers stood aside.

Foolish bravery, thought Eriff of Amot. *But bravery nonetheless.* That moment, for reasons unknown to Eriff, he suddenly realized the contradiction in Lord Ralador's orders to him: cozy up to Order Valkyrie command elements, yet humiliate both them and the Kith they so adore by stealing command of the mission out from under their noses. Eriff rubbed his chin as he pondered the wayward notion.

With a firm hand, Amot held Howler in place, away from danger. He squatted down to the dog's level, waved an accusing finger at Howler's nose. "Stay, this time," he said. His own heart was still pounding. The scout glanced over his shoulder. The gryphon had folded its wings and now sat calmly on its hinds. Rainsong had put down her spear and had taken to gently stroking her Ashes. Eyes closed and head tilted sideways, the gryphon nuzzled her like a kitten to its mother. Queensmen, their squires, and rangers started back to their tasks.

Amot returned his gaze to Howler, drew a deep breath. "Lucky," he said, then scratched behind the dog's ears. With Ashes blocked from view, Howler seemed to be acting normal again. "You can't bark at gryphons. They *eat* dogs like you."

Rix wandered over, hunkered down beside the spaniel and his

master. Amot glanced to his friend, at a loss. "How I am going to bring Howler along now?"

The spotter only shrugged.

"Bring the dog along?" scoffed an eavesdropping queensman. Airy laughter infused his words. "Ha! You're not. Can't you see, dogs and gryphons don't mix?" Casually, he approached. It was Danus Leigh.

Amot nodded to Rix, who immediately assumed hold of Howler. The scout stood up abruptly, ready to confront Danus. The man's face was sour, nose crinkled like a bad smell was in the air.

Already, Eriff was on his way over. The queensman commander seconded his charger. "You can't bring a dog on a gryphon. Are you mad or just plain stupid?"

Berendt retorted flatly, "We need Howler to find and track the scent trail when we get to Whisperwood, if there is one."

The two commanders faced one another. "No, no, that simply will not do," Eriff told Berendt. "Your *men* are for tracking. We must keep the load as light as possible – ask any valkyrie. A ranger should know that. Give the dog a bone and be done with it. The mutt will just get in the way." He turned and called out to a nearby squire: "Tell Lorri to unpack my things and find me a gryphon! And when the time comes to depart, take this ratty creature with you and drop it off at the nearest ranger outpost." He turned back to regard Berendt.

"You see? Problem solved."

Rix spoke up. "Howler can ride with me."

Eriff turned to the spotter, annoyed at the sight of him. "Did you not hear what I just said?" He looked the ginger over and winced. His words were laced with derision. "Let me repeat myself. The dog is staying. We need to minimize the weight and we cannot risk upsetting the gryphons."

Rix shot back. "Me plus the dog still weigh less than your fat ego." Rix's inky swirls brightened.

"Watch your mouth, scoundrel." Eriff's eyes darted over Amot and his Kith commander. "None of you rangers are worth your weight, if you ask me."

Rix's eyes narrowed. "Well, who the hell is asking you?"

The Kith commander interjected. "Rix, that's enough." Berendt scanned his men, making direct eye contact with each, in turn. "That's enough from everyone. We have a mission to attend to. Now get moving."

Stormbringer called out to them from her place next to her gryphon, her voice scolding. "Yes, stop your squabbling. Amot, you're with me." She turned to another valkyrie. "Catwings, take Rix *and* the dog."

A wave of relief washed over Amot.

Next, she addressed Eriff. "You can ride with me as well. That other queensmen…"

"Marec," offered Spratt.

"*Marec* has been assigned to Catwings," she finished.

"I'm not riding with a dog *or* a ranger," Eriff objected. "I will cast them off."

The spearmaiden huffed. "Fine," she responded, thin-lipped and with her brow crossed. "Eriff, join your uncle with Catwings then, but leave me some gear. Rix, you're with me now. And bring the dog. He's small and can lie down middle-back. It's dead space for riders anyways."

She beckoned Rix and Amot to her. Eriff didn't contest and the rangers obliged. And when Amot and Rix arrived to mount Ladybird, the spearmaiden conceded, "We've actually done this sort of thing before."

"With a dog?" Amot asked.

"Close enough."

⁂

Rix strapped in behind Amot, with Howler in between. The dog seemed to be worn out and rather accepting of his fate.

Amot twisted halfway around. "It's better this way Rix. She's out of your league anyway." Amot made a passing glance across the field to Catwings, smirked. "Way out of your league." He'd noticed the lingering eye contact between the two when they were apart.

Rix grinned. "You don't even know what my league is."

Stormbringer pulled deerskin gloves over her long fingers, then turned and looked past Amot to the spotter. Amot leaned sideways to clear her view. She addressed Rix candidly.

"Before we lift off, Rix, in answer to your previous question – before all the commotion – I will say this: Rainsong is the only one of us valkyries present who has done anything like *that which you mentioned* before."

Rix guffawed, glanced to Amot. Amot made wide eyes back, nodded slightly. *Yes, Rix, she's talking about how they fight.*

She went on, "Catwings might be inclined to follow suit one day – her eyes light up whenever the tale of Rainsong comes up in conversation. Personally, I don't think she has it in her."

Rix raised an eyebrow. "You might be surprised." Then he looked the spearmaiden square on. "And you?"

She laughed. "The risk-takers ride the Harpies – the battle cats. My Gold's more of a mellow, long-distance flyer."

Rix folded his arms. "That doesn't answer my question."

Amot felt the gryphon stirring underneath, eager to take flight. The Gold spread its great wings. The spearmaiden kept a restraining grip on the reins. The griffon chealped in protest.

"And we haven't been properly introduced," she added. "Spearmaiden Stormbringer."

"Spotter Rix Caledon," Rix replied. "Soon to be a deadeye."

"Hold on tight, Spotter."

Stormbringer turned to face forward. Amot glimpsed a private smile creep across her face as the gryphon's wings began to thump. Her voice rang out loud and clear.

"Valkyries, on!" she cried. Her comrades joined in chorus as Ladybird sprang into the air. Amot glanced down at the glade as they rose over the treetops. Then he tilted his gaze up to the dark, rolling clouds.

Stormbringer indeed.

Cloud lightning flashed above. Violent crosswinds gusted against the squadron of gryphons as they joined formation.

Hail pelted beast and burden, beginning soon into flight. Amot pulled his cloak tight around his body, but the streaming bits of ice still stung his face and burned his eyes. There seemed no protection from the elements. Beneath him, the extreme musculature of their mount labored on. Ladybird swayed and tilted as she fought to stay on course against the turbulence.

Rix hollered from the rear of the gryphon. "Shouldn't we head back? Wait this out?"

The Wilder glanced over his shoulder at the spotter, keeping low and clinging tight as the hailstones whipped into him.

Stormbringer craned her neck around. "I don't think this will last long."

Amot raised his forearm to shield his face. "At least it isn't raining."

"It's a good thing rangers don't mind a bit of weather." Stormbringer took stock of the other three gryphons, then turned forward again and tucked in.

Amot checked on the other gryphons as well. He watched as the hailstones bounced off their backs. The valkyries flew in two staggered pairs: The forward element consisted of Stormbringer's Gold as the flight leader and Catwings' Harpy elevated to the rear left. The Harpy bore two queensman passengers, along with the wind rider. Amot could barely make out the second pair of gryphons, behind and to the right. Galewind's Gold led the rear element with Rainsong's Harpy trailing to the lower right. The knightmaiden carried two rangers with her, while Rainsong had only one queensman – in order to make room for all the gear, one had to be left behind. In the end, the choice had come down to Tallman or Spratt, and the command elements – even Eriff – unanimously decided they couldn't do without Tallman. "Amot, easily," had been Eriff's snide remark, "but not Tallman." Both Berendt and Galewind blocked that from happening.

Stormbringer twisted her body around with something to say. The scout leaned into her.

"The formation," she called over the winds, "makes us difficult targets and makes it easy for the two groups to split off and attack or defend as separate, coordinated units. Harpies defend first, then the Golds swoop in."

Amot nodded. *Defend against what?* he wondered. "How did you know I was looking at them?"

"I could feel the load change," the spearmaiden answered. "You shift the balance every time you move. You're not exactly a featherweight."

The hail let-up slightly and the turbulent winds abated. Catwings took the opportunity to sway in close, riding high on Spree's withers to make room for the two queensmen on her Harpy's short back. Her eyes were narrow slits in the stormy conditions. Bronze-rimmed goggles hung loose around her neck. She'd donned a cloak to cover her slim-fitting armor. Eriff, one seat back from her, wore a bloodless and pale expression, his gripping knuckles white as the hail. Behind him, Marec huddled in close, just forward of riding the gryphon's loins. He kept his head down, sheltered by the width of his nephew's armored shoulders. Bits of ice rang off the queensmen's plated armor.

Catwings yelled over, "We'll be all right. I've been through a lot worse."

Amot raised his hands to his mouth, funneled his voice to the queensmen. "I thought you'd enjoy this," he bellowed, "being such great horsemen and all."

Eriff lifted a hand to shield his face. "Loving it," he shouted back. His voice began to waver. "Cannot get enough, really. In fact, I think I will trade in my horse for one of these cat-things when I get back."

Catwings looked over her shoulder at her riders. "Sorry, girls only," she teased.

Eriff glanced behind him. "What do you think, Uncle?"

Marec jerked his head up, face pale as a ghost. "Aye. Couldn't be better. But I wouldn't want to deprive the ladies of such wonderful flying creatures. The Order Valkyrie can keep them, as far as I'm concerned."

Catwings made eye contact with Amot and Rix across the swirling expanse that separated them. A one-sided grin drew across her lips. She raised her goggles to cover her eyes, then called back to her passengers.

"Did I ever tell you my gryphon's nickname?"

Marec responded, "Your gryphon has a nickname?"

"Yeah, 'Diver.'"

Eriff's head jerked back. "Diver?"

Catwings leaned forward, tucked her body in close to her mount. "Here, let me show you. Hold on!" She pulled down on the reins.

Amot caught glimpse of the queensman's gaping mouths as the Harpy dropped and dove past the Gold, before spiraling into a roll and leveling off. An undulating "whaaaa… aa… aa… aaaaa!" filled the air.

Rix slapped his thigh, bursting with laughter. Howler joined in with his own blend of rawling. Stormbringer kept to an even composure, while Amot subdued his own urge to chuckle along with Rix and the dog.

Below them, Catwings glanced over her shoulder again. She called back to the queensmen. "Still loving it?"

Amot spoke into Stormbringer's ear. "Pompous ass, that Eriff," he said. "I kinda feel sorry for his uncle though."

She nodded in response. "Yeah, Marec's not so bad."

Rix leaned forward, stretching over Howler. "Stormbringer, can we try that?"

"No," the spearmaiden stated flatly. She followed-up in a softened tone "Gold Gryphons aren't really made for that sort of thing."

A somber quiet filled the air. "Oh," the redhead said, not hiding his disappointment. "That's okay," he added. "Just asking… whaa?"

The Gold's wings suddenly tucked. The animal veered sideways, then shot straight up. Amot held on tight as Ladybird looped around in an inverted arc, leveled, and then beat her wings hard, accelerating to reclaim her lead position in the formation.

"Whoa!" Rix screamed. "That was great! Wait a minute. Where's the dog?"

Amot's heart stopped in his chest. He felt behind him in a frenzy, twisted around, frantic, only to find colorful Rix laughing straight at him, his hands grasping Howler.

Amot breathed a heavy sigh. "Funny," he said. "Can we go back and get my stomach now?"

Rix's face was aglow with daring Wilder colors. "Again!" he cried.

Although nowhere near as dramatic as Catwings' drop and roll, Amot had a strong feeling that Stormbringer wouldn't risk any more aerial acrobatics.

The spearmaiden signaled to Catwings, and the wind rider's Harpy slowly rose above them to the usual wingmate position. The two valkyries exchanged knowing looks.

When the crosswinds picked up again, Stormbringer called to Amot. "Move up a bit," she said. "It'll be easier on Ladybird."

Amot obliged, shuffling towards her along the gryphon's back.

"A little closer," she added.

Amot continued to shuffle a little more, until lightly pressed against Stormbringer's back. The straps he gripped were now at awkward angles behind him, and good handholds were lacking beside and in front of him.

The spearmaiden caught on to his dilemma. "Just put your arms around my waist, if it's easier," she told the Wilder.

Amot let go the straps, leaned into her. He adjusted his position as Stormbringer had suggested, and gently wrapped his arms around the spearmaiden's strong and narrow waist.

As they flew on through the storm, the scout's mind began to drift. *How old was Stormbringer?* The scout knew she had to be several years older, but looks-wise the age difference would even out eventually. Heck, by Amot's thirties they'd look about even, before youthfulness tipped in her favor once she started her rejuvenation cycles…

Face numb with cold, Stormbringer welcomed the warmth the young ranger imparted on her back. The valkyrie half-smiled to herself at how good Amot's strong arms felt around her waist. She wouldn't complain if he leaned in a little closer still. Catwings had shot her more than a few secretive glances about the arrangement already. With the queensmen teasing over and done with, the wind rider now respected her place in the formation. In a strange way, Catwings' spontaneous maneuver had broken the ice between her and her passengers, and fragments of the lively conversation that ensued carried to Stormbringer's ears.

The spearmaiden craned her neck, peered over the side, down and to the right behind her. She scanned the whitewashed skies for signs of the other two gryphons. *Nothing.* Straining her eyes, she tried to make shapes out of the milky swirls of snow and ice in the air. *Still nothing.* Stormbringer's body tensed. She pumped out a screeching wail to the ice-laden winds – the call of the valkyries. Catwings soon joined in chorus.

After a long time-gap, in the distance, Rainsong returned their calls, signaling that all was well. Stormbringer sighed. "Thank you, Norwin," she whispered to the winds. *As long as we stick together, we'll be fine.* The spearmaiden let the relief sink in for a minute, then contemplated the weather they faced. The blustering winds had died down some, but lightning still flashed in the clouds above. The temperature had dropped and wet snowflakes had begun to appear among the bits of deflecting ice. *We're entering a different phase of this weather system,* she surmised. She glanced back over her shoulder.

"All this trouble just to find a sword?" she asked Amot. His face was only inches away. "Why don't you just get another one?"

The scout shifted in his seat. "It's not a regular sword. What have you heard?"

"Not enough," Stormbringer said. "Trying to piece a few things together. A lot of it's hush hush."

"Well, the strikers are unique weapons," Amot stated. "Lumen Hadamard from the Grey Quarter created them, based on Jhinyari legends. But even he doesn't completely understand all the forces at play."

"Hence our predicament," Stormbringer remarked.

Amot grunted back in agreement.

Stormbringer paused. "I heard the blade 'dances,'" she said. "What does that mean?"

"I guess one could say that." There was a long pause before Amot answered, fumbling his words as he spoke. "Hmm… not really… sort of… well…"

"Well, what?" Stormbringer said. "Are you afraid to say? Held to secrecy?"

The scout hesitated. Stormbringer had a good idea why. He was weighing her need to know. She waited patiently for him to sort it all out in his head. After another extended pause, he continued.

"Yes," Amot said, "it is secret. But based on what you told me about the gryphon slaying, you should know too. In case one falls into the wrong hands and is used against the valkyries."

A heavy feeling came over Stormbringer. She twisted around more fully, directly meeting his gaze. He pulled back slightly. "The Jhinyari swords," Stormbringer said, "at Fortune Bay. They're real, aren't they – the ones believed to have cut down the two male gryphons?"

"Exactly. Yes," Amot said. "Do you see why strikers are so important now?"

She turned forward, eyeballing the weather and the path ahead. She let Amot's words soak in for a long minute as she did so. *I need more,* she decided. Stormbringer twisted back around. "How far is their reach?"

Amot shrugged. "Nobody knows how far the blades can project, really. There seems to be a sweet spot around a hundred yards for targeting by farseeing. Closer confuses the senses; farther… is more difficult all around. I don't know what the limits are."

The spearmaiden glanced up and down her sides to confirm her sisters' places in the formation, then to the ranger again. "How many of these swords are there?" she asked.

"Six were made, as far as I know," Amot replied.

"So, how did you lose one way over in Whisperwood?"

"I didn't. I was in Tetherport when it happened."

Confused, she faced the scout squarely. "Tetherport… in Seventh Kaeda?"

"Yep."

Stormbringer gasped. "Really?" By his expression, she knew Amot wasn't jesting. But the scout's claim would make the true distance incalculable – any travel to the Otherworldly Realm involved a portal that was not well understood.

In disbelief, the spearmaiden turned back around, focused her attention on the course ahead. The weather was changing yet again, and she had to stay on top of it.

Chapter XV

SEPARATE WAYS

(Stormbringer, Amot, Galewind)

WHITE OUT.

Stormbringer crouched low behind Ladybird's neck to shield herself from the rifling winds that'd blown up. Curtains of snow whirled all around. Everything was covered in it. She wiped the wet coating from her brow. Her eyes darted about.

Ahead, white. Behind, white. Above and below, white; and white again to either side. Worse, the light of day had begun to fade. *More trouble coming.* Rix called out.

"How will you know when we're there? I can't see a damn thing."

Stormbringer glanced behind her to the spotter. His hair was white. He was covered in snow. "I caught a glimpse of a rocky peak a while back. I think we're nearing the Dim."

"I saw it too," Amot said.

The spearmaiden glanced to the navigation instruments mounted on Ladybird's harness: a ball compass, a chronometer, and levels all covered in sleet. She wiped them, turned her head slightly. "Valkyries can fly blind if we have to," she told the Wilder, still nestled in. "You never know what you might get off those north peaks. When it's this bad, it doesn't usually last very long."

Amot nodded in acknowledgement. Stormbringer swung her gaze forward facing, then ducked down low again.

In a close huddle – Stormbringer to Ladybird and Amot to Stormbringer – the spearmaiden and the scout minimized their exposure to the elements. Snow and ice beads streamed over the pair, collecting in areas of exposed cloth and hair. Stormbringer's firm tugs on the reins and sharp commands spoken directly into Ladybird's ear kept them on course. The gryphon struggled for steadfastness against this latest, sudden onslaught of wintry conditions.

Amot did a quick shoulder check on his dog and his Kith brother who'd tucked himself close to Howler. Rix's bright ink markings were nearly invisible in the frigid conditions. Poor Howler had transformed into a shivering ball of frosted fur.

The scout broke away from his comfortable position momentarily. Leaning back, he lifted his hands from Stormbringer's plated coat where he'd been keeping them warm, brushed a patch of snow off Howler. He gave the dog a consoling rub.

Rix said, "At least he has f-f-fur."

Amot brushed himself off while he was at it, along with the gear beside him, and everywhere he could reach on the Gold's side and back. A frozen mix of ice and snow matted the gryphon's fur. He reclaimed his protected position, in close with the spearmaiden.

"You're freezing," she said.

"Ladybird is taking on weight," he told her.

Stormbringer paused, then called out to her wingmate. "Catwings," she shouted. "I'm dropping down to see if I can spot the river."

"I'm with you," she replied. Then Catwings called out behind her shoulder. "Galewind, did you catch that?"

Amot heard a faint affirmative, drowning in the winds.

"Hold on," Stormbringer said. She pulled down on the reins. Ladybird ducked into a shallow dive.

Amot's felt his body lift away from the gryphon's back. Rather than pull Stormbringer along with him, he released his hold on her one hand at a time, stretched out to the nearest straps and grabbed them tight.

The leather was thin, but strong. Howler whimpered and whined as they dropped, struggling against his bonds. They fell that way for the longest minute.

Stormbringer swung her gaze to where the other gryphons ought to be. She noted at least one dark shape descending along with them.

When Ladybird finally leveled out, the spearmaiden scanned the expanse below. Across the winds, she yelled out to her wingmate.

"See anything?"

Catwings veered in close, peering out through her bronze rims into the blanket of white. She wiped the snow off her googles, peered again, then responded with a quick shake of her head.

"A little lower then," Stormbringer shouted.

"Careful," Catwings shouted back. "We don't know our elevation."

"Higher yet than any tree," Stormbringer assured her, "but keep watch for the peaks. I think they're behind us, but…"

Catwings nodded. Both gryphons dropped deeper into the swirling mess beneath them. Not a second later, they passed through a boundary layer. The pattern of wind and snow suddenly changed. A grander and calmer flow of air dominated the new zone. Puffy snowflakes circulated in a long, slow rotation. The two gryphons sailed down until a small break appeared in the weather.

Rix called out. "I see something!"

Stormbringer strained her eyes to solidify her view of the terrain below, but only blurs of grey emerged. Then she swung her gaze forward to where the horizon should be. The evening was waning and the sky had begun to darken. During a second break in the weather, she noted a succession of tiny points of light in the distance, with somewhat regular spacing.

"I see it too," Stormbringer said. She scanned the flight instrumentation. The compass and chronometer affirmed her instincts.

"Turnsby is a few leagues southwest," Amot said.

Stormbringer glanced back. "What can you see?"

"Not much," he replied, still looking down. "Just some trees, back a ways."

"I saw lights," Stormbringer said. "I'm sure of it."

"Lights!" yelled Catwings, from the left wing.

"Yes, we saw them too," Stormbringer yelled back. She steered her gryphon slightly south. Catwings hesitated, then veered to follow.

"No, no," called Catwings, shaking her head. "I mean lights! It's getting dark."

Stormbringer watched as Catwings pilfered a lantern from her sidebag, handed it to Eriff. "Spark this up," she told him.

In turn, Stormbringer struggled with her own leather sidebag. It had shifted awkwardly low. She stretched her arm out, felt through the bag, got hold of a metal corner and tugged. The stupid thing wouldn't slide free.

"Here. Let me help," Amot offered. His strong hand slid alongside her arm. Grunting with the effort, Stormbringer yanked the lantern so hard the straps nearly popped. It came loose, flew out of her hands.

"Amot!" she screeched. The thing bounced off the right wing on an upward beat. Rix's hand shot out, grasping the lantern mid-bounce. Stormbringer huffed in relief. "Ekkon's Wheel!"

"Don't worry. Rix has it," Amot assured her. "I'll handle it. Just concentrate on keeping us airborne."

Amot opened his palm to Rix, who passed him the lantern. The scout spun the contraption around in his hand, but had no idea how to light it. The lantern was nothing more than a small glassy ball, wrapped in a wire mesh and mounted on a cylindrical bronze base. One half of the ball was coated with a shiny metal. He passed the contraption back to Rix.

"Any idea how this thing works?" he asked the spotter. Rix took the lantern, rolled it in his palms a few times examining it closely.

"Nope," Rix said.

Duelist Marec called out from Catwings' gryphon. They'd finally managed to fire up her lantern. "Look for the sparker," Marec suggested. "Takes a few clicks."

After flicking half a dozen times, the lantern flashed and yellow light spilled forth. Rix discovered a lock-hook that swung out, then found a place to attach the light.

The spearmaiden twisted around. Her arm stretched out past Amot. "No," she said, wiggling her fingers. "Give it to me."

Rix unhooked the lantern and handed it to her. Stormbringer swiveled back around to face forward. She clipped the lantern low on Ladybird's headcollar, lighting the path of shining white streaks ahead of them.

Catwings had a different way of doing things. She'd removed her winged helm from a sidebag, snapped the lantern onto it then placed it on her head. The beam shone everywhere she looked, like a miner's headlamp.

A third light flickered into view, to the rear right and below. Amidst the sea of white, Amot could just make out the milky form of Galewind's large Gold and its three riders. The gryphon arced up and pulled into tighter formation.

Stormbringer piped out a command. "Rainsong, spot."

A long moment passed. There was no reply.

"Norwin's Breeze." Galewind's stomach was in knots. *Damn storm. Lorenz was right, again.* She looked down, eyes squinting as she tried to see through the snow. The Harpy was nowhere to be seen. She swung her gaze to Stormbringer and Catwings, riding the winds ahead and above her. The knightmaiden's throat hurt. Her voice was hoarse and choppy. She rasped out a call to them.

"Where's Rainsong?" she said, as loud as she could. "Ashes was right behind me."

Berendt, seated behind Galewind, squinted into the storm. "Yes," he gruffed. "They were there a minute ago."

Without pause, the three valkyries cried out in unison. Seconds ticked by, but the call of the valkyries was met only by the howl of icy winds. They tried again. Nothing. Another minute went by. "Rainsong... Ash-es...," they yelled in turn, but there was no response. All eyes scanned the snowy expanse around them.

Over the racket of beating wings and wind noise, Queen's Guards and Kith Rangers alike bellowed out at the top of their lungs. The male voices paled in comparison to those of Catwings and Stormbringer – like trained opera singers, the two of them.

"Galewind," Catwings called, "what happened?"

The knightmaiden hollered back. "I don't know," she rasped, straining her throat. The desperation in her voice only made it sound worse. "Rainsong kept wandering off but she always swung back, and already I could barely make out Ladybird or Spree." She hesitated. "I should have stuck closer to her."

Galewind squeezed her eyes shut for a long moment. *Please be all right. I can't lose another one.* She looked to her spearmaiden. "One of us could hang back. I'll do it."

"No," Stormbringer called, insistence in her tone. "We can't afford to lose another gryphon. And what about those two rangers you're transporting? What is the mission without them? No. We press on."

Galewind firmed up her own tone. "I insist," she replied.

Stormbringer huffed. "Remember our commands? Three wings. This is my wing. You stick to yours and I'll stick to mine."

The knightmaiden turned her head away, sighed heavily.

"You can overrule her," Berendt said.

She fought the urge to do just that. Galewind rewrapped the furs around her neck. *Get a grip,* she told herself. *Rainsong can take care of herself.* Yet, a voice inside still nagged at her insides. *You can't afford to lose another one… or go through another judicial.* She called out again.

"Might I remind you, spearmaiden, that I am the ranking officer."

"Sisters!" Catwings scolded. Then she softened her voice and reassured them all: "Rainsong has the lightest load and the strongest gryphon, she'll be fine."

"And Danus is a strong and capable charger," Marec added.

"Maybe if we fly slow, they'll spot the lanterns," Rix said.

Eriff scoffed. "I can barely see yours from here. Pity a queensman is lost with her and not a ranger. We are already down a queensman, and we only really need one good ranger."

Berendt grumbled, "We don't need any queensmen."

Galewind composed herself. "Stormbringer – you're call. Lead on."

"Enough then!" Stormbringer piped back. "These cats aren't getting any drier. Rainsong will have to catch up. She knows the heading." The spearmaiden paused. "And Norwin's Breeze, double the damn lights!"

With the winds now less volatile and a steady course being held to, Amot became normalized to the gentle undulation of the gryphon's rise and fall on currents of air, and the rhythm of Ladybird's muscular heaving as her great wings beat on.

The flurry had thinned some. Yet still, there was no sign of Rainsong. She eluded even the Kith – all expert spotters – peering into the whirling snows.

True to purpose and her word, Stormbringer kept her bearings straight. She led the three remaining valkyries along yet another descent, this time as low as she could go, nearly skimming the treetops. For a long while, the thinned squadron flew on that way, having moved to a simple V formation with Stormbringer in the lead, Catwings on left wing and Galewind on right wing. Each gryphon bore two illuminated lanterns.

At one point, Stormbringer signaled to her wingmates, tracing out wide loops with her arms. Her sisters knew exactly what to do. The two wingmates veered off in search of the lost gryphon and her riders. All the while, the spearmaiden concentrated on keeping to a steady bearing as the other two valkyries arced away and then reappeared after a minute or so in perfect formation. After looping back, they shook their heads solemnly, waited a few minutes, and then struck out again into the wild snows.

After half a dozen loops in this fashion, the two wingmates flew straight up to look, only to return again and again with the same sad news. Catwings and Galewind followed that alternating search pattern for some time. Eventually though, the three cats crossed a river. The treetops beneath them vanished.

The river could only have been the Dim River, and the treeless flats had to be the wide field that lay between the town wall of Turnsby and the Wulver-infested forest of Whisperwood. Amot remembered the terrain well, from his youth – at ground level though. He'd never seen it from above like this. A long hill came into view.

They had arrived.

Chapter XVI
MESSENGER

(Lorenz)

THE FIRE BURNED low in the beastmaster's chambers. *When will we ever get that extra help?* Lady Apsarla had promised to bring in two or three stable hands, but that promise seemed to have died with the recent tragedy. He spoke to the winds, howling outside. "My bones are getting too old for this... to do everything."

At his age, nearly sixty-two, Lorenz was already picking and choosing what to do and what not to do. All of the Order's focus had shifted to replenishing the valkyrie ranks. *As it should, I suppose.* The beastmaster winced when the image flashed in his mind, the image of two fresh, wide-eyed celestes falling to their deaths.

He scoffed at himself. "I should not complain. I will serve as I am able." Lorenz contemplated burning the broken chair piled into the corner of his one-room quarters. It had been that way for three years, since last he had a visitor.

A loud knock rapped the window pane overlooking the falls. A sudden, heavy feeling came over him. *Oh my. Not again. Norwin's Breeze.*

Lorenz pushed himself up from his good chair, the one that was not broken. Stiff and sore, he hobbled over to the door, straightening his back as he did so. He swung it open, ducked his head under the archway, and stepped outside. Buffeted by a strange, downward gust, the beastmaster limped around back, suffering the pins and needles that tingled in his legs. He swiveled his gaze to the stone floor, beneath the window.

Sparrow.

He groaned with the effort of crouching down beside the window, stabilizing himself against the outer wall to keep himself from toppling over. His sinews cracked loudly in protest. He squinted at the small shape in the darkness.

Broken neck.

There was no saving the bird, and he understood the message it relayed. Lorenz gently picked the carcass up, held it in his palm. *Please,* he pleaded, *no one I know.* But the beastmaster knew his wish was empty, because whatever happened had already happened and there was nothing he could do to change it. He closed his eyes and meditated for a long minute.

"May Shroud's Well reward you," he whispered to the winds that would carry his words. Then Lorenz swiveled his gaze up to the sky. He uttered a prayer to the Guardian of Human Souls. It was the least he could do for a friend of the avians.

CHAPTER XVII
TOUCHDOWN
(Catwings, Stormbringer)

FOLLOWING HER COMMANDER'S lead, Catwings urged her mount to veer a hard right and descend. The ground materialized below. On completing the turn, Spree leveled off. The three remaining valkyries raced over a grassy field. Catwings fought to keep her end of the formation tight. The heavy load had degraded her Harpy's maneuverability. And the queensmen passengers had been awkward, shifting their bodies in all the wrong ways for the glides and turns, especially the sharp ones.

Amot hollered out, pointing. "There! Dead Gnarl's Knoll!"

The wind rider traced the ranger's cue, fixed her eyes on a low hilltop. Snow-laden winds whipped past its summit, skimming the surface.

Stormbringer shouted a landing order. In unison with her sisters, Catwings drew back on her gryphon's reins. The three beasts cupped air in their great wings and slowed to a near hover over the hill, rearing up to a half-normal pitch.

Ladybird was the first to break formation, eagle forelegs reaching as she touched down. Electra came next, landing with a jolt. Catwings sent Spree on a sideways tilt, sailing over the others. The Harpy set down next to Electra, soft as a floating feather, even burdened as she was.

The wind rider double-checked the safeties on her talon daggers before removing her helm and clipped-on lantern. Then she slid the bronze goggles off her eyes to rest on her forehead.

She had questions. Many questions that had burned in her mind since Rainsong had disappeared. Before even dismounting, Catwings swiveled to a sidesaddle position. She fixed her gaze on Galewind. And although gentle nudges and prods were more her nature, Catwings had to try not to glare, try not to be angry. She shouted over the howling winds.

"So, Galewind, what in Shroud's Well happened back there?"

The knightmaiden brushed her dark, tangled hair away from her face, her pale skin ghostly and her expression apologetic. Her voice was scratchy.

"I lost Rainsong's cat when trying to follow the forward unit, Catwings. The winds were so strong up there, the snow so blinding. Before I knew it, we were separated. I'm lucky not to be lost myself. Having a couple of rangers aboard helped with that. Tall Hallman here spotted your lanterns. Berendt guessed Stormbringer would be dropping down to get under the weather. When I shouted back to Rainsong…"

Catwings felt her throat constrict, her chest tighten. She breathed a shallow breath, held it. *Rainsong will be all right*, she tried to convince herself, then exhaled.

Rix, still atop Stormbringer's cat, picked up where Galewind had trailed off. "Rangers are good that way." He shifted his gaze to just behind Catwings. "You're right, Eriff. Too bad a ranger wasn't with Rainsong. They'd still be with us."

The queensman scowled.

"Rainsong can take care of herself," Stormbringer said. "If worse comes to worse and she doesn't find us, she'll sneak by Harrow's Gate and head northwest to the second wing rendezvous point, on the hills overlooking the Malevuin."

"My spearmaiden is correct," Galewind said. "The best course is to carry on and meet up with her as soon as possible."

Eriff asked, "Are you sure she knows where the next rendezvous point is? You valkyries seem to change these things last minute."

Catwings huffed, turned to regard Eriff. "*We* all managed to meet on time. The only one *truly* late was you. What were you thinking, going off on your own like that anyway? I flew all over Deepweald to get the message out. Why didn't you arrive with the other queensmen?"

Eriff fumbled what might have been a response but couldn't seem to find the words.

From atop her mount, Stormbringer commanded, "Kith, Queen's Guard, listen up. To those of you tasked with the recovery wing of Diamondback, this is as far as we take you. Get off my cats and don't forget your packs."

The two rangers on Ladybird were quick to untie the dog after the spearmaiden's comment, while everyone else dismounted and began unhitching their gear. Everyone, that is, except Marec and Catwings. Free of the barrier that was Eriff between them, the older queensmen initiated a conversation, opening with an exposition of the complexities of training and handling gryphons in comparison to thoroughbred horses.

Ekkon's wheel, will he ever stop talking? Catwings smiled politely, listened attentively for several long minutes, until he came to a pause to catch his breath. The wind rider interrupted in a whispery tone. "You should remove your gear before Stormbringer gets on about you." She glanced over to her commander and feigned a cross face. "Spearmaidens can get quite temperamental, you know."

Marec reacted abruptly. "Oh. Yes. Thank you, dear Catwings." He started fidgeting with his straps. "I quite agree. Unfortunately, much of my gear is with Rainsong. I'll see what I can salvage though. We must pick up where we left off, sometime soon." Eyebrows raised, he prompted her, his head frozen in a half nod.

Catwings smiled back. "Yes, that would be very… nice."

Marec shrugged, suggestively. "Perhaps I might visit the Aerie someday…"

"Sure, Marec," Catwings replied. "We'll talk then. Beastmaster Lorenz would be pleased to show you to the stables when you come by. He can talk for hours about his gryphons."

Marec clasped his hands together. "Splendid. That would be wonderful." His eyes darted about the gryphon's tie-ons. "Now, where did I hook in that rapier? Or was it… hmm… this sort of thing is what squires are supposed to be for. A funny story… Ahem…"

When he turned around, the wind rider had already disappeared. She heard him call out.

"Catwings?"

The wind rider giggled to herself like a tween. Pretending not to hear his call, she made a mad dash towards Rix, already busy setting up lanterns on retractable posts.

"It's okay girl," Stormbringer consoled, brushing away snow and removing clumps of ice from Ladybird's lower portions and haunches. The build-up was far worse than she'd imagined. Rangers had swiftly unloaded the packs and the gryphons were nearly ready to fly. Her gut clenched momentarily when she thought of Rainsong not being there.

Amot happened by after his quick sweep of the hill. No signs yet of Wulvers or missing swords, she'd overheard. The spearmaiden called him over.

"Yes, Stormbringer?" he said. Amot approached her until the two stood face to face.

He looks so young, she thought, then got on with what she needed to say. "I have to get these cats in the air," she started, "before they take on more ice." *I wonder how old he is? Must be in his early twenties, at least.* "I just wanted to say, may Ekkon's Wheel favor you in your search for the dancing sword of the luminaries."

"Thanks," Amot said. He smiled a half-smile in return, but there was seriousness in his eyes, and more. Something void, subdued. He reached to Ladybird, stroked the cat behind her ears. "They're quiet – the gryphons."

"Tired and hungry." Stormbringer regarded Ladybird, gave her a few solid pats on the belly. "No deer for you tonight."

The gryphon raised her neck feathers, firmly nudged the ranger's hand. Stormbringer smirked. "I think she likes you."

Amot raised his eyes skyward and gazed into the falling snow. "At least the wind has died down some." Stormbringer's eyes tracked his. The ranger continued, "I don't think the flight will be so bad going north."

Stormbringer replied, "Yes, should be easier." Both lowered their heads until their eyes met again. "You will face the greater danger," she told him bluntly. "I hear stories about these Wulvers – not just the children's tales. Don't underestimate them."

"I know what I'm doing."

"Do you?"

Amot nodded. "I do. And I know the difference between fiction and reality, but I still feel as though I'm about to live one of those tall tales."

Stormbringer let out a soft laugh. "Maybe someone will make a story about your Wulver adventure."

"Maybe." Amot added a touch of rasp to his voice, and quoted an excerpt from *The Moonlit Feast*:

> "*In the woods, the man-wolves waited for*
> *the stray travelers to arrive,*
> *To mount them on a spit and then roast them alive.*"

"I just felt a chill run up my spine," Stormbringer said. "I haven't heard that one in a very long time."

"The story originated in Turnsby," Amot said, "just a few miles south from where we're standing."

Stormbringer sighed. "Maybe it's time for a new story, with a better ending."

Amot took a half step towards Stormbringer. He took her by the arm and pulled her aside, behind the gryphon and mostly out of sight from the hustle and bustle around them. He spoke softly. "Keep a safe distance from the trees in these woods."

"I know," she replied. "It would be so easy to hit one on a hill or something."

"That's not what I mean," Amot said.

"What *do* you mean?"

He paused.

"Because of Wulvers?" Stormbringer prodded. "Or because people say the forest is haunted? The two are probably one in the same."

"The *ghost pines*," he told her. "I don't know why, exactly. I was very young, but my grandfather knew these woods and he always told me to steer clear of them."

"Okay, I get it," she said. "We won't skim the treetops. And don't worry, we plan to scout out the high ground for our base camp. It's terrible we lost Rainsong on the way. This is more her territory than anyone else's. Knightmaiden Galewind ran patrols a decade ago, but things have changed a lot since then."

"Rainsong will show up," Amot said. Then he repeated her name. "Rainsong. Why Rainsong? It's an unusual callsign, even for a valkyrie."

Stormbringer replied, "She's the only one of our order who ever successfully handled a gryphon in full rain for an extended period. That's partly why I'm so confident she'll be all right. On one of her first solo patrols, she kept Ashes in the air by singing to her. They'd been hit by a terrible storm, but it was important to press on. They barely made it back that day…"

Stormbringer hesitated. Amot tilted his head, waiting for her to continue.

"Some people say she can sing in such a way that only the gryphon's ear can pick up the tune."

Amot smirked. "Can you get her to sing to Howler for me? He doesn't listen to anything I say. I don't even know where he is right now."

"Listening and obeying are two different things. Plus, you have a quiet voice. Howler probably just hears a bunch of mumbling and then his name pop up occasionally." The spearmaiden looked directly into Amot's eyes. His face lit up.

"What?" Stormbringer said.

"I expected blue," he told her.

She wondered how he'd missed noticing her eyes before.

"It's the blonde hair," Stormbringer offered. "What color do you see?"

"All I can make out is… a cloudy grey."

"I haven't heard that before. Well, I guess it makes sense… I am, after all, the *storm bringer*."

Amot smirked again. An awkward silence followed.

The scout's ink began to sharpen. She examined his forehead, his cheekbones…

"Your face…" Her right hand reached up to touch his temple. She gently traced down to his cheekbone with one finger.

"I know," Amot said. His eyes fell to his boots.

"I like it. The soft color… and the pattern." Her heartbeat began to race. She placed a finger under the Wilder's chin to raise it. His eyes met hers again. She felt a mental rush; it flooded through her body and almost carried her away.

No. Stormbringer dropped her hand, stepped back, averted his gaze. "Umm… if you ever want me to ride… need a mount… to fly… when this is all over." She couldn't stop fumbling her words. "There's been some talk around the Wing Table… we might need a ranger."

Amot smiled with confidence. "I'll find you if I need you. And if you need a ranger, come find me. May Ekkon the Wanderer guide your way tonight."

"Ekkon? I was thinking more Norwin, maybe, but I could use all the help I can get."

Stormbringer turned to mount her gryphon, but the farewell was far from over. Eriff, it seemed, had been lurking in earshot. Eriff, it seemed, had a few bones to pick with Order Kith and Order Valkyrie alike.

Chapter XVIII
ASHES

(Rainsong)

RAINSONG RECOVERED CONSCIOUSNESS in a jolt. She gasped, opened her eyes.

Darkness. She was sprawled out on the ground. *Cold, wet ground.* Rocky. Forested.

Ashes' warm body pressed against her. *Heavy.* On her.

My leg. Numb. Trapped. An image flashed in her mind.

Crashing. Snapping. Loud. Branches breaking, rocks sliding.

She jerked. Pain shot through her body. She called out.

"Ashes, are you okay girl?" No sound. No movement.

Rainsong's neck didn't feel right. Contorted. *What about my arms.* She lifted her arms. They were numb and tingly, but at least they moved. Then she felt above her head. *Fur. Ashes.* Soft. Feathery. *Light.* The wing. She tried to move. *Stuck. The harness.*

The wind rider undid the straps. With both hands, she gripped her trapped leg, jerked it free from under the gryphon. Using every ounce of strength in her, Rainsong pressed the large wing up and off her body. She wormed out from underneath, then dragged her way onto a rocky slope.

Her leg throbbed. The wind rider could barely turn her head. She rubbed her throat, glanced up. Dark pines loomed overhead. A veiled moon shone through. In her peripheral, Rainsong's eyes caught the glint of steel. She turned her head. A shadowy, partial form took shape.

"Danus," she tried to say, but her voice came out a whisper.

The form was hunched over. Rainsong got down on her hands and one knee. Keeping the throbbing leg outstretched, she half-crawled her way around Ashes' wing to reach Danus. She nudged the queensman. He barely moved. She glided her hand along his back, felt a branch jutting out. *Impaled. Shroud's Well. A lot of good all that armor did him.* She clambered up beside Danus, felt for breath. Her shoulders dropped. She pinched her eyes shut. *Dead.* Rainsong rolled onto her back in despair. A horrible thought hit her.

Ashes! Her heart skipped a beat. *She's still warm,* Rainsong reminded herself. *Breathe.* Everything seemed fuzzy, drifting, spinning. The wind rider tried to take a deep breath, but took another shallow breath instead. She rubbed her throat again, looked over her gryphon. She didn't see any branches puncturing her girl.

The wind rider dragged herself to the head of her gryphon. She felt for breath. *Warm. Alive.* She patted and shook Ashes. *Out cold.* The wind rider wrapped herself in her poncho, huddled in close to her Harpy. She let the side of her face sink deep into the gryphon's fur. *Comfort.* Then she gently stroked her cat's nape and began to sing. She sang softly to Ashes – soft whispers, for her voice would not reveal itself.

A sudden urge came over Rainsong to sing about the Great Eagles of old, and especially the foremost among them: Norwin of the Dawn. And as she sang the gentle words, a strange sensation overtook her. She felt the beating of Cold Death's wings carrying on the wind, like a vibration. A shiver ran through her bones before she passed out, mid-song.

CHAPTER XIX

MISSION COMMANDER

(Eriff, Amot, Stormbringer)

ERIFF WAITED PATIENTLY as Marec's gloved finger slowly traced down the master list of provisions and equipment. When it finally reached the bottom, his uncle looked to him, grunted, and cleared his throat.

"Not bad," he grumbled. "I expected worse."

Eriff swept his gaze over the remaining load on Electra one last time, calling out anything new to his uncle. Galewind had stolen away with the ranger commander while he did so, as if they hadn't spoken in private enough already.

"What's the damage?" Eriff asked.

Marec rubbed his collapsed chin, spiked with widely spaced stubble. He made a pained expression. "One battering ram; that's the main deficiency. Maybe it went with Charger Danus."

Eriff scoffed. "Doubt it."

"Why? Did you see it elsewhere?"

Eriff shook his head. "No."

"Do Wulvers even use doors?"

"That is exactly the question," Eriff replied. "I suspect not. The battering ram might have been left behind deliberately – did you not hear Rainsong complaining about the load? – or it simply could have been forgotten. That utter foolishness that played out in the glade grossly disrupted the preparations."

"Not exactly a confidence builder either." Marec paused. He suddenly became animated. "Bah!" he bellowed out, throwing his arms. "Neither was losing a gryphon!"

Eriff shushed his uncle.

"What?" A confused, guilty look washed over him.

"Be wary, Uncle," Eriff warned, as he cast a series of darting glances to determine who might be within earshot. To one side, he caught Knightmaiden Galewind look away at the last possible instant. Hers was the final gryphon they'd inspected on their stiff accounting circuit. To the opposite side, and closer, Amot and Stormbringer spoke casually, so enamored with one another nothing else in the world seemed to matter. *Ranger-valkyrie pairs are springing up everywhere. Even Catwings is cozying up to Rix*, he noted. The pair were farther away, near Spree. *This isn't some Shroom District meat market. Lord Ralador was right. The wrong alliances are forming right under our noses.* Annoyed, Eriff swung his gaze back to Marec. "Leaving one queensman behind was bad enough, but with two down, proper mission control is at risk."

Marec turned his head slightly and narrowed his eyes at his nephew. "Control? Do you mean…"

Eriff reached into his belt pouch, pulled out the bone scroll tube Lord Ralador had given him. He used it to tap his uncle's shoulder, then jerked it away when Marec made a grab for it. Eriff held the tube just out of reach.

"In good time," Eriff said. "I see your point, though, Uncle, about the valkyries. I had assumed they knew how to keep track of one another."

Marec grunted a second time. "That's not all." A discomforting waver entered his voice. "You might not have noticed, but… well… my rapier has gone missing."

Eriff shot a glance to Marec's waist. "Your rapier? Uncle, you lost your sword?"

Marec shrugged, apology blanching his face.

"Was it with the missing gryphon, somehow?" *Truly, a tragedy. A duelist without his sword is like... a lover without his penis.*

"No, nephew. I'm afraid not."

Eriff just shook his head, then locked eyes with his uncle. "Unbelievable. Catwings then? And her gryphon acrobatics? I could have easily lost a gauntlet myself when…"

Marec crinkled his nose at the suggestion. "I don't think so. Catwings assured me she packed everything my little wonder boy handed to her. Thing is, the squire didn't hand her a sword, that's all. She must have assumed I had it on my person. And with all the distractions…"

"It was Snaithe, wasn't it?"

Marec nodded. "Unfortunately, yes. Squires these days, they just can't be relied upon. I should've known better than to pick a Snaithe. We got along so well. I remember when—"

Eriff broke in with a huff. "Uncle, that is why they are still squires: they make mistakes. BIG ones. They cannot help it. They are STUPID. Stop being so chummy and start screaming 'bloody murder' every time Snaithe screws up, and then browbeat the sniveling reprobate whenever he steps out of line. Otherwise, how will he learn?" Eriff looked his uncle square on. He added an air of sympathy to his voice. "What is your plan if you run into trouble?"

Marec chuckled to himself, waved Eriff off. "Bah… lower my head and ram them with my helm, I suppose."

"You laugh now but wait until you're up against a skin-peeling giant in the Harrowian Guard. They really are merciless, you know."

"And dumb as a rock, don't forget. Do you suppose one might be sporting enough to toss me a sword, in all fairness?"

Eriff sighed. *I give up.* "There is no helping you, is there?" He smirked, slapped the shell of his uncle's armored back. "What am I going to do with you, Uncle. We'll find something. You might have to make do with a ranger hatchet."

Marec snorted in disgust. "I'd sooner swing a limp buttercup."

"I hear you," Eriff said. "My sentiments exactly."

The two queensmen chuckled at the notion. Then something caught

Marec's attention. With a flick of his chin, he cued Eriff to it. "See those two over there?" he said. "Plotting out *their* command, I'd say."

Eriff followed his uncle's lead to Galewind and Berendt, then scoffed. "Not for long."

Marec was right. *They are planning.* The conversation between the pair had taken on a serious tone, and they were well off on their own. *Hmm… and they did not even think to invite me.*

Marec interrupted Eriff's thoughts. "They're very much alike, aren't they?"

"Too much alike," Eriff replied. He discreetly motioned to Amot and Stormbringer, and the two queensmen tuned their ears to the soft words spoken between them. It wasn't difficult to guess the tone of the exchange. "Those two as well, not to mention that ginger and Catwings. It has become apparent to me that without solid Queen's Guard leadership, this mission will go to the dogs and the will of Aelish will not be respected. I am putting a stop to it."

"How, exactly? The scroll? What is written on that scroll of yours, anyway?"

"You shall see, Uncle. You shall see. I daresay that I will enjoy this."

Marec raised an eyebrow. "Taking them for a ride, are you? You haven't changed a bit."

Eriff didn't answer. *I have, Uncle. Very much so.*

⤜

With a confident stride, Eriff sauntered over to where Amot and Stormbringer had gathered to say their goodbyes. The spearmaiden stood poised and flexed, ready to re-mount her gryphon, one foot in Ladybird's stirrup and the other on solid ground. Amot stood beside her, ready to assist her upward bearing. *Both gentlemanly and self-gratifying, all rolled into one*, thought Eriff. He recognized the subtle game of body posing and gratuitous physical contact astir between the two.

When the queensman spoke, he projected his voice loud enough so that everyone would hear the belittlements on his tongue. In his mind's eye, his future father-in-law's face beamed with anticipation.

Eriff halted in front of the ranger and the valkyrie. They swung their heads to regard him. He faced them squarely.

"I am extremely fond of you too, Stormbringer." Eriff adjusted the armor about his midsection in about as rude a manner as he could muster. "But it really is a challenge to show you, with all this chain skirting on. If only I could change color… a nice shade of coral, perhaps? What is your favorite color, anyway?"

The spearmaiden glared back at him, silent and frozen in place, eyes cold and expressionless. Her ranger sidekick crossed his thick eyebrows. He shot Eriff a stern, unapproving look. The queensman laughed inside as the Wilder colors quickly drained from Amot's face. He felt a rush of elation on the verge of giddy.

This is too good to be true. I haven't even told them yet, and look…

Amot stepped forward, arms crossed. He drew in uncomfortably close. *A challenge.* Eriff raised his chin. The ranger stood taller, but Eriff was not in the least intimidated. Amot glowered at the queensman, defiance in his stance.

"I believe you owe Stormbringer an apology," he said.

Eriff puffed out his chest. "Ha! Well, I believe *she* owes *me* an apology. She lost one of my gryphons."

"They're not your gryphons," Stormbringer retorted. Her tone was firm, her resolve measured.

Eriff grinned back at her. "Oh, but they *are* mine. At least on this mission, they are."

Amot spoke thin-lipped. "Get… lost." His tone was flat and guttural.

Eriff shook his head slowly. "You will not be able to get rid of me that easily." Out of the corner of one eye, he saw that he'd drawn the attention of Rix and Catwings. He rolled his eyes and huffed.

"Yes, scoundrel, I see you. And I will be keeping you close on this mission. Someone must keep you honest. And do not fret, boy, you are going to like me, I promise. You will like me so much you will just do whatever I say."

Rix scoffed. "I don't think so, Sir Braggart!"

"You shall. The Lord of the March insists. And not only here. Afterwards, Spotter Rix Caledon, you shall accompany me to Ironeagle."

Rix cocked his head sideways, narrowed his eyes. "What are you talking about?"

Eriff paused to savor the building unease around him. Berendt and Galewind had become cognizant of the exchange. A few muffled words passed between them. At the height of the moment – when it must've seemed clear to all that the queensman wouldn't answer Rix's query – the Kith commander growled to Eriff in a thick, odd voice.

"Have you forgotten, Champion Haulik? We have a knightmaiden among us. She outranks you; she outranks me… all of us. Last I checked, you and your uncle are under her command. Queensmen are to assist the knightmaiden's valkyries in any way possible to seal the northern limits of Whisperwood and ensure that no one enters or leaves."

Eriff regarded Berendt directly. He let out a quick, disgusted snort. "*Gallant* Haulik to you, ranger."

"Since when?" Rix demanded, but Eriff ignored the low-ranking rascal once again. Instead, he concentrated on Galewind's face, committed her wan look to memory. It was like the blood had drained out of it. Contrasting her, Berendt grimaced heavily, while gnawing on his pipe. His eyepatch was flipped up and his dead eye seemed to fix upon Eriff. The deep scar scratched into his face folded in on itself with the strain.

"That still doesn't put you above her," Berendt grumbled. "The two of you are at equals."

Galewind touched Berendt's wrist.

Lovely, thought Eriff. He swept his gaze over everyone as he spoke.

"Only the Earl can overturn the order that I command this mission."

Stormbringer broke in, "And exactly what order are you referring to?"

Eriff waved the scroll tube in front of her eyes.

Amot's tracings flushed. *Now that's a good one to mention to Lord Ralador*, Eriff thought. *My, my, the poor lad must be fuming on the inside.* The scout hadn't budged, while Stormbringer had removed her foot from Ladybird and now stood firmly planted beside him.

"Oh look," Eriff sneered, eyeing Amot. "Love the displays of color. First for Stormbringer and now me. Do you have a thing for authority?"

The scout clenched his teeth. The edges of his wilder ink sharpened. Red slashes bled through as though glowing hot. *Markings of rage.*

"I've heard enough of your insults," Amot spat.

"Try me, Kith-boy," Eriff said.

A surge of energy washed over the queensman. *The Senses of Aelish. Uninvoked.* He hadn't even asked for them, but they were there. Soon, he understood why. Eriff suddenly became aware of every subtle motion in his vicinity – the uneasy shuffling of the gryphons, the wind picking up again, the contempt of the rangers, and the agitation of the valkyries. Tension elevated around him. He felt the all-seeing eyes of Aelish on watch, looking out for him. The silence drew so tight it could snap in an instant.

Stormbringer cut through it all, harsh impatience in her voice. "Amot! Eriff! Stop this! We're on the same team. Remember?"

Hearing this, the tall ranger that rode with Galewind stood up from his crouched position, beside Rix Caledon, where he'd kept himself busy sorting through his very large pack. He flipped up the shaft of a two-handed, double-bladed battle axe as he straightened. Tallman casually leaned on it for support, like an old man's cane.

I get the hint.

So did Eriff's uncle. Seeing this, Marec instinctively raised a hand to rest on the pommel of his rapier, the way he always did in touchy situations. Only, the rapier wasn't there for him.

Amot shifted his weight slightly to a more solid stance. *One swing*, he told himself. He imagined putting his full body into the delivery; every fiber of every muscle leveraged to power an uppercut. But Eriff had to make the first move, so Amot provoked him. He snarled as he spoke.

"Beating you to the ground at Tetherport obviously wasn't enough."

Eriff only scoffed at the remark. "A beating? Hardly."

Amot pointed to a spot about ten paces away, north of the knoll. "I was right about there in the simulation," then he waved his hand towards the opposite side, "and you were *cowering* somewhere on the other side of the hill."

Eriff flapped a hand in dismissal. "Cowering? I might have, if you had not lost your sword in the process."

"I shattered your shield into pieces. You were lying on your back, desperately holding up the shards of it to fend me off. The fight was over."

"A flimsy pine shield, not a real one," Eriff countered. "A proper shield would have turned your girlish taps."

"What did you say?"

"Besides, I disarmed you."

"What? You did not. The sword was—"

"Pulled from your hand? Yes, I did that. It was a simple disarm maneuver and you fell for it." Eriff flicked his hand. "It is all in the wrist. You Kith rangers are novices with a blade. Hack, hack, slash, slash. A sword is not an axe, you know."

"So, *you* are the cause of all this?" Amot felt his jaw drop. It just hung there while he fumed on the inside, glaring at Eriff.

The queensman shrugged. "What else could I do? My shield was broken and you were swinging a dangerously sharp object around like a mad girl with a frying pan. Besides, a fighter must learn how to hold on to his, or *her*, sword. Better to learn that lesson in an exercise than on the battlefield."

"You are to blame," Amot stated, in a perfectly controlled tone.

"Oh look, he's turning color again."

Amot felt his fury bleed through into his wilder ink. He drew in slow, steady breaths. *Stay calm.* "Let's finish this right here, right now." *C'mon, make the first move.* Berendt would go easier on Amot that way.

But the queensman did not lash out, nor did he back down. His eyes didn't even narrow in defiance. Eriff was many things, but reactionary wasn't one of them. Neither was cowardice.

Berendt interrupted. "Never mind who is to blame, Amot. It's more important to figure out exactly how the striker was lost and where it might have landed."

Amot took a deep breath. He wanted this to work and he needed his commander on his side. *Eriff isn't going to take the bait.* The scout loosened his grip, turned his back to Eriff and Berendt. He stepped away, ran his fingers through his hair. Then he cursed quietly to himself and turned back around. He nodded to his commander.

Eriff, eyeing Amot carefully, swung his gaze to Berendt. "Shall we move on then?" No one objected. The queensman cleared his throat and began his announcement the same way he always addressed those around him – every word wrapped somehow in implicit superiority. That triumphant, smug look that he'd worn all along only grew more prominent as he spoke.

"By order of the Lord of the March himself, empowered in this matter by the Earl of the Gorge, the Queen's High Commander, I am to provide purpose and direction to the rangers on this leg of the mission."

Eriff popped the tethered cork off the bone tube he'd been holding, removed the parchment inside. He raised it high to show to everyone. "This is the order, signed by Lord Ralador himself." Eriff backed away one step from Amot, lowered the scroll to eye level. He cleared his throat again.

"Ahem. THE THIRD LINE STATES: 'GALLANT ERIFF HAULIK SHALL ASSUME FULL COMMAND OF OPERATION DIAMONDBACK.' Period."

"What!" Berendt stormed over to Eriff. "Let me see that." The queensman held the decree just out of the ranger's reach.

"Not just yet," Eriff told him. Then he addressed everyone. "For those of you at unawares, *this* is Operation Diamondback, and we – *you* – are all charged with recovering the lost striker – a hand-and-a-half sword that disappeared yesterday, due to ranger carelessness during the Diamond Saber exercise, and which is believed to be in this vicinity. You are to prevent the lost striker from falling into Harrowian hands by following your prescribed tasks, and ultimately, by any means deemed necessary and at *any* cost."

He scanned the faces of the group, then focused in on the rangers present. "Might I remind you that your Kith Commander's rank, although high for a ranger, amounts to a mere champion in the Guard – no offence, Uncle."

"None taken," Marec responded. "Command was never my thing."

Eriff continued. "My status equates to Ranger Knight-Errand in your system."

Berendt shook his head. "I already fought this battle. Everyone agreed this was a Kith op, including Lord Ralador."

"As you know," Eriff said, "this order makes *null and void any preceding orders that might conflict with it.*" He divided his gaze between Catwings and Stormbringer next. "And to the valkyries, by rank I equate to your knightmaiden, as Berendt pointed out. However, I have been assigned command by the highest authority. Clearly, I am the high-ranking officer on this mission. From now on, you will take orders from me."

Stormbringer did not look impressed. Catwings shrugged at her.

Berendt growled back to the knightmaiden. "Galewind, what is your take on this?"

She let out a heavy sigh. "Unfortunately, he's right. Order Valkyrie has not received any specific instructions from higher command elements. The request for assistance came directly through Ralador. The letter stands."

Eriff offered Galewind a polite nod. "Thank you, My lady."

Stormbringer interjected. "*If* it's official," emphasizing the word "if."

Eriff guffawed at her suggestion. "Are you calling me a liar? I will have you know—"

"No," Amot cut in, "she's calling you sloppy." He turned to Stormbringer. "I saw it too."

Eriff challenged them on the spot. "Whatever are you two going on about?"

"Stormbringer?" Amot said, deferring to the spearmaiden.

"I don't see a seal," she responded. "Why aren't there any wax seals?"

"Seals?" Eriff said. "Pff. You're grasping. There is no specific need for a seal."

Stormbringer rested a hand on her hip. "Then how do we know Lord Ralador really signed it, and how do we know the order traces back to the Earl? To be valid across the domains, the order requires Lord Ralador's seal and an inked impression of the Earl's original seal from the original order."

Eriff huffed. "Nonsense. You are talking technicalities. Unnecessary technicalities, especially given the expediency required. We all know where the orders originated."

Galewind spoke up. "I don't. How do we know you are even a Gallant? Your promotion seems rather timely and sudden. Lady Apsarla will back me on this."

Amot snatched the parchment from Eriff's hand, held it behind his back, flapping in the wind. "If I just let this go, there'd be no record at all of the change in orders."

A devious smile crept across Rix's face when he saw what Amot had done.

Eriff's eyes went wide at the bold gesture. "Might I remind you that destroying this order, or disobeying it, is a serious offence, punishable—"

"Do you really think we care?" Rix said.

Eriff slowly scanned the faces of the group: rangers, spearmaidens, and queensman alike. He fixated on Tall Hallman for a long moment, looked to his own uncle, then breathed in deep. "Very well," he puffed. "I will take command of the recovery component. I had planned to put Marec in charge of the border seal, but I have changed my mind. I doubt he wants it anyway. I now leave that to you, Knightmaiden. Do we have a deal?"

Galewind regarded Berendt. He grunted his disapproval but nodded anyway. She shifted her gaze back to Eriff, accepted his terms with a nod. "Only I command the gryphons," she stated flatly. "And stop belittling everyone."

"Agreed," said the queensman, without hesitation. Eriff raised his voice again to address the group. "Does anyone have any other questions about who is in charge?"

No one answered.

On behalf of his nephew, Marec examined the faces of the group. "I'd take that as a 'no,' nephew," he said. The duelist wiped melted snow from his brow, let out a long sigh of relief. "I'm glad that's over with."

❧

Stormbringer carried out one last check to ready her gryphon for flight. She wanted no part in anything that had to do with her new commanding officer. *Pompous jackass.* With little more than a stern glance, she signaled to her remaining wind rider to do likewise.

Catwings carried out the silent request, then mounted Spree. Stormbringer had hoped Galewind would follow suit so they could be on their way, but instead the knightmaiden remained locked in a serious conversation with her favorite confident: Commander Garondi, of course. He'd tucked his pipe away after Galewind's comment that her gryphon might not take well to the smoke, and he'd put his eyepatch in place as well.

Stormbringer had no idea the two were so close, and wondered about their history. She had the perfect vantage point, atop Ladybird. The spearmaiden watched and waited as the ranger-valkyrie pair exchanged words, heads tilted in towards one another, voices too low for anyone else to hear. Finally, they paused, looked to one another squarely. Berendt nodded and Galewind left him to ready Electra. After a casual glance this way and that way, the Kith commander produced a dull metal flask and downed a swig, before stowing it away somewhere on his person.

Stormbringer appreciated the ruffian Berendt, and she could see what the knightmaiden saw in him. Sure, he was rough around the edges, and maybe smoked and drank too much for his own good. But Commander Garondi was sensible, genuine, and dependable, three simple traits she admired that seemed to be lacking in so many. In fact, most of the rangers she'd met were like that – not thieves as Eriff so enjoyed characterizing them as. Additionally, she felt that Kith skills and know-how were greatly understated in terms of value to the Hidden Kingdom, and that those of the Queen's Guard were generally overstated, relying more on past glory than present accomplishments.

When Berendt returned to Eriff, he did so with level-headed composure, exactly as Stormbringer expected him to do. From her seat high up, the spearmaiden was well positoned to overhear their conversation. And since they'd gathered between Ladybird and Spree, Catwings was in the same situation. A grin from her together with a subtle nod confirmed that the wind rider planned to listen in as well. Berendt's voice was low and rutted.

"Gallant Haulik," he gruffed, "since you're going to be with Recovery instead of Border Seal, I'm sending one of my men to the camp along with the valkyries and your queensman." He motioned to Galewind's gryphon. "We don't know if the missing gryphon and her riders will make it to their post. You might be down a man on that front, and you could use a ranger out there, regardless. I already discussed this with the knightmaiden and she is all for it."

Eriff rubbed his chin, glanced at his uncle, beside him. Marec responded with a series of quick, bouncing nods.

"Agreed," Eriff responded.

Berendt swung his gaze away from Eriff and straight to Rix. The spotter was clearly oblivious to the decision hanging in the balance.

Really? thought Stormbringer, watching from above. *We get a scrawny ranger and a swordless, middle-aged man? That won't work.* She discreetly signaled Catwings, who was perfectly in line with Rix's field of regard. Catwings understood immediately. She waved at the young spotter, raising a finger to her lips to guarantee a hushed response. Rix took notice, returned an awkward wave and a confused sort of smile. At Catwings' prompting and gesturing, he eventually clued in to his commander's attention on him. Taking her cue, the spotter regarded Berendt and shook his head in a vehement "no," completely faking his understanding of the situation.

Berendt sighed, and by some immeasurable instinct quickly glanced at Catwings, who, suddenly by all appearances was simply tending to her gryphon's comfort. He then swept his gaze away from her, skipping over Amot who was busy trying to coax Howler onto the hill, and then let his eyes rest on the tall ranger.

Fine with me, thought Stormbringer. She grinned as she nodded back to Catwings, who'd raised a hand to her mouth to keep her wide smirk undercover.

"Tallman!" barked Berendt.

"Commander?" he responded. Tall Hallman already had his pack on and looked fully ready for ranging. He stood a full head taller than

Rix, and much the opposite in appearance. He had dark wavy hair, a square jaw, and a well-rounded physique. He wore darker browns and tans instead of bright colors, with barely a trace of wilder ink to show.

"You are to accompany Marec and the valkyries north. Help select a forward operating base in reach of Harrow's Gate. Your primary roles will be scouting and close combat. Bring along that guillotine you call an axe."

"Yes, Sir. Understood," Hallman said, without hesitation.

"And keep an ear open for whispers," Berendt added. "We need to keep comms open."

Awesome, thought Stormbringer. Her spine tingled with the thrill of hers and Catwings' success. *Just as we'd discussed at the Wing Table.* Overall, she'd rather have had Amot along. *His place is here though*, she sensed, *plus that dog complicates matters.*

Hallman simply shrugged the pack off his shoulders and straightaway got to repacking some of his gear.

Next, Berendt turned to the spearmaiden. "Stormbringer, when are you planning to come back for us, and where do we meet you?"

"We'll come when you call, now that we have Hallman," she started. "But we should set a no-later-than date. We can pick off a few deer in the lowlands to sustain the gryphons for up to a week. After that, they need to get back on their regular diet."

"Three days then?" Berendt offered.

Stormbringer looked to Eriff for a response.

"Three days, *maximum*," he replied. "And perhaps a flyby or two if you are able, just so I know you are still out there, independently of what the rangers tell me."

Berendt scowled at the demeaning remark.

Stormbringer simply nodded. *I'm not getting in the middle of this.*

"I'll send Catwings. She can shoot along the river at night or weave through the terrain for cover."

Galewind added her thoughts on the matter. "Assuming fair weather, we'll fly along the river course – the Malevuin, not the Dim – to keep a low profile. We'll touch down at the very edge of the forest and take cover along the tree line. There's a small creek there and an abandoned tower."

"And if we get more of this weather?" Eriff asked, palms open as he gazed up into the night sky.

"It won't stop us," Stormbringer said. "But if it rains heavily…"

"We just wait," Galewind said. "It's all we can do."

"If Catwings spots you on one of her patrols, she might just drop in," Stormbringer added.

Eriff shook his head. "No. Do not drop in unless you see trouble or an obvious signal. You might give away our position."

Fine. Stormbringer nodded, but left him with a bitter look. Galewind returned to Electra and mounted. Stormbringer waited patiently while Tall Hallman strapped in with her, and Marec with Catwings. As soon as her sisters confirmed their readiness, Stormbringer drew in a deep breath.

"On valkyries!" she cried out. On the hilltop, the queensman and the rangers shielded themselves from the heavy flap of gryphon wings, as forced air buffeted the landing party. Snow swirled up from the ground around them. And while the beasts sailed across the fields and arced up over the tree line, valkyrie cries resounded in the night sky. They called out repeatedly, until the landing party's freshly lit lanterns winked out of sight behind them.

Chapter XX
DEAD GNARL'S KNOLL
(Amot, Eriff, Rix)

Facing north, Amot swept his gaze over the forest's edge a good hundred and fifty yards off, then to either side. He couldn't see much through the blowing snow. But he knew the area and that there wasn't much to see anyway – a handful of broken farmsteads and not much else. Inroads from the quarantined Scarsands and the frontier lands of Ironeagle helped to define the region's jaded past, a natural nexus for smuggling refugees, slaves, and forbidden goods, alongside the more practical industries of logging and trapping out of the walled town of Turnsby, behind him. The scout pulled his cloak close around him – his grandfather's old ranging cloak.

Howler broke the moment, whimpering and nudging Amot's legs for attention. The scout knelt beside his weary companion.

"I know, Howler," he told he dog, roughing up his fur. "Tough day, wasn't it? Dogs aren't built for flying."

The canine dropped to the ground and rolled onto his back, belly up, in full expectation of the usual fussing over.

Eriff quickly grew weary of Berendt's rambling on about his preplanned mission, pointing at the faded grey boundaries on his leather map and the yellowed regions in between, wiping off snow with his sleeve in the jittery illumination. Rather, the gallant turned his attention to Amot, consoling his dog. Then he watched the scout stroll over the hill to Rix and interrupt actual work – getting the supplies together. Eriff could barely hear their words over the whooshing noise of the winds. Something about setting up camp for the night, followed by exaggerated claims about valkyrie wooing. *I have to put a stop to this.*

The gallant scoffed. Berendt stopped talking.

"If these were queensmen," Eriff said, "they would be charging into the forest by now and setting it aglow with torchlight. Wulvers would be fleeing in droves, dropping their belongings behind them as they bounded straight into a kill zone."

Berendt responded by rolling up his map and tucking it away in his cloak.

Those two pissed away valuable time chumming around with girls, Eriff thought. Irritation flaring, he abandoned the lead Kith and crossed over the knoll. He approached the young rangers.

The gallant addressed the ginger when he got there.

"You want to set up camp here, now?" Eriff scowled. "It is barely into evening and we are situated in the middle of a field exposed to the enemy and to the elements. What are you thinking?"

"You're right." Suddenly, Rix's eyes bulged with enthusiasm. "We could head to Turnsby for the night. It's not that far. Nice, dry inn, warm meal, fresh linens and all. Get an early—"

"No, no, no." Eriff huffed. "Are you mad?" *Is he toying with me?*

"Hold on," Berendt cut in, following over the hill's summit, Rix's pole lantern in hand. "That might not be such a bad idea."

The spotter grinned.

It isn't even the lad's fault. Flawed leadership, obviously. Minding his promise to Galewind, Eriff kept that thought to himself. Plus, he needed Berendt on his side, at least so long as the mission lasted.

"I know it isn't what we planned," the Kith commander continued, "but if we sent someone into town, we could hire a guide – a Stout trapper maybe – or at least talk to one. We'd gain time in the long run. Some of those old-timers know the forest inside out, including where NOT to venture if you value your hide. It's exactly those places we need to find."

Eriff shook his head vehemently. "No one should even know we are here. This territory is out of the queen's authority for anything unrelated to treaty enforcement. And besides, we could not ask for better cover than this unseasonal storm. I say forget the guide." He addressed Berendt square on. "You and your paltry crew here *are* the professional guides on this mission. So, rangers, guide me into the forest. Isn't that what you do?"

The looks the rangers gifted Eriff in return were Ralador-worthy: Rix's startled face, Amot's pressed lips, and their commander's grimace while scratching under his eyepatch. "Queensmen fight; rangers point them in the right direction to the next glorious battle."

Berendt sighed heavily, lowered his fingers from his patch to his chin, then rubbed his beard. He met Eriff's gaze with his good eye, nodded, then regarded his scout. "Amot, what did you turn up? Anything we can use?"

"Not much," Amot answered. "A dozen or so interconnected trails weaving their way through the grasses, to and from the hill." He gestured in the direction of the nearby town. "The fresh ones lead either to the wall or the landing at Dim River." He waved a hand west. "A couple of older paths fan out towards the Upper Malevuin River." Amot paused, eyed Berendt straight on. "The rest wind their way towards Whisperwood. I didn't find any bones or signs of man-wolves or the sword."

"So, you found basically nothing," Eriff said, arms folded.

Berendt replied, "We'll do one last scan of the area around the knoll for signs of the missing sword or the man-wolves that might have taken it, and then proceed from there based on what we find."

"I want new eyes on the next search," Eriff demanded.

Berendt cleared his throat, "Rix and I will do the next circuit, but we should wait until daylight to enter the forest. That'll allow my rangers time to limber up and have a bite to eat. Set night watches. Start fresh, early in the morning – and I'm talking wee hours."

Eriff sighed heavily. *Am I conversing with bricks?*

"No, no, no," he implored. "We will make for the forest immediately. You can get a head start on tracking where those thieving mutts ran off to."

Rix interrupted. "Track? We can't track in this! It'll be black as pitch in the woods."

Eriff retorted, "You have lanterns, use them."

Berendt turned to the inexperienced spotter, growled back to him. "Tracking isn't the issue. We can do it if we have to." He turned to Eriff and continued. "We'll get more done if we hunker down tonight, finalize our search plan, and put in a long haul tomorrow. We have days to work with here, and we have to be capable of dealing with the threats we encounter on clear terms. Not stumbling around in the dark."

"Nonsense," Eriff rebutted. "Your scout didn't lose some ordinary sword. This mission is too important to simply linger about while man-wolves and Harrowians are on the prowl. We start tonight." He looked to Berendt's one eye. "There will be no further discussion on this point."

For a long and silent moment, the one-eyed ranger stared back at the man from whom he was forced to take orders. He inhaled deeply, turned to his colorful spotter. "It won't be easy, Rix, but with a little luck we could pick up the trail literally anywhere. That's what Howler is here for."

The queensman, suddenly feeling chummy towards his prospect, sauntered over to Rix, dealt him a hefty pat to the back of his ice-encrusted cloak. Where the shards flew off, the green underneath shone through like spring grass. "There now, scoundrel," Eriff told him. "All settled. Now get to it. Follow the damn dog." *The boy needs to dispense with that defeatist attitude,* thought Eriff. He wondered if Lord Ralador might have been wrong about this Caledon.

Berendt turned to his spotter and began reaffirming the next steps. "Rix and I will scour the hill again." He shifted his gaze to his scout. "While that's getting done, Amot, you need to step through *exactly* what happened back at Seventh Kaeda, during your… altercation with Eriff." He regarded the queensmen. "Then we head out."

Wow Commander, way to stand up to the Royal Quarter, Rix thought. He tried his best to contain himself but wondered if it was even possible. *No way a Queen's Guard should be running a ranger op.* It just didn't seem right.

Berendt called Rix aside while Amot and Eriff went off to do their re-enactment. "Now Rix," he grumbled, in his hoarse coaching voice, "Wulver trails will have their own distinctive markings, defined by their habits, body dimensions, and patterns of movement."

Rix felt like he was back at spotter's school. He widened his eyes, nodded, did his best to appear attentive.

Berendt went on. "It's the simple things – an obvious shortcut across a glade, a convenient passage to water, a dry way over wet ground. I know you haven't completed your training for the next level up, but think it through for a minute anyway, and then *you* tell *me* what some of those distinctive markings might be."

Rix knew nothing about Wulvers except that they were wolf-like people. He took it from there. "Well, let's assume Wulvers imitate wolf behavior as much as they can," he began. "They're too tall to behave exactly like wolves, but they might instinctively crouch to stay low when they go creeping through the woods." Rix paused.

"Not bad," Berendt said. "Go on."

"The wolf in them suggests they travel in small packs, single file, and in straight lines." Rix thought carefully for a long moment, staring at the grassy terrain. "So, deeper cuts than if they were spread out everywhere."

Berendt nodded, motioned to Howler. "Unlike Ding-a-ling over there who runs in circles chasing his own damn tail. Imagine tracking that mutt."

Howler's ears perked at hearing his "other" name. He glanced at Berendt momentarily, saw that there was nothing obviously beneficial to dogs happening, then swung his snout back to the tree line and gave the air a quick sniff.

Berendt grunted. "But does any of that help you track Wulvers in the dark?"

Rix shrugged. "I bet they leave bits of fur and dung behind wherever they go. Even if we can't see it, Howler should be able to pick up the scent."

Berendt acknowledged the statement with a slow nod. "Now you're getting it. You know more than you let on, Spotter. You'll make scout soon enough. Everything you said is true. Even with good illumination though, you're not likely to see a nice clump of fur dangling in front of your eyes on some branch. It just doesn't happen that much. Dung maybe, that you might come upon or kick up by accident. Definitely, the scent trail is your best bet in a situation like this."

The mocked-up environment in the Netherdome had been conjured up by Djinxarai projectionists, based off an old Turnsby map. And a dead ringer for what Amot saw around him, apart from obvious deficiencies that couldn't be helped. After all, constructing terrain out of shiro beetles and the corpse of a long-dead Colossus had its limitations.

It didn't take long for Amot to locate exactly where the weapon had disappeared in relation to the hill, and once he'd done so, Eriff soon found his own position at that crucial moment.

"This has to be it," Amot said. His eyes scanned the ground around him. "Nothing here."

"Amazing," Eriff said. "I am impressed. The Netherdome version of Dead Gnarl's Knoll was almost identical." He waved his palms over the ground at his feet. "This is the very hollow I was lying in." Eriff tilted his head, squinting as he peered at the hillside. "Wait, what is that?"

Amot crouched down and pulled a clump of hardy grass out of the ground to mark his spot, then crossed over to Eriff's side of the knoll. The depression in the earth that the queensman had been standing over jutted further into the hill than the Djinxarai rendition.

"A small cavity," Amot said. "A dugout."

Eriff stepped back, knees bent. His sword hand rested on the handle of his cutting rapier. He raised his buckler slightly to defend.

"Wulvers?" Eriff asked, poised to draw.

Careful and quiet, Amot squatted, felt out the ground around the entrance. The wet soil made for easy pulling. He tore out tufts of grass in clumps. "Maybe an old den," he commented, then grunted as he scraped out clumps of soil with his fingernails. "Seems like it's blocked."

"Have they barricaded themselves in?"

Amot tried not to snicker. "No. Wulvers don't live here. Maybe they were sniffing around… listening for mice or rabbits."

Eriff removed his hand from his sword, stood more upright. "So, what does that mean?"

"What it means is… I don't think anyone really knows what it means. But if Wulvers took the striker, they'd have gone back to the forest."

Eriff scanned the team. "We're leaving."

⁂

Amot coaxed Howler to the old dugout, got him to sniff around, and then told the dog to "fetch" before the pair made their way across the field with the others. Howler leapt about the scout's legs, barking with muffled excitement.

No one attempted to be quiet or stealthy in the field, the way a Kith ranger normally would. Between the rambunctious Howler, the clinking queensman, and the lanterns carried by Eriff and Berendt, there was no point in pretending. Instead, the troupe crossed in Queen's Guard fashion: brazen and defiant, inviting of hidden watchers to test their might against them, if they dared. Only the shushing winds gave answer to the party's challenge, sending blowing snow, leaves and bits of fall debris their way as they pressed forward to haunted Whisperwood. Low-hanging clouds, indigo dark, streamed by overhead, thin and stretched. A small, persistent bright patch hung in the sky where the moon shone through. Strong scents of pine and creek water filled their nostrils as they neared the forest's edge.

Chapter XXI
Ghost Pines
(Amot, Eriff, Rix)

The Wilder and his dog closed in on the northern wall of shadowy pines ahead of the others. Cold winds wailed between the trunks. September leaves blew up from the ground, stirring the sickly scent of rotten wood in the underbrush. There was no telling what might lurk ahead on the forest floor, or dwell within the confines of overhanging branches, or lie hidden in dark tree hollows unseen to all but the most prying eyes.

Howler stopped to sniff among the grasses. Amot waited patiently for the spaniel to move on, watched as the moon slid back behind the clouds. Rix caught up just then.

"Find something?" he asked.

Howler cast a glance to Rix, then put his nose back to the ground. Amot shook his head. "If only we were searching for anthills. You?"

Rix shrugged. "Ditto."

"The wind and ice pellets did a number on this field. You'd be lucky to see anything." The scout glanced over his shoulder to the others. Two blotches of yellow light marked the progression of Berendt and Eriff, cutting across the field.

Rix put his hands to his hips, arced his back and gazed up at the looming treetops. They creaked and groaned above them, silhouetted against a rogue patch of brightness in the night sky. His wilder markings came off muted grey in the dim light. Amot could see by the spotter's placid expression that something was bothering him, something that Amot had also sensed.

History.

Presence.

Folklore… Meaning.

Amot broke the silence. "A Kith channeler from the eastern tribes once told me these woods are warped beyond compare, in every sense of the word. Yet, in the winds that whisper through the distorted branches live the earliest echoes of the ancient Hurlorns."

Still staring up, Rix let out a gentle huff through his nostrils. "Sounds like that crazy Wilder druid minding the L-O-C with Bitterhelm." He tilted his gaze to regard Amot. "Do you believe all that? I always found the druids to be a bit over the top."

"Well, they do come here to perform certain rituals," Amot replied. "That's all I really know. But I wouldn't discount it. Druid mysticism is right up there with luminary thaumaturgy, and that's real. Otherwise, we wouldn't be here."

"True enough." Rix grimaced, tipped his head to one side. "How far is the Harrow line from here?"

Amot hesitated. "Officially, the line of control is a few leagues due north. Practically though, we could push it to the northern edge of the forest, which breaks out onto the Western Tor, past Harrow's Gate."

"Giant territory?"

"Half-giants, mostly, belonging to a handful of the Tor Lord houses. They don't normally venture into the forest. At any rate, we have lots of ground to cover between here and there."

Howler let loose a muffled groan, started to claw at the earth. Rix glanced down, then back to Amot with a bright-eyed look.

"Do you think he has something?"

Amot shrugged. "Hopefully not another field mouse." With an airy voice, fast-tempoed, he addressed the spaniel. "What is it, Boy? What is it?"

Howler sprang up at the prompting, then quickly sat. Eyes darted from his master to Rix and back again. The dog whimpered as it shuffled back and forth around the same patch of ground, tail wagging.

Infused with excited tones, the spotter added, "What is it? What'cha got?"

Howler let loose another muffled groan, punctuated with a sharp bark. He looked again to his master and Rix, head cocked, eyes pleading, as though to say: "C'mon, use your little snouts. Don't you get it?"

Eriff eyed Amot's ridiculous animal as it spun about full circle, before plunking its nose to the ground. The two junior rangers stood over the canine, chumming around it seemed. The queensman nudged Berendt, striding beside him. He pointed a gauntleted finger.

"Over there," he huffed between forced breaths. "Why aren't your rangers doing anything? Do I have to assign them a task from one minute to the next? And what is that mutt doing?"

Berendt let out a short, raspy chortle. "Howler picked up a scent and he's tickled about it. That's why he's dancing around. Amot and Rix, well, they're just trying to make sense of it."

Rix's voice rang out over the field. "Go get it, Howler. Fetch!"

Amot hunkered down beside the spaniel, rested his hand on the dog's back. "Don't encourage him too much," he scolded Rix.

Eriff sidestepped a gopher hole, then glanced to Berendt. "What does the dog smell?"

The ranger paused, gauging his response. His rough words were measured. "With any luck, that dog picked up a Wulver trail, but…"

"But what?"

"Howler isn't specifically trained for this. He's more of a… typical pet dog. Amot rescued him from—"

"So, the scent could be anything?"

Berendt grimaced, offered a shrug. "Just about."

Unbelievable. And they call themselves professionals. Eriff bit his own tongue to hold it firm, then spoke under his breath, "What I would do for one good queensman right now."

"What was that?" Berendt gruffed, before his foot clipped an anthill on his blind side. He stumbled.

The question hung in the night air, unanswered, until the awkward silence was broken by the sound of something crashing through the woods.

Eriff pointed. "Look! The dog!" He'd only turned his attention away for a second.

Amot dashed after the spaniel, dropping gear as he went until he toppled, fell flat.

Berendt called out to his men with a grumble, "Don't let the dog get too far ahead."

"Howler, wait!" Amot cried, scrambling to his feet. He limped forward.

Howler shot up a rocky outcrop. From the high ground the dog stopped, craned his head around to stare back at his master. He tilted it curiously. Ears perked, the look of inquisitiveness the spaniel wore was almost child-like.

Taking careful steps and uttering calm reassurances, Amot approached. "Take it easy now, Howler," he pleaded.

The dog turned.

"Nope," Berendt said to Eriff, in a low voice. "Not gonna happen."

The lead Kith was right. Howler bolted through the trees, deeper into the woods.

Amot's shoulders dropped. "Damnit, Howler!" He gave chase into the bush.

"It is more fun to ignore the master than obey him," Eriff announced as he and Berendt came upon the scene. The edge of the forest lit up with the lanterns they carried. Eriff tilted his gaze upwards, gasped at the crooked trees that loomed overhead, gnarled and disfigured like crumpled bodies, and each one a pine.

"Shroud's Well, what a hideous place! Not exactly a stroll in the park."

Berendt seconded the gallant's sentiment with a grunt. "You called it."

Sweat stinging his open wounds, Amot halted in the woods, called, then made his way back to the small, rocky outcrop that Howler had disappeared from. He squatted down, felt out the damage from his stumbling fall. *Bloody knee. Scraped elbow. Stiff ankle.* Rix joined him.

"Did you sprain something?" The spotter swiped a lantern from his handbag, got started lighting it. Amot found a flatter space on the bedrock where he could sprawl out.

The scout grabbed his right foot with two hands, pulling and rotating. He gritted his teeth and winced with every motion. "Damn anthills. Stupid dog. I don't think it's sprained. Just… bruises and scrapes."

Rix shrugged. "Not bad, considering you went down like a brick." He lit the lantern, handed it to Amot. "Here."

Amot set the yellow light beside him. "Yeah, I stepped in a gopher hole and face-planted on an anthill." Amot swiped at the sand still stuck to his face, then swept his legs for the tenth time. "They bite."

Rix chuckled. "You're paranoid." He glanced up at the trees overhead. "Eriff's right though. This place creeps me out." He shrugged off his pack, set it on the bedrock, then started shuffling back down the rock slope. "I'll get your stuff."

"Thanks, Rix." Amot stretched out his left leg, grunted with the pain. His knee made an odd sort of click. Then he shifted his position and hollered again into the woods for the dog. It was no use.

While Amot flexed his joints and tended to his scrapes, his two superiors entered the rocky clearing. Keeping to themselves, they discussed what to do next – something about what approach to take when they encountered Wulvers, and how they might avoid a fight. Amot didn't pay close attention to their exchanges. Even in the cold, he could feel the sweat evaporating away from his wet skin.

Mind buzzing with the numbing pain, Amot inclined on the rock, gazed up at the trees around him. The grueling day came crashing in all at once. Stiff. Sore. Tired. It'd been non-stop since before dawn, and that was after a sleepless night worrying. The pending tribunal. Screwing up this mission. Amot was exhausted. He let his eyes relax, unshut. The voices of his superiors took on a hollow quality, as though in a tunnel. Far off. His vision blurred yet widened at the same time. Opened.

In the yellowy glow of the lantern and with his vision thus altered, the pines took on a different character. Their limbs twisted in, out, and around, without good reason. Wood creaked. Leaves rustled. Shapes coalesced in the shadows. Contorted. *A jumble of body parts*, he thought. The pines he'd known were always tall and straight. But not these.

Slowly, a chorus of hushed voices welled up around him. He felt too tired to be alarmed. Frail. Wanting. Bitter.

Distorted faces appeared in malformed burls. *Damned souls?* he wondered, as though it were a routine occurrence.

The buzzing in his mind intensified. Rising. Undulating. Throbbing in his ears. But the power wasn't just there, present and contained. No. The power was mostly… elsewhere. Larger. A deeper sensation pulsed through his body, reverberating in his bones. *The power is in the reaching*, he realized. *Something here is reaching.*

Patience wearing thin, Eriff removed a gauntlet, dropped it on the rocky ground, then scrubbed his face while he listened to the Kith commander go on and on about excessive details. This operation just wasn't moving fast enough.

"Like we discussed on the way," Berendt explained to him. "We need to focus on two things: set up a base camp that is hidden and defensible, and scout for a Wulver encounter."

"How do you suggest we deal with the Wulvers when we find them?" This was Eriff's biggest unknown. "Kill on sight? Attempt to parley?"

Berendt rubbed his grizzled chin. "If we pick up a trail, shadow them. Get an idea of their numbers, locations, how they behave…"

"And in a contact situation?"

"We need to be in a position to interrogate, barter, bribe, intimidate… if that's even possible. We have to be prepared to do whatever it takes to get the information we need."

Eriff shrugged. "That should be easy enough. How soon can we get to that part?"

Berendt grunted back. "Hold on now. I'll bet hundreds of Wulvers are creeping around in these woods. My guess, they break out into small packs just shy of a dozen, but numbers could be twice that. Wulvers aren't wolves, after all. Now, assuming we track them to their dens—"

"Like the one I saw?"

"Sure, why not? Wolves burrow dugouts under small hills and larger tree roots." Berendt hesitated. "It's either that or natural caves, but you won't find many of those around here. This terrain is all sand, carried in by river water over time."

"We could be overwhelmed, then, quite easily," Eriff said.

Berendt tilted his head. A pained expression washed over him. "I'm not so sure. I doubt the different packs work together. But then again, these are Wulvers, not wolves. It depends on how human they are, I suppose. Anyway, if it does happen, that's when we retreat to our defensible base. We sure as hell can't outrun them."

Eriff sighed. *I should have insisted on bringing in more of my men. We would have gone in and out fast, instead of wasting all this valuable time sneaking around.*

"If there is no other option…"

Berendt grunted. "We can't expect to fight our way through every pack of Wulvers we come up against."

Eriff nodded. "Right." The gallant thought carefully about all the Wulver tales he'd heard as a child. A common theme shone through nearly every one of them. *Fire.*

"Send Caledon to gather deadfall to pile along the perimeter of this outcrop," he told Berendt. "Then have him soak it in lantern oil for a quick light. If we run into trouble, as you say, we shall retreat to this position and fend off the Wulvers by torch and flame. They do hate fire. Am I right?"

Berendt nodded. "I gather they do, but again—"

"They are Wulvers, not wolves. I understand." The gallant pondered such a skirmish. "In a fight, what exactly do I have to work with? Your rangers, I mean."

"Well, you already know Amot."

"I need more information."

Berendt paused for a long moment. "Well," he started again, "let me think." He glanced to the meadow where Rix had gone, then to Amot, tending to his wounds nearby. Berendt continued in a low voice.

"Rix is quite the sneak and an accomplished marksman," he said, his hoarse voice barely audible. "Plus, he can wriggle his way into just about any cover or climb a tree in no time. He can shoot on the run and plug three arrows off in the blink of an eye."

Eriff nodded. "And Amot?"

"Amot now… well, Amot is aggressive and can do just about anything you might need him to do to get the job done. He's a bit of a wildcard, but he'll rise up to any level. Point him in the right direction and let him do his thing. He'll shoulder the operation in ways only he can shoulder. Just don't try to control him too much. He needs leeway or everything falls apart, trying to follow orders instead of doing what comes natural. That said, reel him in hard when he steps too far out of line."

Eriff nodded again. "Got it." He stooped over, picked up his gauntlet, pulled it back on. "That makes it easy. No matter how bad a plan I come up with to defend this rock, just put Rix in a tree and fill in the gaps with Amot. What about you?"

Berendt grunted. "Cover and overwatch seem fitting. It's too easy for a situation to get out of hand. I need to be in a position where I can pull everyone out when the operation goes to hell."

"A comforting thought," Eriff remarked. *One-eyed overwatch.*

He always gets himself into these messes, Rix thought, lugging Amot's gear back to the outcrop. Berendt once told Rix that he stood to learn a lot from Amot. The Kith commander was not wrong, except to say that what the spotter learned mostly came from Amot's mistakes.

The scout had barely moved by the time Rix returned. Amot sat sprawled out on the bedrock, staring blankly at the canopy above. The spotter plopped the backpack down next to him. He stretched his arm out, grabbed his Kith brother by the shoulder, gave him a gentle shake.

Amot jerked back, shook his head, blinking. He stopped when he spotted the pack, stared at it as though focusing.

"Are you all right?" Rix asked.

"Yeah. Thanks," Amot replied. He rubbed at his eyes, then ran his fingers though his hair to push the rogue strands away from his face. "I guess I sort of shut down."

"No problem," Rix said. "It's been a long day." He paused. "What should we do about Howler?"

"He always comes back, eventually."

"Sorry about… coaxing…"

Amot sighed. "Don't worry. He would have bolted anyway. He never listens."

A sudden rustling sounded at the edge of the clearing. Rix backed away in a crouch. Amot pushed himself to his feet. Bushes in front them suddenly parted, leading into the woods.

"Did you invoke that?" Rix asked.

"Not me," Amot said. "You?"

Rix shook his head. "I don't even know how to do that yet." He swung his gaze to Amot. "They're here, then?"

Amot knotted his brow in response. "That's definitely a Hurlorn path." He paused. A pained expression crept over his face. "Something's not right though. Not for here. Not for these parts."

Rix asked, "Why not?"

Amot cupped his hands to his mouth in the shape of a funnel. "HOWLER," he yelled.

Eriff shifted his gaze from the grimacing Berendt to the scout. Amot cupped his hands to his mouth again, ready to yell.

"Enough of that," Berendt barked, before Amot could get the call off. "You'll give us away."

"If he hasn't already," Eriff remarked. The gallant took a long look at the parting of the bushes directly ahead of the two junior ranks. He'd seen the phenomenon only once before.

"Splendid!" he said.

Amot dropped his hands to his side, looked over to the lead ranger and the gallant. Rix's gaze followed. They seemed unsure about what to do.

Puzzled, Eriff turned to Berendt, beside him. The ranger's expression was just as grim. "What's the problem?" Eriff asked. "Isn't this exactly what the forest does for you rangers? Find the path? Show the way? You don't even need to track. The trees have done it all for you."

"Hurlorns. Not trees," Berendt gruffed.

"Whatever," Eriff responded. "They look like trees, and they act like them until you walk up and chop one with an axe."

"I'm a bit leery of anything in this forest," Berendt grumbled. "We don't get much in the way of comms out of Whisperwood, but what we do get is sketchy at best."

"I don't like it either," Rix said.

"I don't care, I'm going to follow the path," Amot said. "It'll lead me to Howler. That's what was on my mind. The Hurlorns must've—"

"You can't trust it," Berendt broke in.

"How else am I going to find Howler?"

Berendt grunted in response. "He'll be back once he has that scent out of his system. He knows where we are."

"Does he? Will he?" Amot clearly was not convinced.

Berendt muttered something incoherent, scratched at the skin around his eye.

Eriff addressed Berendt directly. "I agree with your scout," he stated. He swept his gaze over the young rangers. "Proceed, Amot. And Rix, you are to accompany him." He turned his attention back to Berendt. "You can gather the wood."

Berendt scowled, then hoarsely cleared his throat. His words were as firm as they were gruff. "Gallant, if those two are going, then I need to go with them. Amot will take the trail. Rix and I will run parallel lines to either side, about fifty yards apart. While we're doing that…" The Kith commander's patient, unbroken stare conveyed his sense of persistence on the matter.

Unwavering.

"Very well," Eriff replied. "I shall remain behind, gather firewood, and make the necessary base camp preparations. Report back as soon as you find anything, or send that Caledon. I bet he can run like the wind."

Berendt nodded, "They both can." He turned to face his rangers, barking orders even as he pivoted. "Rix, get Eriff another lantern out of the bag. Amot, you first on point. I'll count to thirty and head out. Rix, back to you, bring up the rear in sixty."

"And stealth mode," he said sharply. "Birdcalls to signal and echo-locate. Whispers only in an emergency – you know the kind I mean. Amot, wait a hundred yards before calling for Howler, and keep it down." Berendt paused, took a long look at his rangers. They gazed back at him, waiting on his words.

"Ready, Kith?" Berendt barked.

"Ready," Amot replied.

"Ready," Rix said.

Berendt began pacing out his fifty yards away from Amot, while Rix pulled another lantern out of his handbag. Eriff removed his buckler and gauntlets.

The Kith commander called back over his shoulder.

"Birdcall?"

"Owl," Amot replied, stepping onto the Hurlorn path.

"Owl it is," Berendt added with a hoot.

Rix hastened to Eriff, handed him matches, torches, and the lantern. Eriff weighed the lantern in his hands, nodded. It was full of oil. The spotter nodded back and started off to pace his own fifty yards.

"Remember," Eriff called out to the rangers' backs, "if you run into problems, warn each other and execute a controlled withdrawal back to this position. The defense will be ready."

Berendt called back over his shoulder, "Keep that fancy sword of yours handy."

CHAPTER XXII
NATURE'S LURE
(Howler)

Canine?
Canine.
Female?
Nice Canine.
Run.
Run.
"Howler!"
Master.
Ignore.
Canine.
Female?
Run.
Run.
Stop.
(Sniff)
Where?
Near.
Where?
Oh, there.
Canine?

(Look)
Not canine.
Person?
(Sniff)
Person-canine?
Play?
Sharp!
Pain!
Bite.
Run?
No.
More. Circling.
Bite. Bite.
Fine?
No.
Lie down.
Wet.
Blood.
(Sniff)
My blood.
Sharp! Held.
Move.
Held.
"Howler."
Faint.
Master.
Come.
Fading.
Dark.

Chapter XXIII
THE FOREST DARK
(Amot)

THE HURLORN PATH ended abruptly. Amot halted. Behind him, the bushes sprung back to their natural positions. He examined the forest floor, spotted a half dozen tracks breaking into the thin crusts of patchy snow. He traced them to a mud-filled stretch, glistening in the pale moonlight. Beyond, the ground was uneven and pitted with rocks and roots.

Hail drove the deer out of the field, Amot surmised. He crouched to examine the tracks more closely. *More than one… a pair.* Both sets were on the small side and narrowly spaced. *Young bucks or does,* he concluded.

Amot shifted his gaze to the mud. A half-pawprint there caught his eye. *Wolf? No.* He tilted his head to better catch the moonlit gleam on the wet surface. *Howler.* Amot would recognize the dog's prints anywhere. *Must've picked up the deer scent after all.*

Amot stood up. Hands to his mouth he hooted his best owl call. His voice didn't sound quite right to his ears though… subdued and hollow in the night. He tried again – same. Neither of his Kith brothers responded. A branch cracked in the distance – that sounded normal. He tried the call once more. Again, no response.

Shroud's Well. Where are you two? Something about the hush around him seemed artificial. Filtered.

A stick snapped – close. A scrabbling of claws on the forest floor followed. The scout ducked down, froze, heart thumping hard in his chest.

Drawing shallow breaths, Amot peered into the gloom. He held his gaze for a long minute. *A smaller animal?* he wondered. *Going about its normal routine?* The night had a way of amplifying minor sounds.

He let out a muted whistle – the spaniel's special call.

Another stick snapped. He called out softly, just in case…

"Howler?"

A moment later, the forest went eerily silent around him, like November come early. A tingling washed over him. Neck hairs stood on end. *I'm being watched.* Still crouched, Amot quietly undid the sheath on his belt, gripped the handle of his hunting knife. Without drawing the blade just yet, he contemplated his next move.

Do I push forward, risk losing the others, and risk confronting Wulvers? Or do I return empty-handed with Howler still out there? Amot figured he must've covered nearly half a mile on his traverse.

He waited a long minute, watching, listening. *Still nothing.*

A wolf howled in the distance.

The scout sighed. *They're out here somewhere.*

"Keep going," he urged himself, barely audible. He kept the knife in hand.

The deer trail led him deeper into the forest. Hard ground soon gave way to spongy moss underfoot. Large branches barred his path, in various stages of decay. *Seasonal windstorms,* he'd assumed at first, until he noticed the earth torn up around him. This despite a lack of actual, uprooted trees. *No, something's different here.*

But as much as the terrain was just getting interesting, the trail seemed to be leading nowhere in particular. The scout couldn't be sure if he was even following deer anymore. The hour was getting late. No traces of Howler or Wulvers. No owl calls from his fellow rangers had reached his ears.

Amot halted. He let go his knife handle, fastened it, then rubbed his arms. They were nicked and scraped. So were his legs from stepping and slipping on moss-slick rocks and logs. It was time to report back what he'd found, time to hear what the others had discovered so they could put it all together. Teamwork.

Just one more bend, Amot promised himself. And then another. And another.

Amot pressed on, spongy steps crunching on layers of dead pine needles and twigs. It had become impossible to move quietly. After a few long minutes, he stopped to make one final call for his dog.

"Howler?" The scout followed up with a whistle. And as he stood waiting for a response, a rustling sound jolted him. Abruptly, he turned his gaze to look. The bushes had parted.

Hurlorns. They're back.

Heartrate rising, Amot projected his voice into the dark woods around him. "Are you friendly?" he asked. The scout wiped sweat from his brow, felt more trickle down his back.

Hearing nothing in response, Amot called out a melodic greeting in Treesong, waited. The wind picked up. A branch crashed in the distance and thudded on the ground. Then a twig snapped close by. Too close. The scout homed in on the sound, swung his gaze – it came from the direction of the new path. *I'm being lured.* Several more crunches on the soft ground followed. *Heavy sounding, like me.*

"Rix?" he said, uncertain. "Berendt?"

Next, Amot caught a whiff of smoke on the wind. Without a moment's time to process the sensation, a vaguely canine outline appeared in the shadows, on the very edge of visible, bright eyes watching.

"Howler?" Amot repeated. But as his eyes made better sense of the shape, he knew it couldn't be his dog. Large. Sleek. Fur shimmering in the night. Slowly, Amot inched his hand to his side, felt for the hunting knife again. He undid the retaining snap and gripped the handle.

In place of the affectionate "Rawl, rawl, rawl" he'd hoped to hear, there came a low, rumbling growl instead.

"RRRRU… RRRRSH… RRRRT…"

The animal crept a step closer, head low, eyes glimmering. Then it crouched out of sight behind ground cover. The scout drew back to a thick-trunked pine. He scrambled down into the moist darkness of a hollow, between the tree's roots. Knife in hand, Amot waited. Tense. Ready.

The growl sounded again, closer. Amot could almost decipher words, garbled as they were. The guttural voice sawed through the air, rough and serrated; the tone accusing: "RRRROU… RRRRSH-NOT… RRRRBE… HEERRRR."

Amot peered between the roots. The creature rose from the under-story and stood up on hind legs. Amot caught the glint of eyes – a person's eyes, but on a wolf's face, narrow and sleek that somehow had a feminine look to it.

Wulver.

Slowly, Amot showed himself, one palm raised as a calming gesture. "I mean no harm." He muscled up and out of the hollow. "I am in search of something lost in this forest."

The she-wolf responded with a single, drawn out syllable, straining her vocals with the effort: "Lo… rrr… st?"

Hollow voices in the dark echoed the word. Far and near, high and low: "Lor-st… Lo-rst?… lost?" Amot's eyes darted about him. The sounds came from everywhere.

"What is this?" Amot looked to the shadowy form. "Are you doing this?"

The Wulver raised her voice above the chatter, monstrous sounding. Straining with effort, she crafted a more complex phrase. "Lo… rrr… st, says the man. That's ho… rr… w it begins. They aarrr arrlways lo… rrr… st, and then threy a… rrr… e dead."

Amot's unease heightened. *Is she threatening me?* Sounds around him intensified. *Or warning me?* Wood knocked; branches whipped. That smell of smoke lingered in the air. Whispers flooded the woods around them, above them. *Foreign?* No, not quite – a dialect of Elder-kin, Hurlorn style. Difficult to make out. Their own unique tongue.

"Never found, never found," said one Hurlorn with a wicked wom-an's voice, old and malignant.

"Shut yer hole, y'old snag," another voice retorted, with an old man's ring to it.

"LOST, Lost, lost," came chants and echoes from all directions.

As the words faded into the night, a booming Hurlorn raised its voice above them all. "Lose yerself next time," it cried, and then cackled. All the voices cackled.

Without warning, the ground beneath Amot shifted. The Wulver ducked down. A loud tear sounded, and then a crackle. Roots exploded out of the earth. Amot stumbled forward. The knife flew out of his hand. Thwunk! It stuck into a tree.

"Ooo," exclaimed the wicked Hurlorn above him. "That tickled."

Amot heard the knife thwunk again somewhere else – maybe real, maybe imitated – and then again.

A branch whipped through the air. The scout's knife flew past his head, stuck into the tree beside him.

"Yipes!" screamed another Hurlorn. "That does tickle."

As mayhem brewed in the branches, on all fours the Wulver crept cautiously towards Amot, eyes darting to the treetops. The Wilder stood his ground as she rose up on hind legs, a head taller than he. The beast tilted her jaw up, raised her voice to the trees.

"Enough," she snarled, narrowing her eyes and shaking a fisted paw. "I'll tearrrr the barrrk from yerrrr limbs. I'll carrst the fires up-pron you!"

"Where's your flame?" called a mocking voice.

"Don't yrou smrell the smoke?" she replied.

Out of the blackness, a whipping branch lashed at the she-wolf, striking the back of her neck. She yelped, hunched forward.

"Not there," said a Hurlorn.

A second branch whipped her side.

"Not there either," another followed.

The Wulver glared at Amot. The scout held her gaze. Steady. Branches lashed. Roots whipped around them. His muscles tensed. He braced for a brawl. Bare-fisted, he could smash her snout, gouge her eyes, grip her throat, or lock her in a hold.

A massive Hurlorn branch swiped at him, low and fast. Amot

leapt out of the way. It bashed a tree behind him. The old deadwood uprooted and fell over.

Non-threatening, the Wulver approached with caution, stopping at arm's reach. The scout kept his composure even, showing neither aggression nor fear. An almost pleasant snarl crept across the Wulver's face – very near to a serious grin. She spoke again, words slow and practiced.

"They rrlike r-rrou even mrrorre than they rrlike me," she growled.

Another large branch swung, straight down. This time, at the Wulver. She easily sidestepped the strike. It smushed into the soft earth, then withdrew.

"Are you sure about that?" Amot said.

She growled. "They might h-r-ate each other mrrorre than the trruu of us put together-rr." The creature extended her paw. Except it wasn't quite a paw. It was very much like a human hand. Her forearm was long and slender, with smooth fur that shone like a piece of the pale moon.

The white Wulver. Mystical or deadly, or just another person you meet traveling – Amot didn't have a clue what to expect of this creature. Tales had Wulvers feasting on young, plump townsfolk as a rare delicacy after luring them into the forest. On the other hand, over the years a handful of hopelessly lost Glebe Stouts out of Turnsby claimed to have been helped by a Wulver. They were called liars and attention-seekers.

"This r-rray," she said. "Hur... rrey. Irt is not safe herrre."

Do I trust her?

She was right though. Where they stood was not a safe place to be standing around and chatting in the dark. But to go with her would be to defy orders. Amot had a duty to return to base camp and report the encounter.

Every length of quivering bone, every fiber of tensed muscle, and every hair that stood on end urged the Kith ranger not to go with her. And yet he hesitated. The Wilder gazed deep into the she-wolf's eyes. They conveyed a core sincerity to him that could not be masked. He'd seen the same in Howler's eyes, so many times.

Above, below, and all around, wood was on the move. Groaning.

Creaking. Ripping through the earth. Branches swept this way and that way. One massive limb struck that of another pine, broke off and went crashing to the ground. Hurlorn targeting Hurlorn. A flurry of curses followed. Deafening smaller strikes resounded in a flurry. Ghost pines cursed in unison at the "flesh-ed ones" in their midst, then moments later swore vengeance to one another.

We're mice on a battlefield, Amot thought, as he ducked and dodged. *Mice about to be stepped on.*

He had to make a decision.

Amot reached out, accepted the outstretched paw-hand. He took his first step to follow. It was an implicit trust, the same way he trusted man's best friend.

She led him away.

And like mice, they made for the nearest cover.

CHAPTER XXIV
LOST

(Eriff, Rix)

ERIFF DROPPED THE armful he was carrying onto the main pile of fallen branches he'd collected, then stood back to survey his work – rows of seasoned deadfall along the perimeter of the rocky outcrop, with breaks in between, plus a central heap for replenishment. The oil, he decided, could be spread on top and lit moments prior to a confrontation. *That should do the job,* he thought, wiping sweat from his brow. He brushed the bark and pine needles off his chest and arms. *Defensible enough.* Eriff actually enjoyed the task, even in armor. The exertion. The cold air infusing his blood. *Invigorating. Like working the family stables.*

And as the queensman stuffed torches into a convenient cleft in the rock, he heard the rangers returning, traipsing through the bush.

Berendt climbed the rock dome first, panting, covered in sweat. Soon after, Rix joined him in a similar state of exertion, stepping out of the shadows and into the lantern light. Eriff paused, waiting. He peered into the dark woods behind them.

"And where is Amot?"

The Kith commander flipped up his eyepatch. "Still out there," he gruffed. "Amot hasn't responded to any of our calls."

"The owl thing?"

Berendt nodded.

"Just send him one of your ranger whispers." *Do I have to tell them everything?* "Amot will hear it and get back to us. Is that not a major part of what you do, whisper to one another over long distances?"

Berendt grunted back. "Well, Eriff, it isn't so simple. Not in these parts." The ranger's good eye held Eriff's gaze, while his dead eye seemed to stare past the gallant. "Information gets twisted passing through these parts. Plus, there's another, more general risk involved." He scratched at the scar tissue.

Eriff tried not to watch.

"You see," Berendt explained, "whispers are widely broadcasted. We don't think anyone's listening that shouldn't, but for an operation this sensitive…"

"But surely," Eriff said, "when one of you is lost…"

The ranger folded his arms. "This is exactly why we don't go fumbling around in the dark, unprepared. We should've…" Berendt trailed off with a huff, took a deep breath and gave himself a long moment to compose himself. He winced when he scratched at his scar again, then continued.

"Of course," he assured Eriff. "Overriding priorities and all. We can always find a way to disguise the true meaning of our messages. We need to locate Amot and determine if he needs our assistance. He should've been back to base by now, even if he couldn't find Howler. Unless… unless he already encountered Wulvers." He swung his gaze to his spotter. "Rix?"

"We all heard the wolf calls out there," Rix replied. "I didn't see any tell-tale signs of Wulvers in the immediate area though." He made a pained expression. "But something's not right."

Berendt grunted. "Explain."

"I could've sworn Amot didn't stray far at all. I could hear him nearby and Howler too, up ahead, right up until just before I gave the owl call. You heard that, right? Then everything went quiet."

Berendt nodded. "Couldn't miss it."

"Strange," Eriff said. "I could hear you all quite clearly."

The Kith commander did a double-take on Eriff. "That's impossible." He shook his head. "In fact, neither of you should've heard a damn thing, except maybe Rix picking up Howler mucking about. You can't train that animal."

The spotter swung his gaze back to the deeper woods, eyes squinting as he scanned the limits of the lantern light. "Sound has a funny way of carrying in this forest."

Berendt rolled his good eye. "It's the damn wind," he gruffed. "Do you think Amot isn't answering on purpose? How far out were you?"

Rix scrunched his brow. "Half a mile, tops. No. That wouldn't be like him. Unless, like you said—"

"Unless he *had* to be quiet," Eriff finished. "Now that I think about it, I could hear you in the bushes up to a point, then nothing until you were nearly back to the rock."

Berendt scrubbed his face with one hand, rested it on his chin. "Wulver's ought to have the keenest ears. If you could hear us..." He chewed at his lip, turned to Rix. "Get a damn whisper out, Spotter. Pronto. Think up a code he'll understand."

Rix hesitated. *He knows I haven't done my trials yet.* The spotter could only trust himself with basic words and a handful of common phrases.

Berendt scowled at him, "What are you waiting for? Get to it. Just make it something simple. Simple and discreet." He turned to face the queensman. "Now, Eriff," he began...

While his superiors argued next steps, Rix crossed to the far end of the rock dome and entered the woods to concentrate. Gusty winds shuddered through the branches overhead. He kept going until the voices behind him became muffled and faded. The light dropped off quickly away from the lanterns.

Simple, Rix repeated to himself. *Discreet.* The last thing he wanted was a repeat of Amot's now legendary disaster, all due to incorrect phrasing.

Only one word came to mind for the message he'd send, and Rix happened to know its Treesong rendering. One word, but five times longer in that sylvan tongue and finicky as hell. He sounded out the translation twice before committing, matching the initiating tone as best he could and singing out the syllables at a fast tempo – finesse the spotter was still getting used to. The damn meaning could change with the speed of utterance. Pushing aside his lingering apprehension, Rix cupped a hand to his mouth and whispered into the woods: "*Goo-khwa-wah-khoo-hoo.*"

The spotter felt a disturbance in the air, which he interpreted to mean the whisper had been taken up. Satisfied, he returned to base. Eriff met his gaze when he got there.

"So, what message did you send him?" he asked.

"Owl."

"What?" Eriff shrugged, showing his palms. "Another owl call?"

"Not exactly," Rix replied. "Just the word 'owl.' If Amot hears the whisper, he'll know I'm calling out to him. If anyone else hears it, they'll probably just think someone saw an owl."

Berendt grumbled, "Not bad," then he nodded to Rix.

That, apparently, was a compliment.

"Now get out there again, Spotter," he went on, "and keep your eyes and ears open. Stay close. And call out once in a while. I want to know everything that gets picked up on the back of that return message, everything that's out there. Even if it makes no sense."

Rix returned to his place in the woods. He let out a five-syllable test call.

His commander responded with the appropriate acknowledgement.

Eriff waited a few long minutes for something to happen. Patience wearing thin, he turned to Berendt. "I haven't heard anything back yet. Have you?"

"No," the ranger gruffed. "It takes time."

Eriff sighed. "I'm not sure I trust all this ranger awareness sharing."

Berendt continued, "And you won't hear anything. You're not trained." He sounded irritated. Eriff ignored the ranger's ill-tempered disposition, prodded him anyway.

"Surely, my ears can hear as well as yours. Perhaps better – I am younger by a decade." *I'm being generous,* Eriff thought, looking the rugged man over.

Berendt sighed heavily, as though explaining the concept for the hundredth time. "Picking up whispers is a trained skill and you have to be initiated into it – part of the Eightfold Way that we Kith follow. Even then, the skill is more about picking the signal out of the regular jumble of noises you might hear in the woods – wind, leaves rustling, that sort of thing. Once you hone your senses on the message, the Hurlorns do the rest."

Eriff scanned the trees around them, each one warped and crooked. "I wouldn't trust a person so bent out of shape and decrepit looking."

Berendt grunted. "We rarely have any problems. Hurlorns pass messages rather instinctively, for the most part. But I have to admit, sometimes the content gets filtered. And information gets picked up along the way – not all of it good. Especially if there's a Spirit Hurlorn in the loop. But usually, what extra we get is either harmless or oddly useful later on."

"Obviously, the Hurlorns are helping you, or trying to." Eriff paused, having heard something in the wind himself. "Wait, what was that?" He cocked his head, listened intently.

Berendt shot him a skeptical look. "It's nothing – a reflection is all. It happens sometimes." He called out to his spotter, "Rix, did you catch that?"

"Nothing here," he replied.

"Well," Eriff said, "I heard 'owl' plain as day."

The Kith ranger's eyes narrowed, gauging. "Can't be."

"I did," Eriff said.

"Treesong, do you know it?"

Eriff scoffed, "Why bother to learn Treesong? I would sooner have a conversation with a rock."

Rix called from his place in the woods, "I hear something now."

A bellowing voice rose like woodwinds above the gusts in the branches and the rustling of leaves.

"Man-flesh, dog-flesh, which one first?"

A second voice responded, that of a fluty old woman.

"I can't decide how to quench my thirst."

The first broke rhythm, spat back to the second, "That's because your head's too rotten to hold a thought!"

The woods knocked and rattled.

"Rix, get back here," Berendt barked. He flipped his patch down.

Eriff turned to the Kith commander, "A cantankerous lot, these Hurlorns."

Berendt tilted his one-eyed gaze to the high branches. He stared at the dark, looming forms outside the clearing, as though gauging a storm brewing. He grabbed his chin and growled. "These aren't normal Hurlorns, if the legends have any truth to them."

Rix showed up beside them. "We need to find Amot. NOW." He cupped his hands to his mouth to yell out.

Eriff gripped his arm, yanked it from his face. "No," he stated. "That's an order."

Rix looked to Berendt, wide-eyed.

The Kith commander grimaced. "Eriff's right. That won't help. It'll only draw them in."

"This is all a distraction," Eriff said. "We need to focus on the mission – find the Wulvers, retrieve the sword."

Berendt sighed. "You might be right. In which case, these Hurlorns are in on it. That, or they're just being a royal pain-in-the-ass." He glanced at Eriff. "No offence."

"None taken," the gallant replied. He regarded Berendt. "Get everything ready. We shall enter the forest. Either we find the Wulvers or they find us. Either way, we make contact. The sooner the better."

Eriff expected the Kith ranger to push back, to say they needed to rest first, or try more calls, or whatever. None of that happened. Instead, Berendt simply nodded. His good eye shifted between Rix and the queensman.

"Although I can't think of a reason why these ghost pines would have anything against us, be mindful of every word you hear out there. Assume that deception is highly possible – even with normal vocal contact between us. If you don't see lips moving, think twice before acting."

"I suppose I'll leave my helm off then," Eriff responded.

"With that huge double-visor of yours?" Berendt let out a gravelly chuckle. "Yep. Pack it. We're goin' in Wilder style."

CHAPTER XXV
SHE-WOLF GUIDE
(Amot)

HER FOREPAW WAS like a human hand, but it didn't feel that way in Amot's grip. The leathery underside was warm and calloused, and the fur that Amot wrapped his fingers around was thick and coarse to the touch. For the few moments he held it, he felt like a child being led through a shady part of town.

The she-wolf let go her grip. And with her awkward hind-legged stride, she guided the Wilder through the dark and dangerous woods, weaving out-of-the-way paths between the sparring tree spirits. The Hurlorns appeared too preoccupied with one another to notice the soft footpadding through their territory. Lithe branches whipped overhead; great limbs crashed. Tree roots upheaved, destabilizing the ground.

The Wulver reverted to a more wolf-like stance. As did Amot, keeping to a low profile, crouching in hollows and ducking behind boulders. The scout shadowed the she-wolf's every move. And at every turn, without so much as a word or a growl, she stopped to check on him. With silent gestures, she communicated the path ahead. Slowly, the scout found meaning in her somatic cues: a turn coming, an obstacle to be circumvented, look for danger ahead…

Out of nowhere, the crashing noises subsided. Hollow voices arose from back where they'd started. Like woodwind instruments, they rang clearly through the woods.

"Where'd the flesh-ed go?" one of the pines asked, sounding much like an ornery old man.

"Huh?" boomed another, low and sonorous.

"Clear the cobwebs out o'yer eye sockets," came a younger man's voice, with a coastal accent. "They's right there, like the post says."

"Your head's gone rotten! Where's the flesh on a boulder with moss on it?"

"Boulder?"

"Boulder."

"Moss?"

"Moss."

"Well, how am I supposed to know?" The voice grunted with exertion. "*He* made me think it." Again, wood smashed and knocked, amidst spite-ridden arguing impossible to follow.

Amot and his guide dropped into a ravine that cut through the forest floor, then followed it. Nearing a small bluff, the she-wolf glanced back over her shoulder at the Wilder. She stretched out a forepaw, palm down, lowering it in stages to get him to crouch. Then her clawed fingers daintily pointed out a tripvine, and a protruding root to avoid stumbling over in the dark.

The pair slunk along the bluff's craggy base, then climbed up the other side. Behind them, the crashing died off again. Another Hurlorn cried out into the night air.

"So, where is they then?" the voice boomed.

"They was there a minute ago," responded another.

"You're supposed to be smart about it, not stupid," said a third, an old woman's voice. "Are you sheep-flesh?"

"I thought that were him too," cried yet another.

The bickering continued as the Wulver and Wilder quietly departed the ghost pine territory. Amot could see that the higher ground was no longer torn up. The trees there appeared rooted and normal. Soon, they came upon a swift and cutting creek, deep, boulder-laden, and choked with trapped sticks. Its banks were overgrown with bushes.

A windy roar rose above the quarreling voices behind them, angry and hateful.

"Fools! Find the flesh-eds! Find the man-flesh!" A loud whack followed.

Down on all fours, the Wulver darted over a fallen log to cross the creek, then gestured at Amot to follow.

A deafening thump sounded through the night air, then finally a silent pause. Amot craned his head around to peer through the trees. Heavy groans and wood creaks sounded, slow and regular, many at once. Then whipping sounds.

They're on the move. He glimpsed something in the shadows, too veiled to make sense of. In his mind's eye, he imagined large limbs swinging. Listening intently, he could hear the ghost pines meandering about and rummaging through the underbrush, followed by the knocks and scrapes of rocks on rocks as the demented tree spirits pushed aside boulders and felt out crevices.

The she-wolf called to him in a loud whisper: "Psht!"

Amot jerked his gaze to her. Again, she beckoned him to follow, standing tall now and fronting a thicket of thorny briar. Amot picked up on a new sound from her direction – clinking metal.

The scout hesitated. *Where is she leading me? Is her kindness genuine, or is this a trick?* The she-wolf easily could've left Amot to the whims of the ghost pines and saved herself, but she didn't. *Definitely a good sign,* he decided, *but kindness can also be a lure.*

The Wulver cocked her head at him, sensing unease.

What would she do if I bolted? Amot could try to lose her in the ghost pines, race back to his comrades and report all he'd seen. They could formulate a plan. By all rights, Amot knew he should do just that. But something kept him from acting. A gut feeling, the kind he got before every big change in his life, at every crossroads where the most basic content of his future hung in the balance. A faint fragment of Treesong resounded in his mind. The Green Dragon's song. *This is one of those moments.*

She cares. Amot could see it in her eyes. *Deeply.* His fears washed away. Again, the clinking sound carried on the wind, like rattling chains.

Undeterred, the scout crossed the creek. He crossed to the scratchy grass and underbrush on the other side. And as he came face to face with the Wulver, she began to gesture with her hands again, slow yet complex. Amot watched curiously, his mind scrambling as he struggled to interpret her signals. He pieced the concepts together one by one.

Under the brush... round to the left... then right... then straight through. Amot nodded in understanding. She pinched her thumb to her fingers in her right hand, gestured to her mouth as though to eat. After a short pause, the she-wolf raised her hand, traced out a high arc. In Amot's estimation, she meant to convey reaching over the top of the thicket and touching down on the other side.

The scout's reading of this latest signaling left him uncertain. Two versions bled through: "My den is just beyond this thicket" or "I'm going to eat you when we get to the other side." Assuming the first, the scout nodded to her again. She returned the gesture, crouched down on all fours, then ducked under the briar. Amot glanced over his shoulder at the shadowy Hurlorns still crashing about. He shrugged, then followed suit.

⌁

Amot tilted his gaze to the high branches as he approached the Wulver's glade. He quickly learned the one important thing missing from the Wulver's silent descriptions – chains. Many, many chains, swaying and rattling in the wind. Heavy, hanging, they draped down from branches high above. Iron spikes anchored them to a ring of boulders on the ground, and to rocky outcrops. The chains didn't just hang loose, they'd been woven together in a grid to form a kind of barricade.

How is this possible? Amot wondered. By all appearances, his guide and the village beyond the metal lattice were as primitive as could be. The chains, it was apparent, were not meant to stop other Wulvers or even people from entering the glade. Only the ghost pines would be barred passage.

With a friendly growl and a swinging-head gesture, the she-wolf enticed Amot to pass through the iron mesh. He did so unharmed. Next, she enticed him to follow her into the glade. It was a lumpy clearing, choked full of old logs and crisscrossed with narrow trails. No other Wulvers greeted him in the open field, dimly lit by the veiled moon. But they were present. Eyes glimmered from den openings as he passed.

Last, she led him towards the largest wolf den, dug into the largest mound at the heart of the Wulver territory. Smoke billowed out a shaft atop the hill, puffing up over the treetops. A pile of wood had been stacked near the entrance, with an axe sticking out of it.

Before entering, Amot took in the sights around him. The greater forest beyond the chained perimeter had grown even more twisted and hostile in the waiting. The ground underfoot trembled and shook as spiteful ghost pines stomped their giant roots, and branches clashed in the woodlands as they sparred. Chains rattled while some tested the perimeter. They cursed even their own kin, and routinely blamed "the flesh-ed ones" for the woes of a dozen lifetimes. Then they blamed each other. It was not a good place out there. Not a safe place either.

The Wulver grasped Amot's hand again, warm in the night. She crouched down in front of the entrance to the den, gave him a tug. The smell of animal was strong. The scout thought back to his interpretation of the hand signals she'd given him at the creek.

The Wilder hesitated, sighed heavily. *I've got to be crazy*, he told himself, as he crouched to his knees and scrambled in after her.

CHAPTER XXVI

URGENT PACT

(Rix, Haar)

D ISEMBODIED VOICES MURMURED in the dark. They spoke as one.

"Dead in the woods."

Cold energy blossomed at the base of Rix's skull. The chill ran down his spine, spread across his shoulders.

The whispers wouldn't stop. They kept coming in, carried by the cool, night air. The spotter bit his lip hard. He did his best to ignore them as he led the way through the shadowy gloom of the woods, composite bow gripped in one hand. Berendt followed and then Eriff, single file. With each spongy step, the layers of pine debris crunched underfoot. The moss-coated terrain was marred by upturned trees, littered with rocks and fallen branches.

"Are we even going in the right direction?" Eriff said, his voice colored by the sort of irritation people like him reserved for substandard servants.

"We're heading north," Berendt grumbled back, "the same direction Amot chased Howler and the same direction we heard those crashing sounds."

A whisper rose out of the darkness ahead, "Blood on the wind."

Rix halted. *Enough.* He snatched three arrows from his side quiver, nocked one to his bowstring and gave it some pull. He peered into the darkness.

"That sounded close," Eriff said.

"Too close," Rix replied.

A new whisper welled up from behind them, "The Wulvers tore him apart."

Rix spun around. Eriff ducked as the spotter raised his aimpoint high, to the upper branches of the shadowed pines.

"Show yourself," Rix cried into the night, "whoever you are. My three friends would love to meet you."

"Tore him apart."

Rix swung left. *Nothing.* He added draw-weight to his arrow.

"Tore him apart."

He swung right, waited, bow bent. *Next time, I will shoot.*

But the voices multiplied. The same words repeated again and again from different directions.

"Stop!" he yelled.

The forest went quiet.

Eriff scowled at the spotter. "Put that thing down. Are you even holding it right? It looks like your arrows could go flying off in any random direction."

The spotter ignored the slight. *What does he know? A bow to him is a bent stick.*

Berendt grimaced, spoke coarsely, "Don't let the voices get to your head, Rix. That's what they want, to get to your head. We need to keep moving."

"How do we know they're not Wulvers?" Rix asked, eyes still scanning the woods. "They could be surrounding us."

Berendt grunted. "They're not. Animals hunt, they don't taunt."

Rix kept up his guard.

"You heard the man," said the queensman. "Stand down. This is nothing more than one of your ranger whispers gone twisted."

After a long moment staring into the gloom around them, seeing nothing, the spotter sighed. He relaxed his grip on his composite.

"Keep an arrow nocked anyway," Berendt advised him. "Just in case. And I'll keep a bolt in my hand crossbow."

Rix nodded, gathered his bearings, and started off again.

The first thing Haar noticed was how the tree devils were acting strange when the man-fleshes strayed into Haar-wulf territory. Grizzer had told Haar it would get that way. Grizzer had been the first to hear the man-fleshes, the first to catch their scent, and the first to introduce Haar to a new type of smell that only Grizzer had caught a whiff of, once before. No Wulver had believed his grumbling tales about a vicious long-haired cat-bird, until now.

But it had been Haar who ordered the ambush. *These man-fleshes have no place in my woods*, he decided. Baruush he could tolerate, Nali to some extent, but not man-fleshes. More than half his pack had crept through the woods in search of a place to crouch low, a place to lie hidden. A place to linger and wait for his sign.

Haar nudged Grizzer, then moved to position himself in the path of the intruders. Grizzer followed. Haar knew that man-fleshes were easy to group. *They clump together. That makes the hunting easier.* Grizzer had argued for slaves, but Haar dismissed the notion. He could smell that they weren't ones to submit, that they'd be trouble. They were not the little ones from the town, or the starving ones brought up from dark caves, or the sick ones that came from the West, over the mountains.

The smell of youth and cloth preceded the one guiding the small man-flesh pack, walking on his hinds like all man-fleshes do. Haar narrowed his eyes as he watched the three of them thumping and cracking loudly through the forest. Cat-bird smell was in the air, but not so strong as the waft that had blown in from the field when the day was still fading. From his hidden place, Haar looked the lead man-flesh over, sniffed him out. A sneer formed on the Wulver pack leader's lips.

Scrawny and hungry, that one, thought Haar. *Last-eater.*

When Last-eater came within a few leaps of Haar and Grizzer, the man-flesh let out a yelp to the others.

"Wulvers!"

The man-fleshes came to a stop. Haar pricked his ears to the dull brushing sound of metal over wood from one of the rear ones, standing tall in the shadows. *A weapon.* It was followed by a sharp metallic click from the other.

Last-eater glanced at Grizzer first, but quickly shifted his gaze to mighty Haar. He yelped again, waving a bent stick around.

"Who are you, and what have you done with Amot?"

Amot? The Wulver cocked his head, carefully examined this strange Last-eater. *A whipping branch?* The bent wood that Last-eater held was too far away to whip Haar, but the Wulver pack leader still didn't like it. It was bent so tight he could hear the tension creak. *I don't trust man-flesh devices, especially the ones that don't make sense.*

The scrawny man-flesh with the whipping branch spoke again. "Well, Wolf, tell us. Where is our friend?"

Friend?

Haar pricked his ears for what was important. He pricked his ears for the footpads of his fellow Wulvers creeping among the trees. Grizzer couldn't wait though. The dark-haired Wulver growled a challenge at the man-flesh before it was time, before Haar's pack was in place. *He wants to clamp down on a man-flesh leg*, Haar told himself, *and feel the blood squirt between his teeth.* Grizzer was still in his middle-dark years, virile and strong with the scent of a roughneck, like himself. *I feel it too, Grizzer. I feel it too.* Haar knew he had to watch his own neck around Grizzer though, and let him strong-jaw the other Wulvers to satisfy his urge to show strength over them. When Grizzer glanced to Haar for approval, Haar stared back firm and did not encourage him. *That's not how we hunt.* Then he swung his gaze back to the scrawny man-flesh and growled.

"R-rr, I am no wolf."

Another man-flesh stood behind the lead, wrapped in shadows. Haar made out the vague shape of his face. It swiveled one way and then the next. *You won't find my Wulvers*, Haar thought, *but they will find you.* The man-flesh raised a steady hand and croaked out a command.

"Stand down, Rix."

Haar didn't know what that meant until he saw Last-eater lower his bent stick. The dull brushing sound came again, followed by a soft knock. *He put his weapon away.* A one-eyed man-flesh wearing hides stepped forward from the shadows. He kept his hands raised where Haar could see them. *Man-flesh's can't flatten their ears, so they do that instead.* The Wulver knew much about how man-fleshes reacted to fear. Yet, despite the gesture, Haar backed away slowly. He growled out a warning with a low, steady rumble. *That's close enough, One-eye.* He'd come within one leap.

Grizzer joined in chorus. He always joins in for that sort of thing.

One-eye stopped, as he should, and waved his hand to usher the next man-flesh forward. That man-flesh – with a soft face and metal skin elsewhere – clinked and swished with every step. Haar had already heard that one half a forest away. When Soft-flesh came into the open, beside One-eye, even in the gloom of night Haar could see that his eyes were as blue as a pup's.

With temptation like that in front of him, Haar understood Grizzer. He'd tasted man-flesh before. The pack leader wanted to sink his teeth into this one's limbs and tear the bare skin off too. *So easy it would be, if I could get my jaw underneath that metal skin. No real hide past that.* But one thing worried Haar. Haar did not smell fear on this clinking man-flesh, like he did when confronting others with soft skin like him. He didn't smell it on One-eye either, but One-eye was more of a roughneck. Maybe Last-eater, but not much.

Haar swung his gaze to Grizzer, lifted his nose subtly to him.

Grizzer – the best sniffer – acknowledged with a return ear-twitch. Grizzer waved his muzzle up and down twice, sniffing at the air as he did so. "Their fr-r-riend… Lusii-wulves."

The soft one spoke. "Do you know where he is?"

Haar grunted. "Wulver-rrs have him, yes. R-rr, a vile pack."

Last-eater blurted out, "Where are they?"

"Hold your tongue," One-eye scolded. Haar imagined Last-eater's ears flattening to his head. Less rounded they were, than the others.

"My name is Eriff," the soft one continued, "son of… and…" The man-flesh went on using words that Haar didn't recognize or care about. The pack leader cut him off.

"Haar-rr," he growled.

Soft-flesh turned to One-eye, expecting.

One-eye gruffed back, "He says his name is Haar."

"Trespasser-rrs," the pack leader went on. "Haar-Wulver-rr lands."

Soft-flesh spoke. "Haar. Yes. We are here to find our friend and recover something that is ours – a lost sword. When we find them both in good order, we shall leave."

One-eye spoke next. "Will you help us?"

Haar looked the three over, gauging. *Easier to rip their throats out.* He regretted that the Cutter had already left the forest. *Good trades, these man-fleshes.*

Soft-flesh spoke again. "We can make it worth your while."

Worth my while? Haar'd heard that before and it was a lie, or he didn't understand it right. *But they have metal things.* Haar liked metal things – all sorts of them. He liked the sharp edges. He liked how they cut through soft flesh, even the old rusty ones, even better than teeth, sometimes.

Haar grumbled back. "Rrr-what metal things do you have?"

Soft-flesh answered. "We have lots of metal. If you help us find what we seek, I will give you…"

Haar roared, "A swor-rrd? A sword for a sword?"

"Yes, you'd like that?" Soft-flesh said. "And in exchange for our friend…"

"Armor-rr," Haar growled. "Armor-rr for the man-flesh that would fill it."

Soft-flesh glanced to One-eye, then back to Haar. "Yes, exactly. Armor."

Not as miserable as Cutter, Haar thought. *Blood from a stone, that one.*

"Lanterns," Last-eater added. Whatever that was.

Haar ignored him.

One-eye spoke next. He sounded the most like a Wulver.

"Haar," he gruffed, "can you lead us to what we seek?"

The Wulver turned away from that one eye staring at him. It made him uncomfortable. Haar knew something was going on. Not far, his mate and her young sisters had killed a man-dog as a gift to Haar. *To raise the status of her pups*, he surmised. The pack leader had many mates and sired many pups. He looked to Grizzer to help him decide what to do.

Grizzer had been waiting for just that. He strode close, nudged Haar. The pack leader grumbled, "R-rr I know what you want, Grizzer-rr." *You want me to say 'yes' and then kill them. Take everything they have.*

As the pack leader contemplated the offer, wondering if he should sound the howl to attack, a strange thing happened. Voices called to him from the high branches. Tree devil voices, in unison, high-pitched and whispery.

"Maa'rii, who throws fates, is the one who took the sword," they told him. Haar's eyes darted about – it seemed like the man-fleshed hadn't heard the voice.

Haar grunted. *Sounds about right.* He knew well of the bonethrower Maa'rii and also of his mate, Lusii, a pack leader. He couldn't help but snarl to himself at the thought of a female ruling a Wulver pack. *I hate those two and their greedy pack: the fires they will not share and the chains that keep the tree devils out.* The voices went on.

"Bring down the chains."

Haar gazed at the man-flesh's faces as they whispered amongst themselves, using many words he didn't quite understand about "lines" and "control." *They don't hear the words of the tree-devils. Man-flesh's ears are weak.*

Haar growled to interrupt. He addressed Soft-flesh, although he had more respect for One-eye.

"R-rr the Lusii-wulves found something. They pr-rr-otect man-flesh things they find. Value them. They will not shar-rre."

"Where are these Lusii-wulves located?" Soft-flesh asked.

Grizzer growled out an answer. "The Lusii-wulves take slaves," he lied.

We take slaves.

"That's wher-rre your man-flesh will be. They kill some."

We kill some.

"They use their-rr fire to burn the flesh."

Hate fire. Grizzer spoke well.

The tree devils' voices rose up again. "Lusii-wulves have an axe. They cut us and torture us. They're brutal and they deserve to die."

"Shut-up, you deser-rrve it," Haar grumbled back.

One-eye cocked his head, squinted that one eye of his. "What was that?"

Haar hesitated, then he made up his mind. "Thr-rree swords and thr-rree armor-rrs," he growled at last. *For those I would take.* "Thr-rree swords for the sword you seek. Thr-rree armors for your-rr friend and your-rr trespasses."

Soft-flesh didn't agree right away, like he did the other times. He turned to One-eye again, but One-eye was staring at Haar. He stared at Haar long and funny, and Grizzer too, for a moment. Haar stared back, trying to get a sense of him. *Hard to figure out, man-fleshes, behind the eyes,* thought Haar. *And this man-flesh only has one of them.*

One-eye scratched at a big scar down the tough half of his face. "We must discuss, in private," he grumbled. Haar showed his agreement by backing away with Grizzer. He pricked his ears in anticipation of hearing everything. Haar hoped they wouldn't use any more words he didn't know, but right away they did. *It's always Soft-flesh.* The metallic one talked about lines and control again with One-eye, while Last-eater looked on because he is submissive and talking might get his tongue cut out. He'd heard of that happening. The thought made the pack leader shiver. One-eye shook his head when Soft-flesh said something about "opportunity" – a word that Haar understood very well.

The tree devils interrupted Haar's eavesdropping. They had another high message for Wulver ears only.

"Not now!" Haar growled. But they whispered at him anyway.

"Take the fire, carry it to the Chainmaker and burn him down. Burn him down and take his man-tools."

Haar grunted. *I don't take orders from tree devils.* But the prospect was not without its benefits. The Chainmaker was by far the most dangerous of the tree devils, and a bane to the Haar-wulves.

Soft-flesh approached. He slid off the metal covering one hand. "Deal," he said. "And I'm feeling generous tonight, Haar. There is a way you can obtain more swords and more armor for your tribe, but you will have to wait for it." Soft-flesh extended his hand, the one without the metal. "Exactly how many Wulvers do you command?"

Haar paused, uncertain about the gesture.

"Scratch it," Grizzer gruffed.

Why would Soft-flesh give me more? Haar felt as though he was missing something.

"Scratch it," Grizzer gruffed again, "or I will."

Haar jerked his head to Grizzer and snarled, baring his teeth. "He's going to want something," he growled.

The younger Wulver didn't back down though, like he usually does. *Not good.*

Grizzer snarled back. "Give them slaves if they want mor-rre, and get mor-rre in return than the Baruush offer."

Haar turned his head back to Soft-flesh. The hand still hung in the air in front of him. Slowly, Haar raised his own paw-hand. He took the man-flesh's palm in his.

Sooo soft. A droplet of drool formed at the corner of Haar's mouth. It took all his strength to ignore it. "R-rr deal," Haar said, scraping his claws gently across the flesh.

And the pact was made.

Chapter XXVII
Sit

(Amot)

THE SHE-WOLF SLIPPED farther into the tunnel and disappeared into the dimness, smooth as a shadow. Amot always prided himself on his ability to read animals. But a Wulver, well...

The hollowness in Amot's chest wouldn't go away. It'd been there since he'd passed through the chain mesh and entered the glade. And as he crawled after her on all fours, barely into the tunnel, his mind churned with the ramifications of his decision to follow.

The signs had all seemed right. But Amot wasn't about to make himself an easy target. He glanced back. The eyes that had been watching from the next den over blinked out and disappeared. In a split-second decision, he crept back to the woodpile and wrenched the axe from the chopping block. If he had to fight off half the Wulver pack to get out of the glade, and then half the forest to get back to the base camp, he'd rather not have to do it bare-fisted. The scout lightly ran his thumb across the blade. *Sharp*. He crept back to the den opening.

Other than the fresh tracks on the ground and the disturbed earth at the sides, the entrance to the den was not much different from the dugout he'd examined at Dead Gnarl's Knoll. It was barely large enough for a man to squeeze through. The she-wolf, although taller than Amot when upright, had a narrow build and a funny way of elongating herself. Now it was his turn.

Amot peered into the den. Ambient firelight flickered at the bottom of a steep descent, where the tunnel bent right. The scout clambered through the opening, nudging the axe just ahead and bracing himself so as not to slide. The warmth of the crackling fire wafted his face, while at the same time a fresh, cool breeze flowed past him from behind.

Inside smelled like earth and damp dog, mixed with the scent of burning pine. Howler immediately came to mind. Amot paused. "Be safe, boy," he whispered to his spaniel, in spirit. It occurred to him that the dog might be respecting marked Wulver territory and keeping well away. A wise choice. But he couldn't deny that something in his gut felt rotten about not finding Howler. Something in his gut felt rotten to the core.

Rotating to one side, Amot squeezed through a pinch-point in the tunnel, blocked by a tree root as thick as his leg. He wriggled along the curvature, then peered around the bend. The tunnel opened to an earthen chamber, a hollowed-out den with a central fire pit. Another stack of firewood, smaller, sat near the opening. Three freshly killed hares hung on the snapped branches of a bloodied post.

The she-wolf was waiting for him, alone. The heat of the blaze swept over Amot as he forced himself into the chamber, leaving behind the axe. Newly-placed wood burned high. Hairs on his bare arms curled as he crawled a bit closer.

Through the flames on the opposite side of the pit, Amot's guide sat with a forward lean, cross-legged. Her pose appeared most un-wolflike, her greeting not but a stare. The two eyed each other with caution, fire roaring between them.

Amot glanced left and right to size up the place. It was big enough to hold a cozy score of Wulvers, and must've hollowed out most of the hillock. The wide and roughly circular base of the chamber had a tapered ceiling and a hole at the top to funnel rising smoke up and away. Elsewhere, gnawed roots protruded from the walls and ceiling, while woven mats of leather cord and deer hides lay scattered over the bare earth. Other simple belongings were strewn about: flint tools for preparing meat, ratty blankets for lying on, and clay bowls lined earthen shelves. Small, crude figures of woven bark hung here and there, firelit and rotating slowly in the convected air. They depicted wolves and Wulvers, Stouts and Outlanders, forest animals, trees, and symbols of unknown origin. Dug out pockets held all manner of worthless throwaways from the civilized world. A collection of crude spears leaned against the wall.

In the side tunnel to the left, a yearling lay in partial slumber, eyes barely open, jaw resting on a single paw.

The Wilder rose to his feet, slightly hunched.

The yearling's head jerked up for moment, eyes fixed on the intruder. *Wulver or wolf?* It was impossible to tell just looking at it in isolation. But its fur was as white as the she-wolf's. Amot looked to his guide again. The fire cast a red glow upon her face, and the shadows revealed the true extent of her wolfish features. Very little about her appearance was human. Her face was slender and long with a wolf's snout, smoothed fur, and perfect symmetry.

The young Wulver gave the she-wolf a questioning glance. She, in turn, responded with a reaffirming nod. Back down went the head. The yearling's eyes blinked and narrowed, but never quite closed for long.

The she-wolf turned her attention back to Amot. She seemed to project an air of refinement in her long and lean body proportions. Her coat was even-toned, silky and healthy looking. Younger days had passed her by though – that much was evident from her eyes. They were not eager, playful, or full-of-expectation. No, they reflected something somber and knowing.

Acceptance... intuition. But there was something more to them, something that reached further beyond her canine appearances.

What does she know that I don't?

With inviting arms, the she-wolf waved Amot in closer. Her clawed finger traced out the path for him.

Walk around the fire to me, Amot gathered. He almost fell for it, but caught himself.

"Come, *Kirrth*," she compelled. "Sit wrirrth me. Wre talk. Just tarrlk."

The heat was sweltering. *That's how the stories all start*, Amot told himself. He wiped sweat from his brow, stalling. *And they don't end good. They don't end good at all.* His heart began to thump as he considered the danger he could be in. Wulvers could be piling into the entrance tunnel to block his escape. *What does she really want with me?*

The she-wolf cocked her head as she had before, at the creek, and examined his face. "Such color-rrful man-flesh." Her words came off not the slightest bit eerie. And he wasn't sure about the thin smile she wore. He didn't know if he was flushed from the heat or if his colors were showing through. Amot widened his stance.

"What i-rrs the matter, *Kirrth*?" she said. "Trell mre."

Is she mocking me? A shuffling noise sounded from the entrance tunnel. Amot casually stepped aside, back to the wall beside the spears, to deny access to them. He eyed the axe. It'd become a liability.

"Wrill you not sit writh me? Come sit writh *Lusii*." The she-wolf patted the earth beside her.

The stories, the legends – they came back to Amot in a rush. *Hunger. Deception. Shroud's Well, they eat children.* Amot responded with a raised voice. "Why should I? So you can rip out my throat? How can I trust a wolf?"

The Wulver jerked her head back.

"Hrow crould you thrink such a thring, man-flesh? I helped yrou in the forrest."

"Did you?" Droplets of sweat beaded on Amot's forehead, rolled down his brow. It wasn't just the feverish heat that caused them. If the Wulver's intent was to lure him into the chamber and devour his flesh like the wolf-men of legends did, she would attack soon and others would follow. Why else would she call him "man-flesh"? Images of battle flashed across his mind.

The scout cast shooting glances between the she-wolf and the entrance tunnel. He had it all planned out: grab the axe, then leap across the fire pit to gain the element of surprise on his host before being outnumbered. Then back to grab a spear and defend the entrance, taking out the first Wulver to come through. Others following would be blocked. If overwhelmed, he could snuff out the fire with the she-wolf's dead body, scale the sloped ceiling by the protruding roots, then escape through the smoke hole.

No matter what, he would prevail. He did not fear.

The she-wolf's eyes fell to the entrance. She took a long look at where the axe was stashed. The handle jutted out.

She knows.

Her shoulders dropped. She sighed heavily, bowing her canine snout. Amot recognized the look. It was the same demoted face Howler wore after being shamed. Then she raised a hand-paw to her forehead, covered her eyes. *Is this a ploy? Is she gathering her resolve?*

It was the yearling that broke the tension. Eyes now fully closed and eyelids pumping, the young Wulver let out a series of small, high-pitched "woofs" and a pathetic growl. Amot glanced over to see the whelp's body twitching. He couldn't help but smirk.

Motherly fondness in her eyes, the she-wolf swung her gaze to the yearling. She spoke in an excited whisper.

"Sick'em Maa'iing," she said. "Go get'em."

Amot sighed. *How could she possibly be a monster?* A wise question, and not a moment too soon.

"Chasing rabbits?" he said.

She turned her gaze to the Wilder. The kindness never left her eyes. "Hre's a good chaserr, and a grood little tr-rracker too."

"I bet he is." Amot felt ashamed. *Silver platter*, he thought. His speech was broken. "I'm sorry. I..." He shook his head and sighed. "It's just that..."

"Ver-rry wrell," she said. "If you wrill not sit, be gone writh you then, Man-flesh. Back to the wroods for you." The she-wolf leaned sideways, fixed her gaze on the axe, shook her head.

"Hrow am I supposed to trrust a man-flesh w-r-aving my own axe around at me!"

Her words were hurt, angry, and... perfectly faked.

"But—"

The she-wolf raised a staying hand – no excuses. She stretched out and pulled a mat closer to her. Like an insistent girl, she patted it gently.

"Sit," she insisted, with motherly firmness. The she-wolf tilted her head down slightly, her gaze steady.

It was the first time a canine had suggested to Amot that *he* be the one to sit.

Amot decided to be a good man-flesh and obey.

CHAPTER XXVIII

FIRE AND WULVER

(Amot)

Amot moved the axe to lean against the earthen wall with the spears, then took his seat beside the she-wolf. New logs snapped and popped in the fire pit as he made himself comfortable. He swung his gaze to the Wulver.

"Your name is Lusii, then?" he asked.

"Yres, Lusii." The she-wolf's voice was very much a growl, but the more she spoke the more her words improved. She sniffed at him with her nose in the air, the way a regular dog might.

"My name is Amot." The scout raised his palms to the fire to gauge the heat.

Lusii stopped sniffing and nodded. "Kirrth."

"Yes, Kith ranger. You knew before I told you."

She turned her gaze to watch the flames. "The heartwoods whrisper. So Amot, whry yrou trust me now?"

The scout hesitated. "Well, you led me from danger. And I can see you are good natured and that you have strong bonds with your family. Most of all, if you were anywhere near as vile as the Wulvers in songs and tales, you would've made all sorts of outlandish promises to convince me to stay. You did the exact opposite when you saw that I was… uncomfortable. That is why I trust you."

She shot him a sidelong glance. Orange and red reflected in her eyes. "Is that whrat man-fleshes horrwl on about all night? Hrow bad Wulver-rs arre?"

"It's not like that…" The Wilder turned away, fumbling his words. Actually, it was exactly like that and he knew it. By the Wulver's expression, she knew it too.

"Hrrmph," was her response, staring back at the flames. "Wre do the same."

"About us?" Amot said. "About… man-fleshes?"

"No, no," she admitted, then sighed heavily. She turned to him, placed a paw-hand on his shoulder. "Not srro much. Sometimes. It's Wulver-rrs, always Wulvers – wrre hrowl just rike the man-fleshes about *other* Wulvers. Bad packs. Bad stories. Haar-wulves."

"But not your pack?"

She withdrew her paw-hand. "They hrowl about us too, forr sur-rre." The she-wolf scoffed, shook her head, then changed the subject entirely. "Whrry are yrou here, Kirrth?"

Amot shifted in his seat, unsure what to tell her. "I'm here for a very good reason."

Lusii snorted. "Sro are the heartwoods. So is Haar." She shook her head. "Irrr… don't like their grood reasons though. Nrot grood at all."

"I am looking for something lost." Amot leaned in close, spoke in a low voice to convey the seriousness of the situation. "Something very important."

"Hrrmph," she growled in response. It was an empty growl, the feigned complaint of a woman masking her appreciation of what she must have taken for a small sign of affection. Lusii adjusted her sitting position, and in so doing inched a little closer to Amot, nonchalantly. Her fur brushed up against the skin of his arm. He wanted to rub her side, give it a solid pat, and call her a good girl. Amot wondered if she, in turn, felt the urge to nuzzle his hand for a scritch, or lick his face. *Not likely.* Dogs learn that sort of social behavior through interacting with their masters. Lusii had no master.

She looked Amot directly in the eyes. "The Chainmaker shraid you would come."

"Chainmaker?" Most unexpected. Amot tilted his head, fur-rowed his brow at her. "Who is the Chainmaker? How did he know I was coming?"

"The Chainmaker is the r'one who did not say you wrould be such an ass." She forced a throaty growl that ended in a choppy laugh, then continued. "Maa'rii says the wrorld is not frull of answers for the taking. It just is as it is. The Chainmaker knows what hre knows."

The she-wolf turned her gaze back to the fire. "That is hrow Ir knew to rlook for yrou."

Amot had no idea how to respond to that, so he defaulted to the obvious.

"Did the Chainmaker make the chains around your glade?"

"Of cour-rrse, whro else?"

"To keep the Hurlorns out?"

She jerked her head back. "To keep the *heartwoods* out. You man-fleshes arsk some rearly obrvious qruestions."

"Can I meet the Chainmaker?" Amot asked.

"You hrave to. Hre has whrat yrou seek."

The news hit Amot like a wood plank. *Unbelievable luck.* It was almost too easy. And no fighting. *This could fix everything.* The scout took a deep breath, let the air out slowly. Without thinking, he patted her on the back. Pet her, more like. Then he caught himself. "Oh, sorry." He retrieved his hand.

The Wulver shot him a strange look. "Yrou can relax nrow," she said. "Yrou are too uptight."

Lusii was right.

"Can we go see the Chainmaker now?" Amot asked.

"No," she said flatly.

Amot nodded his acceptance. After all, it was the middle of the night.

"Who is Maa'rii?"

"Yrou will see."

"Any orther questions, man-flesh? Irr'm getting hrungry."

Amot assumed correctly that her comment was not a reference to *him* being dinner.

Lusii rubbed the leather over Amot's stomach. "Aren't yrou hrungry, man-flesh?"

Amot was a tad unsure about Wulver fare. He looked to the hanging hares and then to the fire. *Good signs,* he thought.

"A bit," he replied. He definitely was hungry again. Apart from his rushed breakfast and the quick snack he'd downed just to keep himself going after landing in the meadow, Amot hadn't eaten.

The scout very nearly blurted out, "Where is the sword now?" But before the words came out, he stopped himself, realizing that he hadn't yet told her what he was looking for. *Does she actually know?* A passing thought came to mind, that her comment about the Chainmaker having exactly what he was looking for might have been a clever lure to gain information. He thought of another question instead.

"Can you describe what was found?"

"Nro. After wre eat. Final question."

Amot paused for a long moment. There were at least fifty different things he wanted to know about the Chainmaker and his whereabouts, and another fifty about Wulvers, their history, and how they survived being driven away from civilization to live among the ghost pines. But rather than pursue any of them, he decided to revisit a minor detail that the she-wolf had avoided telling him.

"You said 'Bad packs. Bad stories,'" he prodded. "I want to learn about your pack… your stories."

"Hrrmph," she snorted. "Stories ar-rre either bad or there's nothring to tell."

"When did you start using fire?" *That can't be bad.* "Everyone who knows anything about Wulvers says they hate fire."

A sly smirk grew across her lips, a smirk that bared her teeth. She seemed to like the idea of the question. "The man-fleshes ar-rre right," she said. "Wulvers hrate fire. But some hrate ghost pines more, and other Wulver packs more, and er-rr the cold bite of deep winter more still."

"And your pack?"

"We hrate *Haar* the most, and Haar hrates us the most. Hre is the strongest. All orthers scattered. We leave him be. He is the r'one you fear. He r-rrips out our throats, and he r-rrips out the throats of man-fleshes too."

She looked away.

"Many thr-rroats. Some fled the for-rrest, never to return. We hrope for them. Some he caught. Hre makes them slaves. Some join him."

"Haar sounds very bad."

"Hre is the one man-fleshes hrowl about. His father-rr the same. Takes man-fleshes for slaves, or worse. Tr-rrades them to other man-fleshes for blades. Cuts our thr-rroats with the blades if he smells us near."

Lusii took a long look at her offspring, then glared at Amot, eyes ablaze with firelight.

"My pack was sur-rrounded, to the last r'eight. Desperate. Two ran to break fr-rree. Haar-wulves cut them down with blades. Wre had nowher-rre to run but up a big tree. Tried to scratch our-rr way up the bark. Couldn't. But the tree…"

"A ghost pine?" Amot said. She gave him a so-so nod.

"It helped us. The Chainmaker helped us. Picked six up and stomped on a Haar-wulf. Screamed so loud, Haar-wulves tucked their-rr ears and darted off, hrowling in the night."

The Wulver took a long minute to withdraw from her story. She stared into the crackling fire, eyes far off. The flames had died to embers. Amot felt a draft of cool air, small relief from the unrelenting heat that had filled the underground cavity.

"But where did the fire come from?" Amot said.

She continued to stare at the hot coals in the pit. "Chainmaker. The Chainmaker taught us fire. Hre knows everythring about the bur-rrn."

"I have never heard of a Hurlorn starting fires."

"The Chainmaker is nrot like orther heartwoods."

Amot sat back, leaned against the earth wall. *And that is the story of how a Wulver pack discovered fire.* He felt as though he'd learned a great secret, a secret that might shatter standing legends and change the way people thought of Wulvers. The scout prodded for more details, but all he was able to get out of Lusii was that since then, Haar's pack no longer bothered them. And ever since, the ghost pines kept their distance as well. Besides that, her pack now cooked their food. She said they could hardly eat raw flesh now, and the young had become even more accustomed to it.

Amot nodded slowly. "I grew up in a forest where the Hurlorns are good to man-fleshes. They would be good to your Wulvers too."

The she-wolf's eyes lit up. "Is this for-rrest ver-rry far?"

"Not very far. I could take you there… across the river. We call it Deepweald Forest."

"My pack wrould like that."

"What is your pack called?"

"Lusii-wulves." She put a paw-hand on the scout's shoulder again, this time leveraging it for support to prop herself up on hind legs. When standing, she glanced down at him.

"It is time, Amot."

With that, Lusii lifted her head, yelped to where the yearling lay sleeping. The young Wulver rose with a jolt, quickly glanced left and right, and responded to Lusii with a "rawl-rawl-rawl," tail wagging. *A male*, Amot observed. Even in full view, there was little to distinguish this "good little tracker" from a wolf, at least not by firelight. Two younger whelps from deeper in the same tunnel bounded up beside the white pup. Their coats were similar, but marked with a spattering of grey and black over the white.

Next, the she-wolf looked straight up, howled at the ceiling.

"Wrait here," she told Amot. Lusii left the scout with a sturdy branch in hand to stoke the fire, then disappeared into a side tunnel. Amot added a few logs. Soon after, the she-wolf returned with more mats and more hare posts. When Amot was done flipping over charring logs and poking the new ones into place, he wiped the sweat from his brow, slid away from the fire to cool off. Before long, snarls and grunts sounded from the main entrance, followed by a steady stream of Wulvers spilling into the chamber on all fours. Several came through the opening; adults and juveniles alike. The original pack of six had grown in numbers. They circled the chamber at first, keeping a safe distance from Amot, only ever approaching Lusii from the opposite side. Amot kept to himself as they sniffed at the air and shot squinty glances at him through the wavering flames, all the while reacquainting with one another through friendly snout nudges and tail sniffs.

Some Wulvers carried a hare or two on a stick clenched in their teeth, until they stood up and hooked their catches onto one of the new posts that Lusii had fetched. Others bore autumn apples in woven baskets, or an awkward armful of berry-laden branches that they passed to others in greeting. Amot didn't get one. A silver and black Wulver dragged the hind portions of a deer behind her as she entered.

At some point, each of the adults barked or grumbled a greeting to Lusii, and the she-wolf in turn growled back at them. She nodded her approval at whatever the offering. Unlike the adults, the juveniles and yearlings seemed to operate on the premise that anything goes. They ignored their elders as they chased one another or sparred over a shredded blanket. Some even brushed by the quiet scout, unconcerned.

A full dozen adult Wulvers had crowded the chamber – standing room only in some quarters. Latecomers had barely enough space to squat a comfortable distance from the blaze.

A particularly strong looking one, whom Amot took to be the dominant male, entered last. Exactly why the pack was Lusii's and not this Wulver's escaped the scout. Pack members made way for the hulking man-wolf to pass. He took his seat on the other side of Lusii, opposite to where Amot sat. The alpha male eyed the Wilder from head to toe, as though sizing up the competition. He shared a hushed and growly exchange with the she-wolf. Amot couldn't make out the gnarring tongue they used, but he could still read the she-wolf's insistent demeanor against the alpha-male's stiff stance, scowling rebuttals, and the way he raised and lowered his voice.

She's convincing him of something, Amot told himself. *And he's not being particularly receptive.*

While their discussion continued, one of the whelps, who'd been watching Amot curiously, stopped at a safe distance to sniff him out.

Amot eyed the pup with the same kind eyes he reserved for Howler. "Waiting for an invitation?" he asked. The white Wulver sat, watched silent, attentive. The scout couldn't remember the name Lusii had mentioned.

"I hear you're a good tracker," Amot said. He reached out to pet the pup, but the young canine scooted backwards to avoid his hand. So, instead, Amot held it there, casually outstretched, for the Wulver to investigate on his own terms.

The room went quieter. Not silent, but definitely quieter. Without taking his eyes off the pup, Amot realized that the activity in the chamber had also dropped off. He'd drawn an audience. That audience included the alpha male, his conversation with Lusii having paused.

One cautious step after another, the pup inched forward, stretched out its neck, then gave the hand a quick sniff. A moment later came a wet-nosed nudge, then the yearling began to lick Amot's fingers. Full-growns grumbled and muttered to one another coarsely, in low tones.

The scout flipped his hand over, palm up. A Wulver gasped. Amot followed through uninterrupted, and tried to scritch the young Wulver behind ears like he would Howler. The yearling snapped at the hand, jerked back. Angry snarls arose from the resident Wulvers. Amot's eyes darted about the growing ruction. Some dropped into a prowling stance, others bared their teeth and growled. All eyes fell now upon him. Angry eyes. Wolf eyes.

Amot ignored their stares and their growls, and his own racing heartbeat, and his own tensed muscles. He focused on the young.

Oblivious to the attention and the perceived risk by the pack elders, a minute later the pup was back, romping and playful. Dashing forwards and back again, the pup suddenly invented a new game of keeping itself just out of reach of Amot's outstretched hand.

Amot twitched a finger, the pup sprang back. Full-grown Wulvers let out barking laughs. And when the pup inched close to the scout's hand, Amot feigned a quick grab. The pup sprang away again, then charged back snapping. Wulvers roared at the display, and even more laughter erupted when the other pups joined in on the fun. The play evolved to the point where Amot did his best to politely keep all of the Wulver pups and yearlings from jumping all over him and gnawing at his shins. He exchanged a quick glance with Lusii. She smiled thinly at him. The alpha male's arms were folded across his chest, his expression pinched and unconvinced.

~

With the entertainment having peaked and then settled to become the new norm, the full-growns took to skinning hares. A few skillful movements were all they needed for each: a claw slice here, another there, and a few strong tugs. The deer took longer, but with three on it at once, they still made short work of the carcass. The Wulver next to Lusii fed sweet-smelling herbs to the fire from a bundle that he carried in his satchel.

Amot and the Lusii-wulves feasted though the night. And although he didn't say much, partly due to a new kind of dizziness he experienced from the smoke, the scout's spirits were lifted greatly in that firelit hole, deep in the ground. And when the Wulvers around him barked and howled in chorus, he wanted to howl along with them. He gained an appreciation for their language as they carried on, growling and harr-harring until the light of dawn. The Wulvers tended to express themselves mostly in a gestural manner, mixed with a scattering of grunts and "man-flesh" words. He noticed that tone of voice often meant far more than the actual words spoken, even to the point of contradiction.

All went hush when Lusii began to tell of a legend. She claimed the story had never been heard by man-fleshes, about a pack that lived in the mountains among giants. And then she told another she said was new, about a forest where the trees helped a Wulver to catch a deer. She favored Amot with a sly smile during that one.

By feast's end, Amot experienced the pull of a new brotherhood. He felt wholly connected to these man-wolves, and fully accepted by the extended Lusii pack. And when the fire burned down to coals again, with the fresh wood in the chamber spent, the scout finally laid himself to rest on a woven mat beside it.

On an overfull stomach, his mind churned with thoughts that never could have existed inside his head before that day, or anyone else's head for that matter. The whitecoat yearling and a few other pups nuzzled up against his side. In the end, the Kith ranger dozed off, clumped together with the lot of them. *As* one of them. He didn't wake until the mid-morning light beamed through the smoke hole.

CHAPTER XXIX
BREACH
(Valkyries)

ATWINGS DIPPED BELOW the morning cloud cover, then leaned over the side to fix her eyes on the terrain beneath her. As Spree descended through the misty haze, a strip of thin and sickly pines sharpened into view. They edged a meandering tributary of the Malevuin River. The wind rider glanced left to verify her bearing against the southern tip of the rocky tor, where they'd set up camp. *This is it.*

She coaxed her gryphon to tip its wing, then leaned hard into the banking turn. Oriented due north now, Spree leveled out to a smooth glide, just above the watercourse. Catwings urged her mount to beat its heavy wings and propel them forward. *Faster. Faster.* She scanned the tree line to her right as they whizzed by, scouting for patrols entering the forest or Wulvers leaving it. She saw nothing more than a few stray deer.

Jagged hills soon appeared in the distance, cradling the far shores of Dim Lake as it stretched out towards her. Having reached the northwestern tip of Whisperwood, Catwings veered east and skirted the forest's northern edge, keeping to within a few wingspans of the outlying branches. Far to her right, above the treetops, peaked the twin towers of Harrow's Gate. They marked the city-state's southern border.

The wind rider dipped down again to run the tree line, to keep low and out of sight. Well within Harrowian territory, she couldn't risk being spotted for anything longer than a blurred minute.

Electra rode the cold streams of winds over the Mire Steps – a small line of hills jutting west out of Deepweald.

Nothing, the knightmaiden told herself, again. *Where could they be?* The rock-feeling in her gut caused Galewind to dip down and circle back one more time. She'd retraced the lost valkyries' flight path as best she could, to no avail. Into the turn, gusting updrafts beat against her, whipping her hair into her face as she slipped between the two highest peaks of the Mire Steps. *Rainsong had to have made it at least this far west*, she surmised.

Beneath her, the lowest-lying areas showed a mess of bog patches and deadwood, while the higher ground was steeply sloped, thick with brambles, rocky underneath and littered with fallen trees. *It's impossible to spot anything in this*. Ashes splotchy pattern of grey and white wouldn't make the task any easier, either. And the wind. The wind dried out the knightmaiden's eyes like she couldn't believe. She'd forgotten about that minor annoyance of prolonged flight.

On Galewind's command, Electra banked low around a hilltop. The knightmaiden called out to the hills, but her hoarse and airy voice was lost to the winds. The gryphon must have sensed her purpose though, for Electra let loose a piercing wail. Galewind pricked her ears, waited for a response from below. A call, perhaps, from Rainsong's strong and carrying voice. Anything. Electra cocked her head, gazing at the ground with a single eagle eye.

Another bleak circuit, Galewind realized. Eyes suddenly bleary, she closed them tight for a long moment, let the darkness absorb the shot of pain that charged through her. The pain of another loss under her watch. She let out a heavy sigh, leaned forward.

"Up and away," she rasped into her Gold's ear, stroking the gryphon's nape. Electra cried again, then swung westward, beating at the air with her great wings. They climbed high again, into the morning air.

Rainsong awoke again, in a jolt. She'd dreamt of the eagle's cry. No, a gryphon. A Gold to be precise. *Electra.*

She jerked to a sitting position, called out, but only a grating sound issued forth. She tilted her gaze to the sky. A dark shape rose into low-hanging clouds. Rainsong pushed herself to stand. She scanned the skies, expectant.

Only, the shape didn't reappear. She called out again, rasping. Her bad leg teetered. Stiff and sore as it was, she held her balance. After a long minute, the wind rider swung her gaze to Ashes. The Harpy's eagle eye stared back at her. Relief poured over Rainsong.

"You're awake!" she gasped, high-pitched and wheezy. "I was so worried."

Ashes scrambled awkwardly to her feet, ruffled, then took a bad step on the rocky slope. Her wing shot out to counterbalance.

"Easy now," Rainsong rasped. She gave the gryphon's head a firm rub as the beast found its footing. "You'll be all right."

Instinctively, the wind rider checked over her mount, head to tail. "Your right wing," she whispered. Ashes was favoring it. Not only that, she was clearly caught. A chill ran up Rainsong's spine.

"Norwin's Breeze," said the wind rider. "I have to cut Danus loose."

Stormbringer swept overhead of the unlikely pair – a middle-aged queensman in full armor but practically unarmed, plus an over-sized ranger. Both were attempting to be stealthy. *Their scent likely gave them away long ago*, she thought. Another twenty strides and the two of them would be at the entrance to the cave – the valkyries' first choice for a base, until discovering it was already occupied.

Wulvers. White Wulvers, at that, of the kind spotted through the Djinxarai farseeing contraption, according to Galewind. *However reliable that thing is.* The knightmaiden had explained to the rangers how the device converts sound to imagery somehow – at least that's what one of the projectionists had told her.

Ladybird swung around to begin the next loop. Stormbringer scoffed to herself as her mount tilted into the wide turn. *I don't care how that Djinxarai thing works. If it was so great, they could've told us exactly where to look.* She'd already decided that these man-wolves couldn't be the same ones they were looking for. Not unless they'd bolted straight north-northwest the second they grabbed the sword, then ferried it across a river, only to climb to a height unimaginable for Wulvers. All so they could hide in a cave. Actually, Stormbringer knew nothing about these beasts. It could be the sort of thing they do. *But why would they go through all of the trouble?* she asked herself. It made no sense. *No, it isn't them*, she knew, *no matter how you angle it. Nonetheless, due diligence demands…*

Ladybird flattened out, lining up their approach to their second-choice location for a forward operating base. The spearmaiden peered ahead, shook her head. *Nothing out of the ordinary.* Normally she wouldn't check so often, but the location was lower in elevation than she would've preferred, was situated close to Harrowian territory, and lacked adequate cover to hide their stores.

She instinctively cast a glance towards Dim Lake's Iron Tower and the city nestled around it on the lakeshore. *Harrow's spies, where are you?*

A sudden feeling of cold gripped her core. What she beheld across the flood plain shocked her, as new as the light of day. *It can't be.* She did a double take. *It is.* Suddenly, her heartbeat raced.

A regiment had amassed in the night, just outside the city. This was no exercise. Harrow would soon be on the march. *But where to?*

Spree swooped up to clear a line of alders, jutting out of Whisperwood and into the flood plain, then quickly dipped down on the other side. "Whoah!" Catwings cried, gasping at what she saw. Adrenaline flushed through her body. *Dead ahead!*

"Spree," she called feebly, veering into the forest. Branches lashed as the Harpy broke the tree line. Tilting and dipping, the heavy flap of wings diverted their course at every obstacle. The wind rider brought the Harpy down in a small clearing. She drew in a quick breath, let go the reins and put a hand to her chest.

She'd spotted heads turn her way, but did they see her? If so, did they know what they were looking at?

Catwings knew what she had seen, at least.

Harrowian guardsmen, six or eight. But what was that with them? Two enormous shadows from what she could tell, sweeping up the slope from Dim River. Catwings took a long breath, let it out slowly.

Giants, she realized. *I'd better tell Stormbringer. Harrow is sending a pair of giants into Whisperwood…*

What do they know?

CHAPTER XXX
BLOOD ON THE WIND
(Amot)

AMOT DIDN'T WAKE easily.

Before the dawn, he'd ignored the rolling growls of the she-wolf from the adjoining tunnel. And when the rough tongue of one of the pups licked his cheek, Amot'd rolled over to bundle up in his cloak and bury his face in his arms. The pup gave in, went back to lazing by his side. Later, much later, a rasping voice jarred the scout awake, rattling his eardrums – the alpha-male, the Wulver who'd been at Lusii's side during most of the night's festivities. Amot's eyes were too glued shut to open straightaway, but his ears were keen to every sound.

Lusii had referred to her oversized mate as "Shaman" and also "Maa'rii." The two Wulvers were fond of one another, that much was clear. A close couple. The shaman sucked in heavy breaths between his rough words. He huffed them out as he spoke.

"I have been most busy in the night… Man-flesh… divining visions… of what will come for our pack." This Wulver's speech, although slow and deliberate, was more refined and clearer than Lusii's. The alpha-male nudged the scout's shoulder. "Ar-rre you awake?"

Amot himself stirred, while the warm bodies of the slumbering pups lay undisturbed against his side. He was comfortable and wanted to stay that way. His lack of a complete response wasn't enough to deter Maa'rii.

Perhaps because the shaman knew Amot was cognizant, he simply carried on.

"The Chainmaker," he gruffed. "We must confer-rr with the fier-rry heartwood… A great thing happens today."

Amot perked up at that. "The Chainmaker?" he repeated, voice feeble, rubbing his eyelids. *I need to know this.* The earthen chamber was dim and blurry when he rolled over and pried his eyes open. His head felt fuzzy.

The Wilder's first sight was a cutting beam of white light through the smoke hole, illuminating the pit. Next, the alpha-male came into focus, looming over him, hunched and imposing. His fur was mostly light grey, with charcoal streaks on his haunches and two silver patches above his eyes. He seemed to have grown since just last night, or his fur had puffed out. The shaman's gaze was steady on the scout.

"Yes," Amot continued. "Lusii told me about him… the one who makes all the chains."

The hulking Wulver shrugged. "Who else?"

The she-wolf called out from a side tunnel with her usual growls.

"Mor-r-r-ning light shines. Maa'iing! Rarr'sha! Naw'naw! Get up!"

The she-wolf ambled into the chamber and propped herself up on hind legs, partly stooped. She approached Amot and her younglings.

Maa'rii reached over Amot, prodded the pups. "Get up," he repeated.

The young Wulvers promptly sprang to their paws, bounded to Lusii in a jumble, then leapt and danced about her legs. The she-wolf growled praise as she nuzzled each in turn. She herded them to the tunnel and shooed them out of the chamber.

"Blow the smroke off y-r-ourselves," she called after them as they scrabbled up the slope.

Amot regarded Maa'rii. "A lively bunch."

The shaman grunted, eyeing the tunnel from his place amidst the mats, sitting casually. "They run in circles most of the time."

The she-wolf dropped down to all fours, glided around the pit to her usual spot next to Maa'rii, then made herself comfortable lying beside him. "They'll be back," she said, resting her head on his lap. Amot addressed the shaman.

"You said a great thing happens today."

Maa'rii nodded back with all-convincing seriousness. "Yes… I saw it in the fire." He glanced down with tender eyes at his mate.

"Lusii… you beheld it with me while Man-flesh dozed." He scratched the she-wolf behind the ears. "The flames danced like battle, didn't they?"

Lusii gazed up into the shaman's eyes. "Threy did. I-r-r liked that. Tell h-r-im what happened after."

The Wulver sawed out a laugh, turned to face the scout.

"Yes!" he gruffed. "Of course! Whrat happened after was more than before! I saw that same battle again in truth-smoke when the fire died, and the image came to me once more in the throw-bones. See for yourself, if you like. I left them for you!" The Wulver gestured to a spot on the floor near the wall where a loose pile of avian bones lay. There must have been twenty of them.

Amot sat up for a better look, eyed them carefully. To him, the pile of bones was exactly that – a pile of bones. And he could see no discernable patterns among them. He turned back to the dominant male.

"What kind of battle, exactly?"

The Wulver clenched his jaw before he answered, then snarled, raised his voice. "Battle with man-fleshes like you." Maa'rii shook his head several times, upper lip twitching, one reflex away from bared teeth. Lusii had to stroke his fur to calm him down. After an airy growl, the male Wulver seemed to regain his composure. He drew in a long breath before speaking. "Never just one… Always, there are more."

Hairs stood on end, something in the shaman's tone. The scout rubbed the back of his neck, thinking through the plans of his fellow Kith in the forest. His skin crawled when Eriff came to mind. Fighting when deemed necessary, Amot knew, was part of the operation, and just about the only part Eriff understood.

The Wilder grimaced. "You might not be wrong," he admitted, although he was not convinced of the shaman's methods.

Maa'rii grunted back. "There wras another thing." He hesitated before continuing. Lusii gazed up at him, savoring the comfort of his body warmth.

"Rr-what is it?" she purred, as she studied his expression. The she-wolf gave the bonethrower a reassuring nod. "Tell h-r-im."

Maa'rii sighed heavily, raised an open palm over Amot's head. Slowly, he waved tight circles, spreading his fingers as though feeling for something in the air. Then he clenched his hand into a fist. His hoarse words came out paced and purposeful. "A darkness… swirls about you that must be addressed. The bones tell me so."

Amot paused, searching for meaning. "You speak of rage."

Maa'rii nodded. "Not bad, for a man-flesh." The shaman opened his fist, laid a paw-hand on the scout's shoulder.

"But w-rr-e can change all that," Maa'rii rasped. "Eve-rr-ything. Y-rr-ou will help… Help to stop the battle before it starts. Man-flesh, you are… one of *them*."

Amot shifted how he sat, locked his elbows around his knees. "How do you know that what you see in the smoke, the flames, and the bones means anything?"

The shaman's brow lowered. He shot the scout a slicing glance, raised his growly voice again. "Are you calling me a liar?"

"No," Amot responded. "I believe that you saw battle in the flames, just like you told me. The smoke too, and the bones… just… how do you know it means anything?"

The shaman nodded with understanding. "You seek the *reading*," he said, airily. "I cannot say enough to tell you whrat you seek to knrow… even in a whole season of rain if I tried. But I can say this much. I knrow because once I awoke from a terrible dream. I beheld a flame withering on spent wood. When I threw bones, they hit a rock under the earth and bounced away. There wrere no deer and no hare that winter. Many starved. I should have known."

Maa'rii covered his face with his paw-hands, in utter anguish.

"Had I acted…" The shaman trailed off.

Lusii calmed him. "It's a-r-l right," she said, rubbing his back.

After a long moment, Maa'rii lowered his hands, stared into the spent coals. "I could have moved our pack to better hrunting grounds, before the cold set in."

After a long pause, he sat up straight, locked his fingers to form a vertical curve with his hands, and showed Amot.

"Another time, I saw the flames bend into the shape of a red moon, and that came true as well. That night, the moon went pale red, like smeared blood on white-stone. No act of mine could have changed that.

This time though… this vision… is the third I have seen. It is like the first, not the second. It may come to pass or it may not. I may sit idle and do nothing, or I may walk on all fours and do little, or I may stand and act."

The scout knew there existed forces in the world that could glimpse the future with some measure of clarity. He also knew that the shaman's method could not be one of them.

There seemed no point, though, in arguing that the entire notion was nonsense, that what the shaman saw in the flames and what later happened were nothing more than creatively linked coincidences. And that neither the fire, the smoke, nor the bones told the future. It was *him*. Whether he knew it or not, the Wulver was focusing his thoughts and making the predictions. Maybe it was based on what he'd observed over time, or something he'd heard, or something his dreams had helped point out to him. Either way, it was Maa'rii. Had he asked a Hurlorn… now that would be different.

On top of that, there seemed no point to argue because the shaman was undoubtably right, in the most uncanny way. What the Wulver "saw" was already partially fulfilled and would come true, to some extent. After all, the ranger's detachment had come to the forest to retrieve the lost striker, ready to fight. Even if battle were to be avoided, in the Wulver's mind it would've been avoided because he acted, and nothing would convince him otherwise.

The younglings came pouring back through the entrance tunnel. Maa'rii ignored them.

"We must seek the Chainmaker," he implored. "To seek the Chainmaker, we must pass through the ghost pines. As my dear said, 'the mor-r-r-ning light shines.' They wrill not bother us if we move swiftly and do not bother them."

One of the juveniles, who'd started digging next to the fire pit, began to growl. Another approached. Moments later, the two were engaged in a full-out tug of war over an unearthed bone.

"I have to return to my people," Amot said. "They will be looking for me. Can we go to the Chainmaker now? If we make it quick…"

The Wulver grunted, and in one fluid motion he and Lusii rose to all fours. "It will be quick," he promised.

"Rawl-rawl-rawl," growled the one pup to the shaman. It was the white one, tail wagging and hind shuffling atop the mat he sat on. Amot knew the dance – the expectant yearling was fully aware an outing was about to happen. His clueless siblings were still fighting and rolling about.

"Very well, Maa'iing, you may come too," said the shaman. He turned to Amot. "He likes to track. Maybe he'll pick up a scent and run half the day away." He smiled a grey-fanged smile.

The yearling trotted over to Amot, lowered his head, waited patiently for a scritch.

"There you go," Amot responded, obliging. "Good little tracker… good tracker."

Lusii nuzzled her mate. Her words came out soft and caring.

"Crome back soon, so wre can r-rrun togetherr," she said, then snapped at his neck. The shaman's head jerked away. He responded with another toothy grin and sawed out a laugh.

"Feisty, ar-rre we?" he replied. "We'll see if you are just as feisty when I r-rreturn."

With that, the three departed. The yearling dashed through the tunnel ahead of Amot and Maa'rii, so excited the scout thought the young Wulver might pee himself.

The hulking shaman defied geometry. He had a chest like a barrel, yet managed to squeeze through the tunnel unhindered. It could not have been any smaller. When Amot emerged on the other side, he saw Maa'rii standing on hind legs. The scout stood up alongside him, and to his surprise found himself taller by half a hand. The white pup sniffed the ground as he scurried about randomly.

The morning was damp, grey, and plagued with an icy breeze. Amot massaged the new kink in his neck as he looked down to the axe, returned to its place on the chopping block.

"If the ghost pines give us trouble, that axe will help," Amot said.

"Fire works best." The shaman glanced at Amot's waist. "Don't man-fleshes knrow enough to carry their own blades? They are the makers of them."

As they spoke, the pup crouched at their feet, rawled, then let out a small bark. He sprang up high, body arched, then landed in a crouch, ready for another spring and barely able to contain his energy.

Amot ignored the attention-grabber as best he could. "I had two blades and shed them both getting here," he told Maa'rii. "One I lost in the forest when the ghost pines harassed me, and the other is sitting in my pack, which I dropped in a field."

The shaman responded with a slow nod. "You should be more careful. Good blades are har-rrd to come by." Then he glanced down to Maa'iing, now sniffing Amot's leg.

"Are you sure you didn't lose something else?" said the shaman.

"What do you mean?" Amot asked.

"Maa'iing can still smell the dog on you," he said. "So can I. That is why you lost your pack, isn't it? Chasing a dog."

Amot shrugged, half-admitting the assertion with a small nod. "Maybe we'll find Howler on the way." The thought made him even more eager to get moving.

The shaman addressed the pup in a commanding voice.

"Man-dog smell," he told the young Wulver. "Remember it, Maa'iing. Come tell me whenever you smell this."

The pup barked, sniffed the air. In response, the shaman lifted his muzzle to the air as well, and spent a long minute holding it there. When he was done, he turned to face Amot. His grinding words told of something Amot did not want to hear. Something grim.

"There is blood on the wind," the Wulver gruffed. "Blood and dog-flesh."

The pit of Amot's stomach felt rotten again, and hollow; guilty for not having gone out to search for Howler in the night. He felt guilty, and he was guilty.

Maa'rii tilted his gaze up to the sky.

"Oh, Spirit of the Wolf. It has begun!"

Chapter XXXI
ALLURE
(Valkyries)

THAT MEANS TROUBLE – even for Catwings, thought Stormbringer the moment she spotted her winger gliding in, low and fast. She hastened towards the landing zone. The moment Spree touched down on the hilltop, Tall Hallman was there to settle the feisty Harpy down and tie it in. He'd just returned from a foot patrol with Marec.

The wind rider dismounted with a light hop from her saddle. She landed in a crouch, cat-like, then straightened to face her superior. Her face was tense. Her breaths burst in and out as she spoke.

"Spearmaiden," she said, huffing.

Stormbringer grasped the wind rider's wrists, looked into her eyes. "Catwings, what is it? What happened?" Feeling the leather against her palms, she took mental note of the gloved contraptions the young valkyrie wore.

"Harrowians." Catwings gulped, her words rapid. "They're coming." She glanced to her outfitted hands, then rotated the retracted claw-daggers slightly for Stormbringer to inspect. "From Lorenz…"

Stormbringer nodded, then got back to business. "I spotted Harrowians too. Don't tell me they've entered the forest." *A mess if they did. And risky.* The spearmaiden locked eyes with Catwings, anticipating the answer.

"Not yet," Catwings replied. "Heading south though, pretty much straight for Whisperwood… two groups."

"Horseback?"

Catwings nodded. "Four riders along the river. But… another two on foot seemed to be splitting off. And…"

Here it comes, the complication. Stormbringer stood stiff. "And what?"

"Two giants."

Stormbringer gasped. "Shroud's Well!" Her mind scrambled to process this new dilemma. *Can this get any worse?* She closed her eyes for a brief moment to compose herself.

"Armaments?" she asked, as calmly as she could muster.

"The foot soldiers are archers," Catwings said, between breaths. She drew in a long, deep one, swallowed, then slowed her speech to a more normal pace. "The horsemen, I'd say swordsmen. Light armor all around; barding for the horses too."

"And the giants?"

"Hides and clubs."

"Did they see you?"

Catwings winced, gently tugged for her wrists back. *Oh my.* Stormbringer released her grip – more forceful than she'd realized – then took a step back. The wind rider lifted a hand to her chest, still heaving slightly.

"I don't think so," the wind rider said. "But it'll be hard to keep out of sight from Harrow's Gate. Every time I pop up over the treetops, I see those stupid towers."

Tall Hallman kept an outstretched hand attentive to the gryphon as he addressed Catwings' concern, his voice low and sonorous. "Don't worry about the Gate." The ranger's tone was confident. "The watchmen's eyes will be fixed the other way, on those entering Harrow. You'll be coming in from behind. Just don't be too obvious."

"Why giants?" Stormbringer murmured, more to herself than anyone else. "I hate giants."

Catwings shrugged. "That's all I know."

Stormbringer said, "I saw a regiment preparing to march, gathering on the lakeshore."

The ranger drew his eyebrows together, face glistening with sweat. The morning light added a slight shimmer to his Wilder markings – dark green and runic, subtle against his tanned skin. "What Catwings saw is a patrol to support the gathering forces," he said. "They're scouting the Dim River for the regiment about to pass through. Standard operating procedure."

Stormbringer regarded him squarely. "Scouting for what, exactly?"

"Snipers. Spies," Tallman replied. "Technically, Whisperwood is a line of control."

"Yes, we all know that," Stormbringer said. "We still fly the line, but we rarely see any movement. We've cut back our surveillance to about once for every three times we fly the Deepweald lines with Harrow and Ironeagle." She made a rolling gesture with her hand. "The question is: why the need for giants?"

"The giants will enter the forest," Tallman stated, "possibly to clear a path but more likely to flush out anyone harboring in the woods near the river. Harrow suspects that Gan maintains a presence in Whisperwood and doesn't fully realize the Kith abandoned that L-O-C years ago."

Stormbringer said, "Really? When you say it that way, it makes me think Harrow might blame us for the haunting."

Hallman scratched the scruff of his chin. His eyes narrowed. "No, I don't think so. Most of those stories predate the L-O-C."

Catwings asked, "So the horsemen I saw, they'll keep to the river then, right?"

"They should," said the ranger, "if they know what's good for them. They'll spread out as they go and take advantage of their speed to quickly gang up on anything the giants scare out. They're probably carrying horns or maybe flags to alert one another."

"Ahem," came a polite voice.

Duelist Marec approached, adjusting his gear as he stepped. Stormbringer noticed him reach to adjust his nonexistent scabbard as well, seemingly forgetful about losing the rapier. He brushed over it, smoothly correcting the action to tug at his belt. Finally, he spoke.

"Those Harrowians will have small rivercrafts out and about, I'm sure." Marec hesitated, exchanged a knowing look with Hallman. "Shall I?"

The ranger spoke up. "Spearmaiden, we have more bad news." He gestured to Marec, passing the explanation to him.

Stormbringer let out a long and heavy sigh. She regarded Marec directly. "What now?"

An apologetic look washed over his face. "Harrow is not our only problem… We did what we could."

"Just spit it out, Duelist," Stormbringer responded.

Marec continued, "For starters, one of the Wulvers we were tracking got away."

Shroud's Well. "The sword?"

"No sign of any weapons, Spearmaiden. We encountered three Wulvers and they were on us the second we entered the cave. Straight for the throat. Vicious creatures. Tall Hallman here made short work of one with his knife; no room to swing that giant axe of his." Marec glanced up to his kithblade companion, gave him a nod of appreciation. "Thanks for that, mate."

Stormbringer tilted her head back, gazed up at the man. He stood expressionless, stoic even.

"The smallest Wulver bounded past me and bolted," Marec continued. "The third squirmed into a tight crevice neither of us could fit into, panicked, then got itself stuck. Maybe even suffocated, because we stopped hearing panting after a while."

The ranger interjected, in his baritone voice. "I tracked the runner halfway down the slope," said the ranger, "but couldn't get in close enough for a grab. The Wulver disappeared into a gully, probably hiding scared."

"The young Wulver wasn't carrying anything," Marec added, "but it might know something. Tallman and I need to find the creature, interrogate it."

Stormbringer asked, "Will communication be a problem?"

Tallman answered. "We'll get our message across, one way or another."

Stormbringer paused to think.

Marec winced, "If we leave any loose ends…"

Stormbringer closed her eyes momentarily, then nodded. "We shouldn't, but even the scouting parties are too much for us to handle."

Catwings cut in. "We should wait for Galewind to return. Maybe she found Rainsong. And she might have some ideas about the best way to proceed."

Heat flashed over Stormbringer's brow. "No," she said, firmly. "If the scouting party penetrates Whisperwood, it could cause problems, especially if we lose them. And once those archers spread out in the woods, they'll be hard to track, and deadly. We have to act now."

Tallman said, "I can send a whisper to warn the others."

Stormbringer approved with a nod, then turned to the queensman. "Marec?"

"I could sure use Danus right about now," the queensman answered. "But you are correct, Stormbringer, we have to do what we can *immediately*; outmatched and undermanned as we are."

The duelist hesitated, raised his pointing finger. "Stormbringer, did you see anything to indicate which side of the river that regiment is likely to march on?"

"No," she replied. "I can't say for sure, but I only observed forces on our side."

Marec raised an eyebrow to Catwings. "And we don't know if Harrowian scouts are present on the opposite side of the river… do we?"

Stormbringer looked to Catwings for confirmation.

The wind rider shook her head. "I didn't see anything, but I didn't search carefully that way either. The towers…"

Stormbringer addressed Marec. "Do you think…?"

The duelist fanned her thought. "If King Taeglin found out about what the luminaries lost out there, he could very well be planning to occupy the forest with a large force and take the sword for his own, once he locates it."

"More reason not to wait." Stormbringer sighed. She paced to the edge of the bluff, swept her gaze out over the land. Whisperwood stretched out below her. "But we can't halt an army. We're too few."

Lady Apsarla's words resounded in Stormbringer's mind that

moment: "Do not try to do everything yourself, Stormbringer." She swung her gaze back to Marec. He alone had followed her.

"What do you recommend, Duelist?" she asked.

"We don't need to halt an army, Spearmaiden," he said, a hint of optimism in his tone. "We just need to buy time."

"Go on."

"Harrowian scouts are entering a forest believed to be haunted, or traveling alongside it. If they disappear without a trace, morale will plummet and the colonel in charge of the regiment will think twice about going in."

"How in Theia do we do that?"

Marec smirked. "Pick them off one by one, lure them into a kill zone, incapacitate them and hide the bodies… those are the options."

"And the remaining Wulver?"

"Spearmaiden, you'll have need of Tallman's axe on your end to deal with the foot patrol."

She addressed Tallman. "Can you handle giants?"

The ranger inhaled, puffed out his chest slightly. He firmed up his stance and stiffened his expression. "I am a kithblade," he stated flatly.

"They're not half-bad," Marec remarked, "as hackers go." He hesitated. "My recommendation, Spearmaiden, is to take Tall Hallman here along with you to introduce to the giants, and send Catwings to deal with the widely dispersed riders – I hear gryphons love a fresh horse, and what's a little extra topping? Leave the Wulver to me."

Catwings shot up above the forest for a quick look, with Stormbringer trailing on Ladybird, staying low. It was risky, but the wind rider had to see the lay of the land. Not far away, she glimpsed a hole in the treetops, what looked to be a clearing. Her gaze drifted to the river. She shot up higher, fixed her eyes on a promising site along its banks, around a bend.

Perfect, she told herself. A hidden meadow for staging the op against the giants, and a spot by the river for her own op against the scout riders. She made a mental map, plotted her vector to the clearing, then dipped back down and veered into the trees. *This will take some maneuvering.* It was nothing for Spree – one of the smaller, more agile gryphons – to weave her way through the pines, but Ladybird…

The wind rider glanced back. *Good, she's still with me.* The larger gryphon had trouble zigzagging without hitting the branches. Catwings did her best to guide Stormbringer and Tallman, to lay out a smooth, wide path for them to follow. A dried-up creek bed did the trick, part of the way.

Catwings pushed aside the fact that she had no idea what she'd do when she got to the river, how she'd pick off the scouts one-by-one. She sighed. *I'll think of something.*

She found herself wishing Galewind and Rainsong were with them. And they could sure use another Harpy. *Where are they?*

Ahead of Catwings, the trees began to thin. Light filtered through.

Rainsong drank deep from her waterskin, peered through the trees at the two towers and the Harrowian guards manning the walkway in between.

"I don't like this," she whispered to Ashes. She'd come out farther north than intended, following the speck in the sky that could only be one of the Golds, high above and peeking out from the low-lying clouds now and again. Rainsong had tried to signal by flashing a piece of shiny metal skywards, but the sun wasn't strong and she wasn't noticed.

After finding Harrow's Gate in her path, she'd already come to terms with having to sneak along the riverbank and around a bend in order to cross, away from prying eyes. With her injured wing, Ashes was having trouble flying long distances, but with some heavy flapping she could manage considerable "hops."

The wind rider watched as a dozen or more troops exited the tower on the far side of the river, a handful on horseback. Some carried long spears, others crossbows.

No. I don't like this at all. Something is happening.

One of the horses reared. The troops all turned their attention to it. *Smells gryphon, maybe?* Rainsong glanced up to the guards on the walkway. Their gazes were locked on the commotion. *Distracted.*

The wind rider quickly mounted Ashes, strapped in. Her voice scratched when she spoke. "Get ready," she said into her Harpy's ear. She swung the gryphon around to face the river, coaxed her to crouch, ready to spring. Rainsong grinned, gathered the reins and gripped them tight.

"Go now!" She kicked her mount forward.

Ashes leapt into the air, flapping wildly. The Harpy soared across the river and splashed down near the shore, then quickly scrambled to cover behind a stand of birch.

Rainsong glanced over her shoulder to the towers and the troops. A single guard leaned over the parapet, gazed her way. She placed a hand on Ashes' nape. "Stay still," she whispered. A long minute passed before the spotter pushed away from the wall and stepped out of sight.

"Good girl," Rainsong whispered to Ashes, roughing her behind the ears. *I don't think he saw us. He probably just heard something he wasn't used to hearing.* "Now find me your sisters," she said, "and my sisters too."

Rainsong urged her mount to dash into the forest. Into Whisperwood.

❦

The quiet pool looked secluded enough, situated around a bend in the Dim River. But not so secluded it wouldn't be spotted from the river path. *The perfect place to be happened upon unexpectedly,* Catwings thought. A mischievous grin crept across the wind rider's face as she glanced to the birch thicket nearby, where Spree lay hidden, and the rough walking trail that ran past it from the river to the pool. The Harpy's grey and white plumage made for perfect camouflage among the tree trunks.

The wind rider removed her scaled dress, hung it in a tree with her smallclothes. She laid her remaining protective gear out on a boulder, then tossed her bundled up cloak next to it. She only kept three items on her person: her golden sandals, a scant white wrap to keep around her waist, and her talon gloves – just in case.

Catwings tilted her gaze to the sky above, one forearm instinctively pressed against her breasts to cover them. *A little sunshine wouldn't hurt,* she complained silently. The cloud cover was thin but unyielding to the sun's rays. They would not shine through.

She gently lowered herself onto a boulder next to the rocky pool. The water-stained earth around her and the gully leading inland told her that the location was likely the headwaters of a stream, when the river swelled. For now though, it was just a clear and quiet pool, well-suited for bathing in private.

Catwings waited silently; she waited and watched as a gentle cascade of water from the Dim trickled down a mild slope of smooth river stones, to plop onto the pool's surface.

Rix will love this story, she thought, and smiled to herself as she imagined the jaw-dropping expression he'll have on his face when she tells him. *I wonder if he'll even believe me.*

Catwings drew a deep breath and exhaled, pushing aside doubts that her plan might not work, and the implications for her approaching enemies if it did. *They won't know what hit them,* she convinced herself. The wind rider liked it better that way, and she was grateful that Spree could do most of the dirty work.

A sharp eagle call sounded, subdued for a gryphon. *The signal.* Catwings double-checked the safeties on her gloves, reached to the ground to pick up a smooth, plum-sized stone, then stood up. She waded into the pool.

Warmer than I expected, she thought, until waist deep. The temperature cooled as she approached the middle. Turning her back to the path, she began to bathe, cupping water from the pool and gently rubbing it over her bare skin, humming softly to herself. The thud of hooves grew nearer, then stopped.

Catwings felt the Harrowian scout's gaze upon her. She turned, carelessly revealing, as though surprised. "Oh my!"

"Ah… umm… apologies, madame." The scout's voice was young. He wore light armor and a scabbard for a short sword. Most importantly, he was alone. A hand crossbow hung behind him on the horse. It took him a moment to compose himself.

"You should be more careful. It isn't safe to be…"

Polite, but not polite enough to look away. Catwings pressed the release on one of her claw-daggers. The metal blades shot out with a twang. She held up her clawed hand, slowly rotating the gleaming blades.

Infusing playfulness into her voice, she asked, "Who'd be foolish enough to bother me?" She looked him up and down, raised an eyebrow. "Are you a risk taker, Soldier?" Catwings shot the scout a daring look, then casually continued bathing in front of him. She palmed the smooth stone over her body as though it were soap.

The man turned his head briefly to look the way he came, then turned his gaze back to Catwings. He smiled, eyeing the metal blades. "Are you going to use those on me?"

Catwings smirked. "Not if you're gentle." She tilted her head to him. "There's room for two down here. You look hot. Care for a refreshing dip?"

The man took one last look over his shoulder, then dismounted. Catwings heartbeat began to race. *It's working.* He stood at the top of the slope facing her. His stance, wide and relaxed.

"Don't worry. I don't scratch," Catwings assured him, as calmly as she could muster. She beckoned him towards her, slowly manipulating the claws on her outstretched hand, like extended fingernails. The man shrugged, skidded down the stony slope halfway. He glanced at the scaled armor dress hanging in a tree, then back to her.

I'll have to hide that next time, Catwings thought. It didn't seem to faze him though. He'd already made up his mind.

The man asked, "Am I going in or are you coming out?" He removed his scabbard, laid it on the ground. His armor would be next. *Now.*

The wind rider opened her palm with the stone in it. Smiling mischievously at the scout, she tossed it straight up into the air.

"You're coming in," she told him, just before the splash. "Yee-ah!" she called. Spree lunged out of hiding, claws reaching forward.

The man stumbled backwards with a grunt. At the top of the slope, his horse reared back, ready to bolt.

"Hold!" Catwings called to her mount. Spree clasped the man in one talon. Half-hopping, half-sliding down the slope, the Harpy pressed the scout into the water. Catwings backed away.

"Hold," Catwings repeated. The battle-trained gryphon held the scout there, submerged. Catwings stepped to shore, slipped on her mottled-grey cloak. As the man struggled for air, she gathered his horse, led it into the woods and tied it up.

By the time she got back, the man had stopped struggling.

"Release," Catwings commanded. Spree promptly raised her claw and let the scout go.

The wind rider pulled the man to shore. She dragged him onto the rocks, laying him flat on his back, then looked to Spree. "He's not drowned, is he?" The Harpy tilted its head, gave her a quizzical look.

Catwings started pumping the man's chest. "We have to get the water out of his lungs." He spat water.

While he coughed, Catwings rolled the man over. "Hold," she said to Spree again. With measured force, Spree pressed him down while Catwings quickly tied his wrists. When he stopped coughing and started complaining, the wind rider gagged him. She bound his legs and doubled up on the man's wrist bonds. Amidst muffled cries, with Catwings holding the reins, Spree half-led, half-dragged the scout into the woods, and dropped him there.

Catwings tingled with energy from head to toe. "Good girl," she said, stroking her gryphon. "Only three to go." Her knees trembled. Butterflies swam in her stomach.

I'd better reset. The next one won't be long.

Catwings returned to the poolside, re-hung her dress in a less open place and dragged the scout's discarded gear out of site. Then she removed her cloak and stepped back to her boulder. When she sat down, that same pang of guilt she felt earlier shot up again.

It's not like he's dead, she told herself. *This is how I like it. Nobody dies and the gryphon does the fighting.* The valkyrie-seductress took a few deep breaths to compose herself for the next rider.

The next to come along took more coaxing. Catwings even removed her claw-daggers for the thin, timid man, and made promises she knew she wouldn't keep. She questioned if he was actually a scout or just some passerby. Ultimately, he suffered the same fate as the first scout. And the third… he was rugged and handsome. Hesitant too. Catwings shrugged when he refused to venture into the water, shot him a sly smile. "Okay, I'll come out then." She became so drawn into the role-playing, she jumped back, as surprised as he was, when Spree sprang out of the trees to fulfill her role. The Harpy held that one down too long. Catwings took him for dead for a good twenty seconds before bringing him back.

The last rider arrived quicker than the rest. Catwings had barely composed herself. This time, she submerged her whole body into the pool when she heard the horse was near, then rose up from a squatting position. As she rubbed at her eyelids, she allowed ample time for the water to trickle down her body, in full view.

Catwings shrieked when she opened them.

Galewind swooped low over the hilltop base camp. No one was there and everything was either gone or hidden. *Where are they?* She knew her valkyries had been tasked with patrols and that the rangers had gone to scout out a cave system. *They must've seen something,* she thought. The knightmaiden banked Electra into a new turn, northwest towards the caves.

A minute later, she spotted someone on the hillside, and then a glint of steel in the late-morning light. *Is that…?*

The person waved at her with both arms.

Marec?

Chapter XXXII
TRACKER

(Amot)

AMOT TOOK THE axe.

Maa'rii didn't protest the way Lusii had. "Fetch my spear," he told Maa'iing. To a pup, the only thing more exciting than a hike is a hunt. Maa'iing did as his father bade him, dashing into the tunnel out of sight.

While the pup was gone, for the first time above ground Amot took a long look at the shaman. The grey morning light revealed an older Wulver than the scout expected – older by decades than the one sitting across the firepit, it seemed. The eyes said it all, hanging tired and heavy with guck stuck in the corners. The silver patches on his face, so brilliant in the night, showed themselves to be dull and grey. The dark skin around his jaw was stretched taught and receding, enough to expose his gums and a bare row of worn, yellow-grey teeth. The ring of dark fur around Maa'rii's neck resembled an old man's beard.

"Can you track the scent to the source?" Amot asked. He knew wolves were capable of smelling prey from over a mile away, but he was not so sure how a Wulver's senses compared. "My dog is out there. He might be injured."

"Yes, I can," said the shaman, his voice airy and rough with rolling growls. "But first w-rr-e speak with the Chainmaker. Don't worry, Man-flesh, it wrill be swift."

"I can't just leave Howler out there if he's injured," Amot told him. "I'll track him myself if I have to." The scout turned from Maa'rii and strode towards the hanging chains, back in the direction he'd come from in the night.

Maa'rii called after him. "No, you wrill not."

Amot halted, turned back to face the shaman. "Are you going to stop me?"

A sly smile crept across Maa'rii's face as the scout glared at him. "I don't need to. You're going the wr-rrong way, Man-flesh. Wrong way."

Amot threw up his arms in disbelief. "What?" That meant Howler traveled right past the clearing during the night, or as near to it as he could get from the other side of the creek. "Which way then?"

The Wulver did not answer. They stared at one another, at an impasse it seemed, until Amot began to look about. He scanned the terrain for some kind of sign, any sign. Turnsby was due south. Unless the dog doubled back, he wouldn't be that way. Northwards, a high hill bulged above the treetops. *Howler wouldn't have climbed the hill either,* he decided. So, give or take, only east and west remained. Amot felt the breeze on his cheek – from the southeast. The Wulvers were catching the scent downwind, so Howler had to be east or southeast. That also made sense given the course of the creek that he'd crossed in the night, which ran south past the glade and then wrapped around it with a westward bend. Howler could've crossed the creek, but he wouldn't have done so without a good reason.

Maa'rii furrowed his brow. "What are you doing?"

This time, Amot did not answer. The Wulver grunted at him.

At that moment, Maa'iing's hind quarters popped out of the den tunnel. With muffled growls, the white furball stumbled backwards into the open, pulling awkwardly at the spear shaft clenched in his teeth. It was hooked on something.

Maa'rii looked to his son and shook his head. The yearling had somehow decided the best thing to do was to pull the blunt end of the spear along and let the spearhead catch on every rock and protruding root along the way. Red feathers and leather laces dangled from the shaft as Maa'iing tilted his head sideways to gain more torque. His eyes rolled back in comical frustration.

The shaman sawed out another laugh. "Aaarrr… That's the spir-rrit," he growled, then stooped down, patted the yearling's head the way Amot had. "Good boy," he said, the same way Amot would encourage Howler.

Howler. Amot rubbed the back of his neck, closed his eyes and pleaded to his Colossus. *Ekkon, please protect Howler. For just this one small wanderer, I ask a great favor, and for this favor I promise to meet you at the edge of worlds.* He heard the spear drop, opened his eyes.

The shaman twisted the tip free, then paused to nudge the yearling forward. "Now go off for a minute."

Maa'iing responded by speeding away from the den. He looped back and halted, then tilted his head as he stared, anticipating.

Amot regarded the shaman. "Which way?" he repeated. He already knew the answer. The pup had all but confirmed it. But he wanted to hear the words from Maa'rii.

The alpha-male raised his spear high into the air, thumped the butt end firmly on the ground. Teeth clenched and standing firm, he put his defiance on display. It was clear he did not like to be asked the same question twice.

"Man-flesh needs to speak to Chainmaker," he grumbled firmly.

"East-south-east," Amot said. "Is there a crossing that way?"

In response, Maa'iing, well ahead of him, rarr-rarred something that could have been a "yes," and so Amot began to walk in that direction.

After a few steps, the shaman called after him. "Not bad for a man-flesh."

Amot stopped halfway to Maa'iing. The wolfish pup sat propped up and alert. Eyes bright, he let out a half-bark.

From behind the scout, the shaman growled out a sigh.

"Ver-rry well." Then he addressed his son. "Maa'iing, go and hrelp the man-flesh track the dog blood."

The yearling bounded towards the unsuspecting Amot, jumped him, and stuck his wet nose wherever he could find a patch of skin. The scout ruffled the canine's fur, then set him back down on all fours.

"Maa'iing should lead," said the shaman. "His snout is younger than mine."

Amot looked the man-wolf in the eye. "Thank you."

Maa'rii only grunted in response. Then he strode over to Amot on hind legs, leaning on the spear the way an old man leans on his staff. The yearling ran ahead.

⁂

As they traversed the shadows of tall pines, the scout swore he could hear his dog's huffing, or a rawl, or the sounds of Howler's traipsing through the woods in his usual, haphazard way. "Ignore it," the shaman told him. "It is not real."

The three of them came upon the gruesome site. Blood, guts and hair were scattered everywhere. Howler's severed head had been set upon a sharpened post. His eyes were shut, and two thin trickles of blood hung frozen from them, dripping down like crimson tears. With a heavy heart, Amot took the head down from the post.

A whisper came to him in that haunted moment, bringing news from afar: "A queensmen and a ranger killed a man-dog and his family in a cave off Harrow's Gate."

A twisted whisper, thought Amot, gut-wrenched beyond compare, *more ghost pine treachery. Who else would think to use the term "man-dog" like a Wulver would? How dare they.*

Regret pooling in his stomach, Amot gathered what remains he could find and began the grim task of putting his very best friend to rest. He used the Wulver axe together with his own bare hands, pulling and cutting through roots, scooping out sandy earth to dig a shallow grave. The yearling, whose fur had become splotched with blood, clawed at the ground alongside him. Spear in hand, the shaman uttered a solemn chant while keeping watch on the woods.

The scene felt eerily familiar to the scout: The stillness of the trees, the diffuse light at the forest floor. Echoes sounded in the far-off distance – sniffing sounds, whimpering, four paws stepping through the brush without concern, a young man calling in the distance. No mistaking, it was Howler together with Rix's faded summons for the canine.

Amot asked Maa'rii, "Did you hear that?"

"Ghost sounds," replied the Wulver. His blue eyes scanned the kill-site, then searched the surrounding pines. "This is not a new trick."

"I'm relieved that you hear them too," Amot told the shaman. "I thought I might be going mad – hearing voices in my head."

"That's exactly wh-r-at they do to drive you mad. They go on and on about the things that make you wrant to split your brain in two." Maa'rii gave a subtle nod. "It works. They've already done it to each other."

Amot didn't believe in ghosts, but the resident "spirits" certainly believed in Amot, and the scout took that for a fact. They believed in his sense of loss, his fear, and something else – they believed in his lack of will. They believed he would falter, make mistakes, or simply go mad. Covered in soil and drenched in sweat, the scout gritted his teeth together, shook his head at them. He defied their tactics with the stubbornness of a greybeard. *This is pure trickery*, he told himself.

The shaman put his paw-hand on the scout's shoulder. "The time has come to leave this place." Maa'rii paused briefly before continuing. "The Chainmaker awaits. Most of the morning has passed. And you, Man-flesh, have seen all there is to see in this bloodied neck of the woods."

The scout contemplated a *whisper* to let his comrades know about all that had transpired. *Can I trust these ghost pines?* The answer he told himself was "no," and so he didn't try to contact the others. He should have tried. It couldn't have gone any worse if he had.

⚘

They stopped by the creek so Amot could wash away the dirt and his loyal companion's blood before heading off to the high hills. The echoes persisted, mixing in voices with the birdsong, the wind, and the buzzing of insects. The voices he knew, and there were other sounds familiar to him as well. Sometimes they sounded near and full of life, other times they arose as mere whispers from afar. Occasionally, Amot might hear a delighted "woof" and was glad for it, until he caught himself. Other times, a desperate cry invaded the tranquility of the forest, haunting, like a pursued animal. The deep howls, when they came, were the worst. Like moans of agony, they sent icy chills up the ranger's spine, tormenting him.

Amot rubbed his forehead. It helped to keep him focused. "I have to go back," he said, mostly to himself, "go over the terrain one more time. Carefully. I have to do it carefully so I can find out more about who did this." *Wulvers are to blame. That much is clear. But from which direction did they come? The site is awfully close to Lusii's pack, Maa'rii. So close it makes me wonder.*

The shaman shifted his weight and leaned heavily on his spear, gripping the shaft solidly with two hands. "I can tell you exactly who killed dog-flesh and how they did it."

"Howler. The dog's name was Howler," Amot said.

"Horwler," he imitated. He lifted his snout, double-sniffed the air. "I can smell the filth. I could even smell it back at the chains, and I can smell it more now."

"Who then? And why? Why would someone do this?" demanded Amot. Maa'rii answered.

"To make a statement," he grumbled. "They tell you, 'Go away man-flesh, and take your dog meat with you.' Just be thankful you did not find the head of your red friend on a post. Dog-flesh is just dog-flesh. Man-flesh is something different entirely."

Amot would have asked how he knew about Rix, but for the fact he could guess the answer: the Chainmaker told him. *The Chainmaker tells them everything they need to know, it seems.* Instead, Amot stood there. He stood there and let the fury build. His muscles ached. His whole body ached. A sickening thought kept resonating in his head as his suspicions grew. He tried to find evidence to the contrary… something to say otherwise… to point to anything else… anyone else. But how much did he really know about these Wulvers he encountered?

The shaman's jaw dropped slightly as he gave Amot a measuring look. The scout could see the deliberation churning behind his eyes. Maa'rii took a step back, angled his spear slightly forward. *He can sense my doubt.*

But Amot did not try to hide his distrust – what would be the point? It was there. It was true. It was honest. The scout had his suspicions about the Wulver, just like any self-respecting Kith ranger would. It could've been him for all he knew. Amot had to be sure. And Maa'rii was likely considering that mindset. He'd been around for a long time and was no fool.

Maa'rii let out a heavy sigh. "I wrill show you."

The shaman called to the yearling, sprawled out on the ground and licking himself. "Maa'iing," he said. The young Wulver perked up. "Who hurt the dog-flesh?"

Maa'iing raised his snout into the air. "Haar-raar-waar," he rawled.

"He can talk?" Amot said.

The shaman growled up a soft chuckle. "He thinks he can talk," he said. "Do you know what he is trying to say? The little snowdrift is trying to say 'Haar.'"

Maa'iing nodded vigorously, then sat down and began licking his paws and biting a burr on his leg.

The name… Lusii had mentioned it to Amot. He felt the skin on his face go flush. His ink began to show. Hate welled up inside. "Bring me to Haar," he demanded.

Maa'rii shook his head slowly, eyes closed for a long moment. "You cannot fight Haar. I would hrate to see you torn to shreds, Man-flesh."

"I can give you things, things your pack needs," Amot pleaded.

"We have wh-r-rrat we need." Maa'rii glanced around, uneasily. "Haar is twice my size and the chief of the greatest pack. He has everything, and he takes what he wants wh-rr-ile the rest fight for scraps. He even takes man-flesh. None oppose him, none except us, in a small way." He paused. "The Chainmaker helps us. The Chainmaker said he would help you."

"Is that your plan?" Amot glared at the shaman. "Just sit back and take it, and rely on the only ghost pine that isn't fully mad?"

"Wait Haar out," Maa'rii said. "No rr-one lasts forever."

Amot needed to move. He began to pace.

"You must find the calm inside of you, Man-flesh," said the shaman. "It is there, if you rr-look."

Amot struggled to contain his thoughts. After several minutes he halted, stared up into the grey sky. He took a deep breath to calm himself… to reassure himself. Finally, he decided. Amot consciously dropped his tensed shoulders, then turned to Maa'rii.

"Lead the way."

The shaman patted Amot on the head. "Good boy."

"We don't usually do that to people," Amot said.

The Wulver looked confused, then shook his head and carried on. "Strange man-fleshes."

⁂

Echoes of Howler still sounded in the distance. But at least it was behind them. The ghost pines would have their fun, but soon their phantom whispers would fade and dissipate. And when the ranger's emotions leveled off some, he finally asked Maa'rii about the resident tree spirit who'd broken ranks.

"Why does the Chainmaker know so much about me?"

Maa'rii shrugged. "He takes an interest in some, like Lusii. Lusii was the first. Then, after a long time when I became old, he liked me enough to talk to me too."

The Wulver continued. "But you, you he knows because of *the sword*."

"Tell me about the sword," Amot said.

"I brought it to him, and he knew you would come. He called you 'Kith' and he called you 'Son of Fyorn's son.' His hot rocks have been burning high ever since – all through the night. Even now, I smell. He works the metal."

"Metal?" The scout felt his ink flare once again. "He better not… if he so much as… Hadamard will have my hide!" The scout started into a jog.

Chapter XXXIII

CLASH

(Catwings, Stormbringer)

Catwings gasped. *Damn, a woman.* Her stomach clenched.

The final rider to come around the bend was a sturdy looking female, with a grunt face and tight braids in her grey-streaked hair. *What do I do now?* On top of that, she wore a longsword and sat unusually tall atop her mount.

A bit of giant blood in her, Catwings suspected. *So much for feminine charms.*

The wind rider switched her plan on the spot. She barely glanced at the woman, did her best to act casual about the intrusion. Catwings smiled her way and continued bathing, virtually ignoring her. The clopping of hooves ceased.

In her peripheral vision, the wind rider saw that the woman was watching, silently. And there was something about her. She didn't move on and she didn't come down. *Is she nosy? Open to experimentation?* It was impossible to tell. *Waiting for an invitation?* Catwings posed for her subtly, just so.

A muffled cry sounded from the forest. Catwings' heart froze. She swung her gaze to the scout. The woman's brow furrowed, angry eyes scanning the grounds. There were tracks everywhere: hoofprints, boots.

The woman turned her gaze to Catwings, glaring. Her stare had a crazed quality to it, burrowing deep behind the eyes.

"I've been hearing strange noises in the woods… ghost sounds," she told the woman. "Some say these parts are haunted." Catwings offered her an exaggerated shrug. "You kinda get used to it. Not much seems to happen beyond the occasional word or scream. Seems harmless enough."

The Harrowian scowled back at Catwings, looking her up and down. Her eyes narrowed as she then peered through the trees, where Catwings had hidden her gear. "I know what this is," she stated with disdain. The woman pulled a horn from a saddlebag.

Catwings gasped. *No!*

The woman sounded it twice, long and clear both times.

The wind rider stood there, unable to move as the scout drew her sword. Rather than dismount, the woman urged her horse down the slope.

"Yee-ah!" yelled Catwings, then flicked the safety.

Spree lunged out of the thicket, knocking the horse over. The Harrowian toppled, slashing at the gryphon's massive claw as she slid down the slope. Unbalanced, she made slicing contact, then tumbled into the pool. The Harpy backed off, retracting her leg.

The woman stood up in the water, blood streaming down her face.

Catwings slowly backed away, raised her claw-daggers.

The woman spat blood at her. "Worthless whore. The giants will come for you. They'll spread your legs and split you in two." She advanced, longsword raised for a strike. "But not before I cut you a new hole."

Catwings pressed the releases on her talons. The blades sprang out as the woman came at her. With one clawed hand, the valkyrie deflected the sword, then stepped in close. With the other hand, she slashed at the woman's unprotected neck.

Blood spattered out. The Harrowian's weapon dropped from her hand. Wide-eyed, mouthing curses, she grasped her own throat and stumbled backwards.

As she splashed down, a tremendous crashing noise resounded from the forest. Sounds of splitting wood, heavy thumping, and grunting issued forth.

"Spree!" Catwings shouted. "SPREE!"

Startled flapping sounded.

"Spree come back! The giants are coming!"

A horn sounded.

"What was that?" But Stormbringer knew exactly what it was – the river scouts must've found Catwings and sounded the horn. *Norwin's Breeze. What now?* A sinking feeling filled her stomach.

Where are those giants?

Tallman was off tracking them and was supposed to get back to her with some kind of owl sound, to call her in. He'd said they couldn't be far.

Can I wait?

She scanned the tree line surrounding the hidden meadow. There was no telling when he'd return.

No. Catwings needs me now. And if Marec was right, the giants are on their way to her.

I must get to her. Fast!

Stormbringer mounted Ladybird.

"Yaw!" she yelled. "Yaw!"

The gryphon crouched, spread its wings, then leapt into the air.

CHAPTER XXXIV

CHAINMAKER

(Maa'rii)

THE WULVER KEPT to two legs through the forest, not four. He felt small on four in the presence of man-flesh. Maa'iing was different. The pup did not seem to mind being on all fours at all. *He is still young though,* thought Maa'rii. *Pride comes with age.*

Sunhigh had come and gone by the time the shaman led his yearling son and the visiting Kith ranger away from the creek, away from the fouled site where the dog-flesh had been killed. Maa'rii led them with purpose, taking the high ground when he could. But the bearing was nearly downwind and he could still smell the blood-scent on the air. The man-flesh seemed oblivious to it though, and that was good. He needed to forget, for a time.

The terrain at the Wulver's feet was foremost on his mind. *Easy ground for man-fleshes and two-legged stepping,* he thought.

Maa'rii was proud of Maa'iing that morning. His son had tracked well, and displayed his talent for scent matching by being correct about the Haar-wulves. He would make a good scout someday, a good hunter, and maybe even a good shaman or pack leader. Maybe he could be the one to make peace with Haar's successor someday, and learn to trade with man-fleshes like Amot. *Better than Outlanders,* he decided. *Outlanders are cruel and only trade for slaves.* Glebe Stouts from Turnsby want Wulver heads to mount over their fire boxes, according to the ghost pines. He was not sure about what man-fleshes like the Kith ranger might want. Chainmaker spoke well of the one named Fyorn, and now his very grandson was here – Amot. *I will speak well of Amot to my son*, he planned for his future self. *I will revive the memory of this often, and foretell the many futures for him.*

Maa'rii kept a good pace and did not slow down or speed up on his trek, and he did not have much to say to the man-flesh. Amot did not speak to him much either. It was nice to have a break from his questions. *So many questions, and so hard to answer some of them.*

Maa'iing seemed to like his new man-flesh friend. The Kith ranger's scent had become familiar quickly, and the way he used his hands to make a comforting scratch was friendly. Different, but friendly. Maa'rii had tried the technique on Lusii. He smiled to himself at the memory. *She liked it.* In his mind, he focused on the pleasure that he saw in her eyes. It was a good thing to focus on, especially on such a heartsick day.

Maa'rii turned to his son and the man-flesh. He put his index finger to his lips. "Shhhh," he said, then pointed to the trees. The Kith ranger looked about. *Yes, these are Sleepers, Man-flesh. So be quiet.* The shaman eyed his son seriously. *You too, young wolf.* Maa'iing's bright eyes showed him that the yearling understood. He could see that the Kith ranger understood as well. But something was on Man-flesh's mind. Something far away and unfamiliar, maybe a mechanical thing. Maa'rii always got stumped about mechanical things.

It was a full quarter after sunhigh before the clang of iron on iron rang in the distance. Smoke had been on the wind since a long way back, in wafts. Smoke with a metallic tinge to it. Two hare chases later, they came to a steep, rocky hill.

"The smell of smoke is strong," Man-flesh said.

"The Chainmaker's forge is ever-rr burning," Maa'rii replied. "I smelled it half a hunt away."

Man-flesh asked, "What does the Chainmaker forge, besides chains?"

The shaman paused to think of all the things the Chainmaker had fashioned. Finally, he answered.

"Ther-rre are too many to say all at once. I will name some I remember." He paused to sort things out in his head. "Chains were first. Chainmaker made chains for a year. Then he made three axes, three pots, and three pans. I don't know whry always three. He liked three for a while, I guess. Then Chainmaker made Lusii a black collar. She doesn't like the thing. I use it with a chain to hang deer-flesh to dry. He made me a spearhead – my favorite, until I threw it at a deer and the deer ran away with my spear in its hind." Maa'rii shook his head and laughed.

Even the man-flesh laughed a little. *It is good to see*, thought Maa'rii. *My words lift his heart closer to the sky.*

"I don't know what he is making now," the shaman continued. "I hope for a spearhead, but I think not. I think he is doing something fancy with your sword. You will like it… unless it is like the collar."

As they climbed the slope, the clanging grew louder. Maa'rii noticed that instead of looking where he was going, the man-flesh's eyes were fixed to the ground. He seemed confused. The shaman quickly understood why.

"The Chainmaker is always coming and going," Maa'rii told him. "Many places to go, and just as many to come back from."

"The ground here is trampled enough for a dozen Hurlorns," Amot remarked.

Maa'rii nodded. "Flattened like when the first snows melt," he said. "Chainmaker moves more than any dozen I know. Sometimes I come to the hill and he is not here. I see him miles and miles to the north. Sometimes I see him across the great rr-rivers, and in the bogs. He carries things back with him – heavy things r-like logs and boulders. Once he carried seven man-fleshes to the edge of the forest near Turnsby. He said later the Haar-wulves would have gotten them."

The three trackers crested the hill, then began the short descent into the hollow at its summit.

Maa'rii sawed out another laugh. "Look," he said to Amot and the yearling. "I like this. He made steps out of the earth. He did it just for you, man-flesh – he doesn't need them, I don't need them, and Maa'iing here doesn't need them either."

"I don't need them," the man-flesh said.

Maa'rii tried the steps on his hind legs, but they did not feel right to him. He clenched his spear in his teeth – the right way, not like Maa'iing – and dropped to all fours.

A familiar voice greeted them. It sounded like wind through a hollow log, but deeper. The fire pit cave burned hot. "Furnace," the Chainmaker called it. Furnace is a word Maa'rii learned from the Chainmaker. The shaman did not like the furnace, and he stayed well away from it. It was no good for seeing the future either. He stood too close once, it singed his fur. The Chainmaker's bark was black in many places from it.

Chainmaker's hill was the only hill Maa'rii had ever seen that was hollow in the middle that way, like a giant bowl sitting on top. Inside, the grounds were sheltered from the wind. The Chainmaker once said that being hollow that way is what makes the hill perfect. A pool sat near the middle, next to the fire pit cave, its waters always still. Beside the pool stood the Chainmaker's great stone table, and beside that, man-flesh fire tools and chains hung from an old tree skeleton. Maa'rii only knew the name of one kind of tool – hammer. There were many, many hammers. The dead tree that held them never before grew there – Chainmaker dragged it up from the forest floor. He dragged up hardwood and black rocks for the fire as well, from far away. The hardwood he cut with his own huge axe and stacked it near the fire cave. The black rocks he kept in a big wooden box beside his table.

The Chainmaker called the dead tree "Linny" sometimes, and sometimes "old snag." At least once a week, he'd break off a piece to feed to the fire. "That's what you get, Linny, you old snag," he'd say whenever he did that.

The Chainmaker barely took notice of the two Wulvers and the man-flesh, at first. He seemed to be in the middle of something import-ant. He stood at the table, as unnatural looking as a tree could be, with his long spindly fingers gripped around a hammer. His body was set in a hunched over stance, and he wore some kind of leather apron. He stood there banging away at metal on his great anvil. Metal so hot it glowed. Then he put the hammer down, took a grabbing tool and used it to pick up what he was banging on. He carried the hot metal to the pool, dipped it in the water and left it there. Steam rose as he turned away. He strode to the fire cave and pulled out the sword Lusii had found. It wasn't in the fire itself, but in a small space beside it, where he keeps things warm. In one giant step, the Chainmaker was back at the table. He placed the sword on top of it. It was a large sword, sleek and bright like the white veins found in rock.

Before the three entered his workspace, Maa'rii asked the same question he always asks of the fire-scorched Hurlorn before entering. He called out to him.

"Is it a good day, or a bad day?"

"Maa'rii," the voice sang back. "Are you now going to bring me something new every day?"

The Wulver turned to Amot and lowered his voice. "Not all days are good with the Chainmaker," he growled. He turned back to the hollow.

"I don't think so," Maa'rii called back, then he turned to the man-flesh again. "Only yesterday I brought him the sword, today I bring you."

Amot nodded.

"Is it a good day, or a bad day?" the Wulver repeated.

"Good," came the reply. The Hurlorn lifted the sword and held it up high.

The man-flesh whispered something under his breath. Maa'rii heard easily. "He's oakwood," were the words.

"Yes," Maa'rii said back to the man-flesh. "He thinks a little funny, but his heartwood is solid. The Chainmaker is not like the pines."

Amot gave the shaman a strange look.

"Fine workmanship," boomed the Chainmaker in his woodwind voice, paced and measured. "Best I've seen out of Gan. Luminary design, or I'm a fence post. They never do the forging though. That probably still falls to The Riverworks. Someone I once knew spent his young days there, learning the craft… That was another life."

"The blade was forged in Ironeagle, according to a prominent luminary," Man-flesh responded.

"Ahh-haa! I knew it," Chainmaker said. He scrubbed at the blade with something rough.

Amot furrowed his brow as he looked over the Chainmaker's man-things. "The luminary claimed they were the only ones who could work the white metal."

"White metal – of the Jhinyari – aye, so that's what this stuff is. Stouts out there, I hear. I can't see the Bearded Hill folks doing this." The Chainmaker took a closer look at the metal, near the hilt. His wood-like eyebrows raised. "I suppose it could be Stouts, with about a hundred years to learn a few things. The design threw me off – it's a full hand-and-a-half sword."

"A real bastard," Man-flesh said, and smirked. The shaman did not know what that meant.

"Then a bastard she is," said the heartwood.

The man-flesh smiled. Maa'rii had no idea why, but did not ask because he did not want to spoil the two getting familiar with one another. *These names I do not know!*

The Chainmaker turned his gaze to the man-flesh. He had a question for him. "Are there more like this one?"

Amot paused before giving an answer. This man-flesh did that often. He always thinks before he speaks, as if he didn't want you to know all the things on his mind.

"Yes," Amot said. "Just five others. They're called strikers. The Prime Luminary wants every ranger detachment to have at least one. That would make over thirty... he just needs to get the kinks out of these ones first. He calls them 'prototypes.'"

"Striker prototypes, aye." The heartwood gave the sword an examining look.

"I would ask for it returned," Amot said. "I lost that one, and I must bring it back."

Maa'rii cringed. Words like those could go very wrong with the Chainmaker. Very wrong indeed.

"But what about the kinks?" said the Chainmaker.

"What about them?"

"I don't believe they are kinks. They are more like freedoms."

"What are you saying?" The man-flesh looked confused, like Maa'iing when he hears a strange noise in the woods. No words were spoken for the longest moment. Every tree on the rim of the hilltop leaned in to listen.

At last, the Chainmaker replied, "I know what the luminaries are trying to do. I used to forge their designs. I didn't know then what I know now, though. They'll ruin it, just like the Jhinyari ruined their silvery blades."

"I know the swords you speak of," said the man-flesh.

"The path that seems right is not right," said the Chainmaker. "It is often that way, unfortunately. You end up accomplishing exactly the opposite of what you set out to do in the first place."

"I don't understand," Amot said.

I do, thought Maa'rii.

"Just the same," Amot continued. "I must ask that you return the sword to me. I will tell the Prime Luminary himself all that you have told me. He will be very interested. I thank you for keeping it safe. The striker prototype is the rightful property of Gan—" The heartwood interrupted with a wave of his great, gnarled hand, blackened by many flames.

Maa'rii knew that the hand was one of half-a-dozen. Every second time the shaman came by, the tree seemed to have molded yet another functioning hand out of a new branch. Sometimes, an old one would be gone, reduced to charcoal.

"You have met these Wulvers," said the Chainmaker. "You have shared stories with them, and even buried your dead with them. Do you enjoy the company of these Wulvers, Kith?"

The man-flesh blinked. He seemed taken aback by the question. He looked to the shaman, then back to the heartwood.

"I do," Amot said. "Very much so." He took another look at Maa'rii, a long one, and then did the same to Maa'iing. "They are kin."

"Aye," said the tree, swaying his great trunk back and forth, like a nod. Still holding the sword high, he removed his apron with one hand, and with two others picked up a large pot. He dumped its contents over his trunk.

"Chainmaker, what are you doing?" said the shaman. The smell wasn't right. Maa'iing, who'd been silent and slinky the whole time, backed away at a steady pace, up the slope of the hollow. *Maa'iing senses it too*, thought Maa'rii. *Good instincts, my son. Good, raw instincts.*

"And will you protect them from harm?" the Chainmaker prodded, still addressing Amot.

Maa'rii turned to the man-flesh. "Something is wrong. I don't think today is such a good day after all."

"I suppose not," Amot said to Maa'rii. He scrunched his brow and his eyes went all squinty too.

Man-flesh does not understand.

He will.

The Chainmaker looked up to the sky, then to the furnace, and strode over to it. "You might be too late."

Amot took a cautious step towards the Hurlorn.

Maa'rii saw the pounce in the man-flesh's posture, like a lynx. He saw the tensing of muscles, the focus in the man-flesh's eyes. He heard the hand slide along the grip of the axe, and he smelled the aggression. Amot's face changed into a painted one.

"Don't get too close," Maa'rii warned. "The Chainmaker can be dangerous."

"Oh, Maa'rii!" said the Chainmaker. "Such a fine manimal you are. Always protecting, caring, so unlike your brethren. I will miss you the most."

"And I will miss you," Maa'rii said. It was all he could say at a time like this.

And with those words, five hands scooped coals from the fire. Five hands ignited and rubbed the oil-drenched trunk. The trunk erupted in flames. One hand held the sword in the midst of the fire.

Amot raised his arms to shield his face from the searing heat. Maa'rii backed away, and his son crossed over to the hillslope beyond.

And as the Chainmaker burned, he chanted in a low, raspy voice. And as he chanted, words from afar rode in on a whispering wind to chant with him, until there were many voices. They seemed to come from all around. Amot covered his ears. He looked as though he might go mad.

At the height of the Chainmaker's burn, with wide eyes the heart-wood cried out. His eyes were glowing brighter than the flames.

"Maa'rii. Hurry back!"

His voice suddenly became many:

"Essence of fire, consume.

Essence of earth, renew.

Essence of air, sustain.

Essence of water, cleanse.

Essence of metal… bring balance to the world of Men."

When he was done, the Chainmaker went silent and still. The shaman watched as the heartwood burned. Flames leaped and smoke billowed into the sky. The heartwood burned until his wood began to char and break off. In a few minutes, the man-flesh's sword fell from the great hand of the Chainmaker, into the pool.

Careful to avoid the falling fire, Amot wrapped his hand in a rag lying nearby and retrieved the sword. It had been turned jet black, with flecks of the original white metal still shining through. When the ranger gripped the bastard sword, he held it to test its balance. It shone like a piece of the night sky in his hands, and the amber stone encased in the hilt sparkled when it lit up, like the brightest star in the North.

The Chainmaker foresees. Hurry back! Maa'rii grabbed the huge axe. Together, Wulver and the man-flesh exited the hollow, heavy-footed and heavy-hearted about the loss of a great ally and, to Maa'rii at least, a great friend.

The forest knew. The Sleepers in the lands below echoed with laughter. It was not a good day, and it would not be a good night.

CHAPTER XXXV
OUTRUN A WOLF
(Maa'rii)

MAA'RII CLAMBERED OVER the rim of the hollow and began to run, two-legged, down the hill. He fell, and decided it was hopeless. *Four legs are better than two,* he told himself, and so he dropped Chainmaker's great axe. He could run with his spear in his teeth, but not with something so clunky as an axe the size of Maa'iing.

Man-flesh followed, but he was too slow. *No man-flesh can outrun a wolf, even an old wolf,* he decided. It made Maa'rii smile inside. Maa'iing was not so bad. Maa'iing was young, and could follow. When the two Wulvers reached the bottom of the hill, Maa'rii halted. His son did the same.

"Stay with Man-flesh," Maa'rii told him. "It is dangerous. Man-flesh is good." There was no time to say more.

The shaman started to run again, but the yearling followed. Maa'rii stopped again.

"STAY!" he shouted. This time, Maa'iing stayed, but he didn't like it. He rawled and complained, and paced back and forth, until the shaman was far ahead. By then, Man-flesh had caught up to Maa'iing. *Amot is with my son.* Maa'rii felt good about that.

The Sleepers laughed and cackled as the shaman ran between them.

Yelps and screams echoed through the woods. Wulver yelps. Wulver screams. Young and old. Man-flesh voices, other than Amot's. And snickering of the old snags.

Maa'rii agonized over his failure. *I did not change it, AGAIN. I knew better, and I did not change it, AGAIN.*

As Maa'rii approached the glade of his pack, the yelps and screams became real. Other voices arose in the forest, and strange whirring sounds. Knowing these woods well, he sped up, ran as fast as his legs would carry him. Smoke hung strong in the air. When he looked up through breaks in the canopy, he saw it swirling above the treetops. There was too much. Lusii's fire did not make so much smoke.

And blood was in the air again. Not dog-flesh blood. It was Wulver blood, and the blood of man-fleshes.

Maa'rii felt the rage. It had been a long time. It made him feel young again.

With a great leap, the Wulver sailed through an opening in the chains and landed in the glade. Wulvers were running everywhere, young and old. Brothers lay on the ground with arrows sticking out of them. *Man-flesh arrows.* A Haar-wulf was the first enemy he saw living, confirmed by his markings and a smell that Maa'rii had learned to hate. The shaman dropped his spear, sprang upon him. He ripped out the Haar-wulf's throat before the intruder could react.

Another spotted the shaman, came for him growling and swinging an Outlander's curved blade. Out of nowhere, a black blade appeared without a wielder, and cut him down. It was the blade of the man-flesh, but the man-flesh was nowhere to be seen. And then he remembered.

I saw that blade in the burning battle, Maa'rii told himself. *I saw that blade dancing in the flames.*

Maa'rii heard Lusii's muffled cries from the smoke hole. He clamped on the spear and ran towards it. A Haar-wulf tried to stop him, but he faked one way and ran past the other way. It was the oldest trick in the forest. When he glanced back, that Wulver had bent over, holding his stomach, with guts leaking out.

Again, Man-flesh's sword that somehow flies. I owe him for that one, too.

Maa'rii finally reached the smoke hole to his chamber and leapt in, ready to kill any Haar-wulf that dared to be there. He landed in the fire that was no more. Coals and ashes flew everywhere. The flames in the fire chamber were gone, and the room choked with smoke.

Maa'rii dashed to the side tunnel, where he heard Lusii's pitiful calls.

Lusii! No! Not Lusii.

He sunk the spearhead into a Wulver that got in his way, and left it there. He was right to. The Haar-wulf shouldn't have been there.

Haar himself was next, looming in the small chamber. *Our chamber.* Lusii lay injured beneath him. She called out the names of her children.

"Maa'iing, Rarr'sha, Naw'naw." Her voice was strained. Desperate.

Haar turned to Maa'rii, as mean and grisly as an old bear.

"They're dead," Haar said, his voice like the grinding of rocks. "I killed them."

"He lies," Maa'rii said, to ease Lusii's anguish. "He lies, Maa'iing was with me. And he is now safe with Man-flesh."

"Good man-flesh?" Lusii's words were weak.

"Our Man-flesh. Amot."

With no room for spears, Maa'rii lunged at Haar's throat. But Haar knew all the fighting tricks that Maa'rii knew, and at least one more. Maa'rii regretted, for an instant, spending his days throwing bones and reading smoke instead of practicing how to fight better. It might not have mattered though. Haar redirected Maa'rii's lunge into the side of the den. The intruder's monstrous jaw came down from behind, latched on to the back of Maa'rii's neck.

The pack shaman tried to fight back, but his body had gone limp. He lay on the floor. Haar would not relinquish his grip. The shaman tried to speak, but only blood gurgled out.

"We wrill run together, Maa'rii," was the last thing he heard. Lusii said the words, as tenderly as though it were the morning. It was a sweet song to his ears, and he carried the sound of it with him as long as he could… through to the longest and straightest deer trail he ever saw in the forest… as long as he could.

Chapter XXXVI
BREAKING

(Amot)

THE VIEW OF the Wulver glade, fractured and translucent, folded out of sight in front of Amot. To where, he did not know. Whispers taunted him from every direction, a plague of maledictions that rode the air and swirled about him. "Too late… too late… too late. You killed them all." The scout should have ignored those voices, but instead he chose to respond.

"I did what I could," he cried back. But he was looking at Maa'iing when he said it.

The far fencing weapon in Amot's grasp was different now, since the Chainmaker had gotten hold of it. Besides the new black finish, the balance had been altered, the grip was rougher, the knuckle guard refashioned into a chain-link pattern, with finger-rings. Only the slider charm near the guard remained untouched. And yet, the clarity of far-seeing it imparted had improved dramatically. That much was needed. And when invoked, the glassy stone flickered with the same amber light that Amot had beheld in the Chainmaker's eyes, back when they were burning. The image stuck in his mind.

"Your wolves are all meat now," gurgled a voice full of sap and spit.

Can't they just shut up? Amot's decision to abandon the remote battle was not an easy one. After the shaman had disappeared underground, the smoky haze and mayhem in the glade had obscured the battlefield. The scout could easily mistake a Lusii-wulf for an intruder amidst the pale grey imagery of farseeing, and hack the wrong fighter down. In the den, it would only be worse. On top of all that, Amot had seen something else in the glade that he could not explain, or thought he saw it. Bright colors where all else was colorless. They weren't even there before.

Amot tried not to think of all the bad things that might have happened to Maa'rii and Lusii, and the pups, and the other Wulvers in the glade. He didn't want to let himself think that way at all. He needed to be there. He needed to be there to find out for himself. He tensed his leg muscles, ready to dash.

Wait. The yearling.

The scout crouched down to have a quick word with the young Wulver. Bringing Maa'iing to the glade would put the shaman's son in harm's way. Leaving him behind could be worse. Maa'iing could end up like Howler if the ghost pines moved in. *They'd stomp on him, shred him to bits, or at least try.*

With a gentle touch, Amot rested a hand on the yearling's withers, just behind the neck. "You're coming with me, Maa'iing, to the glade. Stay close until we get there, but don't go in. Stay hidden until I come to get you. Do you understand?"

Maa'iing rawled his compliance. Satisfied, Amot rose to his feet, then ushered the young Wulver along as he started into a jog. Maa'iing quickly matched the scout's stride through the tall stands of tortuous souls. Sword in hand and the yearling at his heels, the Wilder broke into a run with all the speed he could muster.

"You killed your own dog, and now you're about to kill this one," hissed a young and feminine-sounding Sleeper. She laughed with soft mockery. "We let them pass," she egged on. "They came for *you*, Kith. We let them pass to kill your dog-meat friends instead."

A loud creak sounded. Amot ducked to avoid a thick, swinging branch. Maa'iing zig-zagged to get past, deking with the agility of a wildcat. *That was a lively one,* thought Amot, heart pounding as he sped. Sleepers are not nearly as animated or mobile as other Hurlorns, usually. He glanced down to the yearling, keeping pace at his side.

"They lie," Amot told the pup, between breaths. "This entire forest has gone mad." The Wulver gave no discernable response. "You do hear them, right?"

"Kith the Killer… Kith the killer… kith the killer," came the muted chants, unrelenting. Amot blocked them from his mind and pushed ahead.

⁂

The Wilder decelerated to a walk as he approached the creek, a good hike from where he'd first crossed. Heartbeat still racing from the exertion, eyes to the ground, he quietly treaded over the cushioned moss and pine debris of the forest floor. Maa'iing stepped beside him, panting. The air was dead and heavy with the smell of smoke. Behind him, the haunting calls of the whisperwoods had faded.

At the nearest pinch-point in the creek, the scout removed his boots and carried them across, wading through the knee-deep water. Maa'iing had to swim part of the way. On the other side, the Wulver's fur flapped and thudded as he shook his body dry.

"Sh-sh, *quiet*," Amot whispered, forefinger to his lips. "Haar-wulves," he said as he pulled his boots on.

The yearling's steady eye contact showed his attentiveness. He sniffed at the air to confirm. "Haar-raar-waar."

Even in mid-afternoon, the forest was dim. The scout smelled grass burning; the smoke heavy enough to sting his eyes. He would've moved faster were it not for Maa'iing. But even as the thought crossed his mind to charge into the glade, his ranger instincts told him stealth was the right approach, for now.

Amot suspected that Wulvers, like their wolf cousins, couldn't see as well as humans. It was their sense of smell and hearing that he had to worry about the most. The smoke and the dead air would help to conceal their scent, at least, and both himself and the yearling were able to move silently. The scout's cloak was grey-green in color and blended well with the surroundings. He turned his gaze to the young Wulver, so low to the ground. He'd be difficult to spot so long as he crept slowly. *That white fur doesn't do you any favors, though.*

The Wilder crouched low and continued to pad softly, with Maa'iing close behind and silent as a predator. They kept to the no-man's land between the creek and the chains, to avoid detection. From the glade came sounds of commotion, arguing, and intense growls as they neared. A sinking feeling settled in Amot's gut. *The ghost pines could be right.*

The scout stopped to listen carefully. It was not grunting or the clinking of iron or the knocking of wood that he heard – sounds of battle. No. Instead, his ears captured the groans of the injured, desperate calls for loved ones, and a rustling sound he could not place. The battle for the Lusii-wulves territory seemed over, with the victors now arguing over spoils.

Maa'iing suddenly halted, face forward along the creek, ears pricked.

"What is it?" Amot whispered.

"Haar-raar-waar," Maa'iing rawled, raising his snout to the air.

Amot nodded. And although he didn't see or hear anything to cause alarm, he knew what the Wulver was telling him.

"Good boy," he told Maa'iing, then raised a hand to him, flat up. "Stay." The yearling sat obediently. Amot left to scout ahead on his own.

Stepping softly, the Wilder skirted the line of thick, overhanging brush that grew alongside the creek. Sure enough, he came upon sounds of digging, and then nothing, and then splashing water. Narrowing his eyes and peering through the brush, the scout spied a scrawny Haar-wulf having himself a drink, at total unawares to the presence of the lurking Wilder. Blood matted his fur and heavy deer hides hung from his shoulders, for armor. The spiked club at his side was right out of a legend. Wulver belongings wrapped in a tattered blanket sat near, next to a half-dug hole.

Spoils, the scout concluded. *He's about to bury them and go back for more.*

To Amot, the scene before him meant that the battle really was over. Otherwise, this one would still be at it. The man-wolf muttered profanities to himself as he slurped water into his mouth, snickering even, with growling words that hinted at participation in some form of humiliating torture, ending in slaughter.

Amot's head dropped. The faces of the Wulvers he'd spent much of the night with flashed in his mind. *Which one?* He closed his eyes, winced in pain. Not his own pain. It was the pain of his newfound friends the Lusii-wulves that burned within; the pack that had accepted him so quickly. He felt sick inside.

Amot's temples began to burn. He felt hot and flushed. And as much as he tried to delay his feelings, bury them until he knew for sure all that had happened, he couldn't. The scout re-adjusted his grip on the striker in his hand. The gleam of the black metal caught his eye. He stared at it for a long moment. And as he stared, the blood inside his veins began to boil.

He admired the blade. *Such a keen edge.*

He glanced to the man-wolf. *Such a deserving target.*

A tingling sensation welled up in his sword hand, like pins and needles. Amot paused as the vibration coursed up his arm, rushed through his spine, his other arm, his legs. The scout's mind raced to understand.

And when the tingling crept to the base of his skull, an image flashed in the back of his mind. Dark and foreboding. A looming silhouette. Perfectly still. Waiting. The image flashed again. Amber eyes brightly lit. Suddenly the world looked very different. Veiled, yet aglow. Amot's vision blurred, then sharpened to a pinpoint.

Focused more than ever, the Wilder crept in close to his target, so quiet even canine ears were numb to his approach. In utter silence, he raised his sword, took careful aim at the slurping man-wolf.

Perfect balance.

The black blade's heavy, forward weight made Amot feel confident about the strike he readied.

Pride welled up from within.

Pride? Why pride?

The Haar-wulf pivoted at the last second, to face Amot. Eyes wide, he sucked in air with a toothy gasp. His head jerked back, but it was too late. With a quiet slash to the neck, the despicable beast was mortally wounded. The man-wolf grasped at his throat with his paw-hands, smearing the pulsing blood over his fur. The creature gurgled, slumped forward into the creek. A cloud of red formed in the water where the body lay. The draw of the current stretched it into a long streak.

❧

"Don't look," Amot told his Wulver companion as he ushered him past the bloody scene. Most of the Haar-wulf body lay buried in the shallow pit meant for spoils, now a grave. The spiked club had floated away, down the creek. The head was another matter. In vengeful fury, the scout had made short work of severing it from the neck. It had hung by a mere thread after his deadly strike, and now stood mounted on a sturdy post, cut from a branch.

"For Howler," Amot whispered into the Haar-wulf's dead ear as he passed. He felt dizzy. The whole idea of it was mad. And although he'd committed the act without reservation at the time, without a second thought, it all seemed unfamiliar to him now. What had transpired took on a blurred quality in his mind, like the content of a fading dream. Conflict rose from within, churning his thoughts inside-out. Amot felt at odds with himself at how he'd handled the situation. He could have apprehended the Haar-wulf, interrogated him for information, and then incapacitated the beast. *Why didn't I do that?* It was another mistake he would just have to live with. He put the feeling aside. He had to. There was too much at stake. *One can't always show control in the heat of the moment*, he told himself, and left it at that.

With Maa'iing at his side again, Amot snuck around to the thicket Lusii had first shown him at the glade's southern periphery, just outside the Chainmaker's mesh. He peered over its topmost branches, gazed into the field. It was crawling with unfamiliar Wulvers, garbed in scraps of metal and hides for armor. Most carried a makeshift weapon of some sort – a heavy stick for a club, a long stick sharpened to a point, or a length of chain with spikes on one end as an improvised flail.

Greedy, sparring Wulvers raided the bodies lying about, even those still moving. Others sorted through odds and ends scattered outside the den openings, with much growling and shoving. A section of the glade was veiled to him by the constant swirl of smoke from smoldering fires and a jutting stand of alders that blocked his view. The Lusii-wulves must have lit fires throughout the field to keep the invading pack at bay. Ultimately, the tactic failed. Amot discovered the source of the sound he'd failed to identify earlier – the rustle of twitching bodies in the long grass.

A quick count showed nearly a dozen Wulvers active in the areas he could see, with more likely underground in the dens. None standing were recognizable from the previous night's feast by the firepit. And while the basic form of the Lusii-wulves, with the exception of Maa'rii, tended to be long and sleek, the majority of these beasts carried immense bulk on their frames. Many sported round potbellies and mangy fur, fitting of the usual description of their kind in legends – unkempt and nasty to the core. They could only be Haar-wulves.

"Haar-raar-waar," Maa'iing confirmed, sniffing at the air again.

"I know." Amot nodded. "I know." All the information he needed was laid out before him. It was time to make a decision. The scout considered his options.

At the simplest level, he could run or he could fight. Amot considered departing for Deepweald with the sword and the yearling. He could leave all of the senseless fighting behind, bring Maa'iing to safety, reunite with his detachment and catch a ride with Order Valkyrie. He would fulfill his mission and be redeemed, maybe even considered a hero. His rightful place among the Kith Quarter would be established. Surely, his name would enter into Treesong, like his fathers' before him. He might even be given a tribe.

But what of Lusii? Maa'rii? The Chainmaker's words resounded in Amot's mind, asking him, compelling him, to protect the pack that the deranged Hurlorn had once cared for. The Lusii-wulves had only him now… a screw-up, a wannabe kithblade.

No. The easy path to success and glory would not suffice. It would be an empty victory, one that he could not stomach to be a part of.

That moment, Amot knew what he must do: free the glade of Haar-wulves, salvage what he could of Lusii's pack, and move them out of the forest, to safety. Anything less, as a Kith, as a Wilder, as his father's son, he could not live with.

Maa'iing let out a whimper as the scout forced him into to the deepest part of the thicket, where he'd remain hidden. Amot removed his grandfather's cloak and draped it over the yearling.

"Good boy, Maa'iing," Amot said, as he patted the Wulver on the head. "Stay low, stay quiet." Maa'iing let out a quiet rawrl, lay down as instructed. Amot gave the yearling one last scratch behind the ears, together with a side-belly rub. "Stay out of sight. Run like a hare if they come for you."

Amot rose and started on his way. He glanced back over his shoulder, to Maa'iing. The yearling's eyes were upon him.

"A *hare*," he repeated, then turned his gaze forward facing. The Wilder carefully stepped through the hanging chain barrier, black blade in hand. Still behind cover, he began to formulate his plan of attack. Cold rage urged him on. Cold rage and cold calculations from the darkest depths of his mind.

The usual Kith procedure wouldn't do: *stealth – observe – plan – critical strike – withdraw – repeat*. No. This plan was about intimidation. Maim a few Haar-wulves in the most terrifying ways imaginable and send the rest yelping back to their dens with their tails between their legs. Cruel on the surface, but efficient and arguably merciful on the whole. *It could work.*

Haar-wulves are bullies, Amot decided, *domineering over the weak but quick to buckle under the strong*. The scout was no brute, but broad-shouldered and lean muscled as he was, and wielding the black blade, he knew he would present an imposing figure to any Haar-wulf. Even Haar himself.

All I have to do is not let them swarm me, not put myself in a vulnerable position.

Amot studied every detail about the Haar-wulves' activities and how they moved about the glade. The closest Wulver, at twenty paces, sorted through a pile of belongings that looked like garbage to Amot. A large axe lay on the ground beside him. *Stolen from a Glebe Stout, no doubt. He will be the first.*

In a pit behind the trunk of a felled tree, several Lusii-wulves lay bound and held. Two moaned and writhed in agony only a few feet from the edge, while others he could see did not stir, either dead or out cold. A pair of rusty-furred Haar-wulves stood guard at the rim, armed with crude spears for poking and prodding their captives to keep them down. As the scout looked on, the larger of the two guards whipped a Lusii-wulf in the head when she tried to prop herself up. She slumped back to the ground. Amot's eyes narrowed. *You're second.*

Elsewhere throughout the glade, two to six other Haar-wulves were visible at any given moment. *A few less than I first thought. Good.* They scrabbled in and out of the various dens, barely able to fit. During his watch, only a few went in or out of the obscured part of the glade. Larger ones, who carried themselves with authority.

A handful of Haar-wulves max then, if my timing is right. At worst, Amot could wait until several wandered to the far side of the glade before charging in. Neutralizing the one with the axe and then one of the guards would probably be enough to scare the life out of the rest. He eyed the captives in the pit. *Freeing up a few more fighters wouldn't hurt either.*

While waiting for the right moment, Amot counted the dead. They totaled nigh as many as the living, among them three with arrows sunk deep into their fallen bodies, sticking out this way and that way. *Where's the archer now?* None of the Haar-wulves he'd seen possessed a bow. Amot knew from experience that a good sniper could turn his plans upside-down. He scanned the tree line. *Nothing.* His armor provided good protection, but like any armor there were gaps, and that meant risks. *I'll charge any archers I see. Cut them down and cut their bowstrings.* Amot noted the hidden portion of the glade, in particular, as a potential threat area in that regard. The smoke there was beginning to thin as the fires continued to burn to embers. But there was no time to scout it out, and one or two more opponents wouldn't alter his plans in the least.

Amot took note of the two Haar-wulves he'd slain remotely, and then of a third that Maa'rii had put down. All three had already been stripped of their gear. Without a closer look at the rest of the bodies, and without entering the open glade, there would be no way to positively identify exactly who was who. That would have to wait. *No,* he contradicted himself. *Most are Lusii's pack.* To think otherwise would be foolish.

Lusii… Maa'rii…

Amot couldn't bear the heavy feeling. He hadn't seen either of his new friends among the dead or captured.

And where are the pups?

He tried not to let himself think about the pups, or Lusii again, or Maa'rii for that matter… or how to tell Maa'iing…

A light-headedness came over him. He felt outside of himself.

Shake it off.

He did. And quickly. Amot re-doubled the grip on his bastard sword. A feeling of power surged through him. He would go in two-handed. The Wilder's sense of focus returned. Sharpened.

"Chainmaker," he whispered, calling his sword by name.

The moment had arrived. Only four Haar-wulves were visible above ground.

Amot drew a deep breath. A cold sort of calm washed over him. Eyes as steady as his resolve, he fixated on his objective.

By the time Amot stepped into the Wulver glade, anyone looking could tell that the Kith ranger meant business. Deadly business.

∽

"CHAINMAKER!"

The Wilder's battle cry resounded through the forest.

Amot charged into the glade, a screaming maniac. He lunged at the nearest Haar-wulf, still sorting through worthless junk. The beast reached for the axe at his side, just as Amot expected. The raging scout did exactly as he'd planned. He sliced down hard on the man-wolf's outstretched arm, leveraging the entirety of his momentum. He severed the appendage clean off, then left the vile creature to scream in terror. The Wulver fell to its knees, grasping at the severed limb.

Next, the Wilder swung his gaze to the two guards at the pit. One held her long spear readied. She would be a challenge to overtake. The other's eyes darted about the glade, uncertain, then settled on the fallen Haar-wulf. His pointed stick shook in his hands.

Easy target, Amot thought. He raised his sword to the high guard position.

With a high-pitched growl, Maa'iing dashed out of his hiding spot in the thicket, towards the same two guards.

"No! Go back!" Amot yelled, but all the scout could do was try to beat the yearling to the pit. He sprinted with all his might, grunting with the effort. The more capable of the two Haar-wulf guards set the butt-end of her spear into the ground, angled firm against Amot's charge. She growled at her comrade, gestured that he take care of the young Lusii-wulf coming at them. But her quivering companion dropped his spear, bounded off in the opposite direction.

A voice called from across the glade. "Amot?" A man-flesh voice. *Ghost pine?* It sounded like Rix. *A trick.*

Amot glimpsed a flash of colors as he charged. *Rix's colors?*

The scout came upon the spear set against him. He knocked the stick aside with the black blade, then cut off the foremost paw-hand that held it. Maa'iing flanked the same Wulver, tore at the other arm. *Vicious.*

The Haar-wulf snarled, gnashed her teeth to take the pain. Her slavering jaws pulled back. She ignored the dangling yearling and snapped at Amot. The Wilder dodged her attack. And with a swing fast and low, he targeted her legs. The ferocious beast went down cursing and growling, grabbing at her hacked appendages.

Maa'iing wrestled the spear away from under her body, clenched it in his jaws.

"You're a fierce one," Amot told him. The fourth Wulver bolted.

Another ghost pine tried to trick the scout. "Amot, stand down," the voice called, rough around the edges. *Berendt?*

Amot hesitated. *No. The pines are on the Haar-wulves' side.*

With the immediate threats neutralized, the Wilder spun around to survey the scene and gauge the invading pack's reaction. He watched the fleeing guard bound into the woods. Not far behind, another followed after popping its head out of a den amidst the screams.

A Lusii-wulf in the pit recognized Amot, from the gathering the night before – she'd dragged in a deer. She stood up on her hinds and called to him. Amot cut her bonds. She picked up the abandoned spear.

It's working.

There were three others in the pit, all Lusii-wulves. One of them was strong enough to fight, another too weak and the third might've been dead. Amot freed the fighter, checked the pulse on the third. *Barely.*

"Amot! Stand down," demanded the ghost-pine version of his commander's voice again. The Rix version called out as well. The scout didn't even look. Instead, he addressed the yearling, gesturing to the just-freed fighter. "Maa'iing, give that one your spear." The young Wulver stepped over, dropped it at the Lusii-wulf's feet.

"Irr'll take that axe instead," the fighter grumbled, eyeing the nearby Haar-wulf's amputated arm. The lean-muscled brute locked eyes with Amot, beat his paw-hand twice to his chest.

"T'saa," he declared.

Amot sized him up, amid shouts from his impersonated comrades. This Wulver was marked by a chewed-up ear and a rear leg with a raw chunk out of it. One eye bulged. He sported a build similar to Maa'rii, but with reddish fur like the Haar-wulves. He grasped the shoulder of the Wulver standing next to him.

"My sister-rr, Kii." She was a smaller female than Lusii, with close-set eyes. Her grey snout was punctured with teeth marks and streaked with ripped flesh, peeling back. Along one entire side of her body, patches of blood-soaked fur blotted her otherwise healthy, grey coat.

Amot nodded to T'saa. "Yes, take the axe. And toss that one-armed sack of shit into the pit while you're at it." The injured Haar-wulf had finally stopped screaming, curled into a ball, stump tucked close to his body and moaning heavily.

T'saa turned from Amot, hastened to the axe and picked it up. He proceeded to drag the injured Haar-wulf back with him.

More Wulvers crawled out of the dens to investigate the commotion. With one strong arm, T'saa lifted the amputee into the air, dangled the body at them. "I-r-nto th-r-e pit for yrou," he growled, then tossed the Wulver. At the same time, Kii made a display of kicking the wounded guard and rolling her down the slope.

Witnessing the carnage, Haar-wulves scrambled to exit the glade. Running blind and fast, they rang the chain barrier before scattering into the woods.

"It's the r-r-other man-fleshes wre have to w-r-orry about," declared Kii. She thumped the butt end of her spear to the ground.

"What?"

Amot turned to face where he'd seen the colors, that scraggly part of the glade sectioned off from the rest. The smoke had thinned. From his central vantage point, he now had a clear view.

It can't be.

Amot stood there, frozen, gaping. The scout shook his head, trying to look in ways that made what he saw not be true... not be seen. But no matter how his mind warped the scene, what he saw was real. There and present. He could not look away.

"Amot, what the hell are you doing?" barked Berendt.

"No," the Wilder muttered to himself. "No... no... no." The scene that emerged from the cover of the smoke stabbed at his heart. It stabbed at his heart and twisted the fibers of his being into a hard knot. Amot shook his head again, his mind reeling.

"No. You were... the voices were ghost pines." *It can't be.*

"What?" come the reply. It was Rix. The real Rix.

Amot's rage had no place to go. He felt his ink flare like never before, burning into his temples. It burned inward until it peeled away the fragile shell underneath.

"What are you doing here?" But as Amot said the words, he suddenly recognized the interrupted operation – a search and clear of the remaining dens: Rix stood on overwatch duty near an opening, arrow nocked, bow slightly bent. He made sideways glances to Amot through the wispy smoke, squinting his eyes in confusion. Over the den entrance stood two Haar-wulves armed with heavy clubs. Their roles, Amot knew, were to apprehend anything that might come out of that hole. One wasn't ready. Instead, he just stood there, club lowered and jaw gaping, looking to Berendt who was situated nearby, as though waiting for a cue.

Other Haar-wulves snarled, narrowed their eyes at the black blade wielder and his rag-tag band of Lusii-wulves. They banded together, stroked and readied their weapons. Teeth bared, frothing at the mouth, they were hungry for a fight.

Eriff first appeared along the sidelines of the action. He held himself with the high poise expected of a Queen's Guard, garbed in his full, intricately emblazoned metal armor. To Eriff's left stood the biggest, meanest, grizzliest looking Wulver the scout could've ever imagined. His huge paw-hand dwarfed the curved Outlander blade he held.

Haar.

Chapter XXXVII
THE ARROW
(Amot)

AMOT GAZED ACROSS the field of blowing smoke and torn bodies, sized up his enemies. Four Haar-wulves in a knot brandishing crude weapons, then Haar. Muscles tensed, the scout readied his sword.

Berendt barked out, "Hold steady. No one move." The Kith commander raised his palms at the two Wulver packs to stand down, each side slavering to get at the other's throats. "Amot?"

They won't listen, the scout thought, *nor will I, if it comes to a fight.* He caught Eriff's stare, eyeing his sword from afar. *That's right, Gallant. I have it.* Eriff wasn't the only one watching.

"The black blade!" exulted a Haar-wulf.

The scout heard a growl beside him. He shifted his gaze to the freed siblings.

T'saa readied his axe and nudged his sister, a glimmer of hope in that bulging eye of his. "That's the rr-one, Kii. I told y-r-ou I saw it. The black blade will lead us to victor-rry."

Kii lowered her head, moaned in frustration. "My pups!" she wailed, leaning on her spear for support. The she-wolf shook her head repeatedly, her words breaking into angry sobs, "No… n-r-o… nuh… nuh… kill yrou all."

Grinding his teeth, T'saa grimaced as he fixed his good eye on the pack of Haar-wulves where they stood. He pointed his axe at his unruly foes, scowled. "What rr-have y-r-ou done with the pups, y-r-ou mangy mutts? I'll carve y-rr insides out."

Haar's Wulvers cackled to one another in response, and Haar himself let out a hoarse laugh. The hunched, hulking Wulver broke away from the queensman, who looked small in his shadow. He sauntered forward.

"Mrr-ove aside, let me speak!"

Berendt stepped back, let him pass.

Eriff made to protest, but Berendt, with a raised hand, stayed his words. Haar's pack-mates nodded to one another in great satisfaction. A club wielder growled back: "S-prr-eak, great Haar-r-r!" The cries of his thuggish comrades rose in gnarring approval. Haar halted after several steps, pointed his Outlander blade right back at T'saa, as though finding his mark. The pack's urgings fell off into saw-toothed mutterings, so their leader could have his say.

"I know yrou, T'saa," he started. "You sh-r-ould have joined us when I gave r-you the chance." Haar's lips snarled with contempt. He leaned to one side, spat. "Don't worry y-rr furry little head, T'saa. The pups are ours now. We'll raise them as our own, prim and proper – you kn-r-ow what that means. The females w-r-ill breed with the strongest males. The males w-r-ill fight their way up in our ranks like every other male, so they can be the strongest and breed too. They won't grow up to be furry little last-eaters like yrou, by the time we're done with them. They might not grow up at all! That's why we are strong and you are weak. What good are y-rr metal chains and y-rr fires now, Lusii-wulf? Nothing."

Haar scoffed, lowered his sword, spat a second time. His Haar-wulves erupted into a cacophony of hoots, cackles and jeering laughter. They knocked shoulders, waved their clubs and spears in the air.

Kii slammed the blunt end of her own spear to the ground. Her sobbing grief had turned to fiery fury. "I-rr wrant to taste Haar's blood and rr-let it drip from my jaw. I-rr wrant to see the flesh on his neck blossom. I-rr wrant him dead with flies buzzing over him."

T'saa nodded, slowly turned to Amot. "And I-r want Haar-wulf blood on this axe. And when I'm done, I'm gonna carve up some man-flesh."

Amot started to speak. "No. Not the man-fleshes." But the Lusii-wulves roared and howled back at the invaders the moment Amot tried to raise his objection. T'saa pumped his axe into the air, and Kii her spear. Maa'iing howled and barked along with them. A Wulver hidden in the woods joined in the chorus. T'saa and Kii went mad with the sound of another brethren come back to fight with them.

"Rrrr-let them fight it out!" Haar roared.

The scout looked to his comrades, stepping back as the Haar-wulves' anger grew, uncertain glances passing between them. *They're going to let this play out, aren't they? Just like the slaughter.* Amot knew they expected him to do the same. He'd already messed up their operation.

With a growl building from deep within his gut, T'saa raised his axe, broke into a charge. His growl turned to ashes as he bounded at his enemies on hind legs. "Lusii!" he roared. Kii and Maa'iing leapt after him. The hidden Wulver lunged out of the woods to join in the assault.

Amot was left standing there. *I can't stop this.* He wanted to, and shouted as much, but his words fell on deaf ears. He had to decide. The sword tingled in his hand. Energy. "Yes, I know," he muttered to himself, or to the sword, unsure which.

In quick succession, Haar-wulves charged to meet the glade's defenders, cackling and hee-heeing manically in their rush. Haar himself hung back with Berendt's crew, folded his arms with a snarling grin.

Tightness seized Amot's chest. The grip of his sword now buzzed with a steady vibration, urging him on. With a reluctant shake of his head, he raised the black blade high with a firm, two-handed grip. He would not abandon the Lusii-wulves. Not now. Not ever. His smoldering rage rekindled.

"CHAINMAKER!" screamed the raging Kith as he cut loose in pursuit.

"KITH! STAND DOWN," Berendt shouted in response.

This time, Amot did not stand down.

Eriff cried out, "Haar, call off your damn dogs!"

The hulking Wulver brushed the queensman off with a look of utter disgust. "Let them fight it out. But four-on-four-rr. None of this man-flesh interfer-rrence."

Berendt yelled again, "STAND DOWN!"

The two packs clashed in a frenzy, clawing and biting, latching on with rabid growls and rolling over the smoldering ground. Clubs bashed, T'saa's axe caught flesh, and makeshift spears jabbed until grabbing paw-hands rendered them inert. Amidst the yelps, the blunt trauma, and the tearing into flesh, Amot hurled himself into the fray.

The Lusii-wulf newcomer sprang in alongside him, jaws gaping wide with ferocity. The scout struck three Haar-wulves immediately, taking only scratches in return before Haar himself roared in protest. Berendt moved in to intercept, longsword drawn in a two-handed grip.

Although not a kithblade, Berendt was a seasoned swordsman, and in a fair fight he was sure to make short work of any Lusii-wulf that came at him. Amot could not allow that to happen. A dark conviction came over the scout as he withdrew from the battle to meet his commander. Amot presented himself as nonthreatening. Berendt fumed, as angry as he'd ever been.

"It's about damn time! Stay outta there!" He freed one hand, reached to grab Amot's arm to lead him away.

With the butt end of his sword, Amot smashed his commander's nose. An unsavory crunch sounded. Berendt reeled back, collapsed to the ground cursing and screaming, holding his face in his hands. Yet he still maintained a hold on his sword.

~ On guard.

The small voice came from inside. A dizziness washed over Amot – confliction. *Shake it off.* Hollow sounds – clangy, fragmented and at regular intervals – began to build over the grunting and clamor of the Wulver battle.

The scout's ears homed in on the quiet clank and swish of heavy armor. Without even looking, he realized it was a bull rush – a queensman's favorite tactic.

Amot might have been confused, but not slow. He dropped flat to the ground, heard a grunt. Eriff's shins clipped the scout's body. He went sailing overtop with nothing but air to tackle, skidded over the burnt grass. Amot sprang to his feet, but stumbled back to one knee, head spinning. Black chaos swirled. He stabbed his blade into the earth for stability.

What's happening?

Amot's vision blurred, went blotchy. Using the sword like a crutch, he pushed himself to his feet. He adopted a low and solid stance, steadied himself. Patches of darkness swam about him, coalescing. He watched as a pattern formed in front of him, a shadowy image. Without warning, the apparition raced straight at him, faster than human. Amot raised his arm in desperation to defend himself… the shadow passed through him.

The next thing Amot saw was his commander's face, smeared in blood. Longsword raised, Berendt came at him in the midst of a lunging attack. The blade flashed, targeting his dominant hand. Amot's off-hand bracer blocked the attempt, effortlessly. The strike had been weak, minimal even, intended to temporarily harm rather than maim or kill. And Amot's bracer had been in exactly the right place to deflect the blow, without him even seeing it coming.

The scout drew his blade from the earth, sliced back the same way at Berendt's sword hand – a risky move in his current state, unbalanced. If he missed…

He didn't. Berendt dropped his weapon, pulled back, clenching his fist to seal the wound. Eriff had scrambled to his feet, but he wasn't fast enough on the draw. *Over-armored,* thought Amot, as he hoofed him down again.

The Wilder cast a glance at the scuffle behind him, eyes darting among the growling Wulvers. The fight wasn't going well for his pack. Weapons lay strewn about the ground, wretched from the hands of their wielders. More Haar-wulves had joined in, clearly dominating. It was only a matter of minutes before the Lusii-wulves would see their last hopes defeated.

T'saa was pinned. Kii stood over his body to defend, lurching and biting at any that dared to come near. The newcomer lay on the ground too, bloodied and trampled. Maa'iing danced around the perimeter, barking and snapping as he darted in and out, as though playing a deadly game.

"Maa'iing," Amot called. "Like a hare!" The yearling turned to stare at Amot, ears pricked. He hesitated.

"Like a hare," Amot repeated. "GO!" In his peripheral, he saw Eriff regain his footing. Amot turned to him. The queensman drew his rapier, held it defensively.

"We thought you were dead," Eriff told him, through clenched teeth. He was limping badly.

"Tell me you didn't do this." Amot feigned a wide swipe at Eriff, forced him to parry, then executed the disarm maneuver the queensman had taught him. Eriff's sword whipped from his hand and spiraled across the glade.

The queensman grimaced. "Now that was unexpected," he said, almost nonchalantly.

The Wilder's fury exploded, unleashed in his barking accusation. "Tell me you didn't just slaughter these Wulvers!" He shoved Eriff. The queensman lost his balance, hopped back and braced himself on his good leg. "Because if you did—"

Berendt answered instead. "Wait. Stop."

Amot could hear the pain in his commander's words, but he didn't care. He didn't care that Berendt was injured and he didn't care about the consequences of disobeying a direct order. He'd had enough of being ordered around anyway. He couldn't care less about Eriff either, for that matter.

Berendt used his sleeve to wipe blood from his face. "We had no choice."

The words seemed foreign to Amot. The voice inside sounded again.

~On guard.

The clamor of the melee around him suddenly took on a far-off quality. Echoey. And yet, the scout homed in on a faint, but familiar sound... the subtle creak of Rix's bow being tensed. *Rix... Rix...* He saw him in his mind.

~Charge him.

Amot's thoughts stuttered. *No.*

~Cut him down and cut the bowstring.

His thoughts stuttered again. *No... not Rix... Rix can't die.*

But if Berendt and Eriff and... and... the archer were responsible, then they are as vile as Haar-wulves. And... and they must all pay. Yes... all must pay dearly.

Amot was surprised to see the weapon he held readied for a strike. Eriff stood in front of him, buckler raised in defense. *No substitute for a proper shield,* thought Amot, *and that armor won't turn this keen edge.* The queensman was saying something. Calming words. Muffled. Amot couldn't make them out. From the corner of his eye, the scout spotted Haar coming at him.

Just then, Amot heard a twang. Something slipped into his back, just beneath the left shoulder blade. The hot, wet of it flooded his skin.

Rix? Rix...

Amot turned to face the spotter. Yes, it'd been Rix. *Of course. Who else?* Already, the deadeye had another arrow nocked and ready to fly, and a third in his shooting hand standing by. *Quick Rix.* But the next arrow was not trained on him. *Haar.*

Amot's shoulder burned. The black blade dropped from his hand. Suddenly, everything became clear. Crystal clear. Except his breathing. That was ragged.

"Wrong," he muttered to himself, "so wrong." The newfound clarity turned in on itself when Amot began to fall. It seemed he fell for a very long time. In his mind, he never stopped.

⇜

Dark dreams passed in troves. Amot woke with a wet, sloppy tongue licking at his face. He pushed the snout away with one arm, wiped off slobber with the other. He rubbed at his eyes. "Howler?" he said. But the canine wasn't Howler.

When the ranger opened his eyes, the first sight to greet him was Maa'iing's expectant gaze. The second was the glossy reflection of the sun in the yearling's eyes, shining through silhouetted pines. Evening had come. The third sight, and the last singular one, was a gentle trail of smoke drifting high into the air.

Amot scanned his immediate surroundings. He lay on his back in the pit meant for prisoners. The bulk of his upper body armor lay in a heap at his side, his cloak lay underneath. Blood marred the trampled earth around him in trails and patches. The yearling came at him again.

"Aaah, get lost," Amot said. The young Wulver tried to nuzzle his way past the ranger's defenses, aiming straight for the face again. With a solid push, Amot kept him at bay. The scout propped himself up on his elbows. Pain shot through his left shoulder. Amot pivoted to his side.

"There are many stories about this forest," stated a familiar voice, too young to be wise. "It messes with your brain, that's for sure." The voice was behind him. "Drives people mad, too. At least that's what Berendt said. Eriff thinks it's all drivel." The voice paused. "That was the word he used: 'drivel.' He makes it sound like the idea slid out of the corner of your mouth, trickled down the side of your face and then dripped down onto your boot, don't you think? Like you were utterly lowly to have even considered such a thing. That's the way he is though. He puts you down in so many ways, sometimes you don't even know he's doing it."

"Rix?" Amot said, his voice weak. The spotter's bow and ranging quiver leaned against a nearby stump.

"You're damn right it's Rix," came the reply. "'Save-your-ass Rix' to you, from now on."

Amot felt his left shoulder, winced. *Tender.* The wound there had been bandaged with spiderweave. "You feathered me."

The spotter edged along the pit so Amot could see him. Once in sight, he just stood there, long arms dangling, red hair matted with dried sweat. Rix's usual smirk had vanished. The spotter tilted his head, curious-like. His wilder ink colors shone as vibrant as his bright blue eyes and as fresh as his freckled complexion.

"Would you have stopped?"

"Stopped?" Amot struggled with the memory. Not a solid thing, this memory. The images in his mind formed and reformed, churned and rolled back, like the nonsense of a dream. The entire notion was unsettling.

"I... I..." A single word was all that came out. *I don't know.*

Chapter XXXVIII
Gryphon Battle
(Valkyries, Marec)

*S*HROUD'S *WELL, WHAT happened here?* Stormbringer didn't ask – no time. Her gryphon's wings cupped air for a drop landing. The loud crashing grew nearer. Ladybird touched down, squatted, bent a wing to Catwings.

"Get on!" Stormbringer shouted, extending her hand. Catwings reached out. She was dripping wet, half-naked, smeared with dirt and blood.

Grunting with the effort, the spearmaiden hauled her up, then cast a glance rearward. A dozen feet of thick-muscled, angry giant broke out of the tree line, deformed body garbed in hides and disjointed plates of armor. Its gnarled hand gripped a great club with foot-long spikes jutting out. The beast halted, cracked its neck.

His enormous head swiveled on a sideways tilt to survey Catwings' battle scene: the pool of red water, the slumped woman, the clothes hanging in a tree. He probably had the height to observe the tied-up scouts and horses nearby, which Stormbringer had spotted on her glide in. The loose horse had galloped off.

The giant raised its arms, shook them, roared to the sky in thunderous fury. Then the beast fixed its gaze on Stormbringer. One huge eye did the gazing, the other pressed shut from a massive black lump growing over it. The giant charged, crashing towards the valkyries, grinding its teeth and growling with effort as its thick legs thudded the earth.

Stormbringer kicked her mount into action. "Go, Ladybird, go!" she yelled.

With a heavy flap of wings, the Gold sprung into the air. Catwings tossed and twisted as the gryphon propelled them above the treetops.

"Tie in," Stormbringer shouted to her.

A whoosh of air sounded. The giant's club missed by a hair.

"Spree!" Catwings called back. "Where's Spree? She didn't come when I called."

Stormbringer didn't answer. She didn't know. *Scared up, maybe.*

Catwings craned her head, searching the skies desperately. Then she scanned the ground.

"Norwin's Breeze!" she yelled. "Tall Hallman!"

Stormbringer tracked the wind rider's gaze. Both giants were on the scene, with Tallman in their midst. The ranger swung his axe at the closest, a miss, then ducked and darted past the beast. He moved fast.

Smart. He was no longer caught in between. But there was another problem.

"Damn it!" Stormbringer yelled back to Catwings. "Look!" Two Harrowian scouts were closing in on the unfair fight. One stopped to cock his crossbow, took aim at the ranger.

"I'm going in," Stormbringer shouted.

"But the giant!"

"One threat at a time."

Stormbringer turned to see if Catwings was belted in properly, let out a gasp. "STOP!" she yelled. Her wind rider was not even holding on, let alone secured. Catwings crouched as though ready to spring off the side.

"What are you doing? Strap in! Wind Rider, that's an order."

Catwings made a sideways glance to the spearmaiden, her face placid as the moon. She squeezed her eyes shut, spoke softly. "Norwin, carry me."

"No!" Stormbringer cried. She reached back to grab Catwings, but too late. Arms spread wide, Catwings leapt off Ladybird's back. She sailed into the air. Buffeted by the winds, she began to plummet. Adrenalin surged through Stormbringer.

"DOWN!" she called to Ladybird, rough handling her mount hard and fast. But she knew it'd be too late. They weren't high enough for a stunt like that.

As Catwings fell towards the earth, Ladybird on the chase, Spree zinged underneath them both. The spritely wind rider flopped onto the gryphon's back. Stormbringer's heart skipped a beat when she saw Catwings clinging to the Harpy, struggling to gain her saddle. *Crazy stupid...* But there was no time to criticize or marvel over the feat. Stormbringer shook her head, shunted Ladybird off the winds and redirected her dive towards the crossbowman. He was loading a second shot. *He won't get a third.*

As Stormbringer propelled forward, out of the corner of her eye she saw Catwings bee-lining it for the giant on Tallman. *Ekkon's wheel, Sister.* She focused on her own target, called on Ladybird.

"Snatch!"

The Gold's claws shot out. The gryphon swooped in, clasped its talons around the crossbowman. He squirmed helplessly as the claws lifted him into the air, ripped into his body. Ladybird raised him to eighty feet.

"Release," Stormbringer ordered. The man fell, screaming.

"No Harpy's going to save you," she muttered to herself.

Out of the blue, another Gold appeared – Electra – bearing two riders: Galewind and Marec. The knightmaiden drove her gryphon to swoop down at the second Harrowian scout. He was wise to her though, got two shots off with his crossbow as she flew in. A bolt plunged into Electra's side. Galewind veered away before she could make the grab.

Stormbringer turned her attention to Tallman, now in a tight squeeze. She watched him sprint, take cover, then slash at the two-eyed, brawny giant who came for him. Tallman dashed to the next hiding spot before it could counterattack. *How long can that cat-and-mouse last?*

But the giant on Tallman kept glancing up. Spree circled in a tight arc. *Catwings is slowing the beast down. She'll drop down on his ugly head the second he looks away.*

The spearmaiden swung her gaze to the one-eyed giant, now kneeling beside the captives and fidgeting with their bonds. *Breaking them out, are you? Not so fast.* That beast wasn't checking the sky at all. *Stupid brute.* Stormbringer swung Ladybird around, urged her mount into a fast dive. *I'll take this one out.* She cast a quick glance to Catwings.

Hugging Spree close, the wind rider was in the midst of dropping down on Tallman's giant, just as it closed in on him.

Fight the gryphon, Catwings told herself.

Spree swooped in, latched onto the giant's back. The Harpy tore at its flesh with her talons, while her beak pecked repeatedly at the back of its massive head, neck, and ears.

"The eyes, Spree," Catwings shouted. "Peck its eyes out."

The giant reeled, twisting and turning. Spree clung on. The giant reached behind, but its hunched-over posture and overbuilt musculature prevented it from making contact with the bird. The giant swiped its mighty club – a miss. Catwings felt the rush of air. *Too close.*

Tallman charged in, axe swinging, slashed the giant's calf. With Spree tearing at leathery skin and muscle, the giant grunted, swung its club wildly at the ranger – another miss.

Reeling again, the giant lunged back, pressed itself against a stand of pines. Catwings dodged the heavy branches, but her exposed torso scraped along the smaller ones. Spree got pinned, let out a squawk. A subtle shift came in the giant's posture, a purposeful twist. Adrenaline surged through Catwings. *He's going to slam us to the ground!* She yanked hard on the Harpy's reins. "Fly!"

Spree flapped heavy against the motion to break free, hooked by her injured claw on the giant's hide armor. The brute began to topple into a controlled fall. But before the giant could trap them underneath, the Harpy freed itself, flapping wildly to push off as the giant slammed to the earth.

"Maul!" Catwings yelled, the rage surging through her. "Get 'em!"

Spree dropped onto the giant's chest, wings spread, hissing, beak wide open. The gryphon raked flesh, pecked at the eyes. A great hand batted Spree away. Catwings was thrown off, landing in a patch of moss and rotten wood. Her gryphon ended up in a tree.

Tallman, who'd come charging, positioned himself amidst the flailing limbs of the beast. He slashed at the giant's neck. His great axe penetrated deep. A torrent of blood gushed out. The giant lashed out in desperation, caught the ranger with its fist. Tallman took a solid hit to the gut and flew back.

Catwings pushed herself to her feet. She glanced at the downed giant, brushed the forest litter off of her bare chest. She ignored a look of bewilderment from Tallman and tilted her gaze up to her Harpy, struggling in the treetops, its weight snapping the branches that held her. Catwings hastened toward the tree. "I have to get her loose!"

"I'll cover you," Tallman said, plainly winded.

Stormbringer urged Ladybird to tilt her angle of approach just so, then slid her spear-like pole arm out of its fastenings. She spun the weapon around so the prong would strike flesh, as opposed to the hammer or spear point. She firmed up a two-handed grip.

One good hit, she told herself. A precision strike was all she needed.

Ladybird sailed silent over the treetops, then dropped down low where the one-eyed giant knelt, completely at unawares. Stormbringer braced herself for the flyby attack, held her weapon steady as her gryphon vectored towards him, aimed carefully. The captives saw, wriggled frantically, muffled voices called out warnings. The giant turned its head halfway around.

The prong made contact, plunged into the giant's head. The wrenching force pried Stormbringer from her mounts' back. Heavy straps kept her in. Struggling to maintain her grip, she held the prong fast as it jammed into solid bone and got hooked. Ladybird and the giant spun before the prong released.

The giant roared in anguish as Ladybird thumped air to get up and away. Blood streamed into its huge eye. In a frenzy, the goliath felt out the ground for rocks, found some big ones, then stood up and whipped them – not even close.

That's right, you dumb oaf, thought Stormbringer. *Waste your damn energy.*

The spearmaiden looped around wide for another pass. She readied her pole arm for a second strike. This time though, she would use the piercing spearhead.

Thwunk.

Stormbringer gasped when she saw the heavy quarrel bury itself in Ladybird's neck. The Gold jerked beneath her, twisting with the hit. Stormbringer spun around as another projectile whipped past her head.

"Up and away," she called to Ladybird. Her gryphon climbed.

Galewind, riding high, pulled up beside her, called out. "We have a sniper."

Marec eyed the hit from his seat, strapped in behind the knight-maiden. "And a good one, at that."

Stormbringer shouted back, "We must take that crossbowman out. Now!"

"Agreed," Galewind replied, across the winds, "but Electra is out of the fight. She took a bad hit. I'll keep her up as long as I can. How's Ladybird holding out?"

Stormbringer ran her hands through Ladybird's neck feathers, felt out the quarrel. "Looks superficial, penetrated nearly crosswise." She looked over the side at the crossbowman below. "Are you able to provide cover fire while I drop down to neutralize him?"

"No," Marec called out. "Drop me off. I'll do it. Me and that ranger."

Galewind protested. "Tallman has a giant to contend with, and you don't even have a sword."

Marec said, "My armor protects me from Harrowian crossbows."

Stormbringer nodded. "Very well, go then," she told him, "but take my spear." She extended her weapon so he could grab it.

Marec shook his head. "Disarm a lady in the middle of a fight? Never!" He smiled and winked. "I'll manage."

Stormbringer huffed, shared a frown with Galewind.

The knightmaiden hesitated, bit her lip hard. A grimness came over her. She glanced back, nodded to Marec. "All right then, as you wish." Galewind redirected Electra to a quick descent, steering clear of the last known location of the sniper. At a safe distance, the Gold touched down.

Stormbringer kept an eye on them as the queensman climbed down from the gryphon's back and thudded onto solid ground. Galewind didn't linger long. Electra was soon beating her wings again, in ascent.

"There," Rainsong told Ashes, pointing. "Two Golds."

She'd watched them in the distance, patrolling the skies, swooping down and then up again. *The Tower Guard had to have seen them by now.* At times they made tight turns, rapid descents – in battle, no doubt.

Ashes sprang forward again, like a grasshopper, flapping as she went. As Rainsong closed in on the action, she could hear frantic shouts. *But who are they fighting?*

After Ashes' next hop, the wind rider had her answer. She came upon a one-eyed giant, looking to the sky and palming a large rock. Blood spewed from its head. At its feet, three Harrowian soldiers struggled with their bonds. One got rid of its gag, shouted at the grotesque-looking monstrosity to hurry up and untie them. But the giant had other problems.

Tallman was making a calculated approach, great axe in hand.

Is he nuts?

Rainsong glanced up and to the right. She spotted Catwings and Spree in a tree, large feathers dropping down around them.

"Norwin's Breeze," she said aloud. "What a disaster."

The giant turned its gaze to Tallman and whipped the rock at him instead. Tallman dove to dodge but didn't quite make it – he took a glancing blow. The giant stooped to pick up its spiked club, to beat down on the ranger who was scrambling to get up.

Rainsong scowled, yelled out. "Oh no you don't!" Her voice felt strong again. The giant glanced her way.

The wind rider's ears pounded as she quickly undid the harness buckles. "Ashes and I are going to carve you up." Her heart beat wildly. As the surge of blood coursed through her veins, pumped into her muscles, her injuries from the night went numb. She leaned forward on her mount, gripped the reins tight.

"Attack," she commanded Ashes.

The Harpy closed in, low and creeping, drawing the giant's full attention. The brute slowly turned, club ready. The gryphon was more its size.

Ashes stopped just out of reach, wriggled into a crouch, then sprang into the air. The giant swung, but too slow. Mid-flight, the wind rider leapt off Ashes back. And as the gryphon pounced on the giant's hideous face, Rainsong tumbled on the ground, rolled to her feet. Muscles tensed and feeling stronger than ever, she drew her longsword. The spiked club dropped to the ground. Ashes scratched and pecked at the giant's single eye, Rainsong charged the beast on foot.

The giant reeled and twisted with the Harpy clinging to it, sweeping its huge arms and tearing at the gryphon to get it off his face.

Rainsong screamed an undulating battle cry as she maneuvered for close combat. Taking quick note of gaps in the giant's armor, she slashed at its calves. A second later, she plunged her sword into the torso. The giant spun around, flinging Ashes to the forest as it toppled sideways. The deformed body smashed to the ground, head knocking with a thunderous crack. The huge eye popped out, bounced once on the earth, then snapped back, fastened by a bloody tether to the empty eye socket.

Marec hit the dirt when he heard crashing branches above. A Harpy gryphon plummeted through the trees, then rolled to his side.

"Ashes?"

The gryphon lay on the ground, stunned it seemed, but otherwise not seriously harmed. The queensman's eyes fell immediately to a scabbard, tied to the Harpy's side.

"Ah," he said. Marec reached out, undid the clasp, pulled the sword from its scabbard. "A rapier." He turned it over in his hands. "My rapier."

A grin crept across Marec's face as wide as any grin. Holding the sword, he scanned the terrain. In his mind he tried to match what he perceived around him to the aerial view of the last known location of the sniper. A particularly tall pine looked somewhat familiar, a few hundred feet away.

There.

Marec walked as quietly as he could on the thick bed of pine needles beneath his feet, which muffled his steps. He moved slowly so that his armor would not swish and clink. As sure as day is day, the duelist came upon the crossbowman from behind, at unawares, just as he'd hoped.

The Harrowian squatted low at the edge of a meadow, crossbow cocked and raised, watching the sky.

A stick snapped, underfoot.

The sniper turned, saw Marec for what he was, fired off a bolt.

Marec felt the impact in his gut.

Grunting with the effort, the queensmen charged forth. The sniper reloaded, but didn't have the time to aim before Marec's sword pierced his heart.

The crossbowman died first.

Marec withdrew his blade, stumbled backwards, then leaned his back against a pine. Slowly, he slid to the ground.

A loud creak sounded, then a knock, and then a hollow voice. "Crossbow-proof, eh?" the voice said, looming above.

"You heard?" Marec replied. He coughed, tasted blood in his mouth, spit it out.

"I hear everything," said the voice. "I am very sensitive to sounds. All sounds."

Marec snickered. "I lied. It was the only way that stubborn valkyrie would drop me off."

"An honorable lie is as good as the truth," said the voice.

Marec closed his eyes, snickered one last time. "Sometimes it is."

His head flopped sideways, limp. The duelist felt a gentle desert breeze on his exposed cheek, then heard a soft voice from long ago, of a woman he'd loved. She tried to tell him something, but he couldn't make out the words. Echoey. Distant. He strained to hear.

"We waited for you, but you never came," the wispy voice told him. "Me and my sister waited."

Marec grimaced slightly, felt a trickle of blood run down from the corner of his mouth.

"Go to hell… fucking know-it-all ghost pines."

CHAPTER XXXIX

SMOKE SIGNALS

(Rix)

RIX ROLLED THE tip of his tongue over the snake bite piercings in his lower lip, tasted the metallic tang of the silver studs. He brooded over his Kith brother's confusing responses. Amot looked like hell – scraped, bruised, bloodied. And a big part of that was Rix's fault. *Did I really have to plunge an arrow into him?* The sick feeling in his stomach told him otherwise. *Maybe I could've yelled instead.* He addressed Amot.

"You were about to go 'wilder' on Eriff, weren't you? With that damn striker." Rix paused, added emphasis. "Again." He shook his head and drew a deep, pained breath. "This is a Diamond Saber replay, except worse. What's the problem? Is it Eriff? Is it the sword?"

Rix waited for the answers, gauging Amot's expression. He'd always managed to get some kind of response out of Amot. Even after the recent raid-gone-bad in the Akedan ruins, the spotter had managed to coax a smile out of him, despite three melted dead and a raging alchemical fire that lit up the bay.

But not today. The scout's face betrayed nothing. Not even that he'd heard Rix's words, much less processed them. Amot sat hunched in the pit, silent and unnaturally still, void eyes staring at the gently swaying chains that lined the glade, through them it seemed, to the pines beyond.

Maybe he reached his limit, Rix thought. And it was a reasonable limit: blood-soaked earth all around, air hanging thick with the smells of burning flesh and singed fur, bodies being dragged out of dens. The spotter scanned the site, wondering where his commanders had gotten to. He needed to get answers before they got back. Before Eriff started picking Amot's story apart. Rix watched as Haar-wulves heaved another carcass onto Berendt's sickening bonfire. Berendt had insisted they burn the dead because they had to get out of there fast and there'd be no time to bury them. Others from Haar's pack led slaves away or hauled loot. The gallant was nowhere to be seen. *Probably 'negotiating' with Haar – selling our souls more like, to buy Haar's.*

The young canine still lay at the scout's feet, refusing to leave his side, resting its snout on its forepaws. Its white fur was marred by grime and blood. Rix was certain the creature was a Wulver. He'd tried a dozen times to shoo it off or scare it fleeing into the woods, until he saw other young pups being dragged away. And while Amot had been out cold, this one's wolfish eyes had tracked Haar's Wulvers as they passed, going about their cruel business of exercising their agreed-upon rights to plunder the dens. The arrangement wasn't something Rix was comfortable with. None of it was. But a deal is a deal, and he was but a peon in all of this.

The spotter prompted Amot again. "Would you have gone crazy on Berendt too? Finished him off?"

This time, the scout reacted. He appeared to realize something had been asked of him. Amot shifted his gaze from the pines and the dangling chains, but still not directly to Rix. Instead, he rested his eyes on a small, bright patch of bare ground in front of him, bright from the sun's slowly retreating rays. It was one of the last bright patches to survive the cool, long shadows of evening that'd crept along the desecrated ground to fill the space around them.

"Berendt," Amot muttered under his breath. He put his face down into his hands, stayed that way for a long moment. Then he spread his fingers wide and ran them through his long locks of dark hair, as though brushing away unsavory thoughts. Seeing this, the yearling rose, sniffed the back of the scout's left hand, gave it a nudge, then wet-nosed Amot's cheek full on. Amot jerked his head back, out of range of the sloppy tongue that tried to follow. In the same motion, his hand reached out mechanically to scritch behind the fur-bearer's ears, while keeping him out of slobbering range.

Rix repeated his question, louder and firmer, waited half a breath, then added, "I know you can hear me." After receiving another null response, Rix sighed. "Berendt's pretty pissed. You'll need to explain yourself to him before he stands you up in front of the Overseer and has you declared 'Unchosen.' Is that what you want?"

No response. Rix raised his voice another notch. "And you'll need to explain yourself to Eriff before he flexes his royal thumb and has Icy Blue condemn your actions." Rix motioned to the barrier around the glade. "You see those clinking chains? That's what you'll be wearing when they send you to Jakka, on the next prisoner transfer."

Amot shifted his gaze to the yearling, roughed up its fur a little more.

"HEY!" Rix crouched, snapped his fingers in front of Amot's face. "What about Eriff? You were about to strike the commander of this mission with that sword, poised for a kill if you believe *his* take on it. Are you going to let *his* voice be the only voice? Are you going to let a *Haulik* win? Eriff's had it in for you from day one." The spotter paused. He had to know.

"So, were you planning to kill him or not? You didn't go that far last time."

Still no response. Rix threw his arms to his side.

"C'mon Amot. You need to explain yourself. To me, at least. What the hell were you thinking?" Rix let out a deep sigh. "Let me help."

Finally, Amot looked up to Rix, eyes shining with defiance. "No, I wasn't trying to kill anybody, even if they deserved it." Then his gaze darted about the glade. What he saw made him scowl, and his voice became laced with venom. "What happened here, Rix? Where is the goodly tribe that made this place their protected home? Where are their young? Where are the Wulvers that were captives in this pit before I became the captive? T'saa… Kii."

Amot glanced to the pile of burning bodies. "Is that where they are?"

Rix definitely didn't want to take on the job of explaining this mess to Amot, or defending it. *Save that for Eriff. This is his mess.* In fact, he felt compelled to fall in line with Amot like he always did, to criticize the leadership, poke holes in the system. But he didn't. He kept his composure firm.

"I'm asking the questions here," Rix asserted. He crossed his arms. "And you better think of good answers, because Berendt and Eriff are going to come over and ask you the same ones. Next in line will be the Overseer. And after that, a magistrate."

Amot brought his gaze back to Rix. "How many dead on each side?"

"Berendt will have those numbers."

Amot narrowed his eyes. "How many did *you* kill, Rix? I saw your arrows."

Rix hesitated. "I killed two and feathered a lot more. That's my job. Satisfied? How many of our *allies* did you kill?"

"Not enough." Amot shut his eyes for a long moment, lips pursed, containing himself and his angry tongue. "Allies," he repeated, calmly. Then he nodded. When he opened his eyes again, he made a sideways glance to Berendt, who'd come into view stoking the fire with a thick branch. Amot did a double take on him.

"Yes, Berendt has the striker. He bundled it in his cloak and slung it over his back." Rix shook his head.

Amot swung his gaze back to Rix. "What is it you want from me, Rix?"

The spotter tipped his chin in the direction of Berendt. "Let's start with that sword. It's the one we came here for, right?" Rix followed up with a quick glance at it. The metal showed through the loose wrapping. "I don't recall it being black."

"You're right, Rix," Amot replied, deriding him in tone like it should be obvious. "The sword wasn't black. The Chainmaker made it that way."

"Chainmaker? Is that what you shouted?"

Amot nodded slowly. "I did."

"The Chainmaker is a demon Hurlorn," Rix stated.

"Says who?"

"Says Haar's bone-tosser."

Amot shook his head. "No. That, he is not. Haar's shaman lies."

Haar lies too, thought Rix. But he didn't say it. He didn't want to say anything that might trigger Amot. And he didn't want to choose sides. Not if he didn't have to.

"Anything else?" Amot said.

"Yeah. Cool down for a minute."

Amot looked away. He tested the mobility of his left shoulder by rolling it, then shrugged it a few times. He raised his left arm straight out, winced in pain. It changed his whole expression, his demeanor. The hate was gone.

"Sorry about that," Rix said.

"Dammit, you feathered me good, too."

"I had no choice. You deserved worse. Think about how you'd feel if Haar took you down instead. You'd be diced."

"Are you saying you were trying to save me? If that's the case, next time don't. Or maybe just holler instead." Amot rotated his shoulder again, slower. "Well, maybe it's not *that* bad." He felt the sutures on his wound beneath the spiderweave, winced again. "I've had worse." His next sentence he phrased like a rhetorical question. "Berendt stitched me up?"

"Yep. Berendt. Right before Eriff stitched him up."

Amot sighed heavily, rubbed his forehead as though at odds with the situation, with himself. But at the same time, he also seemed to be normalizing. To keep him that way, Rix decided to omit mentioning the fact that, as a member of the Chamber of Aelish, Eriff could have sped up the healing process dramatically, but chose not to. *Probably didn't want him to be full strength just yet.*

"You gave it a weak draw, didn't you? The arrow." Another rhetorical question. "And right where that damn gap is, where the shoulder plate meets the cuirass. I've been meaning to fix that. Shit Rix, you're a spot-on deadeye."

"The best," Rix replied, infusing his tone with confidence. "When your left arm reaches forward, the shoulder plate lifts and it's all bare skin underneath. The hole was the size of an apple."

"And the draw?"

"As gentle as could be." Rix added a hint of tease to his voice. "I don't even know why you fell. It was more of a warning shot. A faerie strike."

Amot grunted. "There was blood."

"More than there should've been." Rix kept a straight face and a serious tone. "You bleed easy."

Amot almost smirked. "You're too much, you little shit."

Finally. Rix could feel he was getting through to him. *Maybe he's not so far gone after all.*

Amot patted the yearling on the side, gave him a friendly nudge. Then he rose to his feet.

Rix reiterated his earlier enquiry. "Did you know what you were doing, or not?"

Amot shrugged cautiously, mindful of his injury. "It's a bit of a haze, but I think the sword gives... I think it makes me experience what's happening during combat in a different way, even without invoking the farseeing."

"Farseeing? That would be suicide at close range."

"Whatever happened, it was... disorienting. I can't quite explain it, but I felt I was there – fighting – and yet part of me was somewhere else at the same time... far and near at once, sort of." He looked Rix in the eye. "There's a certain inner and outer reach to how this thing works, y'know..." He trailed off.

Rix waited patiently for Amot to finish his idea. *This might be important.*

"No, I wasn't really hazy. I was... partially displaced? I just... I just needed to shut down, maybe."

"Shut down?"

Amot looked away. "Something like that. It's..." He began to rub his wrists. "I was angry, I guess. I know I wouldn't have seriously hurt any of you."

It seemed to Rix that Amot was talking in circles, looking for ways to justify his actions, denying their consequences. *Amot's dancing around the truth. That's not like him. Not like him at all.*

Amot looked to his wrists, rotated them, examined the red ring of raw skin encircling each. Then he looked back to Rix. The spotter explained.

"Eriff had you bound up." Rix hesitated. "And that's not all. He was willing to let Haar's pack-mates watch over you. Imagine that?" Instantly, Rix regretted his words. He'd let down his guard. Revealed too much. *I shouldn't have said that.* He kept on.

"I volunteered to watch, untied your wrists and I'll probably get in shit for it. I don't trust those creatures."

"Thanks for that. What has Eriff been doing?"

"He sent smoke signals using an old blanket dragged out from one of the dens. Last I saw him, he was on his way to meet Haar."

"Smoke signals?"

"To Order Valkyrie. So anyways," Rix continued, "even if your shoulder really doesn't hurt that much, act like you can barely function because of it. I told Eriff it was a solid hit and Berendt backed me up. I told him the injury would be 'debilitating.'"

Amot nodded his understanding.

"Besides," Rix continued, "I don't want you ruining my reputation."

Amot cracked a smile. Rix took a deep breath, then felt like someone was watching. He turned to see Berendt looking their way. At the same time, Eriff re-entered the glade from his private stroll with the Wulver command elements – the two nastiest of them all, Haar and Grizzer. Eriff glanced over to the pit as well, then marched straight to Berendt. The two began talking amongst themselves, casting heavy glances Amot's way.

Rix stepped backed to where he kept his quiver. "I'm going to get Berendt. I told him I would as soon as you came to, so I'm overdue." He strapped the quiver on.

Amot said, "Who's going to watch me?"

Rix grabbed his bow next, nocked an arrow. "I'll still be watching."

Amot eyed the arrow.

Rix casually tilted his bow sideways in a showy way, met Amot's gaze. "Just an act," he told Amot, with a smirk. "Don't worry, I'm not going to shoot you again." *If I don't have to.*

Amot nodded.

"Don't go anywhere though, got it?" Rix said. "You'll make me look bad."

Amot acknowledged with a nod. The spotter turned about, made off to his superiors.

A few steps in, Amot called out. "Hold it."

Rix halted.

"The dead…" Amot trailed off.

Rix pivoted around to face him. "What about them?"

Amot raised a hand, rubbed at the back of his neck. He seemed overtaken by sudden emotion. "Wulvers expect to be buried when they die." His voice wavered, eyes glistened. "Did you see a… did you see one with…" He blinked, shook his head, then forced out what he had to say. "Did you see whelps? Were there any whelps?"

"Whelps? Some were taken, others escaped into the woods. I don't know why they kept so many *wolves* for pets. I guess it makes sense though – like us having dogs, except the relationship is closer."

Amot opened his mouth to comment, but clearly stopped himself.

Rix winked, signaling that he knew what the yearling was, but also that he'd keep the secret to himself, for what it was worth. He looked to the young Wulver. "I think you have a new companion, Amot." Rix couldn't help but to smile slightly as he continued. "Good luck getting rid of him." He felt a hollow pang in his gut for Amot's dog, for the way he died. But there was something else there. Something positive. *Nothing can replace Howler, but this might be good for Amot.*

The spotter turned and continued on his way, focusing on his next steps. Amot needed him now more than ever. Rix quickly formulated a strategy for dealing with his superiors. *Maybe, just maybe, I can convince them that Amot acted under some unknown influence – a Colossus. Then maybe they'll go easy on him.*

CHAPTER XL
ALIAS
(Amot)

AMOT HAD NEVER been an older brother, and yet considered himself Rix's mentor in an older brother sort of way. *That might have to change, now*, he thought. Maa'iing watched as the spotter made his way towards mission command, then turned his gaze back to Amot, eyes expecting.

"Tracker," Amot said. "From now on, your name is 'Tracker,' do you hear me?" Giving Maa'iing a dog-like nickname might help to protect him and get him out of the forest. The yearling gazed back blankly, as though waiting for some cue that he could actually relate to.

"Tracker," Amot repeated, this time speaking with the same intonation in his voice that he used when saying "Maa'iing."

Tracker drew in close. Amot rewarded him with a side-belly rub. "Good boy," he said. "Good Tracker."

Amot spoke in a low voice, so as not to be overheard – at least not by the humans. "You don't really understand what happened here yet, do you?" The scout sighed. "That's okay. I'll explain everything to you." *Someday, once I find out all the details, and once you're old enough to hear them.* Amot took some solace in the notion that the yearling might be too young to fully remember this day.

Chapter XLI
Unbeliever
(Eriff)

"Your spotter is on his way over," Eriff said, cradling his helm against his breastplate armor. He'd stuffed his white-metal gauntlets into it. Together, the three pieces of armor – gauntlets, plate and helm – comprised a matching set, gifted by House Ralador on the eve of his recent promotion. Each piece still glimmered like new in the dusky light, and each piece bore the distinguished mark of Ironeagle – the most prestigious forgers in all of Theia.

Berendt growled in frustration, struggling with the long branch he'd cut to force a fresh body over the hottest spot in his huge fire. He retracted the makeshift poker, tossed it to ground. "We'll get his report, then start the interrogation."

Eriff turned his back to the fire and the smoke, checked on their rogue scout. "No one is watching Amot," he said.

"We are, Gallant," Berendt gruffed. "Trust me, he's not going anywhere."

Eriff nodded. *Gallant,* he thought. *Has a nice ring to it, especially coming from the likes of him.* Eriff ignored the rangers' deviation from his specific orders about overwatch. *They never quite do anything exactly as instructed.* An annoying trait, but they'd done their job in the Wulver battle, and so he let the breach in protocol slide.

Eriff pondered the favor he stood to gain though his mission's success, now guaranteed for all practical purposes. Upon return to Gan, he could expect to rise from his station as a quick reaction force squad leader to commander of a light infantry in the Queen's 136th Lancer Battalion. Eriff couldn't deny the value of the opportunity. Yet, his enthusiasm was measured. The posting wouldn't be perfect – right battalion, wrong company. He would've preferred a heavy cavalry, or *any* cavalry. But infantry? Anyone bearing the Haulik surname would've considered the appointment a slight, a putdown, a cross to bear until seen through. His family bred Akedan Lord Horses, after all – the most sought-after mounts in any cavalry. Meanwhile, half his men would be green-riders.

I want to see each green-rider fall at least a hundred times, Eriff thought, smirking to himself. *Train them hard – exactly what my drill master would have done, back at the academy.* Dana Leigh-Mignon was her name, from one of the lower houses. Delicate she was not, and Champion Leigh-Mignon had no trouble "toughening up the blue bloods," as she liked to say over a drink. The gallant sighed. *I will chalk this up to character building, I suppose.*

Rix stopped, turned and began to backtrack. He raised a staying hand to Amot as he started into a jog.

Eriff huffed. "What is Rix doing now?"

Berendt gestured right of the pit. "The pup took off to one of the dens, close to some of Haar's plundering Wulvers. Rix is fetching it back."

Eriff sighed. "If it isn't one dog, it's another." His chafed hands felt strangely naked in the cool evening air, contrasted by the heat radiating on his back from Berendt's giant fire. *So much for discretion,* he thought of the fire. Half of Harrow was probably watching the smoke billow up and out of Whisperwood by now. It'd be dark soon, at least. The blunder was just another example of the sorts of minor disasters that tended to happen if he didn't enforce strict control over every single detail.

The queensman's cool eyes swept over the glade: surveying, evaluating. He slid his fingers through his hair, thick and saturated with dried sweat.

The surrounding pines, tall and straight, cast their evening shade over the grounds before him. The patches of scorched earth had begun to blend in with the rest of the field. Beyond the perimeter chains, a smoky grey gloom lay waiting in the forest, its promise of malice only partially fulfilled. Wispy clouds, basking in orange light, stretched across the southwestern sky, and were already dipping their thin edges in purple hues above the treetops. Night would not be patient, and Eriff sensed an air of convergence in its coming; closure after a day of battle. He shivered as the gruesome day flashed in his mind, before he could push it aside.

Nonetheless, Operation Diamondback had gone about as well as it could have, thanks to his skills at diplomacy with the Haar tribe, his efficient planning, and a little luck, which is always welcome. The only blemish was a single mad ranger. Eriff regarded Berendt.

"I had suspected something might be unstable about Amot, even before Diamond Saber."

Berendt scratched under his eyepatch. "I'll be the first to admit he's had his troubles, but this is different."

Eriff scoffed. "Your scout has now proven his misconduct enough times over to seal the military tribunal against him: reckless endangerment, driven by wild emotional swings instead of good sense, confrontational to superiors, disobedience, desertion, and now this — betrayal of his own comrades before having to be taken down."

The lead Kith shut his eyes for a long moment, nodded. The expression left on his face was solemn.

"The man needs to be locked up," Eriff went on, "before he does serious damage to the interests of Gan and Deepweald. I will see to it."

Berendt didn't respond. He just scrubbed his face with one hand, then gazed at the field. Eriff watched with him, eyes swiveling to various locations. Throughout the glade, Haar's unruly and undisciplined beasts still worked the last of the dens, but no fighting had occurred for some time and there were no fresh kills to speak of. Over the minute the pair stood there, one of Haar's own dragged the bloody mess of a Wulver body out of a hole, flopped it onto the burnt grass. The carcass had the common look of a trapper's catch. A second Wulver, larger, baring its teeth and snarling, chased the first one off, then entered the den alone, no doubt to claim the spoils. Eriff shook his head in disdain. *Wild dogs, the lot of them.*

"It's about time," Berendt gruffed. He gestured to Rix and Amot, back in the oversized hollow used for detainment. The scout stooped down, held the pup in place.

The pair watched Rix approach again – third time by Eriff's count. He wondered if there'd be a fourth. Berendt patted his doublet pockets, grunted when he found what he was looking for. He'd be replenishing his pipe weed any second now.

"Isn't there enough smoke here for you already?" Eriff remarked.

Berendt grunted in response, pulled the pipe out of his mouth and tapped it on his knee guard. His face was a mess, and beet-red with the exertion of having fed the bonfire continuously for over an hour. Still more bodies to come from the last few holes.

"It'll be interesting to hear what Quick Rix has to report," the ranger remarked, brushing bits of bark and grass off his person. He proceeded to pick crud out of his blood-stained beard. Berendt had bandaged up the gash on his nose with the same sterilizing, sticky mesh rangers carry with them wherever they go – similar to a non-sticky variant they wore under their armor. He'd made a shabby job of it, and it would've left a nasty scar had Eriff not intervened.

Another scar would have blended in just fine, he thought, glancing at the rough tissue around the ranger's eyepatch. Whatever the case, Eriff's healing touch had to be used sparingly, given his Elder Leviathan's dire condition and the demand from others with higher station in the Citadel. Higher than radiance channeler, at least.

The young ginger strode up to them with a natural glide, composite recurve bow in hand. His high, leather moccasins made his steps soundless – a force of habit with the Kith. Eriff ran his eyes over Rix. It'd taken some time, but the gallant had gotten used to the spotter's appearance – piercings, ink markings, and all. Wilders in general had an edge to them that his Queen's Guard comrades would never have, try as they might.

"So, Rix," Berendt roughed out. "What does Amot have to say for himself this time?"

The spotter grimaced, rested the tip of his bow on the grassy earth. "He's a bit mixed up. Something happened… I don't know what, exactly, but he seems to be coming out of it."

Eriff said, "Happened? We all saw what happened."

Berendt growled in response. "That's not what Rix means. Nasty, twisted whispers, messing with his head. I heard a few that I had to shake off myself."

"I think that's part of it," Rix said. "But he's having trouble remembering too. It seems to have something to do with the striker."

Eriff asked, "Did he tell you how he recovered the sword?"

Rix looked away to the right, bit his bottom lip. Then he glanced back to the slave pit, to Amot.

Here it comes, thought Eriff. *The lie.* Clearly, the two rangers were already covering for their comrade.

The spotter shifted his weight from one leg to the other, then swung his gaze to Eriff. "He had help from the Wulvers that lived in this glade." Rix hesitated. Clearly, there was something more.

"And?" the queensman prodded.

"And he might have had help from someone he calls the 'Chainmaker.'"

Eriff scoffed. "Haar's demon?"

Rix nodded.

Eriff groaned. "The Wulver's story sounded more like superstitious bonethrower nonsense than reality."

Berendt grunted. "I wouldn't be so sure. This has the stink of Colossus meddling all over it." He turned to Rix. "Could this 'demon' have influenced Amot's actions?"

Eriff groaned again. "Now you think he's possessed? Absurd." *That won't go over well in the tribunal.*

Rix shrugged. "I don't know. Maybe."

A trickle of blood ran down from Berendt's nostril. He pinched his nose, tilted his head to the sky. "I told him not to follow Ekkon," he complained. "Why couldn't he have just followed a more sensible Colossus like Aelish the Resplendent or the Green Dragon."

Eriff's patience for this sort of talk was wearing thin. "Ludicrous," he spat. "None of this has anything to do with Ekkon. That beast does not even respond to its followers. Your scout is simply a hellion and a screw up."

Berendt tilted his head level again, let go his nose, sniffed. "Easy now," he told Eriff, looking to the pit. "I'm pissed too, but until we know what happened—"

"No," Eriff cut in. "You need to expel him from the Kith before he completely spoils the already sketchy name. And this is a *Crown* mission, meaning that when we get back, Amot WILL face the military tribunal promised. And I guarantee, once Lord Ralador gets hold of this information, Amot WILL be locked up and sent away in chains – forged by a true 'chain maker.'"

Berendt grunted, gave Eriff a sideways look, eyes narrowed. He raised a hand to his chin and rubbed it. "I don't see it that way."

Rix's eyes lit up at the ranger's words.

Berendt puckered slightly in defiance, shook his head and continued. "The way I see it, Amot just did what we did, Gallant, except better. He allied with one of the Wulver packs, the right one from what I can tell, gathered information on the mission objective and acted on it accordingly. And – don't forget this – *he* was successful. We still wouldn't have the striker were it not for him."

Eriff rolled his eyes. *A ridiculous twisting of events.* "It does not matter that he recovered the dancing sword. We would have done so anyway, and it appears as though he has gone and damaged the blade. It does not matter that he made friends with a few man-wolves along the way – we have forged an alliance with a more dominant tribe that could be pivotal for the future of our influence in this region, smack on the borderlands of Harrow. Amot is through. Done. Get it? Through!"

Eriff could plainly see that his comments didn't sit well with Berendt, or Rix for that matter. *Too bad. Suck it up. That is what command is for.*

Berendt lit his pipe, drew in. "Permission to be excused, Gallant."

"Why?"

He took another drag. "I need to talk to Amot."

"I'll go with you," Eriff said. "That was the plan and I intend to stick to it. I am not about to stand by while you all scheme your way out of this."

Berendt shook his head. "Better to give me a minute alone first, to prepare him. I'm his immediate commander, after all."

Eriff's eyes darted to Amot, to Rix, then back to Berendt. "You bloody Kith need more discipline," he snapped.

The grizzled ranger's one eye glared at the gallant. Perhaps soothed by the long-awaited pipe smoke, he held his tongue. Berendt didn't flinch and Berendt didn't blink.

Eriff broke the silence. "Very well then, but go alone. I don't need all three of you conspiring against me."

"That won't happen," Berendt said. "We all know who's in charge here and we all respect that."

Eriff scoffed. "Does Amot know? Does he respect command?"

The ranger sighed. "That's part of what I need to find out." Berendt nodded quickly to acknowledge his dismissal, turned, and strode over to the pit. Rix stayed behind.

Eriff watched as they talked for a few seconds, tried to gauge their expressions. He saw Amot glance up at Berendt after Berendt had said his piece, then shake his head as though in regret. The Wilder then took to staring at his own feet.

Amot's playing us, thought Eriff, *and so is this one standing next to me, in a more subtle way*. He glanced at Rix, forced a bitter grin when the spotter returned the look. Then the queensman donned his helm. As he tightened the leather straps under his chin, he made a remark to the spotter.

"You had better not be holding anything back," Eriff told him. *This is fair warning.*

Rix furrowed his brow. "Like what?"

Eriff paused as he fastened the buckle, more for dramatic effect than any other reason. He finished, pulled on his gauntlets, then raised an armored finger to the spotter.

"You tell me."

Rix turned his gaze away from Eriff, ostensibly to observe the conversation underway between his Kith brothers. "There's nothing to tell," he stated flatly, gaze steady. Rix's even composure made his claim believable, if not practiced. Eriff looked him over, thinking again back to Lord Ralador's remarks about him. The gallant's eyes fell to Rix's bow again. An impressive Kith weapon: at least two different types of wood and a layer of animal bone had been bonded together for its construction, bent in unison. The making of such bows by the Wilder tribes was a ritual. And no question, Rix had the dead-eye for using it. *I sure hope the March Lord is right about this one accompanying me in the future,* he thought. Rix clearly had that Wilder edge – primal, yet well-trained; wild-eyed, yet calculating like the cunning stare of a fox. And young enough to be molded. *A part of him will always remain untamable though. Just like Amot.*

⁕

Eriff moved to the pit after Berendt waved him over, stood next to the lead ranger. His gaze fell to the young wolf at Amot's side. "I see you have found a replacement already. Looks like one of the pups that bolted when the fighting started."

Berendt addressed Amot, his tone sympathetic. "I didn't get a chance to say 'sorry' about Howler…"

Eriff scoffed. "Not an easy task while parrying a sword-swinging maniac." He shifted his gaze to the scout. "I told you not to bring that dog. You should have listened."

Berendt shot Eriff a scornful look.

"I guess I deserved that," Amot said, eyes lowered.

Berendt nodded slowly. "We saw the aftermath of what happened to the poor bugger, Amot. Haar told us they'd seen that sort of thing before with stray animals from town… part of a pattern – lure a dog or take down an unprotected pack animal, then kill it."

Eriff added, "Don't forget the part about putting the head on a stake to ward off intruders. When Haar brought us to the kill-site, we saw the bloodied stake, but the head was missing. He growled to us that your Wulver friends decided to eat the entire carcass."

"Maybe he doesn't need all the details," Berendt said. A long, uncomfortable silence followed. Amot was shaking his head though.

"That's not how it happened," he said softly.

Eriff countered. "Haar just showed me one of his Wulvers mutilated the same way, near the creek – head on a post. That confirms he was telling the truth."

Berendt scowled. "That doesn't confirm anything."

A shadow passed over them. Eriff glanced up. *Order Valkyrie. We need to hurry.* He regarded Berendt. "Are you two finished your talk?"

Berendt nodded. Amot didn't respond.

Eriff backed a safe distance away from Amot and the pit, gesturing to the Kith commander to join him. "Berendt, the blade," he said. "We need to verify that it is what we think it is."

The ranger reached back over his shoulder, undid the makeshift fastenings, and produced the bundled sword. He placed it on the ground, began unraveling the cloth it was wrapped in.

Eriff drew his own weapon. He discreetly double-checked that the slider charm assembly cover was properly in place. Instinctively, he also patted an inner pocket to check that the insertable stone was there. *Yes.* When Berendt was finished unraveling, Eriff showed him his own sword. "The two blades should have originated from the same forge – the finest in all of Theia – and they should both display the highest craftsmanship, the highest standard in balance and precision. The hand of the very same Stout blacksmith, or a close relative, is like to have fashioned both blades."

Berendt grunted. "And applied the same stamp, no doubt."

"Of course." Eriff hunkered down, laid his war rapier on the cloth, parallel to the black blade.

From his squatting position, the ranger eyed the two swords carefully. "Dead ringer style-wise," he gruffed, "apart from the obvious structural differences and miscoloration. Fine work. Gem looks intact."

Eriff scrutinized the blades as well. "I do not know what in Aelish's name could have tarnished the black blade so, but the mark of Ironeagle looks identical to me. And I can tell by looking that the craftsmanship is superior. Do we agree that the mission has been accomplished?"

Berendt itched at his scar, swung his gaze to Eriff. He narrowed his eyes. "Are you sure that rapier of yours isn't a striker? The metal looks identical to the Jhinyari white metal."

I have to be firm on this point. Eriff tried not to sound uncomfortable.

"The Stouts of the Ironeagle Forge infuse white metal into all of their finest weaponry," he stated plainly. "No doubt, you have never seen it. More importantly in this case, as you pointed out the black blade has a slider charm – the luminary stone that makes farseeing and far fencing possible. I do not see a slider charm on my rapier. Do you?" Eriff prided himself on his handling of Berendt's intrusive question, how he skirted the truth about the swapped rapiers.

Berendt responded with a grimace.

The gallant repeated his earlier question: "Do we agree, then?"

The ranger nodded reluctantly. Eriff suspected his agreement was insincere.

The gallant stood up, sheathed his rapier, then extended his sword hand to Berendt. "Call your man over," he told the ranger. Berendt handed the queensman the black blade, then did his bidding. And when Amot climbed out of the pit, Eriff stiffened his stance, displayed the black blade, and addressed the scout eye to eye.

"I don't care how you retrieved the striker, Kith. But whatever you did, whatever you had to go through, whatever great deeds you might have accomplished, you won't be anyone's hero for it. Not now. Not ever. Your life will be in shambles."

Amot kept his gaze steady. "You're welcome, Sir," he said, his tone unemotional.

Is he mocking me?

The scout shrugged. His voice softened. "It was nothing, really."

In his eyes, Eriff caught a glimpse of something much greater than "nothing." Something wild and uncontrollable, lurking just behind them. *A hint of Ekkon's influence after all, perhaps.*

CHAPTER XLII
FRETFUL BIRD
(Catwings, Rix, Amot, Eriff)

CATWINGS HAD SEEN smoke trails before, streaming over Whisperwood. But usually at night when they were harder to spot, and never quite so thick or widespread as this one. *It has to be them*, she thought. *But why expose their position… unless…* The valkyrie dipped a wing, banked towards the head of the billowing plume for a second pass.

Although not unscathed, Spree was the only gryphon to have escaped serious injury during the mission, the slash to her talon easily dressed by the resident ranger. Galewind's Electra and Stormbringer's Ladybird weren't so lucky. They'd both drawn fire and suffered crossbow-shot wounds, while Rainsong's Ashes was on the mend from a badly injured wing. Galewind had judged that the two Golds could still bear a light load back to the Aerie, and agreed with Stormbringer to ferry what rangers and queensman they could, on the condition they depart immediately. The gryphons' wounds required the beastmaster's earliest attention. They also insisted any bodies be put to rest on the spot, by fire or by earth, rather than be carried across the skies.

Catwings' task was to arrange a firm and fast pick-up. If Eriff and the rangers weren't ready to leave by tomorrow morning, she alone would remain to bear two of them back to Gan. *Eriff and Berendt*, she figured. *The others would have to make the journey on foot.*

As the wind rider approached the site, a familiar voice called out to her. She spotted Rix through the smoke, waving his gangly arms her way. Catwings adjusted her borrowed clothes, then scouted for a place to land.

"Catwings! Over here," Rix hollered. He swung his gaze to Eriff, behind him. "I think she saw me that time."

"Are you certain it is her?" Eriff replied. "I barely can make out her gryphon through all this smoke."

"Of course it's her," Rix responded. "That's a Harpy Gryphon – grey with white patches."

The queensman sauntered over to share Rix's vantage point.

"And Catwings' riding style gives her away," the spotter went on. "I'd recognize it anywhere." He'd paid close attention to how she'd handled her Harpy during the flight in.

"Well, the plan was to have her check in on us." Eyes squinting, Eriff's gaze followed the wind rider's track through the sky. "It's the way she rides, isn't it? She crouches, but still keeps a high posture."

Rix nodded. "Something like that, but there's more to it. The way she flies the gryphon: sharp, fast movements, yet fluid. Hardly ever a steady glide."

"Yes, she seems to give her mount abundant room to maneuver," Eriff added. "As it should be – a gryphon is not a flying pack mule."

"Catwings! Spree!" Rix called, jumping and waving to the sky once more.

The wind rider slipped around the smoke plume, then plunged towards them.

"She definitely saw you that time, scoundrel," Eriff said.

Rix watched as the magnificent beast swooped in, fur and feathers aglow in the dwindling sunlight. Spree made a low pass overhead. Beating her great wings fiercely against her vector, the Harpy slowed to a near hover on the far side of the glade, as far away from the fires as possible. For a suspended moment, the wind rider and her mount hung in mid-air.

Abruptly, the gryphon's talons shot forward while its paws shot backward in perfect alignment. Spree dropped down suddenly, landed with a soft thwunk but nearly toppled over, favoring one leg. Catwings shifted her balance, the Harpy stabilized, then folded its wings.

Eriff made his way towards Catwings and her gryphon. Rix slung his bow over one shoulder and started after him. On the way, the queensman complemented the valkyrie.

"Nice recovery," Eriff said as he drew near.

"Thanks," Catwings called back, "I've had better landings." Suddenly, the front legs of her gryphon shot up. Giant talons raked at the air.

Eriff halted. The wind rider held strong as she was flung back.

"Oh, Spree," Catwings groaned, unruffled by the gryphon's complaint. Her mount dropped back to all fours. The beast shifted, unsettled, eyes darting about the glade. It made a high-pitched screeching sound that made Rix cringe. The spotter broke into a jog to lend a hand.

The wind rider applied a series of long strokes behind Spree's feline ears. "She's uncomfortable here," she explained. The gryphon chealped another scratchy complaint.

As Rix was about to pass the queensman, Eriff grasped his shoulder.

"Leave it to me," Eriff told him. "You have another duty." He flicked his eyes back to the pit, to Amot.

"Who him?" Rix said, nonchalantly. "He's fine." Rix twisted forward, squirmed out of Eriff's hold and kept on. "Don't worry," he called back, making light of the maneuver. "Amot's not going anywhere. Berendt has him now."

Rix didn't give the disregard he'd shown to his superior much thought. *Keep going,* he told himself. *It's only Eriff — not my 'real' commander. When everything gets back to normal, this won't cost me more than a grumble.*

From his place back in the hollow, Amot tracked Eriff and Rix as the bickering pair made their way towards Catwings. Near the rim of the pit, his commander shrugged off their antics, then turned his head to address Amot.

"I don't know what's gotten into those two," he gruffed. Then Berendt shook his head, squatted, and began the process of rewrapping the striker. "Actually. I don't know what's gotten into any of you."

Amot didn't have the sort of answers his commander was looking for. All he had were questions. He watched Berendt, whose back was to him, then spoke his mind. "Maa'rii and Lusii… two Wulvers that helped me locate the striker. They're here somewhere."

Amot shut his eyes, bit his lip. *Dead, I'm sure.* He opened them again, spit out what he had to say. "They wouldn't want to be burned like the others. I know them. A proper burial in the earth was important to them. One was a bonethrower. To him, bones were mystical."

Berendt's shoulders dropped. He paused, then continued to flatten the cloak. He moved the black blade to the center and folded the cloth once each way. Then he grumbled back to Amot in a gravelly voice.

"Ask me again, later."

Amot sighed, put his sentiments on hold and began with other questions.

"Why did you do it… attack the glade? What did these Wulvers do to deserve that?"

"Damn it," Berendt exclaimed, shaking guck off his hands. The cloak had become soiled with a morbid mix of mud and life's vital fluid. "Why the hell didn't Rix bring the sheath? He was doing supplies. It would've saved me a lot of trouble." Berendt paused, glanced the gryphon's way, then turned and rested his eyes on Amot. He spoke low so as not to be overheard.

"It wasn't anything they did or didn't do, Amot… we just… we needed an *ally*, and that's what we found in Haar and that strong arm of his, Grizzer. Eriff cut them a deal."

"What kind of deal?"

Berendt grunted, "Rix and I were both against it. I wouldn't have dealt with them that way." He shifted his stance sideways to Amot, then focused his attention back to rolling up the bastard sword.

"That doesn't answer my question," Amot said.

Berendt grunted again. "Of course it doesn't." He stopped what he was doing to scratch at the scar that ran down his face. It'd gone patchy, red and swollen. Berendt winced in discomfort. "Despicable creatures, I have to admit. But they had us by the balls, Amot. Haar led us to believe he knew where the striker was. When we told them you were unaccounted for, he insisted you'd been captured and put on the menu of the Wulvers living in this glade. He said they feast at night, but that you might be kept fresh and ready for the next roast… or at least most of you."

Amot repeated the word. "Most?"

"You know how the stories go. A limb here to gnaw on, a toe there…"

"And you believed this Haar? With no proof?" Amot had always known Berendt to be good at assessing one's character. *How could he be so gullible?*

Berendt sharpened his tone. "Do you know what it's like hearing that about one of your men? And it's not like we had anything else to go on, except demented whispers and camp-side stories. If anything, they just corroborated what Haar was saying." He sighed, looked Amot over fully. Then his tone softened. "I'm just glad you're still in one piece."

The Kith commander paused to look about the glade before continuing, always keeping tabs on what was going on. At the moment, that didn't amount to much.

"Now here's the thing, Amot," he gruffed, back on track. "As if that arrangement wasn't enough, our new friend Haar said he had slaves that he might be willing to sell us. Bragged about a batch he'd just sold to the Baruush. Said they left the best one behind. Some old lady."

"The best?"

Berendt shrugged. "Couldn't figure it myself. Eriff was keen on her and tried to get a name out of the beast. Haar asked Grizzer and all that he growled out was 'Lad-ryleess' something-or-other." Berendt produced a leather strap to wind around the cloth. He drew it tight to complete the makeshift scabbard. "Grizzer said the old lady kept yammering on about being royal. The Baruush didn't believe her and they had no use for an old lady."

Royal. Amot pondered Grizzer's words for a long moment. Only one name came to mind. "Lady Elise?" *It can't be.*

"That's what it sounded like to me too," Berendt said. "I have my doubts, but it's not impossible. She never returned from Harrow."

"Nor did her betrothed, for that matter," Amot said.

"Right," Berendt responded. "And a royal triton at that, which makes the story even more alluring, given they were last seen sailing out to the Dim Sea about sixty years ago. Hard to resist a tall tale about a sailor and his lady."

Amot paused to ponder the revelation, unsure what it might mean – nothing except for the fact that the very same name had come to him during Diamond Saber only moments after the striker had been torn from his grip. Moments after it'd been lost. Then again, he was half in a daze.

Berendt continued, unhindered by the scout's pensiveness. "After we dealt with Haar, Eriff let on that, according to his uncle, the wedding between the two went down in history as the most magnificent ever, with more coin spent than you or I will ever see in our lifetimes."

Amot asked, "Despite the fact they were no-shows?"

"Because of it," Berendt replied. "The event was already planned and… well, the families decided to hold some kind of grand artistic ceremony to honor their children's everlasting love – put on by the finest minstrels in all of Gan… probably anywhere. Eriff didn't get into the details."

"The Group of None?"

Berendt nodded. "Where else can you find three-hundred-year-old poets?"

A sense of the surreal came over Amot, to be discussing the particulars of a tragic love story within the bloody mess that was the glade, every breath infusing his lungs with fumes of the day's butchery. Amot's stomach began to harden. He shook his head. *Find out about the Wulver deal.*

"So how does this affect us? What will Eriff do?"

Berendt paused, one hand resting on the bundled sword. "Like I told you, Eriff cut a deal with Haar. Supplies and weapons in exchange for everything we wanted: the striker, the slaves, whatever was left of you, plus a promise to shift the pack's hunting grounds north, away from Turnsby."

Amot struggled with the last point. *Why would he want the Wulvers to move north?* The scout began rubbing his brow. He stared down at the spot where the yearling lay. Then it hit him. *I hate Eriff, but he is clever.* "You mean to stir up trouble along the line of control."

Berendt nodded. "Harass the Harrowians instead of Glebes, pure and simple. One more bartering chip for Gan when the Union finally takes effect. There's more fighting on the Harrow lines now than ever before, and I suspect Taeglin is propping up the Baruush to the east. Speaking of bartering, Haar insisted we 'give him' the fire and show his Wulvers how to use it. There's something he wants to see burned."

Insolent little scoundrel. Eriff fumed inside, at a loss for words as he stood watching the scrawny ingrate with the wind rider. He had no choice but to stand back – two attendants approaching the Harpy might've spooked the beast. And as Catwings struggled with her mount, she swept her gaze to Rix and smiled a grateful smile, one that should have been *his* to receive. But then she looked past Rix to Eriff. Her eyes locked with the gallant's and all at once his irritation diffused, replaced with dread.

The valkyrie's sweet stare dug into him, wide-eyed and steady. It dug so deep a sick feeling came over him. He looked away, grateful for his helm to partially shield his eyes. He had to. He'd seen that look before, on those who bear ill news. It could only mean one thing.

No. I don't need this right now. Eriff shook his head. *Aelish, give me strength.* But the radiance channeler could sense that Aelish had none to spare that day, not for him.

Eriff turned, faced the opposite direction. He breathed deep of the smoky air. The Wulvers had all taken cover at the gryphon's arrival. Peeking over logs and around mounds of grass, their suspicious eyes monitored Spree's every move with great interest. Eriff ignored them. With slow and heavy steps, he decided to wander the glade.

Have your fun, Rix, damn you, and then report back to me.

Again, the gryphon's eyes darted about the glade. She was ready to rear up. Rix reached for the headstall and latched on. "Got her," he told Catwings, wrestling against the beast's every move.

Spree protested with a loud, throaty squawk when she couldn't get her way.

"Hold her firm," Catwings said. With the wind rider reining her in as well, Spree finally settled. The Harpy still tugged, but the effort was half-hearted.

Rix swept his gaze over Catwings' slight build – handling a testy horse would be difficult enough for her, never mind a massive gryphon. Of all the valkyries, Rix thought she had the softest look to her. Not as physical as Stormbringer or Rainsong, both of whom he'd witnessed wrestle their gryphons into submission when they began to stray towards disobedience. Nor was Catwings as hard and unrelenting as Galewind could be.

Privileged soft, thought Rix of her, although he noticed a few new scuffs and scrapes. The sentiment was not meant as a put-down, weighted with the baggage of resentment the way such words often are. No, it simply expressed how much Rix was enamored by the quality, as though it were a rare and precious thing in such a place. And so congenial by the way she carried herself, Rix suspected Catwings didn't have it in her to be overly firm or domineering to her Harpy. *That's probably why she gives Spree so much freedom.*

Catwings tipped her helm back, wiped her forehead; her skin glowing wet. "Thanks," she said, with a coy smile. "I'm afraid the calm won't last long… one moment." Bracing herself, the wind rider started to undo the straps that held her in. But the gryphon had other plans. One unopposed tug was all it took for the Harpy to become uncooperative again.

"Whoa," Catwings called, struggling to maintain balance. "What's gotten into you?"

She regarded Rix again. "I can't dismount. I fear my noble queen has departed and left this fretful little bird in her place."

As if to prove her words, the gryphon let out a vengeful squawk. And as Catwings redoubled her grip, the beast half-spread its wings. Rix backed away as much as he could, while still holding on.

"I saw your signals," Catwings said, doing her best to maintain control. "Can we pick you up in the morning? We could do it tonight if you're done."

"Tomorrow is perfect," Rix replied. "We have a few things to sort out between now and then."

"So, you're done? You found the dancing sword?"

Rix nodded. Keeping a firm hold on the gryphon, he quickly ran through the raw facts of what had transpired in the glade. Catwings listened intently, narrowing her eyes and grimacing at times as she struggled to piece it together. Then, with Spree thrashing beneath her, Catwings smirked and told him she had a story just for him, one that he'd find particularly invigorating. First though, she quickly summarized all else that had transpired along Harrow's border, including Marec's untimely demise. Rix's mind raced with the implications. He could hardly believe his ears.

"That's terrible about Marec. How do we tell Eriff?"

Spree bucked. The wind rider lurched forward.

"I'd better go," Catwings said, shuffling in her seat. "Sorry Rix, please give Eriff our condolences." She tightened her straps.

Rix asked, "What about the story you promised?"

"Another time," she replied.

With minimal formality, the two parted ways, ranger and valkyrie, both wide-eyed and speechless at the other's adventures.

CHAPTER XLIII
PACK OF LIES
(Amot, Rix)

"Each line of control is marked in crimson," Amot's grand-father had explained, back when the lines were all active. He'd loomed over Amot, one heavy hand resting on the boy's shoulder, "… to signify the blood spilt there by Wilders in defense of the Hidden City. The bureaucrats like to say they are no-go zones for soldiers on either side. But in reality, each force hunts the other." The military map was still vivid in Amot's mind, beige and yellow and water-stained, rolled out on the single table of his grandfather's one-room cabin. Two of the red slashes on the map appeared in Deepweald Forest – one near Ironeagle and the other near Dim Lake. The third was in northern Whisperwood, extending west from Harrow's Gate. And when his grandfather had said "Wilders," Amot knew that he really meant rangers and tribal warriors – his kinsfolk.

Eriff wants to add Wulvers to the list now, Amot thought. He shook his head in disbelief. *He should consider adding himself instead.* He snickered at the notion. *Queensmen? – never. Their blood is blue anyway.*

A grunt sounded nearby. Amot looked to the rim of the pit, to his superior. With the bundled-up sword now slung over his back, Berendt extended a hand to Amot. "Get outa there," he barked. "This has gone on long enough."

Since he first laid hands on the striker, Amot had felt a change brewing inside of him, an awakening. But it was more than that now. The kernel of his being had twisted into a new form. This new form could perceive things from many angles.

Amot couldn't be sure what it all meant. But he'd quickly gained a new perspective on his superior, so casually carting the black sword of the mystic Chainmaker around on his back. A sword Amot would soon claim. A sword Amot would soon use to slay Haar. It all made so much sense.

The scout refused the hand, clambered out of the pit on his own. Tracker followed. Amot stood tall and faced Berendt, whose eyepatch was flipped up. The leathery skin about his rough-cut scar burned scarlet from his compulsive itching. His bad eye peered out of the inflamed, patchy mess, a smoky haze in its midst. The spiderweave over his nose was thoroughly blood-soaked.

Amot called out the situation the way he saw it. "You've been fed a pack of lies," he told Berendt, straight up. "Haar knew nothing of the striker, those demon-wolves killed Howler, and you teamed up with them to wipe out the only decent Wulvers in existence. Don't expect to get those slaves and don't expect the Haar-wulves to move north and change their hunting habits. Pack of lies. All of it."

Berendt's rasping voice hardened. "I aired my concerns about Haar."

Amot snapped back, "You didn't stop it from happening."

Berendt sighed, shook his head slowly, yet kept to his grim but steady composure. "That's not what a command is, Amot," he explained. "You should know that. We made a more-than-generous offer to liberate those slaves. It wouldn't pay for Haar to renege on that deal and lose everything."

"Really?" Amot gripped his forehead, massaging the pressure points, the temples. "You know nothing of Wulvers. They just don't think like us." The scout shook his head, removed his hand and eyed Berendt. Amot knew he was right. He knew that throw-bones, an ominous looking cloud, or the whisper of a crooked ghost pine could turn any situation on its end when dealing with Wulvers. But he also knew Berendt wouldn't listen to any of that. So, Amot pointed out the obvious.

"Let me get this straight," he went on, hardening his tone. "You're telling me that after this complete shit-storm, Eriff returns to Gan having recovered the lost dancing sword and having rescued one of the most beloved royals of all time."

Berendt grimaced. "You missed one." He reached into his side-pouch, pulled out his whiskey flask. "More than one." He undid the cap, tilted his head back and downed a sharp swig. Then he let out a sigh.

Amot's mind raced through the possibilities. Berendt huffed a laugh in the meantime, rough as a saw blade. Finally, one of the missing pieces came to Amot.

Shit.

"He'll take credit for reopening the line of control at Harrow's Gate, won't he?"

Berendt took a second swig before he answered. Then he wiped his mouth dry with the back of his hand. "That's one." He stretched his arm out, offered the flask to Amot. A gesture of shared pain. "Better drink up. It gets worse."

Amot asked, "What could be worse?"

"Quick Rix will be right up his arse," Berendt gruffed.

"Rix would never join forces with Eriff." A lump formed in Amot's throat. *He despises Eriff.*

"He won't have a choice." After a long pause, the Kith commander nudged the scout's shoulder with the flask. "Take it. Today was a shit day."

Begrudgingly, Amot accepted the flask, drank from it. He swished the stinging fluid in his mouth, surprised how well the taste of the whiskey mingled with the smoke already coating his palate. He swallowed and let the burn of it soothe his throat.

"Why Rix?" Amot asked. "The Queen's Army has plenty of archers and heavy crossbowmen. What's one scrawny ginger to them?"

Berendt shrugged, shaking his head. "Ekkon's Wheel," he growled. "All I know is that for some reason the Queen's Guard has taken a liking to our deadeye. Can't tell by the way Eriff treats the poor bugger though." He raised his eyebrows. "Galewind wants him too, incidentally. Lady Apsarla's lookin' to get a whisper capability for Order Valkyrie patrols and ops. The two orders will play tug-o-war, I suppose."

Amot took a second swallow, let out an audible breath. The whiskey went down cleaner and stronger this time. He winced at the burn. "What about all this? What about everything that happened here, in the glade?"

Berendt puffed air out of his lungs, grumbled a response, "You can scream 'murder' from the highest rooftops if you want to, but no one will listen. Eriff will shoot straight to the top, regardless. The Lord of the March wants to make a hero out of him, an example to aspire to. It serves Ralador's interests, it serves his family, and it serves the Hidden City." He grunted. "That's what I figure, for what it's worth."

That can't happen. Amot wiggled Berendt's flask from side to side, almost empty, then downed one more swig of whiskey. This time, the buzz numbed his mind. In that instant, he understood exactly why Berendt kept his flask handy.

"Good stuff." He passed the swill back to his commander. Berendt nodded slowly, took it from his hand. But something in the commander's far-off expression didn't quite add up. It almost looked like the sort of disgust right before you puke, but it was hard to tell, buried under all of his wounds. *There's still more to this,* thought Amot. Then he remembered the conversation at the lake.

Amot said, "The Queen's Guard will offer you something too, won't they?"

Berendt paused before he downed the backwash. "With a bit of luck, they just might."

"Looking to rejuvenate?"

Berendt grunted. "They can bring in nearly anyone these days." The Kith commander gauged the scout's expression next, then swung his gaze away, to the fire. The bodies were burning down. He tipped the flask to his mouth, then put the cap back on.

"I'm on the brink, Amot," he said plainly. "I've already turned forty."

"I'm on the brink as well, Commander," Amot responded, "except

I'm being taken down. I did what was right, yet I'm the one getting court-martialed."

Amot waited for his commander to dispute the claim. All the man had to say was that it couldn't be right to turn on your own comrades. But Berendt didn't go down that path.

Instead, his grim expression turned doubly so. That, together with his silence, conveyed all that was needed to be conveyed. Berendt would leverage the incident as best he could to make it easier on Amot. But a complication lay in the waiting. *Would he go so far as to jeopardize his acceptance into the Queen's Guard?* Amot believed he would.

Across the glade, the heavy flap of wings sounded. Amot swiveled his head to watch the Harpy gryphon lift off, bearing its valkyrie rider. Rix backed away from the beast and crouched down as Spree took flight, then swept over him. The gryphon passed low over Amot and Berendt next, buffeting the two rangers with forced air. And as the valkyrie and her mount slipped beyond the billowing column of smoke and banked north, Catwings rang out a battle cry. Amot wondered if she fully understood what had transpired that day.

Nervous Haar-wulves slowly rose about the glade, starting with Haar himself. Then, his second, Grizzer. They watched intently as the gryphon glided out of sight. Grizzer growled at the majority still hiding, called them cowards. One by one they showed themselves, and soon the glade was once again crawling with Wulvers. Thin in numbers though, compared to earlier. Some never returned.

Rix watched the wind rider and her mount disappear over the treetops, as though something lost. A fresh breeze drew air from the woods – a welcome break from the smell of burning flesh. He turned his attention back to his surroundings, scanned the Wulver field. Straightaway, he spotted Eriff, standing alone at the edge of the glade. Rix breathed deep. *This won't be easy.* Catwings' news, like his own, had been a mix of good and bad, but mostly bad. He lumbered across the field, mulling over exactly what to say and how to say it. On the way, he iterated through a variety of condolence phrases in his mind.

Just the cold facts, he told himself. *Keep it short. If the words don't come, stop talking.* As he drew near, he could sense Eriff had been waiting for the grim news, bracing himself. Fully armored, the queensman passed him a sideways glance.

"Scoundrel, look here," he told Rix, something different in his voice, reflective. When he said "scoundrel" this time, the word came off as more of a nickname than an insult. Eyes squinting, Eriff gestured to the iron mesh hanging from the trees in front of him and chinking in the wind. "What do you see?"

Rix swept his gaze over the dangling barrier, shrugged. "Chains to keep the ghost pines out."

A flash of disappointment crossed Eriff's face. "This section, right here," he said, taking hold of a portion of the chain. "It's scorched." The queensman paused, waiting for some kind of response.

Rix had nothing to offer.

"Well?" Eriff asked. "What do you think it means? Use your ranger skills."

Rix examined the chains closely the second time. They were black iron everywhere. But the dim light picked up a slight difference in the glint of the metal, the dullness. The outline of dark staining became evident, from top to bottom. "It means a tree burned down here at some point. Or… maybe a lightning strike?"

Eriff nodded. "First answer. Clever, these Wulvers. When they hear the chains rattle, they come running and set fire to the offending ghost pine. Don't you think?"

"Something's missing," Rix said.

Eriff's eyes lit up. "Good on you, scoundrel." The queensman stooped over, pulled up one of the many dangling chains at the end of the mesh, lying unorganized on the ground. Some were anchored, but not this one. And this one was quite long. He raised the end of it to about neck height, each link nearly half the size of his fist. The last link in the chain was actually a heavy hook with a tension lock.

Rix nodded in understanding. "The Wulvers hooked the ghost pines in, torched them, and then removed the remains. That is clever."

He regarded Eriff directly. Rix made sure his tone was clear and purely professional when he spoke, the way Berendt always complained it was not.

"Gallant Haulik Sir, I have tidings from Catwings of the Valkyries."

Eriff locked the hook into one of the links. It slid in easily and clicked when all the way through. He gave it a tug: the hold was solid. He responded without making eye contact, his tone equally professional.

"Report, Spotter Caledon."

Rix opened with the good news: "Catwings promises to return at first light with the Golds. And Rainsong managed to meet up with the other valkyries. Her gryphon is wounded, but should recover in short order. Both gryphon and master are on their way back to the Aerie, with Tallman trailing on foot."

Eriff nodded, staring at his boots. "I see."

Rix paused. *Now for the so-so news.* He briefly described the Wulvers encountered in the cave and the successful neutralization of the Harrowian patrol along the river Dim. The young spotter's voice cracked when he began the last part, the bad news. The Queen's Guard Commander stood stiff at the sound, went silent when Rix announced Danus' death due to the crash landing of the Harpy bearing him. Then Eriff's eyes glistened when Rix informed him of the loss of his Uncle Marec, in battle with the Harrowian Guard. Neither body could be recovered at the time. Eriff shifted his gaze to the forest depths, eyes hardly visible to Rix by the visor of his helm.

"Sorry, Sir," Rix said at the end, heavy-hearted. "The valkyries send their condolences."

Eriff paused for a long moment. Still looking away, he responded. "Danus and Marec served the Hidden Kingdom faithfully and with great honor. Their bravery and deeds embody the spirit of the Royal Queen's Guard. They will not be forgotten. You are dismissed, Spotter Caledon."

Rix left Eriff standing there, blank eyes staring into the woods.

Sweeping his own gaze across the glade, the spotter set his sights on the Kith commander next, conferring with Haar, Grizzer and a scattering of dominant Wulvers. *Berendt needs to hear this as well.* He started towards them.

From behind, he heard Eriff call softly into the wind.

"Aelish, collect their valiant souls."

A decision brewed within Amot, a big one, and it brewed in his gut. But he needed to be sure. He needed to know more. Strangely, that's when the whispers returned, and then some.

Mere minutes after Berendt had left the scout alone in order to "clarify a few loose ends" with the Wulvers, Amot's ears filled with a familiar sound. It began as a low, random noise, like the whisper of rustling leaves. Then it rose abruptly, stronger and louder as though the door of a crowded room had suddenly opened, filled with chatty people.

Ghost pines, Amot thought at first. He hadn't been concentrating on receiving. But the scout soon realized the content of the overlayed messages didn't quite fit the usual pattern of attempted deception and ridicule. They flooded his mind with information: One feed from an unknown source revealed a conversation between Rix and Eriff about valkyries. Amot also received feeds from beyond the forest – Harrowian Guard patrols, Rainsong's and Tallman's whereabouts, activity along the lines of control within Deepweald… and more. Everything to be expected from all of the usual sources, plus new ones added, some in Treesong and others, like snippets of conversation, cast in their original tongues. Amot absorbed it all. And in the case of Rainsong's journey, a grey and grainy view of the valkyrie atop her gryphon formed in his mind, until the gryphon suddenly leapt out of sight and the image faded.

Dark messages tangled in with the news.

Can I trust them? They sound legit. Ghost pines seem to be terrible at hiding their intent, unable to stop themselves from delivering cruelty. These whispers were different.

Death tones circulated in the dozens. Details were mostly sketchy, non-specific, but not in all cases. The heaviness Amot already felt in his stomach went hard when he heard the name "Duelist Marec Haulik" uttered. An image of his slumped over body flashed in Amot's mind, seated at the base of large tree. There was no denying it was him.

Amot sighed. *He was decent, for a queensman.* Indeed, Marec was one of the few of his Guard the scout felt he could've actually gotten along with. Amot might've even felt a pang of guilt for the way he'd treated Eriff lately, being Marec's nephew and all.

At the same time, the scout also caught on to another message, something about Wulvers that Marec and Tallman had stumbled upon in the hills. The outcome had been grisly.

The stream of information continued to flow. Kill by kill, the fighting of the day was revealed. Some of the fallen had names, others remained anonymous. A second queensman made the list of the dead: "Charger Danus Leigh."

When the whispers began to repeat themselves, the scout tuned them out. They dropped off quickly, and Amot began to focus on his next task. With only slight reservations, Berendt had granted him leave to roam the glade freely in search of Lusii, Maa'rii and the younglings.

᷍

Amot remembered the words of the Chainmaker. He muttered them to himself.

"Essence of fire, consume."

The scout drew in close to the fires, peered into the flames.

"Not here," came a whisper.

He strode through the ransacked glade, Tracker at his heels. And when Amot neared the den with the smoke hole, he led the yearling to the stack of wood nearby. When no Wulvers were looking, he pushed Tracker behind it, raised a hand.

"Stay," he said. The young Wulver inched forward. "No. Stay here. You can't follow me now. I'll come back to get you." Tracker stared up at him with sad eyes, then backed away and made himself small.

Amot turned away, got down on his hands and knees and crawled through the opening. The victors clearly hadn't plundered the main den of the Lusii pack yet – otherwise there'd be odds and ends scattered everywhere. *Reserved for Haar himself,* he surmised. A Wulver lay impaled at the bend in the tunnel, rounding to the inner chamber. As the scout's eyes began to adjust to the dimness, he made out a spear shaft jutting out of its gut. *Haar-wulf,* he thought, judging by the body's mass and shape. Amot nudged it. He felt along the shaft, gripped the feathers dangling from its end. *Maa'rii did this.*

Amot peered over the carcass. Beyond was the familiar fire chamber, illuminated by a curtain of fading daylight that shone through the smoke hole in the ceiling. The fire itself had long been doused and the room's contents scattered. He squeezed past the body, made his way inside. Amot scuttled to the small, dark room off to one side – the main sleeping chamber. He peered into the gloom, but it was too dark to see in. When he entered, his hand bumped something.

Amot ran his hands over matted fur. When his eyes finally adjusted to the greater darkness, the sight confirmed what he already knew. His heart sank into his stomach: Lusii, who'd rescued him from the fury of the ghost pines; and Maa'rii, his spirit guide to Howler's remains and later to the Chainmaker's forge.

The two bodies lay strewn on the floor like discarded sacks of meat; not arranged in any special way, nor did either hold any revealing sort of pose. Simply dead.

Amot spoke to them, his voice barely more than a whisper. "Nothing can take away who you were." He closed his eyes, let out a sigh, then uttered a small prayer. "Shroud, bear these souls as one, to Ekkon's Wheel."

Heavy hearted, the Wilder gathered the two broken bodies. He wrapped them in old mats from the fire chamber, dragged them one by one out of the den. Before exiting, he told Tracker to "stay" again, and "don't look." When he thought no eyes were upon him, he dragged the bodies across the field and beyond the chains.

Secluded and with a broken shield to dig with, Amot dug into a knoll of soft sand just outside the glade. He brushed the fallen branches aside and dug until the shield came apart. Then he dug with his hands until his fingertips bled, and until his arms felt like they'd fall off if he went any deeper. Sweaty and buggy and covered in sand, he laid the two Wulvers to rest in the scraped grave. Tracker came to his side, eventually, and when he did the Wilder expended the second of his five charms, gifts from the Chainmaker.

"Essence of earth, renew," he uttered. Together, Amot with his bare hands and Tracker with his claws, they pushed sand over the bodies.

By sunset, the two sweet lovers were in the ground. Amot smiled at the colors he beheld, bleeding into the air around them. The beauty of souls rising seeped into the winds and painted the sky.

Chapter XLIV
BLAME
(Amot, Eriff)

Amot stared into the dark forest, entranced by the unnatural quiet. He had no intention of budging from his seat atop the burial mound. Every muscle ached. Shards of the scrap shield he'd used to dig lay in pieces, scattered about. Tracker curled up in a warm ball at his side.

The image of Lusii and Maa'rii burned in his mind. How he'd found them in their sacred den, bodies tangled in a bloody mess. It spoke volumes about their last moments, helpless but together. And the way the Chainmaker had departed this world burned there too. *Why go out in such a mad and fiery blaze? What reason could there be behind it?* Amot didn't have the answers.

And then there was Danus… Marec. *To what end?* He shuddered at the thought of Howler's last moments in the company of brutal Haar-wulves. Terrifying. Amot sighed heavily. *I bet he yelped out for me, wondered where I was.* Eventually, the scout came around to thinking about what to do with Tracker.

Amot knew the answer to that question, at least. But there were bigger questions. Bigger than all of those: why the dancing sword *led* him to Whisperwood. Yes, he believed he'd been led there. Amot was certain he'd felt something when the striker was ripped from his grasp.

A surge or a wave had passed through his body at that instant, flooding his senses and pounding so hard his eyes nearly burst out of their sockets. Then, as quickly as it had risen, the pulse subsided, never to return.

From the glade behind him, the Wulvers' warning chains jingled.

Then came the grind of heavy footsteps on pine litterfall, the rubbing of plate on plate made soft by leather of the highest quality, and the slight swishing, with every step, of tightly riveted mail. It could only be the queensman. Eriff approached the gravesite with the confident gait of a true horse lord.

Amot didn't turn to look. He hoped the queensman would be smart enough to pass him by.

Broken branches crunched, the ones at the base of the sandy knoll. Amot sighed. *Shroud's Well, that'd be asking too much.*

Eriff called out to Amot's back. "So, this is what you were doing all that time?" The gallant halted to scrutinize the disturbed ground and the broken shield used for digging. Even with the night chill coming in, he felt hot and sticky under his protective gear, confined. He removed his gauntlets and set them down with his helm. His damp skin tingled in the fresh air. Then he adjusted the collar of his cuirass, stepped about halfway up the mound until he loomed over Amot, from behind. He waited.

The scout didn't answer.

Eriff glanced down at the mangy pup, curled up beside Amot. "You cannot go a day without a dog, can you, Scout?"

Again, no answer. Amot sat still as a tree stump, staring between scraggly pines into the northern reaches. All Eriff saw that way was messy, lumpy ground cluttered with deadfall, brushes and long grasses. Nothing stirred.

Finally, Amot spoke. "This was wrong," he said, his voice flat in an accusing way.

Eriff folded his arms, ready to set the ranger straight. But as he drew in the breath to speak, he stopped himself. He puffed the air out slowly. Instead of coming down on Amot, he infused his voice with reluctant invitation.

"What were they like?" he said. "Tell me about your…" Eriff huffed slightly, forcing himself to remember. "What were they again? … Lusii-wulves. Tell me something about the Lusii-wulves."

Amot glanced back over his shoulder, his expression defiant. "Furry."

The gallant squeezed his eyes shut, pinched the bridge of his nose. "You called this tribe 'civilized,' right? The Haar-wulves are anything but civilized from what I've seen, so the notion that your Lusii-wulves are any different is a hard sell. Savage, cruel, power hungry, bullying – yes, but civilized, not on your life. The whole lot of them are despicable. The leader, Haar, he is the worst of them all."

"Pack," Amot corrected.

"Pardon?"

Amot turned halfway around. "They live in packs, not tribes."

"What's the difference?"

"Do you say a pack of birds? No. Birds flock to one another, so you call them a flock. Blood unites a tribe, or some common cause does. A pack is just for whoever shows up. They show up and get along with one another as a group. One displays dominance and the rest follow because they don't know what else to do that's any better, or they don't have a choice. Wulvers form packs."

Eriff contemplated the distinction for a long moment, shook his head. "Packs then… whatever."

"The Wulvers here *were* different," Amot went on. He locked eyes with the gallant. "The Wulvers that lived in this glade were…" He hesitated. Eriff waited patiently, trapped by his stare. "The Wulvers in this glade… one of them, Lusii, helped me out of a pinch with the ghost pines. She put herself at risk for me without hesitation. Maa'rii, their spiritual leader and protector, accepted me into the pack despite strong reservations. They were considerate, thoughtful… some might consider them wise."

"Wise?" Eriff repeated. "That seems unlikely."

"Yes, wise," Amot said, firming up his tone.

How do I make Eriff understand? There was little more Amot wanted to say to the queensman about the Wulvers of the glade, but more and many things he could have said. Nothing seemed good enough. Nothing Amot could say would do Maa'rii and Lusii justice.

"They treated me like… family," he blurted out at last.

Eriff's head flinched back slightly, eyes narrowed, nose scrinched. "Family? Well, you must have quite the family tree then."

"I do," Amot said. He glanced to Tracker. The yearling's ears pricked to the sounds of small critters, scurrying in the underbrush.

Eriff shook his head, dismissively. "Scout," he started, in a tone to reset the conversation. "You need to come back with me to the other side of the chains. I am going to need another strong arm. Haar and his top dogs are coming to negotiate."

"Negotiate? You already have a deal. Berendt said—"

"That was more of an… understanding, shall we say, to get things moving. Details need to be sorted out… the slaves, future relations. Everything was contingent on a successful recovery."

"I see," Amot looked away, stared into the woods again. "Why do you need me? You already have Berendt and Rix."

"If there is one thing I know about these Haar-wulves, it is that they only understand one thing – brute force. I need every man of mine standing behind me when I negotiate. Your commander looks like he's been beaten with a heavy stick, and Rix is a scrawny ferret."

"I'm unarmed," Amot said.

Eriff huffed, impatiently. "Use your brawn. Grimace a little, flex, give them the evil eye… you know. I've seen the Wulvers eyeing the 'Black Blade,' as they call it, on Berendt's back. They are absolutely terrified of it. And they are terrified of you, its wielder."

Yes, its rightful wielder.

"You don't trust them," Amot said.

Eriff scoffed. "Trust a Wulver? Are you mad? If Haar so much as snarls, cozy up to your Kith commander and gesture to the striker. They'll get the hint."

Amot's core tightened, the pressure building inside. He gave Eriff a sidelong glance. "Why should I help you?"

The queensman drew his legs together, stiffened his stance. "LOOK up," he commanded, sharpness in his tone.

Amot met his gaze. Eriff's lips pulled back in disgust, he raised his voice a notch.

"STAND with your Kith brothers," he said firmly, "one last time. Demonstrate to me, to your commander, and to the Overseer that you *have* come around, that you are ready to change. Perhaps then, I will put to record that you obeyed orders *after* the questionable incident with the sword; that those 'tree-witches' – or whatever you like to call them – got inside your skull." Eriff paused to roll his eyes, draw a breath. "It might even help with your commander's brewing story of… temporary insanity induced by Colossus meddling."

The scout said nothing, but kept his gaze steady.

Eriff went on, in answer to his question. "Why should you help me? – because I can help you, Kith, no matter what you are planning for your defense."

I'm not planning a defense.

Amot nodded anyway. "Understood," he said.

"Good then," Eriff responded. "Come when I signal. I want a dramatic entrance – you will be my reserve force for when I wish to make a strong point." He looked away, nodded slowly. His stare took on a far-off quality. "Yes, a strong point." Eriff shifted his gaze back to Amot. "Swagger into the glade at unawares, looking as though you are full of confidence and teeming with rage, just like you did in the battle."

"Oh, I will," Amot said. "You can count on it."

Eriff narrowed his eyes. After a slightly awkward pause, the queensman donned his gauntlets but not the helm, then turned away. He ducked under the chains and strode back into the glade, towards Berendt and Rix.

When he was out of earshot, Amot whispered to Tracker. "Have you ever been to Turnsby?" The yearling just stared back at him. *Of course not.*

Amot pushed himself to his feet, paid his final respects to Lusii and Maa'rii. Tracker whimpered a single whimper as he did so, clawing at the earth. The ranger bent to one knee, faced the pup and held its head firmly in his hands so that Tracker could not look away.

"Your parents will rest here, in the woods forever," Amot said. "Do you understand what I am telling you?"

The Wulver tried to look away, as though to say "stop talking about it."

"Good boy," Amot said. "They loved it here, and they loved you very much." Tracker became restless, eyes darting. Amot held him firm. "You can come here to visit whenever you like, but we have to go right now. This place isn't safe for you. Your father asked that I take care of you, so you are going to follow me all the way to Turnsby."

Tracker made an odd sound: "T-r-r-n-r-ee."

"That's right," Amot said, then enunciated: "Turns-bee."

Tracker backed out of Amot's grasp. This time, the scout let him go. Snout down, the yearling clawed at the earth one last time.

Amot rose to his feet. He swept his gaze over the glade, saw that his unit was gathering with the Haar-wulves. *It's starting.* In the midst of exchanging words with the Wulver Chieftain, Eriff discreetly waved a staying hand Amot's way.

Not yet.

Without hesitation or even looking back, and with Tracker on his heels, Amot turned in the opposite direction, headed into the woods. No one noticed his departure until it was too late.

Chapter XLV

LAST DANCE

(Haar, Rix, Amot, Eriff)

SOFT-FLESH SPOKE MANY words Haar didn't care about. He didn't care until the words "worth your while" came out of his mouth, the same words from when they'd first met among the tree devils. Good words. Last time, those words came out just before the ones about getting things, like weapons. Haar liked them a lot, but he still didn't know what to do when the man-flesh stopped talking. The pack leader was distracted. Soft-flesh had extended his pale hand, as though in offering, except sideways. *What?* wondered Haar. He swung his gaze to Grizzer, beside him. *Am I supposed to scratch it again? Sniff it?*

Grizzer had something else on his mind, clearly, straddled on all fours. *He's that way,* but Haar knew better. Haar knew by the way Grizzer glared at the tender flesh that he wanted to sink his teeth into it, thrash the hand about, use it to drag the man-flesh under him, then lunge for the throat. Grizzer could do it, too – Soft-flesh wasn't wearing metal on his head. Haar had two strong tearers behind him if it came to a fight, more in nearby dens waiting for his signal.

The pack leader ignored Soft-flesh's gesture, looked to One-eye standing next to him. One-eye tipped his snout to Haar. That, the Wulver understood, and tipped his own back. Last-eater stood behind them both, as he should, whipping branch slung around his shoulder. The pack leader had seen how Last-eater whipped sticks with it and plunged them into the flesh of Lusii-wulves. *I don't like man-flesh devices,* he thought again.

Grizzer let out a throaty growl. *What has gotten into you?* thought Haar. He swung his gaze to his second-in-command. Grizzer's narrowed eyes were fixed on One-eye, but with a different glare than for Soft-flesh, not like a deer for the taking. *No, something else.*

Haar looked back to One-eye, caught a glimpse of the black blade's grip jutting up from behind the man-flesh's back. *That must be it.* The sight made him sneer too. Haar didn't like that man-flesh device either – something else that whipped through the air and cut into Wulvers – and he didn't like the missing man-flesh who'd swung it in battle. *Hard to kill, and he kills too easy.*

Even so, Haar turned to glare at Grizzer, twitched an ear his way. *We need to make a good deal, not a bad deal.*

Grizzer stopped growling, at least loudly, but he never took his narrow eyes off that black sword on One-eye's back.

The spotter cast a discreet glance at the large, dark Wulver next to Haar. *I don't like the way that Grizzer is snarling at Berendt,* he thought. Eriff and Haar had begun negotiating about slaves and goods.

Slow and quiet, Rix slipped his bow off his shoulder, gently rested one end on the grass. He made eye contact with the Haar-wulf while the two leaders talked. Rix shifted his stance, slid his quiver from behind his back to his side. Then he drew three arrows, held them in plain sight of the dark Wulver, but occluded from the others' view. The beast ended its low growl, turned its predatory gaze on the spotter. Then it widened its forelegs, hunched its shoulders, and lowered its massive head, in a crouch. A chill shot up Rix's spine, the target of that steady glare. *Marked prey.*

Eriff's bartering on slaves and goods went rather smoothly, from what Rix could hear. The queensman was generous and included bonuses for services rendered and compensation for pack losses, which Haar readily accepted. In exchange for a base supply of weaponry, leather, and metal plates for armor, Eriff went on to secure first pick for new slaves, as long as he or a representative 'man-flesh' showed up in time. Rix listened as the negotiations progressed to the next phase: "tribe relocation" in Eriff's words. On this point though, the pack leader wouldn't budge, and Rix could sense Haar's roughnecks behind him turning restless at the notion. Worse, the spotter caught glimpses of a dozen bright eyes peering from the various dens in their midst. *How many lay in waiting?* he wondered. Rix hadn't kept track. It could be half the pack for all he knew.

The dark Wulver began to snarl at Berendt again. And as Eriff did his best to convince Haar that moving the pack was essential to their continued relationship, the Kith commander glared back at Grizzer. He even rested his sword hand on the grip of his longsword, wiggled his fingers for show. Grizzer was undeterred, so Rix tapped the end of his bow on the ground, flashed the orange fletching of his arrows to the Wulver. This time though, Grizzer didn't back down. Eriff kept talking anyway, over the low growls, doing his best to ignore them.

The queensman told Haar they could discuss relocation later, then hit another snag – concerning Rix's lanterns, of all things. Haar wanted fire. On this point, the queensman widened his stance, pulled his gauntlet back on, folded his arms. He raised his voice. "No fire for your pack, Haar," he stated firmly, "unless you relocate to the north." The ruffians behind Haar only became more restless. Rix nocked an arrow.

Berendt leaned over to the spotter, his voice low and gravelly, "Spark up one of them lanterns, would ya."

Rix grimaced, slid his arrows back into their quiver, slung his bow back on his shoulder. He pulled a lantern out of his sidepouch, lit it. Eriff and Haar went silent, looked over. The Haar-wulves snarled, crouched low, shifted about at the sight of the lantern's yellowy glow. Even Grizzer turned his attention to the fire.

With the pack leader distracted, Eriff discreetly raised a hand, waved a "come here" to the woods where Amot was last seen. But the scout didn't show like he was supposed to. Rix scanned the perimeter. *Shroud's Well, he's gone, or wearing that damn cloak.* Eriff gestured again, more obvious. *Pff. Amot would have to be blind not to see that.*

Rix nudged Berendt. "This isn't right."

"I know," he gruffed back. "Keep that lantern on high burn."

Amot strode through the woods as he'd been doing for several minutes, until he heard Berendt holler his name, muffled in the distance. The scout halted, expanded his chest with a full breath, held the air in for a long moment before letting it out. He bent to one knee, eye-level to his wolfish companion.

"Stay, Tracker," he said softly. Amot ran his hand along the yearling's spine, then gently pressed his hinds down. "The time has come to even the score."

Tracker sat, let out a sad whimper. Amot knew the young Lusii-wulf wouldn't understand. *It's better that way, at least for now.*

Amot rose, turned away from the yearling. He found an open area with enough space to swing a sword. The scout's heartbeat began to quicken as he settled into the clearing's center. There, he closed his eyes, breathed deep, and exhaled slowly. Amot bent his mind to the Lusii-wulf glade, exactly as though he were farseeing during Diamond Saber, or during the battle with the Haar-wulves. But with one crucial difference – this time, no striker.

While concentrating, Amot also invoked the familiar Whisper of the Hurlorns. He'd never put the two together before – farseeing and Whispers – but it had occurred to him to do so. There was no reason why he couldn't, or shouldn't.

First, there arose a noisy, buzzing sound around him. Moments later, the noise turned to flashes in the Wilder's mind. A mental image began to form, colorless, enveloping. But this image was not the broken-glass view of farseeing. It had gained a sense of solidity. And he could hear sounds, in his mind.

A fusion of farseeing and whispers brought him into the sphere of the negotiation taking place. Amot fixed his sights on Haar and the wolfish brutes that backed him up, facing Eriff and Berendt. Rix hung back slightly, holding aloft a lantern. Eriff was going on about using Harrowian superstitions to harass patrols and border guards.

The pack leader's second began to look about, as though distracted. Haar hesitated, did the same.

They sense something.

Amot focused his thoughts on the rift between him and the striker. Between, but connected. In a sudden rush, he felt an acceleration. At once, there seemed no tangible distance between him and the black blade, nothing in the way of him simply lifting it off Berendt's back. The only odd thing was how the sword jittered in front of him, like sunlight on rippling water. Amot reached out, grasped the handle. The rough metal of the grip cooled his hands.

He tugged, felt a slight resistance. Adding force, with a quick pull Amot slid Chainmaker from its makeshift scabbard, held it high. The dancing sword materialized in his outstretched hand, fully in the clearing, black blade shining like the night sky above. The striker's energy pulsed through Amot's palm, coursed down his arm and through his body. With whispers rising in his midst, the scout shifted his stance into a high guard position, then flipped his focus back to the glade. He glimpsed his commander reach behind his back, feel for the sword. Berendt spun around, looked to the ground.

That's right. It's gone.

Rix stood wide-eyed nearby. He scanned the glade.

Stay out of the way.

Amot projected the striker through the rift.

The spotter set the lantern down, nocked an arrow, gave it some draw weight. The uneasiness of the negotiating Haar-wulves turned to open snarls. Heads thrust out of dens, growling, eyes glaring at the trio of human flesh.

Eriff addressed Berendt, "What just happened?"

"The striker's missing again," Berendt replied. "Keep your guard up." A metal *schwing* sounded as he drew his longsword. They all glanced this way and that way.

Suddenly, the black blade slid into view.

"There!" Rix yelled.

It danced in mid-air, not ten steps away. Wulvers yowled and yipped as the sword slowly began to arc around them, tilting this way and that way as it ran the circuit.

Rix glanced to Eriff. He seemed pleased.

Is this part of the plan? Rix wondered.

But the queensman's smug smile turned sour when the sword drifted between him and Haar. It hovered there, threateningly. Too close for comfort.

Haar and Grizzer backed away. "The Black Blade has retu-rr-rned," Haar growled. The roughnecks behind him shifted in place.

They'll bolt, first chance, Rix thought.

Eriff stepped back as well, produced a small leather bag from an inner pocket. He removed an object from it, then fumbled for his war rapier. Not sure what to expect, Rix added more draw weight, raised the arrow tip slightly. Mentally, he marked Grizzer as his first target.

The striker disappeared into thin air.

All eyes – Wulver and human – darted across the glade, searching. Heads turned, ducked at nothing. Rix heard the dull scrape of metal gliding over metal. *Eriff – what's he doing?* Rix shifted his gaze to him. The queensman inserted the object from the bag into a slot in his rapier, below the guards. It flickered. Then he raised his weapon defensively.

Rix did a double take. "What the hell, Eriff?"

Amot waited, watched as the confusion spread. The fear. Then he projected the striker again, this time only a few feet from the pack leader. The Wilder's muscles tensed as he struggled against the forces that would wrench the sword from his grip. Haar saw the blade first this time, let out a yelp as it flew straight at him.

The hulking Wulver turned to get out of the way, but barreled into Grizzer. Grizzer could've moved aside, let Haar pass. But he didn't. Instead, in that crucial instant, and with a hateful glean in his eye, Haar's second-in-command purposely got in the way. He resisted, pushed back at Haar even.

The pack leader glanced back just in time to see the blade up close.

One clean swipe and Haar's throat blossomed red. Haar let out a gargling scream, reached for his neck, then stumbled backwards into his guards. His guards scattered back, away from Haar, away from the hovering dancing sword. All except for Grizzer, that is, who stood defiant. Haar collapsed, contracted into a ball.

Eriff stood poised in a back guard stance, buckler raised, rapier held long and low behind him.

"Where are you?" he said, eyes searching.

You'll never find me, thought Amot. The scout pushed the striker a step towards his unit, then halted, waved it slowly in front of them.

Berendt raised a palm together with his sword in a hands-off gesture, took a cautious step back. He regarded Eriff. "Gallant, I suggest you stand down."

Eriff ignored the advice. Rix trained his bow on Grizzer.

Grizzer, eyeing the floating blade cautiously, lowered his bear-like head and sniffed at Haar's corpse, still twitching. He snarled a satisfied snarl.

"Learn from Haar's mistakes," Amot whispered.

Grizzer's ears perked. He roughed out a reply, "Can't tr-rrust manflesh," he said.

"We can still make a deal," Eriff urged.

"No deal." Grizzer backed away. "If you come near-rr I wrill kill yrou myself." The dark Wulver gestured to his pack-mates, snout waving in the air. Keeping low to the ground, with suspicious stares the Grizzer-wulves retreated, crept out of the glade.

Grunting with effort, Eriff charged the disembodied striker. "Oh no you don't!"

He thrusted his white metal at the black blade, attempted a disarm maneuver. Wild sparks flashed and snapped; electricity forked as the two strikers clashed. He gave his weapon a twist.

The bastard sword slipped out of the rapier's hold, backed off, then circled round.

Surging with adrenaline, Eriff swung hard, this time projecting his blade just behind the sword. He tried to catch the gripping hands. The war rapier swooshed through the air.

By the Will of Aelish, how do I get at the wielder?

The black blade vanished, reappeared near the chains, vanished again.

The strike came out of nowhere, hard and fast. Eriff parried. The air around him lit up, buzzing with jolting power. He tried to disarm again, had a good pull but lost it.

The striker flew back, waved side to side as though in goodbye.

"No," Eriff cried. He projected, thrusted again in desperation.

He's toying with me.

Amot severed the link, lost the image. Exhausted mentally and muscles spent, he dropped the sword, collapsed. He took a deep breath where he lay.

Tracker meandered over, licked his face.

"Stop," Amot said, wincing and grinning at the same time. He freed his face from the yearling. "You won't have to worry about that Haar anymore. I took care of him."

The Wulver's ears twitched at the comment.

"Amot!" came a far-off yell – Eriff's voice. "Bring back the sword, or you will pay dearly." The queensman cursed and cursed when he received no response. "I'll find you," he shouted in frustration.

Through the trees to his left, Amot glimpsed a sword appear, linger, then pop out of existence. A moment later it appeared to his right.

The Wilder grabbed his sword, scrambled to his feet. He looked to Tracker. "We need to get out of here."

The yearling returned his stare. "Rrr… rr-n rlike a hare," he growled.

Chapter XLVI
Norwin's Breeze
(Wind)

THE GREAT EAGLE'S flock banked into a turn as one complete being, to bring them about over the dark forest. High above Theia, riding on Aether winds, Norwin of the Dawn swooped as low as she dared, tilted her gaze to the Bundle's twisted remnants below. The paths in time had fully energized, that much was clear. They pinched and knotted, causing convergences and intensified interactions.

Norwin cried out a thin wail to her stream of followers at the marvel she beheld: all but a few of the paths-to-be had unraveled, many in her favor. Not all were bountiful, but nearly every fiber had purpose now. Purpose that could be read, accounted for… manipulated. Her gryphons and their riders – the Great Eagle's greatest assets – were still strong.

And the Hurlorns had taken advantage of the Bundle's frayed ends, as they often do. That is their space. The meddling didn't concern Norwin – the two like-minded forces were set to play off one another for the betterment of them both, as they had in the past. Still, the Great Eagle's heart sank when she saw the folding of senseless waste in on itself. And the beacon for destruction on a grand scale, a mere flicker at the onset, had graduated to a pulsing light. It pulsed with the flicker of Seventh Kaeda's Starshine, for reasons veiled even to her. This last point required scrutiny.

The one some call the Wind God glided full circle in a wide arc, her Windswept trailing in perfect formation, then angled her great wings against the flow. She beat them gently to halt her advance. Hovering over the forest, Norwin of the Dawn cocked her head and turned all three eyes to focus on this last point. A critical point. What she saw confused her: a small man with his eyes gouged out, a crippled man freed, a freed man with a chained soul, and a young woman amidst a pool of writhing snakes. A wash of warm air pounded down on Norwin as she watched, and the howl of the nether winds filled her ears.

So, for now, the Great Eagle beat her great wings mildly. She sent only a Breeze unto the world, to help along those who ride the winds.

RUNAWAY

(Galewind)

T HE KNIGHTMAIDEN SURVEYED the Wulver glade, still shaded from the early morning sun. *The cats are all packed up,* she noted. The rangers had been quick to get their gear together. Gallant Haulik, on the other hand, had caused delays, insisting that he and Catwings run a patrol in search of Amot. *You'll never find a ranger that doesn't want to be found,* she thought. Unsurprisingly, the search came up empty. Galewind sighed, flipped through her notebook and reminded herself of the initial mission parameters. Then, one last time before takeoff, Galewind read over the final entry in her briefing notes, meant for Lady Apsarla upon return to Icy Blue. She skimmed over the mission background and the left wing that was transport, pausing at the mention of Charger Danus' demise, then looked over the rest carefully.

Recovery mission (Queen's Guard and Kith Rangers): The striker recovery mission failed, but the weapon has not fallen into enemy hands – yet.

*   – A search of Ground Zero implicated Whisperwood as the likely location of the lost striker. Gallant*

Eriff Haulik led a team of rangers into the forest to recover it.

- Scout Amot Rixin went missing during the initial search.

- Haulik allied with a Wulver pack in the area, who claimed to know the whereabouts of both Amot and the sword, held by a rival pack.

- With the help of the friendlies, a search and clear operation of the rival pack's territory was planned and executed. Skirmishes resulted in Wulver casualties but no serious op force casualties. The rival pack was successfully neutralized.

- Rixin appeared during the skirmishing, wielding a modified striker. By all accounts, he seemed taken by the fog of battle.

- The striker was recovered temporarily and verified while in the possession of Kith Commander Berendt Garondi. However, during final negotiations with the Wulvers, Rixin escaped with the striker after slaying the pack leader of the friendlies.

- Rixin's upcoming military tribunal has been augmented with additional charges, including desertion and theft.

- Rixin remains at large, last seen in Whisperwood traveling with a wolf yearling. *Considered armed and dangerous*

Right wing (Valkyries): The northern boundary of Whisperwood was successfully defended, but with losses.

- A regiment had gathered on the plains outside of Harrow. Harrowian scouts were sent along the Dim River and into Whisperwood, including two giants.

- The scouts were successfully neutralized, with one (1) op force fatality (Duelist Marec Haulik) and several casualties, including projectile injuries to the Gold mounts.

- The Harrowian regiment (numbers exceeding one thousand) began marching south on the morning of our departure, along the east side of the Dim River. Their destination is presently unknown. Possibly Fort Abandon.

Tail (Valkyries): A candidate ranger for inclusion in valkyrie ops was identified. However, the Queen's Guard is interested in the same individual.

- Spotter Rix Caledon is well-suited to valkyrie operations. He is a young, lightweight archer capable of delivering and receiving Kith whispers. His shots are unerring, his perceptions keen, and he is a proficient navigator (on land).

- However, the Queen's 136th Lancer Battalion is attempting to recruit Caledon for future operations against the Baruush, to involve strikers.

Risks / opportunities / restrictions going forward:

* Tension between the Kith Rangers and the Queen's Guard proved disastrous. To be avoided in the future.

* The mission into Wulver territory resulted in a rift between the mission team and the dominant pack. This could pose a future threat to the Whisperwood Line of Control, should it become active again. Wulvers are to be avoided.

* Securing a striker for Order Valkyrie is highly unlikely, at least for the time being. Of the original six forged, one is at large with Rixin and has

been altered, while a second is in the possession of Haulik. The whereabouts and condition of the remaining blades is uncertain.

* The mission parameters of the Harrowian regiment are currently unknown. As such, its impact on regional stability can only be speculated.

Next steps:

* The immediate assignment of information collection assets on the Harrowian regiment is critical.

* A follow-on mission to locate and secure all at-large striker prototypes is also needed, including the modified sword in the possession of Rixin and those still in the Otherworldly Realm. Once secured, the active cores - slider charms - must be removed and stored *separately* from the white-metal weaponry.

These missions (information collection and striker recovery) can be combined into a single, multi-wing mission.

Mission code name: ' Operation Runaway' (secret)